Praise for S
Novels o

Living Nightmare

"There's only one way to describe this book to me: fabulous!"
—Night Owl Reviews

"[An] action-packed story of the brooding and angry warrior Madoc and his journey to the future. This series rocks!"
—Fresh Fiction

"Utilizing her ability to combine excellent characterization with riveting danger, rising star Butcher adds another fascinating tier to her expanding world. You are always guaranteed generous portions of pulse-pounding action and romance in a Butcher tale!"
—*Romantic Times*

"Ms. Butcher's written word began to grab hold of my imagination and lead me on a ride unlike anything I have read before."
—Coffee Time Romance and More

Running Scared

"What an entertaining and thrilling series! The characters are forever evolving, secrets are revealed, powers are found, new details come to life, and love is the cause of it all. I love it!"
—Fresh Fiction

"Superb storytelling . . . I am amazed how Ms. Butcher's intricacies and subplots continue to expand the story without bogging down the overall plot."
—Romance Junkies

"This book jumps right in the fray and keeps you hooked till the end and I was unable to put it down. Emotionally dark, this is a wonderful blending of paranormal romance and urban fantasy [with] many twists and turns."
—Smexy Books Romance Reviews

continued . . .

Finding the Lost

"Exerts much the same appeal as Christine Feehan's Carpathian series, what with tortured heroes, the necessity of finding love or facing a fate worse than death, hot lovemaking, and danger-filled adventure." —*Booklist*

"A terrific grim thriller with the romantic subplot playing a strong supporting role. The cast is powerful as the audience will feel every emotion that Andra feels from fear for her sister to fear for her falling in love. *Finding the Lost* is a dark tale as Shannon K. Butcher paints a forbidding, gloomy landscape in which an ancient war between humanity's guardians and their nasty adversaries heats up in Nebraska." —Alternative Worlds

"A very entertaining read.... The ending was a great cliff-hanger and I can't wait to read the next book in this series... a fast-paced story with great action scenes and lots of hot romance." —The Book Lush

"Butcher's paranormal reality is dark and gritty in this second Sentinel War installment. What makes this story so gripping is the seamlessly delivered hard-hitting action and wrenching emotions. Butcher is a major talent in the making." —*Romantic Times*

Burning Alive

"A wonderful paranormal debut... Shannon K. Butcher's talent shines."

—*New York Times* bestselling author Nalini Singh

"Starts off with nonstop action. Readers will race through the pages, only to reread the entire novel to capture every little detail... a promising start for a new voice in urban fantasy/paranormal romance. I look forward to the next installment."

—A Romance Review (5 roses)

"This first book of the Sentinel Wars whets your appetite for the rest of the books in the series. Ms. Butcher is carving her way onto the bestseller lists with this phenomenal, nonstop ride that will have you preordering the second book the minute you put this one down."

—*Affaire de Coeur* (5 stars)

"Absorbing . . . Butcher skillfully balances erotic, tender interactions with Helen's worries, and intriguing secondary characters further enhance the unusual premise. Fans of Butcher's romantic suspense novels will enjoy her turn toward the paranormal." —*Publishers Weekly*

"Ms. Butcher offers fresh and delightfully creative elements in this paranormal romance, keeping readers engaged as the story unfolds. *Burning Alive* is a well-crafted beginning to this exciting new series, and will have fans of the genre coming back for the next adventure in the Sentinel Wars." —Darque Reviews

"An exciting romantic urban fantasy . . . Shannon K. Butcher adds her trademark suspense with plenty of tension and danger to the mix of a terrific paranormal thriller." —*Midwest Book Review*

"*Burning Alive* is Shannon Butcher's first foray into paranormal romance and what a doozy it is! Filled with sizzling love scenes, great storytelling, and action galore, fans of paranormal romance will rejoice to have Ms. Butcher finally join the genre!"—ParaNormal Romance

"A different twist on the paranormal genre . . . Shannon K. Butcher has done a good job with *Burning Alive*, and I will definitely be reading the next in the series."

—Fallen Angel Reviews

NOVELS OF THE SENTINEL WARS

Bound by Vengeance
(A Penguin Special)

Dying Wish

Blood Hunt

Living Nightmare

Running Scared

Finding the Lost

Burning Alive

THE EDGE NOVELS

Edge of Sanity

Razor's Edge

Living on the Edge

FALLING BLIND

THE SENTINEL WARS

SHANNON K. BUTCHER

SIGNET
Published by the Penguin Group
Penguin Group (USA) Inc., 375 Hudson Street,
New York, New York 10014, USA

USA / Canada / UK / Ireland / Australia / New Zealand / India / South Africa / China

Penguin Books Ltd., Registered Offices: 80 Strand, London WC2R 0RL, England
For more information about the Penguin Group visit penguin.com.

First published by Signet, an imprint of New American Library,
a division of Penguin Group (USA) Inc.

First Printing, April 2013

ISBN 978-0-451-23972-3

Printed in the United States of America
10 9 8 7 6 5 4 3 2 1

For Sarah Skolaut, controller of chaos, enemy of entropy, keeper of the calendar, mistress of managing mayhem, and saver of my sanity. Thanks for all you do.

Character List

Briant Athar: Sanguinar
Connal Athar: Sanguinar
Drake Asher: Theronai warrior, bonded to Helen Day
Logan Athar: Sanguinar, blood hunter, Hope Serrien's mate
Aurora: Athanasian servant
Cain Aylward: Theronai warrior, Sibyl's protector
Angus Brinn: Theronai warrior, bonded to Gilda
Gilda Brinn: the Gray Lady, Theronai, bonded to Angus
Maura Brinn: Theronai, Sibyl's twin sister
Sibyl Brinn: Theronai, Maura's twin sister
Canaranth: Synestryn, Zillah's second-in-command
Meghan Clark: blooded human
Helen Day: the Scarlet Lady, Theronai, bonded to Drake Asher
Eron: Athanasian prince
Neal Etan: Theronai warrior
Madoc Gage: Theronai warrior
John Hawthorne: blooded human
Mabel Hennesy: blooded human
Dakota Kacey: Theronai, bonded to Liam Lann
Lexi Johns: the Jade Lady, Theronai, bonded to Zach Talon

Nicholas Laith: Theronai warrior
Liam Lann: Theronai warrior, bonded to Dakota Kacey
Samuel Larsten: Theronai warrior
Thea Lewis: human woman living at Dabyr
Tynan Leygh: Sanguinar
Lucien: Athanasian prince
Andra Madison: the Sapphire Lady, Theronai, bonded to Paul Sloane
Nika Madison: Theronai, Andra's sister
Victoria (Tori) Madison: Theronai, sister to Andra and Nika
Torr Maston: Theronai warrior
Beth Mays: blooded human, Ella's sister
Ella Mays: blooded human, Beth's sister
Jake Morrow: human, member of the Defenders of Humanity
Blake Norman: human, Grace Norman's stepbrother
Grace Norman: blooded human, Gerai
Jackie Patton: Theronai, daughter of Lucien, bonded to Iain Terra
Andreas Phelan: Slayer, leader of the Slayers
Lyka Phelan: Slayer, Andreas's half sister
Joseph Rayd: Theronai warrior, leader of the Sentinels
Viviana Rowan: the Bronze Lady, Theronai, bonded to Neal Etan
Hope Serrien: Logan Athar's mate
Cole Shepherd: blooded human
Alexander Siah: Sanguinar
Paul Sloane: Theronai warrior, bonded to Andra Madison
Carmen Taite: blooded human, Gerai, cousin to Vance and Slade Taite
Slade Taite: blooded human, Gerai, cousin to Carmen, brother to Vance
Vance Taite: blooded human, Gerai, cousin to Carmen, brother to Slade

Zach Talon: Theronai warrior, bonded to Lexi Johns
Iain Terra: Theronai warrior, bonded to Jackie Patton
Morgan Valens: Theronai warrior
Zillah: Synestryn lord

Chapter 1

Kansas City, Missouri, October 29

There was not enough brain bleach in the world to scrub away the things Rory Rainey had seen. Her visions were getting worse, and if she didn't find the person who could make them stop, she was going to go bat shit crazy.

As frequently as the mental images were slamming into her lately, that inevitable insanity conclusion wasn't far away.

Rory kept her head down and her gaze firmly on the sidewalk in front of her. While her eyes saw only dirt and concrete dimly lit by streetlights, her mind saw much, much more. A riot of TV shows and video screens blazed in her head, one image superimposed upon the next, until it was all merely a blobby glow of color and light. Nearby, someone was staring down at a newborn baby. Someone else was reading a book, but there was too much visual chaos in Rory's head to make out the words. Brief glimpses of the same nearby sections of street fired in her mind, repeating over and over as the few people still out at the late hour drove by. As she moved down the street, she got close enough to a couple having sex in one of the surrounding buildings to catch what they were seeing.

The man was all fleshy and sweating, his face red with effort. The harnesses and implements twisting the woman into a vaguely pretzel-like shape made Rory speed her pace until that sight faded.

Ugh. Not enough brain bleach in the world.

She was in a bad part of town hit hard by the recession. The streets were lined with abandoned storefronts and condemned buildings. It was late and cold, and there was little foot traffic for her to collide with as she made her way to the homeless shelter she often visited. She didn't need the shelter—she had her own home. Nana's home. But that shelter was one of the places where she'd noticed the visions recede.

Little, fleeting moments of peace had come to her there. What she saw was *real* and hers alone, making it quiet and oh, so precious. At first she'd thought that she was getting better, that the space between mental barrages was getting longer. But then she left the shelter and the visions were there, waiting for her.

Her fumbling, painful experiments had led her to believe that someone inside that shelter was blocking her curse. If she could only figure out who they were and make them teach her how they did it, she'd be free.

But her potential savior had left, and Rory had never been able to track them down. Once in a while, her visions would fade and she'd know she was close, but she'd never figured out who was to thank for that reprieve.

A flash of hot pink hair and chain-clad leather burst in her mind, making her stumble in shock. Rory's hair was hot pink, and while she wasn't the only one who had that artificial feature, chances were slim there was another woman with her hair and jacket nearby.

Someone was watching her.

Rory tried to sort through the jumbled images to focus on who was behind her, but there were so many flashes, and most of them were so bright, she could hardly see the ground in front of her feet. There were too many people still awake in the city, too many sights slamming into her for her to latch on to a single one for very long.

And just because someone looked at her was no reason to wig out. Lots of people looked at her. That was one of the side effects of having hair louder than a freight train.

Still, her instincts were screaming at her, and she'd learned the hard way that she should trust them. As she continued walking, the hair on the back of her neck rose up in warning. Being out at night was dangerous. There were monsters everywhere, and for reasons she refused to think about, they wanted her.

Rory hurried her pace, anxiety driving her forward. She cut through an alley to get off the street and shorten her walk. The shelter wasn't far now, and while the remodeling wasn't finished, the doors were open, and they were letting people inside to escape the cold.

Bright pink consumed her vision, blocking out the wet pavement at her feet.

That was her hair—her back—and whoever was watching her had followed her down the alley. Definitely not some random pedestrian.

Well, hell. Now she had to do something. No way could she just keep walking, playing the role of prey. She'd never been much of an actress.

Rory stopped dead in her tracks, gripped the gun in her purse, squared her shoulders in a way that shouted she was not some fragile victim, and turned to face whoever was following her. She really didn't want to have to shoot someone, but after what Matt had done to her, she had learned to be more proactively defensive in her thinking. Two days and nights spent in a flooded basement filled with tentacled demons that lived on human flesh and blood had a way of curing a girl's poor decision-making habits.

Anxiety tightened her grip, but she kept her breathing

even, struggling to see the alley looming in front of her over the splashy colors and lights in her head. She saw no one, only a slight flicker of motion she couldn't even trust to be real.

"I saw you," she yelled into the night, her breath misting in the cold air.

Another fleeting glimpse of pink came to her, again showing her the back of her own head.

There was no way someone could have slipped past her. Even with her crazy visions, she wasn't that blind—at least not yet. If the visions got any worse . . .

She wouldn't think about that now. She had to stay positive and convinced that there was a cure for her faulty wiring.

A low hiss rattled out from behind her.

Fear streaked along her veins, and she whirled around to face the threat, gun raised and level.

A demon stood there, black and shiny, easily blending into the wet pavement. Larger than a big dog, its forelegs were too long for its heavily muscled body, pushing it nearly upright. There wasn't a single hair on the creature, but something thick and oily seeped from its skin, leaving smears behind with every step. Its face was disturbingly human, with eyes that glowed a bright, sickly green.

Rory took a step back, unable to control the impulse to flee. The demon's pointed ears twitched as if it heard something, and a second later, in the midst of flashing sights that were not her own, she saw the back of her head again. Only this time it was much, much closer.

There was still someone behind her. Or some*thing*.

She steadied her gun and aimed at the demon in front of her while she spared a quick glance over her shoulder. Sure enough, the demon's bigger, uglier twin was right there behind her, its bright eyes flaring with hunger.

Rory knew better than to hesitate. This was a kill or be eaten kind of situation if ever there was one—something she was way too familiar with these days.

Stupid demons fucking up the city. Someone needed to get rid of them, and while she really wished that someone was anyone but her, there was no one else around.

She fired her weapon three times at the closest demon. Chips of brick flew out as bullets hit a building. One of her shots sucked less than the other two, hitting the demon in the shoulder. It roared in fury and cowered back, twisting its head at an awkward angle so it could lick its wound. From behind her, she heard the other demon charge, its claws scraping across the asphalt. She turned and pitched her body to one side, working to find a clear shot through the flash and sparkle filling her head.

She landed hard enough to rattle her teeth, but managed to stay on her feet. Before she could even steady the weapon, the demon was flying through the air again, claws extended and yellow teeth bared.

The beast really needed a good dentist. That random thought slid through her as she moved on instinct, leaping out of the way. Her shoulder slammed hard against a brick wall, no doubt adding to the bruises she naturally accumulated thanks to her shitty visions.

It was only when she tried to move again that she realized she'd hit more than her shoulder. Pain gripped her knee, scraping along her nerves and digging into her spine. Her leg refused to bend. She looked down and saw a small section of shiny nail protruding from under the side of her kneecap. Attached to that nail was a length of discarded two-by-four that ran back down to a pile of construction refuse. The board was over six feet long, and there was no way she could drag it along with her. But if she pulled the nail out, she'd bleed faster.

Rory knew the folly of that plan way too well. If she bled, these two demons would become the opening act to dozens more.

One of the demons' eyes flared as it smelled her blood, and charged.

She was used to fear. She'd lived with it for years, and had been intimate with it briefly for a couple of horrible nights. That time had taught her how to function despite the terror screaming through her, but that didn't mean she didn't feel it. Her poor ribs were taking a beating as her heart thundered against them. The clammy chill of sweat coated her skin, making the gun harder to hold. But holding it was important, so that's what she did.

She raised the weapon and fired it, sending the greasy beast skidding back on the wet pavement.

That wouldn't keep it away for long. There were only a few more bullets in her gun. She had no choice but to free herself and hope she could run fast enough and reach the shelter before the rest of the demons nearby smelled her blood and came running. Because they definitely would.

She pulled in a deep breath and jerked the nail from her knee. The bent metal was coated in her blood, and she could feel wetness cooling on her jeans.

Both demons were slinking toward her now, their forelegs awkwardly bent to their sides, their muzzles low to the ground as they wove their way closer. One lifted its head and howled, letting out an eerie, mournful sound.

From somewhere a few blocks away, an answering howl rose up. And a little more distant, another. Then another.

Sometimes she hated being right.

Those howls were the dinner bell, and Rory was the main course.

Like hell.

She aimed for the head of the bigger demon and fired. Her shot was clean, and a chunk of oily skin and bone erupted from the thing's head. It staggered and took a clumsy nosedive into the street, legs twitching. Its twin bent down and licked the wound, though whether it was helping or hurting the wounded beast, she had no idea. Nor did she give a fuck.

She hadn't killed it—not if it was like most of the creatures she'd seen. All she'd done was buy some time and increase her odds of surviving, if only from zero percent to one percent. One ravening demon was more than enough to kill her just as dead as two could.

Someone in an apartment nearby looked into a nearly empty refrigerator, and whatever magic curse haunted her decided that she really needed to see a bowl of fuzzy green stuff right now, instead of the demons trying to kill her.

Frustration raged inside of her, but she tamped it down. She had to stay calm and focus on what was real and in front of her. The angrier she got, the more chaotic her visions would become—the more blind she'd become.

Rory shoved out a harsh breath, and backed away from the pair of monsters, easing her weight onto her injured leg. It held, but the pain grew worse with each step. The cold, wet spot on her jeans drooped down farther, reaching her shin now.

Somewhere nearby, a finger bent with age and arthritis dialed 911.

Shit. Poor cops had no idea how to deal with demons. Some ignorant, law-abiding citizen had just sent the protect-and-serve team into the jaws of evil. Literally.

Maybe if she was out of here fast, the demons would go away and not nom on the cops' faces. It was the only chance they had.

Before she could take so much as a step, the sight of dead brown grass filled her mind, sliding past her fast. It was lit by a bright green glow that glinted off of a blunt, shiny muzzle that looked just like those of the demons in front of her. And then the vision shifted and she saw another muzzle pointed down at a dirty street, and another lifted high to stare at the top of a chain-link fence, and another slinking under a parked semi.

Fear chilled her skin and tightened her muscles, and

she had to make a conscious decision not to go into a screaming tailspin of panic. More demons were coming, getting closer. She had to get out of here—both for her sake as well as the cops'.

Rory took another step and her knee buckled under her weight. She nearly fell, catching herself against the wall before she completely lost her balance.

A scratching sound behind her warned her that something was coming. She flattened her back to the wall and split her attention between the pair of demons and whatever was coming now.

It was small—the size of a rat, but hairless and sporting a barbed scorpion-like tail that curved up over its back. Three glistening spines caught a sparkle of streetlight as its claws scrabbled over the pavement, heading straight for her. Six tiny, glowing eyes lit its path.

Rory had no idea what it was, but she knew what it was going to be in a second: dead.

She aimed and fired, finally hitting where she aimed for once. The little demon—or whatever it was—splattered into a greasy stain. Droplets of black blood sizzled across the pavement, sending up thin tendrils of smoke.

Definitely a demon.

She was feeling pretty pleased with herself, congratulating herself for the shot when she heard more scratching coming from around the corner. Not twenty feet away, she saw a faint green glow. And then she saw what was making it.

Dozens of those barbed scorpion-tailed things came scurrying toward her, moving faster than she could run.

She didn't have enough bullets. She couldn't put weight on her fucked-up knee. The only exit was blocked by the pair of greasy black demons. Only seconds had passed since she'd looked away from them, but she didn't dare turn her attention away for long.

She needed a way out. Fast.

Rory leveled her weapon at the biggest threat. The demon she'd shot in the head was back on its feet. The hole in his skull had begun to seal shut already. The smaller demon was several feet closer to her, and she could see flashes of her own face, pale and terrified as it stalked nearer.

She glanced up, hoping for a convenient fire escape, but there was nothing above her but clear black sky and boarded-up windows way too high to reach.

She pulled in a fortifying breath, working hard to shove out some of her fear as she exhaled. The gun bucked in her grip. The closer demon yelped and flinched, but didn't go down. She fired again, and again, each shot sliding it back a bit, but making no real difference. The things kept advancing, and she swore they were grinning at her, their green eyes glowing with malicious intent.

Her gun clicked. She was out of bullets. But she wasn't about to give up and let these fuckers have her. She'd survived worse odds than these.

Of course, she hadn't been bleeding then, either, calling every hairy, slimy, scaly thing nearby to come and take a bite.

Rory dropped the gun and grabbed the long board that had stabbed her with its inconveniently placed nail. The wood was cold in her grip, but it felt solid and real. If she was going down, she was doing it Babe Ruth style.

One of the little things hit her shoe and started crawling onto it. She tried to fling it off with a hard kick, but the pain stalled her out, and the thing held on. She slammed the end of the board into it, crushing its head and her own toe.

Pain sliced through her, stealing her breath for a moment.

Her attention had been shifted to the little scorpion thing for less than three seconds, but as the vision of her own head getting close filled her mind, she knew that had been too long a distraction. The bigger demon lunged for her, and she was completely flanked, and completely fucked.

The world slowed as adrenaline flooded her body. She turned and began shifting her weight to fling herself out of the way. The jaws of the demon were wide open, its yellow teeth only a couple of feet from her head—close enough to see black blood coating them and pulpy bits of greasy flesh stuck between them. The rotten stink of its breath made her gag.

She lifted the board to protect her face, but even as she began to move, she knew she wouldn't be fast enough. There wasn't enough time to get the board in the way before those jaws closed on her head.

This was it. This was how she was going to leave this earth—bleeding, afraid and alone, while the rest of the world moved on as if nothing had happened. The fact that she could see them going about their routines rubbed her nose in just how small and insignificant her life really was. Now that Nana was gone, no one would miss her. As distant as she kept people, chances were no one would even know she'd died. These things would haul her off and eat her, leaving no evidence behind.

What a sad little life she'd led, full of fear and suck.

A metallic sound filled her ears, followed by a solid thwack. The open jaws careening toward her jerked down suddenly and hit her shin, but there was no force behind the blow. The muzzle simply bounced off, and the head rolled away.

It had no body.

Confusion clouded her mind as she tried to figure out what she was seeing. Was this another vision? Something happening nearby? If so, then why wasn't she dead and seeing nothing?

Rory blinked, hoping to sort out reality.

A man loomed a few feet away, too big to be real. He held a wide sword in his huge hands. The gleaming blade was coated in black oil. His giant body moved fast, muscles straining the seams of his leather jacket.

She didn't trust her eyes, and yet this all seemed quite real. It even sounded real. Her visions were silent.

At the man's feet lay the body of the demon that had nearly killed her. Black blood arced out of its neck in a pulsing spray that got weaker and weaker with every spurt. In front of him was the larger demon, staying low and out of range of that lethal blade.

He'd saved her. He'd lopped off the head of the demon and saved her face from being eaten. That wasn't supposed to happen. That wasn't the way her life went these days. Things were supposed to suck, just like they always did.

And yet there he was, still there, not vanished like a fleeting vision.

Rory's world began to make sense again, but the shock of still being alive hadn't faded. A sense of joy filled her up with her next breath. She wasn't dead. The world was still moving on, but she was moving with it.

The big man's back was to her, and he was slowly circling the demon, angling it back into a doorway for an attack. For a moment, all Rory could do was stare. He was smooth, each move flowing into the next in a seamless transition of power and strength. Muscles in his thighs bulged under his jeans, and when he stepped in a shallow puddle, his boot barely made a ripple. Even the mist from his breath curled out slow and lazy, rising into the night as if it had all the time in the world.

Graceful power radiated out from his every gliding step. Shadows caressed him, holding him close in a lover's embrace. He seemed too solid—grounded as if nothing could so much as rock him. And it wasn't just his size that gave her that impression. She *felt* something sliding out of him—a heavy kind of energy that pinned her in place, mesmerizing her. She could stare at his broad back all day and never grow bored.

A sharp pain stabbed her ankle, jerking her attention back to reality. She looked down and saw that one of those little scorpion demons had stung her and was now scurrying away, its barb shining wet with her blood.

That pain made sense. That was how her life was supposed to go. She got a beautiful visual treat in exchange for the low, low cost of being stabbed by a demon.

The board was still in her hands, and she batted it at the little fucker, hoping to squash it dead. Her aim was off, and she only winged it, sending it into a skittering spin.

The thing righted itself and sped off. The others of its kind veered around her and went straight for her savior in black leather.

"Behind you!" she called out, even as she pushed herself forward, using the board as an awkward crutch.

The man spun around in a fluid arc that was way too graceful for someone his size. Between his big, booted feet, she saw the head of the second demon roll across the pavement and bounce into a brick wall.

Whoever he was, she was glad he was on her side. At least he was for now.

Rory slammed her board down on one of the rat-sized things, turning it into a greasy black stain.

The man booted one of them into a wall hard enough to make it pop like a water balloon. The rest of the swarm must have seen it happen, because they moved as one, like a flock of birds, reversing direction to flee. Seconds later, they were gone, back around the corner the way they'd come.

He scanned the area, searching for more signs of a threat. His wide shoulders lifted with each even breath, and that big sword was still in his grip, ready for action. Dim light gleamed off his blade, as if collecting specks of it from the inky shadows. He wasn't looking at her, but she still felt his awareness as keenly as if he'd been staring.

"You're hurt," he said. It wasn't a question.

"Only a little. I'll live."

His gaze hit her then, and drove the breath from her body. His eyes were a deep, earthy green, set below thick, dark brows. The bones of his face stood out, forming rigid, masculine angles. His jaw was a bold statement of strength, the muscles there bulging with determination. It wasn't his good looks that she reacted to, either, though he was a fine-looking man. There was something else in those dark eyes, something potent and stark, with a kind of desperation she'd seen only a few times in her life—usually in those who knew they were about to die. Pain radiated out from him, quivering in the small lines around his eyes, so much a part of him she wasn't even sure he was aware of how obvious his agony was to anyone who cared to see it.

She couldn't look away. His pain called out to her, making her ache in ways she didn't understand. It was as if something inside of him was reaching for her, screaming in torment.

Rory shut her eyes to block out his silent pleas for help. A vision of an elderly woman's sleeping face appeared for a moment before it faded behind closing eyelids.

She pushed aside the visions, trying to concentrate on what was real and looming in front of her—all six and a half feet of him.

He took a step closer, scrutinizing her, and she felt that scrutiny glide along her body, down to her cold, throbbing toes. By the time his gaze had made its path from her head to her shoes and back again, she felt stripped bare, was trembling and defenseless. And that pissed her off.

She knew what he saw: the pink hair, the heavy makeup, the multiple piercings. No one ever really saw her beneath the shock factor, and that was the way she liked it.

At least until now. For some stupid reason, she wanted this man to see her—the real her—all the way down to her bones.

His gaze slid over her face, then lowered to where she was bleeding. She couldn't tell if he was sizing up her injury because he cared or because he was looking for some weakness he could exploit. His face was about as expressive as a marble wall, so there was no way to know for sure. What she did know was that if he sent that sword sailing in her direction, there wasn't a damn thing she could think to do to stop him from slicing her in two where she stood.

His voice was low and deep, rumbling out of him like stones rolling down a mountain. "Come with me."

Chapter 2

Her pink hair was ridiculous. That was Cain's first thought.

Her dark eyes were lined with smudged black makeup that stood out against her pale skin. Multiple silver rings and sparkling crystals decorated her ears, and she wore a tangled trio of chains around her slender throat, along with what looked disturbingly like a spiked dog collar.

His second thought was that she was more than she seemed—more than pink hair and juvenile trappings. That all felt more like a show to him, a disguise.

Her leather jacket was equipped with metal rings, chains and studs, all positioned in a way that looked suspiciously like they'd been put there for the purpose of guarding her against attack, rather than merely being decorative.

She'd kept her cool in the fight, which made him guess this wasn't the first one she'd been in.

That thought angered him and made his head pound even harder. Not even the physical exertion and rush of combat had helped ease the pain this time. It loomed inside of him, large and demanding. Meditation no longer helped, and now it seemed he was losing the slight benefit that fighting gave him as well. Once that was gone, he had no idea what he'd do to stave off the pain of his dying soul.

Death or imprisonment were his only options, and neither one appealed to him. Then again, nothing appealed to him anymore. His soul was fading, and with it his ability to find joy in the things around him.

His ward, Sibyl, who had been like his own child for centuries, had grown up and left him a few months ago. He hadn't seen her since then, and each day he ached with loneliness. Her e-mails from Africa were getting shorter and spaced farther apart. Each time they contained fewer details about her life, as if she were weaning him off of having her around. He knew he had to let her go—that she deserved a life of her own and a chance to find her place in the world—but the cost of losing her was much greater than he'd ever imagined. It was killing him.

But not tonight. Tonight there was still some fight left in him.

Cain held out his hand to the woman. "If I don't get you out of here you'll die. I heard the howls. More demons are coming."

"Thanks, but I'll find my own way home."

Her gaze met his, and the pounding pressure in his skull quieted. The grinding pain of the ever-growing power he contained within him abated. His luceria—the magical ring and necklace he'd been born wearing—vibrated against his skin.

Cain stepped closer, refusing to believe what he was feeling. His luceria would react only in the presence of a woman who was capable of wielding the power he carried. Women of his kind were rare, and stumbling upon one in the dark made hope and suspicion war within his chest. Part of him yearned to believe she was as she seemed—that she was one of the precious few able to save his decaying soul. But mostly, he doubted that which seemed too good to be true.

If the Synestryn had set out to create an enticing package he could not resist to lure him in, this woman would have been it.

She was lovely beneath the heavy makeup. The tilt of her dark eyes, the smooth curve of her cheek, the sweet shape of her mouth—they all invited his gaze to linger a bit too long. The longer he stared, the more curious he became. She roused a restless, hot ache deep in his gut, even as she eased the tightly clenched muscles riding along his spine.

There was a fierceness about her that intrigued him. In the moments before he'd reached the end of the alley, he'd seen her fight. Her fear was evident in her trembling limbs, and yet she refused to flee as most humans would have done. Perhaps it was her injury that held her in place, but something about her attitude made him question that. If his guess was right, she wasn't new to dangerous situations. She seemed far too calm for that. There were no questions about what those demons were or why they'd attacked her. She wasn't in shock. There were no hysterics.

She'd done this before. And survived. Only a true fighter could have done that.

But beneath that fierce exterior, beneath the chains and leather and ridiculous hair, Cain saw something else—something vulnerable and fragile, as if she were protecting some vital, breakable part of herself.

That was what intrigued him most, drawing him in. He wanted to get past all of the trappings and exterior wrapping to the real woman hiding beneath. Only there would he find out if she was the miracle she appeared to be, or some new trick the Synestryn had learned to play.

Cain stepped closer. The wind picked up, dragging a hint of her warm, sweet scent to his nose. Some dormant, crouching part of him woke up, groaning in delight. He breathed in again, desperate for anything powerful enough to distract him from the pain. He didn't even care how it looked for him to lean close and suck in the air around her as if it were the only source of oxygen he could find.

Heat spread down his chest. He felt the branches of his lifemark sway as if seeking a way to get closer to her.

It had to be a trick—some sinister weapon devised by the Synestryn to keep him still so that she could attack.

But she made no move to do so. She simply stood there, staring at him with dark, intoxicating eyes meant to lure him in and render him stupid.

Keeping his voice quiet so he wouldn't scare her away, he asked, "What's your name?"

Her gaze slid to the ground, her posture tightening defensively at his question.

The pain within him swelled again, cutting off his air for a moment. Lights danced in his vision. His hand gripped his sword harder as he fought through the returning pain, shoving it down where he could better control it.

"There's a shelter not far from here, in the old Tyler building," she said, avoiding his question.

She didn't want to tell him her name? Fine. He'd learn it soon enough. After he saw to her wound.

"I know the place," he said. "Can you walk?"

She scowled at him as if he'd insulted her. "Of course."

She used the two-by-four as a cane, but it was too long for the job. On her next step, she tilted wildly, and Cain lunged forward to catch her.

Before his hands made contact, she righted herself. His hands fell to his sides. He was glad he hadn't had to touch her while at the same time regretting the missed opportunity to feel some part of her within his grasp. If he touched her, he'd know for sure if he was imagining his luceria's reaction.

As stupid as it was, he wasn't sure he wanted to know the truth just yet. Lingering in this fog of possibility was nice. There was so little hope left in his life that he couldn't help but wish for it to remain alive for just a bit longer.

He was close enough to her now to see that she was shaking—close enough that his necklace lifted away from his skin, straining to reach her.

He wasn't imagining that. He wasn't simply making up pretty lies for himself. She was the real thing. A Theronai like him.

Or she was causing him to hallucinate.

Cain couldn't take any chances with her life—even if that meant falling for whatever lure the Synestryn had cast in his direction. He had to assume she was as she seemed until proven otherwise. And that meant getting her to shelter. It wasn't safe for her to be out alone and unprotected like this. "We need to get you patched up."

He reached for her, but she hobbled back, leaning on that board for support. "I'll be fine, thanks."

Irritation tightened his mouth, holding back sharp words better left unsaid. Her rejection was as obvious as it was predictable. He'd been through this before—been within arm's reach of a woman who could save his life only to have her deny him. Jackie had chosen another man. Based on this woman's reaction to him, his chances with her weren't much better.

Cain took a long step back. He wasn't going to do this to himself again. He wasn't going to let himself hope for miracles only to have them yanked away from him at the last second. Jackie's choice had nearly killed him. It *was* killing him. He could feel the decay of his soul moving faster with every passing day. If he hadn't been able to convince a woman he was worthy of her vow before, he had little chance of doing so now, with even less of the man he'd once been remaining.

His responsibility to the pink-haired girl was only to see to her safety. Logan would heal her and report her existence to their leader, Joseph. Once that was done, Cain would be on his way.

With that decision made, he felt better. Less unbalanced.

She took a wobbly step forward, trying to make it on her own. If she continued on like this, she was going to hurt herself, and even if she didn't, getting her to safety was going to take entirely too long.

"I'm not going to hurt you," he told her, hoping to ease whatever misgivings about him she had. "My name is Cain. I just want to help."

She avoided his gaze and his invitation to give him her name. "You were pretty handy a minute ago, doing that ninja act. I would have been monster chow if you hadn't come by. How did you find me?"

So she knew about the Synestryn demons—she wasn't one of those people who pretended they were rabid dogs or chimpanzees escaped from the zoo because it was easier to accept.

That made him wonder if she knew who *she* was, too. Several of the women like her they'd found recently had had no clue about who they were. *What* they were. They'd thought they were human.

It wasn't exactly the kind of thing he could ask. If she wasn't even willing to tell him her name, he couldn't expect her to tell him her secrets. And it had to be a secret. If it hadn't been, someone would have known about her—one of the Sanguinar, at least. They meddled enough in the lives of humans to know everything, and if one of them had known, he would have brought her to Dabyr for her protection.

"I was in the area, hunting," he said.

She blinked fast as if trying to clear her vision. "Uh . . . hunting?"

He realized the latent violence of his wording too late. It was no wonder Jackie had rejected him. He sounded like some kind of barbarian. "Those things that attacked you, it's my job to kill them. I was told there was an infestation in this area and came to eliminate it."

"So, you're like some kind of monster exterminator?"

"Something like that. I heard the gunshots. I thought I should check it out."

"You're not the only one who heard them. The cops will be here soon."

At the rate she was moving, both she and Cain were still going to be here when that happened. He really didn't have the time or the patience to wipe the minds of a bunch of human police and send them on their way.

"Please. Let me help you," he offered again, stepping a few inches closer, gauging her reaction to see if she'd balk at his approach. He'd seen her face the demons, and while she'd been afraid, she hadn't been panicked. The spacing of her shots was too even. She'd saved her ammunition until the end. Those were not the actions of a coward.

"Unless you're afraid of me," he added.

Like he'd flipped a switch, her posture changed. She was no longer shrinking away from him, but thrusting her chin out in defiance, her narrow shoulders square and her head held high. Fierce independence radiated out from her dark eyes and Cain felt himself being drawn in, wishing he could get even closer.

Her voice was sharp with anger. "You'd need a hell of a lot more than just a sword to even make my scary meter twitch. Some ugly teeth and at least a few claws for starters."

"Good. Then you won't mind."

Before she could ask what she should mind, he slid her arm over his shoulder and gripped her waist, forcing her to lean on him for support. He didn't want to touch her, but she wasn't capable of making it to Logan without help, and the sooner Cain got her to safety, the sooner he could be on his way.

He was careful not to touch her bare skin with his, but even with the padding of fabric and leather between them, more pain dribbled away, giving Cain room to breathe. He hadn't even realized how bad things had gotten for him until some of that agony eased with her nearness.

He glanced down at the ring portion of his luceria—the magical band that was meant to tie him to a woman, allowing her to wield the power swelling inside him. He'd been on his own too long, and now that power was killing him, crushing the soul from his body.

The swirls of colors in his ring were moving as if they'd been stirred—much faster than they'd ever moved with Jackie. There was no question. Whoever this woman was, she was a Theronai. And she was compatible with his power.

This small, ridiculously pink-haired girl who wouldn't even tell him her name had the power to save his life.

Rory was broken. That was the only explanation as to why she was letting a stranger touch her—especially one as armed and deadly as this man.

She'd lied about his sword not scaring her. The proof of just how deadly it was lay on the ground behind them, leaking black blood. Not that she thought he'd use it on her. She didn't. But she'd learned not to trust her own judgment when it came to hot men.

And Cain was definitely hot.

Pressed up against his side like this, with his arm around her, she could feel just how powerfully built he was. Every step made his muscles flex and bulge as he practically carried her toward the shelter.

He was so warm. Wave after wave of heat sank through her clothes, each one warmer than the last. She tried to stifle her shivers of delight, but she was certain he had to be able to feel them.

"It's cold out here," she said, hoping he'd take those shivers for something other than her drinking in his delicious heat.

He said nothing, but pulled her tighter against his side, sliding his hand a bit lower onto her hip.

Rory stifled a groan of pleasure, biting her lip to hold it back. The urge to lean her head on him was driving her crazy. She was not the kind of girl who snuggled against a man for warmth. Or anything else, for that matter. She'd learned the lesson Matt had taught her. For all she knew this guy was some kind of Renaissance festival freak who lopped off the heads of demons for fun. Slay the dragon, save the girl.

Rory did not need saving. At least not usually. Though even she had to admit that tonight had been a close call.

Flashing police lights filled her head between flickers of *QVC* and some guy surfing a porn Web site. "The police are coming."

"They're the least of our worries. You're bleeding."

"So?"

"You must be blooded. That's why the Synestryn came."

She'd heard Hope talk about Synestryn, but she'd never heard the term *blooded* before. Besides, playing dumb was probably the much safer option here. "I don't know what you're talking about."

A ragged howl echoed off of nearby buildings.

She felt more than heard a low, angry growl emanating from Cain's thick chest, and in that moment, she became all too aware of just how formidable an opponent he'd be. She had no chance of defending herself against him, and hoped like hell that he was telling the truth about wanting to help. Because if he wasn't, she couldn't think of a single thing she could do to stop him from doing whatever he wanted. She couldn't even run.

His arm tightened around her waist a bit more, and she could feel his hand through her clothes, leaving patches of heat wherever his fingers touched. For one brief moment of total insanity, she wondered what his touch would feel like without all the denim and leather in the way.

Great. Apparently she'd lost enough blood to render herself stupid, too. Just her luck.

His hand was shaking. Or maybe that was all her and her quivering idiocy. She couldn't tell. Whatever it was, the vibrating touch felt . . . nice. Right. And he smelled so freaking good, she was sure it had to be her imagination. If she leaned her head against him like she wanted and breathed in his scent, there was a good chance that she might be able to distract herself from the fact that he could be some raving mad, sword-wielding serial killer who wanted to use her skull as a coffee mug.

Their progress was slow and awkward, thanks to her injury. Each step hurt more than the last. The sharp, stabbing pain in her joint nearly stole her breath away, and now a fine layer of sweat was forming on her skin. She made it only a few yards before she could no longer put any weight on her knee. She tried to cover her flinch of pain, but she could feel him staring down at her.

"This isn't working," he said. "I will carry you."

Part of her jumped up and down, clapping its hands at the thought of being in this man's arms, but the rest of her was smarter than that. "We're not far. I can make it."

"Before the demons catch up?"

As points went, he had a good one. Normally she would have protested, but she was worn down by the pain and not at all ready for round two with a demon horde.

Her pride died a little as she accepted the only reasonable option. "Okay, but if you try to cop a feel, I'll punch you in the eye."

One side of his mouth twitched with a hidden grin. "I'll consider myself warned."

He shifted his weight, and a second later, she was airborne. It was a long way up, and the motion spun her head and gave her a brief moment of vertigo.

Her fingers slid higher on his shoulder and brushed the bare skin of his neck.

Rory's world went dark.

All the flashes, all the visions—they disappeared as if someone had flipped a switch. Peace settled over her, clearing her mind of the confusing, jumbled haze and leaving her thoughts blissfully clear.

He moaned, making a deep, purring sound, and said something she didn't catch. She was too busy basking in the visual silence, in the quiet dark of the alley where the only thing she saw was coming from her own two eyes.

Rory's eyelids fluttered shut in pleasure, and she saw nothing. Clear, perfect nothing. It was so peaceful, so beautiful. She didn't dare move. She barely even breathed.

Her throat tightened with gratitude that she couldn't utter. She tried to tell him not to move, that if he did she might lose this gift, but he'd already stopped dead in his tracks. She felt the heat of his body against her left side, felt his arms pull her tighter to his chest. The vibrations she'd felt before were stronger now—strong enough she could tell that it wasn't the trembling of hands causing it. There was something more to it, a kind of living energy pulsing between them.

She felt his body clench. Heard his breath come out in a shocked rush.

She opened her eyes and saw him staring down at her. Even in the darkness she could see longing and hunger in his eyes, as if he'd been starved all his life and had only now found his first meal. And she was it.

The fact that such a crazy notion didn't scare the shit out of her proved just how big a fool she was. Not even the lesson that what's-his-name had taught her seemed to do any good.

Rory started to pull her hand away from his hot skin, but his grip tightened and a look of fear widened his moss green eyes.

"Don't stop touching me," he said, more a plea than an order. "Not yet. Not until I get you to safety."

They were only a couple of blocks away from the shelter, and the truth was it didn't matter if she touched him or not. If he intended to do her harm, she was screwed.

"I won't hurt you," he said as if sensing her worry.

She lifted her chin, giving him a hard stare. "I wouldn't let you hurt me."

"Of that I'm sure. Come on. Let's get you inside and out of those clothes."

Chapter 3

"Excuse me?" Rory nearly shouted.

"That's not what I mean," he said, a hint of embarrassment in his deep voice. "The blood on your clothes will draw the demons. I'm sure Hope will have something else you can wear."

Oh. Well. That was different from what she'd first thought—that he had other, less noble intentions. Though with waves of delicious heat sinking into her wherever he touched, and those tingling vibrations dancing between them, maybe less noble intentions would be fun.

No. Bad Rory. Remember Matt?

Yes. She did. She also remembered those endless hours of fighting for her life, not knowing if she'd ever be free, or if she'd die as a snack for some monster lurking in that filthy water. Matt had caused that torture, and even though he was dead, Rory would not forget that lesson.

"You know Hope?" she asked, hoping to distract herself from hellish memories.

"Yes. How do you know her?"

She could feel the low rumble of his voice all along her left side. He had the faintest hint of an accent—one that came out only with certain words, like he'd been raised somewhere else. She found it intriguing and sexy as hell. If circumstances were different, she would be happy to simply close her eyes and listen to him for hours. It wouldn't even matter what he said. Let him recite his recipe for stewed Rory brains for all she cared—she'd bask in his voice all the same.

After a moment of collecting the few scraps that were left of her wits, she cleared her throat. "I went to the old shelter where she worked sometimes. Before it burned down. Back when Sister Olive—" Rory couldn't finish. Her throat tightened with grief, cutting off her air. She swallowed, trying to work through her feelings of loss and anger at the nun's murder, but she wasn't that strong. It was too soon. Only a few months had passed, but every minute had been lonely and isolated. She hadn't spoken to anyone about what had happened in that abandoned building those demons had converted into home, sweet home.

Words could not make the pain of memories like those go away. Nothing could. She'd carry that grief and terror around with her for the rest of her likely short life.

His thumb slid over her side, clearly an offer of comfort. "Hope told me about her. Her death was a true loss."

Rory nodded, but that was all she could manage. She still hadn't been able to shove away the memories of that night and all its lingering horror.

And monsters had found her the moment she came out of isolation. Story of her freakin' life.

They reached the back of the shelter. The door was locked. Cain tapped it with his boot and a few seconds later, it opened to reveal Logan, Hope's husband, who was way too pretty to have been born a dude. He had silky, dark hair, and silvery eyes that lit with recognition. The angles of his face were too perfect to be real, and he was much less gaunt than the last time Rory had seen him—back on the night Sister Olive had died.

"Rory?" A frown wrinkled his brow for a second, then

his eyes zeroed in on the blood staining her jeans. "Get her inside."

Cain carried her into the big kitchen, but instead of letting go of her like she expected, he pulled her a bit closer against his body, shifting her away from Logan and his intense gaze.

"I left some corpses a couple of blocks over," said Cain. "Police are on the way. I need to go clean up the mess and scrub the cops' minds if they see anything they shouldn't."

"I'm far better at such things than you are. I'll take care of it," said Logan. "Get Rory to the safe room." He waved an elegant hand toward one of the doors leading out of the kitchen.

"Patch her up. She's bleeding."

"I'm keenly aware of that fact, and of just how heavily blooded she is."

"Then take her. Make the bleeding stop."

"Uh, guys. I'm right here. I know the demons can smell my blood. Just put me down and I'll dump some superglue on the wound and plug the hole."

"You'll do no such thing," said Logan.

"We can't have you risking infection," said Cain.

"It's nothing I haven't done before. I'll be fine. Just get me some clean pants or some scissors to cut away the blood, and I'll be on my way."

Logan looked over her head at Cain, clearly dismissing her. "Lexi warded the room when she came to visit. That should cut off the scent trail of her blood, at least for a time. I'll be there in a moment."

"Logan—"

"We're wasting time, Cain. Do as I ask."

Cain's body tightened. Positioned in his arms like she was, she could feel power tremble through him. Until now, she hadn't realized just how gentle with her he'd been—how light his hold on her was. And now that she knew, she wasn't sure if she was grateful for his restraint or feeling deprived that he hadn't held her closer, tighter.

Even more proof of how stupid this man rendered her.

Cain's voice rumbled out in a hard warning. "The two demons I killed aren't alone."

"They won't even see me," said Logan, and then he was gone.

Cain didn't say a word as he hurried through the kitchen, but she could tell by the muscles bulging in his jaw that he was pissed.

"Was Logan born a girl?" she asked, hoping to distract Cain from the tension running through his body.

He stopped, midstride, and looked down at her. The faintest hint of a grin creased the corners of his eyes. "I think you should ask him that yourself. Preferably when I can watch."

Then he moved on through the kitchen, but at least now he didn't look like he was going to chip some molars in frustration.

Rory hadn't been in the new shelter before, but it was much nicer than the old one had been. Of course, the fact that it wasn't a pile of cinders and rubble made it no contest.

This building—previously the run-down Tyler building—had been gutted last spring and was now nearly rebuilt. The modern, industrial kitchen was gleaming and bright, with new appliances and lots of stainless steel. Past the door a hallway led to several offices and a small conference room that were vacant at this time of night.

"In here," said Cain, nodding to a solid wood door with no window. He didn't have a free hand to open it, so she did the job herself and flipped the light switch.

Inside was an organized array of freeze-dried food, big boxes labeled as drinking water, and medical supplies stacked neatly on open metal shelving. A gurney covered in pristine white sheets was tucked against the far wall, near a giant stainless steel sink. A row of oxygen tanks sat in a corner, along with a bunch of medical equipment she couldn't name. On the opposite side of the room was what she swore had to be a kind of oven they used to cremate bodies.

Despite the fact that they called this the safe room, it made her feel anything but. "Looks like they're preparing for the zombie apocalypse."

"Something like that," said Cain as he kicked the door shut behind him.

He set her on the gurney and pulled away.

The moment her hand left his neck, the visions came back, blasting her with a barrage of lights and colors so ferocious her stomach gave a dangerous heave. Pressure built behind her eyes, as if all the sights she'd missed out on for the last few minutes were there, waiting to flood in and torture her.

A shrill sound of pain filled her ears, and it took her a moment to realize that she was the one making that horrible sound.

She clamped her lips shut, and breathed through the assault, letting it wash over her. Slowly, her breathing evened out and she opened her eyes.

Cain was on the floor, his big body shaking. She blinked to clear her vision, wondering if what she was seeing was real.

A flash of an advertisement in a gun magazine superimposed on top of someone washing his hands captured her attention for a second before she could regain a moment of control.

She wasn't seeing things. Cain was sprawled on the white tile, making a horrible choking sound.

Panic darted through her bones, freezing her in place for a long second. Once her heart started beating again, she gathered her senses and glanced around for signs of an attack. No one was here, but she couldn't imagine what could have been strong enough to knock the giant on his ass like that.

Rory knelt down beside him. Pain spiked through her knee as if someone had taken a hammer to it. She felt blood seep faster from the wound, but ignored all of that.

She grabbed Cain's head to keep it from slamming into the metal shelving, and he went still in her grip. Fast, hard breaths rose from his lips.

Once again, Cain was the only thing she saw. No lights, no visions, just his face.

So strange, and yet so very, very welcome.

Concern lined his forehead and sweat dotted his brow. A vein in his temple throbbed and his breathing was labored. "You okay?" he asked, his voice rough and strained.

He was asking about her? "You're the one on the floor. You were thrashing around like you were choking."

His hands covered hers, vibrated against them, and she swore she could feel his ring buzzing near her skin.

"Sorry. I knew it would be bad for me, but I didn't think it would hurt you, too."

He sat up. His face was close to hers now, and for the first time, the lighting was good enough for her to actually see him. He was older than she'd first thought. With a heavy build like his and those gliding reflexes, she'd guessed him to be in his twenties, but now that she got a closer look, she knew that was wrong. He looked like he was in his thirties, but that didn't seem to fit, either. He *seemed* older, though he had no heavy creases or lines, no gray in his hair. There was a kind of depth in his moss green eyes, a kind of awareness or wisdom she'd seen only in people like Nana who'd lived a long, long time.

Several small scars marked his hands and face, supporting her theory. His dark brown hair was mussed from the wind, falling over his forehead in places. A few strands clung to his damp skin. She realized she'd been staring for a long time. Too long.

Rory cleared her throat and looked away. "You didn't think what would hurt me?"

"Breaking contact. I saw your face before I... collapsed. I heard you. You were in pain."

She wasn't about to talk to him about her visions. No way. All she needed was to get patched up and back out there to hunt for the person who could make the visions stop.

The way he did.

Maybe he was the person she'd been looking for. Maybe he was the one who'd stopped her visions before.

"Do you live nearby?" she asked.

"No. Why?"

"Were you ever at Sister Olive's shelter before it burned down?"

He shook his head, frowning at her. "Not that I remember."

"Near it?"

"I don't know. Maybe. Why does it matter?"

"I'm looking for someone." She felt obligated to tell him at least that much. He had, after all, saved her life tonight.

His gaze roamed her face, so palpable it was almost a caress. "Who?"

Oh baby. She could get lost in a man like this. It wouldn't even be hard. She was so used to being invisible—to people merely glancing at the surface—his complete focus was nearly too intense to stand. If he'd tried to make a move, she would have freaked, but he hadn't.

The door opened and Hope walked in, glowing with health and so beautiful it made Rory shrink back so Cain wouldn't compare them.

"Rory. You're safe." Hope rushed forward and engulfed her in a hard hug full of love and friendship. Rory had to blink back tears so no one would see them. She was not sappy. She did not cry, except during that one coffee commercial that aired during the holidays, but that was forgivable. Crying now over some silly hug would not be.

Hope didn't seem to mind showing others weakness, because tears were streaming down her cheeks openly as she pulled back. "I was so worried. You just disappeared after that night. No one knew where you'd gone."

"What night?" asked Cain.

"I needed some time alone," Rory lied, cutting Hope off before she could tell Cain things that were none of his business. He didn't need to know about her captivity. No one did. Her ignorance and shame at falling for such a stupid trick was not something she wanted him to know.

The visions that had been blissfully absent while she'd been held captive had come back before the chaos had settled and survivors were toted away. Not only had the visions come back, but they were stronger. She'd been scared shitless. She hadn't wanted anyone to see her like that, so she'd scurried away like a timid bunny.

Hope wiped her eyes, which glowed with compassion. "I understand."

No, she didn't. No one did. But Rory didn't want to be rude and point that out.

Cain was watching the whole exchange. He was holding Rory's hand, his fingers laced between hers. He hadn't let go, even though they were all on the floor in an awkward heap.

Hope finally saw their joined hands, then her gaze slid up to Cain's throat. A narrow, iridescent band stretched around his neck, hugging it. Colors swirled inside the band, as if it were alive. Shimmering blues and pinks slid in a slow dance around plumes of lavender and darker purples. The colors were way too feminine for a man like Cain to wear, but then Rory figured a man like him could wear whatever the hell he wanted and no one would say a thing for fear of being pounded into pulpy bits.

Shock widened Hope's eyes, and then she looked at

Rory. A grin spread over her face and she dove in for another tight hug, only this one felt like some kind of congratulations.

"What?" asked Rory, confused.

"She doesn't know," said Cain.

Hope looked at him. "But you're sure?"

He nodded, but rather than looking at the stunning woman who'd asked the question, his gaze was fixed directly on Rory. And she felt that gaze all the way down her spine in a thrilling rush.

"What am I missing?" she asked.

Hope cupped Rory's face in her hands. "You're one of us. Welcome to the family."

Family? A family who fought demons and had a "safe" room stocked like some kind of survivalist nutcase? That didn't sound like her kind of family. "Whoa. Hold on a second. I have no clue what you're talking about."

"Let it go, Hope," said Cain. "We'll deal with that after she's patched up."

"Patched up? What happened?"

Rory tried to pull her hand free of Cain's, but he didn't let go. She glared at him while she answered Hope's question. "Just me and my suckful luck with monsters. You know. The usual."

Logan walked in. His nostrils flared and his eyes seemed to glow. "Your bleeding. It's gotten worse."

"That's my fault," said Cain. "I collapsed. She came down here to help."

Logan's mouth flattened as he looked at her and then Cain. "I see. We'll deal with that in a minute. Right now we need to stop the bleeding."

"They're compatible," said Hope.

Cain scowled at her. "Not now, Hope."

Rory's confusion deepened as she watched the silent play between them. Hope was looking like she'd just opened a shiny new toy. Logan was clearly trying to take that toy away, and Cain kept a tight grip on Rory's hand like she was going to float away if he let go.

Rory wanted to mind. She wanted to be pissed off, because that was a lot easier to deal with than all of this unsettling, sappy, tingling nonsense.

Cain rose to his feet in one graceful move. He held on to her hand, his thick fingers laced between hers. In one easy lift, he set her on the edge of the gurney.

He didn't back away, though she could see his body tense as if he was getting ready for her to kick him in the balls or something.

"You need to let go of her," said Logan.

"I know," said Cain in a tone that warned Logan to back off. "I'm working on it."

"Do it slowly. I'll do what I can to ease the pain."

"Pain? Will one of you please explain what the hell is happening here?"

"In a moment," said Logan as he grabbed Cain's wrist. "Just hold still."

"Ease hers," said Cain. "Last time we stopped touching, it hurt her, too."

"Interesting," said Logan, and then he looked at Rory like she were a new and intriguing puzzle for his amusement.

She almost told him that it wasn't pain she felt, but if she'd done that, she would have had to tell them about the visions, and she wasn't about to do that. She didn't know these people. She didn't trust them. Even though she and Hope had been through something horrible together, that didn't mean Rory was ready to be BFFs.

Logan laid his hand on her forehead, and she flinched away from his touch. His fingers were slender and cool, not at all like Cain's. She didn't like the way Logan's hand felt on her. It was . . . wrong somehow, like a kind of betrayal she couldn't understand.

"I won't hurt you," said Logan. "Just relax."

She had no intention of doing any such thing, but a second later, she felt her tension drain away. She sat there on the edge of the bed, swaying and content. Even knowing that whatever he'd done to her was fake, she couldn't find the energy to care.

Cain took several deep breaths like he was about to go free diving, and then eased his grip on her hand. His fingers loosened and slid between hers, inching away. She was sure he hadn't meant it to be a caress, but she felt it all the way to her curling toes. Those heated vibrations trickling into her wherever he touched seemed to cling, wrapping around the tips of her fingers. She swayed toward him, eager to deepen the contact again, but he continued to back away, keeping just enough distance between them that she couldn't make any headway.

Finally, after she was gripping the edge of the gurney to keep from lunging toward him and getting more contact with his skin—wherever she could find it—the slightest bit of his index finger was still in contact with hers.

Electricity arced between them, so intense she swore she could hear it crackle. There was something precious and powerful in that tiny contact—a promise of something she didn't understand, but yearned to possess all the same. She recognized the power, as if a piece of her had been chopped off at birth, only to return to her now in this form.

It was hers and she wanted it.

He broke away, and all thoughts of power were crushed from her head. The relentless stream of images was there, waiting for her, ready to strike. Within seconds, she was completely blinded by the flood of lights and colors that did not belong. Never before had it been this bad. Not even in the daytime. There were too many sights. She couldn't absorb them all.

The flow of images nauseated her. Her head spun. She held on to the bed, but even that solid support did nothing to pin her in place.

She tried not to panic, but terror was clawing at her, tearing at her resolve until it lay in tattered shreds. She had no control, nowhere to hide. All she could do was sit here while the visions slammed into her, driving her closer to the brink of madness.

Chapter 4

Cain's world was engulfed in agony. He'd never felt anything like it before—not even on the night he'd nearly died—the night he'd failed his duties, and Sibyl had been stolen from her bed.

This was different. Deeper. It was more than merely physical pain. It was as if his soul were being wrenched from his body—pried out by a red-hot crowbar.

He held his breath and waited for it to pass, but the longer it went on, the harder it became for him to remain calm. The pain should have begun to fade by now. It should have loosened its grip enough that he could pull in a breath. And yet it went on, strangling him and robbing him of his strength.

And then he heard something weaving between the pounding beats of his heart booming in his ears. Rory. She was making a gut-wrenching sound of frustration and defeat.

Cain lunged toward her, the need to make her pain stop driving him to act.

"No," said Logan. "Not yet."

Someone held him back physically. It took Cain a second to realize that it was Hope who was blocking Cain's progress. She was much stronger than seemed possible, and that shock was the only thing that kept Cain from fighting his way back to where he was touching Rory's skin.

With an effort of will, he forced his eyes open. The edges of his vision were cloudy, fogged with pain.

"Breathe, Rory," said Logan. "You're okay now."

Rory pulled in a stuttering breath, but it was deeper than before. Her dark eyes were open wide, terror stark and pale as it haunted her expression. As he watched, some of the color came back to her cheeks, driving away the ghostly paleness.

"Good. That's it. Just like that."

Cain, once again in control of himself, looked down at Hope. His voice was calm, even though everything inside of him was roiling in chaos. "Let me go."

The woman lifted her hands. "Don't touch her."

It was the only thing he wanted to do, but he knew better. He couldn't walk around holding on to her for the rest of his life. They had to take care of her wound. That had to come first before anything else.

Cain stepped back and shoved his hands in his pockets to remind himself not to touch Rory. But that didn't stop him from watching her and making sure she was okay.

Her eyes were open, but she didn't appear to be able to focus on anything. Her stare was distant, as if she were blind. The silver rings piercing her skin glittered as she shook under the bright fluorescent lighting. Logan laid a long, elegant hand on her brow, and it was all Cain could do to keep from drawing his sword.

Logan was a friend. A healer. Rory needed him, which meant Cain could not lop off the other man's hand, no matter how much of a possessive statement Cain wanted to make.

Slowly, the distant vacantness in her eyes faded as she looked at him. As soon as her gaze connected to his, he felt it all the way through him, warming places he hadn't known were cold until just now.

There was desperation in her gaze, as if she were drowning and he was the only one who could extend his hand to save her. The thought puffed him up, driving away the lingering effects of his battle with the pain of losing her touch. He felt stronger, more solid, like he could go on for years with no rest if that's what she needed him to do.

That sudden flood of purpose left him shaking all the way down to his boots. He hadn't had that in a long time—not since his little girl had grown up and left him. Since then, he'd been floundering, flailing around for some reason to keep on pulling in his next breath. The way Rory was looking at him now, he no longer questioned what it was he needed to do. It was clear.

She needed him to save her from whatever it was she'd just endured.

His lucerla vibrated frantically, celebrating her nearness, clamoring for more.

She looked so small sitting there, so vulnerable. Her bright pink hair, glaring under the fluorescent lighting, was hard to see past, but he did see. Believing was the hard part. Despite her size and appearance, power radiated out of her gaze. He couldn't stop staring.

Her dark eyes sucked him in, making him forget all about the world spinning around them. He knew there were things he should be doing. He simply didn't care. He was content to stay here, staring into her eyes for as long as she'd let him.

She licked her lips. His gaze dropped to watch the path of her pink tongue. He couldn't have stopped himself if he'd tried.

Hot, fast need gripped him. He tried to shove it away before it got a toehold, but he was too slow. His body heated, and sweat prickled along his spine. It was only through a sheer effort of will honed by decades of self-control that he was able to keep his cock from swelling.

He couldn't let himself want her. Whatever inconvenient reaction he was having was simply a trick the luceria was playing on him—a way of forcing him to get closer to her and convince her to tie herself to him.

The idea was compelling, and he had to take another step back to remind himself that it wasn't going to happen. He'd been through this once with Jackie. He knew how it ended.

Logan's voice cut through Cain's fog, reminding him they weren't alone. "I stopped the bleeding, but there's some damage to her joint I must heal."

"How did you do that?" asked Rory.

"Magic. Now hold still. I need to cut away the bloody cloth and burn it."

"What happened to you?" asked Hope.

"I fell on a nail," said Rory.

"She was attacked by demons," said Cain.

Hope gave Rory a comforting smile. "You're going to be fine. I'll find you something else to wear. Be right back."

Logan sliced the leg of Rory's jeans off at her thigh and removed her shoe and sock. He wiped away the smears of blood, leaving whole, smooth skin.

Cain should have averted his eyes and given her some privacy, but even that small act was too much for his depleted willpower. The pale curve of her thigh teased him, making him wish he could see more of her. He wondered how her skin would feel, and how far up she'd let his hand slide before she stopped him.

He hated seeing Logan's hand on her. In fact, he didn't like the Sanguinar anywhere near her. If Cain didn't distract himself, he was going to do something violent and unseemly.

She caught him staring at her leg, and he watched as a blush darkened her cheeks.

The idea that he was making her uncomfortable got his brain moving again. "I'm sorry," he said as he looked away, searching for something—anything—that would hold his attention away from her.

He needed to leave and ensure her future, but he couldn't do that yet. He had to stay and make sure that Logan didn't take her blood. "She's already spilled enough blood tonight. If you need to fuel your efforts, take mine."

"Thanks to Hope, I have no need of it, but Ronan does. He's nearby. Pay him what you would have given me."

"I will," said Cain, feeling the fluttering weight of his vow settle over him, binding him to his word.

Logan addressed Rory. "This may hurt a bit. Try to hold still while I heal the joint. I'll do this as fast as I can."

Logan covered her knee with his pale hand, and it was all Cain could do not to rip the man away from her. This raging possessiveness wasn't normal for Cain. He didn't usually impede someone who was only trying to help the way Logan was.

And then Rory let out a small whimper of pain, and Cain's vision flashed red. He had just wrapped his hand around Logan's arm when she let out a long breath and sagged in relief.

"Better?" Logan asked her, giving Cain a hard stare.

"Yes. Thanks. How the hell did you do that?"

Cain let go and stalked across the room away from her, his body vibrating with his struggle to regain control of his raging emotions.

"Magic, as I said. How does it feel? Any pain?"

"No. It's not even stiff." She jumped off the table and looked up at Logan. "How much do I owe you?"

Hell no. Logan would want blood, and Cain wasn't going to let that happen. "I'm paying your debt."

"No, you're not," said Rory. "I can pay my own way. How much?"

Logan opened his pretty mouth to answer her, but Cain cut him off. "He gets paid in blood, Rory. He'll bite your neck and drink your blood. Is that what you want?"

She blanched and took a step back, bumping into the gurney.

Logan shook his head, giving Cain a disappointed frown. "There's no need to scare her like that. I would have thought better of you."

And just like that, Cain felt like an ass. Logan was right. She'd already been through too much tonight, and here he was, heaping another dose of fear on her.

"I'm sorry. I should go." He looked at Rory. "You'll be safe here. Logan won't hurt you. He's going to take you to a place where the demons can't find you."

"Uh. No, he's not," said Rory. "I'm not going anywhere. I have a job to do. I appreciate you saving my life, and the whole magical healing thing, but I need to get back out there."

"The demons are still out there," said Logan. "I obscured your scent trail, but they won't leave the area until dawn. They're still looking for you."

"I'll find them and kill them," said Cain. "Stay here tonight. It will be safe to travel to Dabyr in the morning."

"Wow. You two must have given up your ability to hear in exchange for all those magical powers. I'm. Not. Staying. There's something I need to do."

"Let us help you do it, then," said Logan. "What is it?"

Her full lips pressed together, a clear indication that she intended to remain silent.

"She's looking for someone," said Cain.

"Way to keep a secret," snapped Rory.

"You didn't say it was a secret. Besides, Logan is good at finding people. I'm sure he'll be able to help." Cain gave Logan a hard stare. "But if you touch her blood, you and I are going to have words."

Rory dug in her purse. "You know, this macho bullshit

is cute and all, but a little goes a long way." She tossed some cash on the gurney and grabbed her shoe and sock.

"You can't leave with that. Your blood is on your shoe. They'll smell it."

She let out a long sigh of irritation. "Those stupid little scorpion fuckers." She dropped the shoe and began unlacing the one still on her foot. "It's not bad enough that the big demons try to eat my face, but the little ones have to go and stab me and ruin a perfectly good pair of shoes, too."

"You were stabbed?" asked Logan, shocked.

"Yeah. They had these barbed tails and one of them got to me before I could squish it."

"I didn't sense any poison."

She frowned at Logan. "That's good. Neither did I, seeing as how I'm still alive and junk."

"You don't understand," said Cain. "If one of them stabbed you, then you could be poisoned."

What if it was something Logan couldn't heal? They'd seen that before. Just the thought of her going through what Torr had endured made Cain's hands shake.

"I'll go out immediately and find one of them, in case you need to devise an antidote."

Logan shook his head. "I'm telling you that there was no trace of poison in her. I would have sensed it."

"What if you're wrong? What if it's something you can't detect?" asked Cain. "I won't let her end up like Torr. Or worse."

"Uh, guys. You're freaking me out."

Hope came back into the room with a change of clothes in her arms. "What's going on?"

"Cain is needlessly upsetting our guest," said Logan.

Anger swelled in Cain's gut, and he had to work to keep from bellowing. "Needlessly? Can you say with one hundred percent certainty that she wasn't poisoned? That it wasn't something new we haven't seen before? That there is absolutely no chance that what was done to her tonight—done to one of our own—isn't going to harm her?"

Logan said nothing.

"That's what I thought," rumbled Cain. "I'm not willing to take the chance that you're wrong. I'm going out there to find one of these things so that you can dissect it and make sure. Understand?"

Hope went to Rory and cupped her shoulders. "Listen to me. You're going to be fine. There's nothing to worry about. We're going to make sure of that."

"Sure," said Rory, her voice heavy with sarcasm. "Gigantor there probably freaks out like a little girl all the time. I mean, sure, he faced down a bunch of demons without breaking a sweat, but I bet that's a first for him. He's probably a total head case that screams when he sees a mouse." She pulled in a long breath. "There's nothing to worry about? Are you fucking kidding me? If Cain says there's a chance I'm poisoned, I'd really like to know if he's right."

"Of course," said Logan. "Whatever you want."

"Good. Then it's settled." Cain looked at Rory, wishing he could touch her, comfort her. But if he touched her, he'd have to stop touching her again, and he wasn't sure he could take that kind of pain again tonight. He had a job to do, and for one glorious moment, he felt like his old self again—driven by purpose and the desire to do what was right. It was a gift he would not squander.

"I'll be quick," he told Rory. "Stay here."

Cain picked up her bloody shoe and headed out to go hunting.

Rory didn't want Cain to leave. That thought hit her upside the head, surprising the hell out of her. At least Hope was here, and the last time Rory had seen her, she'd been sane, unlike the dueling testosterone brothers.

Brilliant flashes of light filled her head. There were people close by, and some of them were awake. Even those who slept were still a problem—sending her random little slits of sight that weren't her own. The visions were now stronger than they'd ever been, but at least she wasn't sick. "I don't feel poisoned."

"I'm sure you're fine," said Logan. "Cain is simply being careful. It's understandable, given the situation."

"And what situation is that, exactly? You guys keep giving each other these looks like you don't want me to know what's going on. I thought I was the one keeping secrets from the world about demons and monsters, and here I am feeling like I'm the queen of clueless."

"Logan," said Hope, "why don't you go and find Rory something to eat. I'll help her get cleaned up and make sure the clothes fit."

Logan nodded. "As you wish, love. I won't go far."

The door shut behind him, leaving the women alone. Rory hurried to change, not sure how long he might stay away. "You're going to tell me what the hell is going on, right?"

"I know what it's like to be the outsider. I can't claim to know everything, but I will tell you what I know. If you promise to stop hiding."

"I'm not hiding."

"The night we nearly died, you slipped away. You didn't even say good-bye."

Guilt hit Rory, twisting her stomach. "I know. I'm sorry. It was just too much to handle. That fuckhead Krag. Being tossed into that den of monsters. Sister Olive."

Hope's amber eyes closed for a minute in sorrow. "I understand. Truly. But we only want to help."

"Cain said I was one of you. What did he mean?"

"Do you have a ring-shaped birthmark?"

Rory paused in the act of sliding on clean jeans. She reached around to make sure there wasn't a hole in her underwear or something. "On my ass. Does it show through?"

"No. It's a mark that identifies you as a Theronai."

"I don't even know what that is. How can I be one?"

"Did you ever meet your father?"

An image of long, elegant fingers opening a can of soup flashed in Rory's head. Logan's fingers. He was making her food.

"No. He was a one-night stand. Mom did a lot of drugs for a lot of years before she OD'd. Nana said she didn't even know my dad's name."

Hope winced at the ugliness, but had the decency to keep her pity to herself. "Chances are he was from another world. Another planet."

Rory's hands stilled at her zipper, as that insane idea shoved every other thought, and every flashing vision from her head. "You're telling me that my dad was an alien?"

Hope took Rory's hands in hers. "If it helps any, my mom was, too. In fact, I was raised on a different world before I was sent here."

A different *world*? Rory pulled away, unwilling to believe something so obviously false. "That's an interesting fairy tale and all, but unless you can come up with a more believable lie, I really need to go." Away from the people who believed they were aliens.

"Is it really so hard to believe that after what you've seen? Demons? Synestryn lords like Krag? Men who can heal with a touch like Logan or kill with the power and ease that Cain can?"

"That's different."

"How?"

Um. Just because she couldn't think of a good reason didn't mean there wasn't one. "I don't know. It just is."

"Please, Rory. Just listen to me. If you are who we think you are, then you can't go out there alone. You're in terrible danger."

"Of that I'm acutely aware. I've run from these things my whole life. I'll keep running until they catch me."

"You said you were looking for someone. Who?"

"I don't know who. Yet."

Hope shook her head, making her blond hair sway around her shoulders. "I don't understand."

"I should just go. I don't want to drag you into this any farther than you've already come. It's my problem. I'll deal with it."

"You're one of us. Your problems *are* our problems."

The idea of belonging somewhere, of not being a freak among these people, was as tempting as it was terrifying. "It's not something I really like to talk about."

Hope took her hand again, and Rory felt a strand of warmth weave up her arm. "Please."

"You wouldn't believe me even if I told you the truth."

"Can your secret really be any harder to believe than aliens?"

When she put it that way . . . what harm was there in telling Hope? No one was going to believe a woman who claimed to be an alien, anyway.

Rory dragged in a long breath and gave in to the urge to spill her guts. "I see things. Things I shouldn't see. I just want them to go away and there's someone out there who makes it stop."

Hope frowned, and it made her only more beautiful, which was, frankly, hideously unfair. "What kind of things?"

"Everything. Random bits of mundane existence. Private things. It all shoves its way into my head and I don't want it there. It's too much. It hurts."

"And this person you're looking for makes it all stop?"

An image of some old dude taking a leak filled her head for an instant before fading away.

"Yes."

"How?"

"I don't know. I don't even know if it's just one person

I'm looking for. Maybe it's more than one. All I know is that sometimes, when I move around the city, the visions stop when I get close to them."

"How do you know it's a person?"

"If it were a place, then I could stand in one location and the visions wouldn't come back. I figured that whoever it is who's helping me must move away. Drive off or something. I can't ever catch up with them."

"It could be a magical artifact."

That was something Rory had never considered. She sat there for a minute in shock, considering the possibility. "I didn't know such things existed."

"They do. I've seen them. Cain's sword and scabbard are both examples of such things. That's why you can't see his sword unless it's drawn."

Now that Rory thought about it, she hadn't noticed his sword since the battle. "So someone could be walking around with a magic ring or something that could fix me?"

"It's possible."

That would certainly solve the problem of how she was going to convince whoever blocked her visions to teach her how they did it, or, heaven forbid, stick by her side all of the time. She wanted a cure, not a conjoined twin. If that was a solution, she could pay Cain to hold her hand for the rest of her life. Which would never work. She needed freedom. Independence. She knew that was going to be an obstacle, but it wasn't one she felt she could plan how to overcome until she knew who it was she would be dealing with.

Logan came in toting a bowl of soup.

"We'll find a way to help you," said Hope. "Logan and I have powerful friends. Like Cain."

Logan set the soup down on a desk near the door. "Are you hungry?"

Rory wasn't, but he'd gone to all the trouble. It seemed rude not to at least take a few bites. "Sure."

Hope let go of her hand, and Rory's arm went cold.

She looked at the steam curling up from the bowl and realized that she had no idea what might be in it. These people wanted her to stay. They wanted her secrets. They could have easily drugged the soup.

She'd told Hope things she'd never told anyone but Mom and Nana. And she hadn't even hesitated to spill her guts just now. That wasn't something Rory did. Ever.

She looked at her tingling hand. There was a pink blotch where Hope's fingers had touched. Drugs? Magic? Rory had no idea, but something had definitely left that mark.

The woman that Rory thought she could trust had done something to her—removed her suspicion somehow. And she hadn't even known it was happening.

Stupid. Careless. Infuriating. Rory knew better than to trust anyone that much.

"I need to go." She grabbed her purse and headed for the door.

Logan sounded confused. "Aren't you going to at least wait until Cain comes back to make sure there's no sign of poison in the creature that stabbed you?"

Cain was as much of a threat as Hope was. That man kept pulling her in, making her want to get closer to him. Touch him. Trust him. It had to be some kind of trick—some kind of magic or bizarre biochemistry she didn't understand. Well, she wasn't falling for it. Not this time.

Rory stopped long enough to write her cell phone number on the wall. "Text me with the results. Don't bother to call. I won't answer." In case they could do that hypnosis thing—or whatever it was—through the phone lines.

"You're scared," said Hope. "I understand. When I thought I was alone, I was scared, too. But you're not alone. We can help."

Hope's voice was so kind, so full of genuine concern. The temptation to stay and soak it up was strong.

"Thanks for fixing my knee," Rory offered, then hurried out the way she'd come in. Sure, there were monsters out there, but she wasn't entirely convinced that they weren't in here, too. At least the monsters out there didn't try to fool her into thinking they were anything but ravening beasts who wanted to eat her face.

Logan held Hope back from going after Rory. "Let her go. I've smelled her blood. If necessary, I can find her later. She needs some time."

Hope's voice was bleak, making Logan's heart weep for her. "She doesn't have any clue how much danger she's in, does she?"

"She's survived this long. I'd say that's a good sign she does know."

Hope laid her head on his shoulder. "Do you think she'll save Cain?"

"Perhaps. Or she may lead us to someone who will."

Hope lifted her head to look at him. "You know something. What is it?"

"Her blood smells familiar. I'm certain I've encountered one of her relatives. Perhaps a half sister."

"Wouldn't you have known if you took blood from a Theronai?"

"Not necessarily. I didn't know with Helen. Her natural defenses masked her from me the way she was masked from Synestryn for a time."

"So there could be another woman like Rory out there?"

"Yes."

"Do you remember where you came across this other woman, this half sister?"

Logan nodded. "She was among those we rescued from Krag's lair."

"Do you know where she is now?"

"There was so much going on then. So much chaos. I assume she went to Dabyr with the others, but Rory slipped away."

"But you had this other woman's blood. You could find her."

"Yes. And I will, but until I do, say nothing to Cain. She could just as easily have shared the same human mother rather than the same Athanasian father."

"Either way, it doesn't matter. Rory is so alone. So isolated. I felt that when I touched her mind. Any family of hers we can find will make a difference, even if that family can't save Cain or one of the others."

Logan stroked Hope's honey-colored hair. "She's one of us now. Part of our family. We will do whatever we can to bring her joy."

She looked up at him, her amber eyes shining. "And that is just one more reason I love you."

Chapter 5

Cain was seeing things—proof of just how far he'd slipped over the past few months. As he walked in through the back door of the shelter, he was sure that he'd seen Sibyl. She'd stood there, staring at him in shock. Her face had been partially hidden by shadows, and he wasn't yet as familiar with her adult face as he had been with her childlike appearance, but for a moment, he'd been sure that it was her.

And then she was gone—slipping out through the kitchen door into the dining area. He followed after her, but there was no sign of anyone passing this way. No lights, no movement . . . nothing but the aching hole Sibyl had left behind.

If he'd slipped down to the point of hallucination, he didn't have much time left. He needed to see Rory settled safely at Dabyr. Now.

He turned and went back to the safe room, carrying a mostly intact demon for Logan to study. As soon as he entered the room, he knew Rory was gone. The space felt empty without her, echoing and lifeless in her absence.

Anger surged and bubbled beneath his skin as he spotted Logan burning her clothes. It sharpened his tone, but he couldn't help that. "You let her go? Alone?"

"It was my fault," said Hope. "I compelled her to trust me so she'd tell me what she was hiding. I'm not very good at that kind of thing yet, and the moment my magic wore off, she knew what I had done. It spooked her. I'm sorry."

"It wasn't your fault, love," said Logan. "Rory is not as susceptible to our skills as a human would be. At least you got her to talk. Now we know the source of her pain."

"Who's hurting her?" demanded Cain. He would find this person or demon and destroy it. Just the thought had his blood pumping through his limbs in eagerness.

Since meeting her, he'd been buoyed by a heady sense of purpose. Her need drove him forward, compelling his actions as strongly as any vow he'd ever given.

Hope shook her head, making her blond ponytail sway. "It's not like that. She has visions of some kind. She's looking for the person she thinks stops them."

"Visions? Of the future?" Sibyl had those, and the knowledge of what would happen to those she loved haunted her. Cain often worried about how she dealt with them now that he was no longer there to comfort her.

"She wasn't specific. All I know is she sees things and these visions clearly hurt her."

That's what he'd seen before his collapse—her face twisted with fear and pain.

The idea of her out there alone was bad enough, but knowing she was out there alone and suffering was too much for him to stand. He had to find her. Help her. He wasn't sure what he could do, but he'd figure out something.

He could help.

The thought whispered through his mind, tempting him with things he knew better than to believe. He couldn't afford to trek up that mountain of hope again. This time the fall would kill him.

His focus had to be on finding her and seeing to her safety. Anything beyond that was too dangerous to risk with him being this close to his end. He had only two leaves left clinging to his lifemark. Once they were gone, his soul would die, and along with it, the fundamental core of him that made him who he was. He couldn't afford to speed up that process by lying to himself. Rory clearly didn't want to have anything to do with him. If that didn't warn him away, he deserved whatever he got.

"I'm going after her." He tossed the small demon on the gurney. "Cut this thing up and figure out if it's a threat to her."

"How are you going to find her?" asked Hope.

Logan set the demon on a metal tray. "Did you leave a bloodmarker on her?"

Cain should have been smart enough to leave a magical tracking mark on her skin, but he hadn't exactly been thinking straight at the time. Once he'd touched her, all he'd been thinking about was how good it felt. "No."

"Then you're going to need her cell phone number. I'm sure Nicholas can track it. And if not, come back here. I've smelled her blood. I should be able to find her if she stays in the city."

"I'll find her."

"And when you do?" asked Logan.

"I'll bring her back here. You can take her to Dabyr."

"You won't claim her for your own?"

Hidden dreams tried to bubble to the surface, but Cain shoved them back down. He refused to do this to himself again. "She may be like Jackie. She may be able to choose who she wants. If so, she should have the chance to make that choice."

"I realize Jackie hurt you, but that doesn't mean Rory would do the same."

Cain hadn't told anyone about that, which meant Logan had gone where he wasn't welcome.

Fury blasted along Cain's bones. He lunged for Logan, but the Sanguinar was faster, darting behind a table, out of reach.

"Don't you dare try to get in my head again," Cain warned.

Logan held up his hands and kept his voice calm. "I meant no harm. You know as well as I do that Jackie's ability to bond with any of the Theronai is a rare thing—one Rory is not likely to possess. You also know that Rory will be far more able to protect herself if she has access to your power. I was thinking only of her safety."

While all of that was true, Cain couldn't let himself be swayed. He wouldn't survive another blow like the one Jackie had delivered. She hadn't done it intentionally, and he couldn't blame her for making the choice she had, but the effect was still the same. He couldn't allow himself to grow attached to the idea of Rory or any of the achingly beautiful things she represented. "I'll bring her back here and you'll take her to Dabyr. Understood?"

"I know how close you are to the end. If you want her to go to Dabyr, you'll have to be the one to take her. I won't help you kill yourself."

Was that what Cain was trying to do? He didn't want to die. He fought as hard as he ever had. The only difference was that now he wasn't doing it to protect his little girl. It was merely habit—something he did because he'd always done it. His vow to protect humans drove him on, compelling him to keep fighting. There didn't have to be more meaning to his life than that. It was enough.

And if it wasn't, he'd pretend that it was until it no longer mattered.

"We struck a bargain," Cain felt compelled to remind him. "I make sure that the demons stay away from Hope's beloved shelter, and you will end my life once I'm imprisoned below Dabyr, after my soul dies."

"I'll uphold my end of the bargain, but I won't make it easy for you to give up. Think of Sibyl. The poor girl has already lost both parents. Does she deserve to lose you, too?"

The wave of guilt punched him in the gut, but he refused to let the Sanguinar know he'd landed a hit. Cain didn't even blink. "She made it clear she didn't need me anymore. She's a grown woman and has a life of her own now, as it should be."

"She's enjoying her newfound freedom now, but one of these days, she'll need advice or help, and you need to be alive to give it."

"Don't you think that's what I want?" Cain bellowed. "I don't have a death wish. But I'm a realist. I know how slim the chances are that Rory would ever agree to be with a man like me."

"Why?"

"You know why," growled Cain. "You know why Sibyl left. I failed to protect her. My sole job was to keep her safe, and I let the demons steal her away."

"Rory doesn't know about that. And you don't have to tell her."

"My failure hangs around me like a shroud for all to see. And Rory sees more than most." Or perhaps he merely felt her gaze more keenly than anyone else.

"So, you're not even going to ask Rory to save your life?"

He had tried with Jackie. It hadn't worked out for him, but at least his brother's life had been saved. He was grateful for that. "I'm not going to discuss this with you. Call me when you know if Rory was poisoned or not. And in the meantime, I'm going to go find her and keep her in sight—the way you should have done."

"Don't push her, Cain," said Hope. "Determination and pride run through her aura as brightly as her fear and pain. She's not like other women. You push her, and she'll push back. Hard."

"Thanks for the advice, but I think I can handle one small woman."

* * *

Maura stayed hidden in the supply closet, waiting for the frantic pounding of her heart to slow. Cain had seen her. She had felt his gaze fall on her, seen it light with recognition. Why he hadn't come hunting for her, she had no idea.

But his easy recognition answered at least one of Maura's questions. Sibyl—Maura's twin sister and Cain's ward—must have been released from the prison of her child's body at the same time Maura had. It was the only thing that Maura could think of that would explain how he'd recognized her so easily.

Maura cowered in her hiding place, straining to hear some sign that she was alone—that the giant, Cain, was not waiting for her in the hall.

She'd stayed here too long. These humans who sheltered her believed she was one of them. Even worse, she was starting to feel as if she belonged. She ate beside them, slept beside them. Never once had they questioned her presence among them.

Not one of them knew the things she'd done to them—to their children. If they had, they would have slit her throat in her sleep, and she would have been powerless to stop them. Now.

There had been a time when even the most powerful Synestryn lords feared her. One touch from her and they'd die screaming in pain. But those days were gone. Her power, her ability to see the future, her connection to her sister . . . all stripped from her the day her mother had died and freed Maura from her child-sized body.

She wore the costume of a grown woman, but inside, she was afraid all the time. She belonged nowhere—not among the Sentinels, and certainly not among the humans. She was a twisted, wicked thing who had turned on her own kind out of rebellion, but not even the Synestryn would want her now. With no powers, she'd mean nothing to them. They'd use her for her blood and drain her dry.

It was better to hide, but she could no longer stay here at this shelter—not when the risk of Cain seeing her was so high. Better to leave now, while she still could, because the only thing she could think of that would be worse than being drained of her blood by demons, would be to face those she'd betrayed and watch them look upon her with pity and disappointment.

Maura slipped from the closet and hurried to her bed, being careful not to wake the few other women nearby. Underneath her bed was a locked suitcase that held a few items of clothing and a little cash. She wasn't sure where she'd go or what she'd do, but there was no more time to linger here, accepting the kindness of those who ran this place. And now that Logan was here with Hope, it was only a matter of time before Maura was found out. She couldn't avoid him forever.

It was time to leave and find her own way in the world. She only wished the idea didn't scare her more than any demon ever had.

For the thousandth time, Maura reached for her twin sister, seeking the comfort of her presence. All she felt was the black chill of utter nothingness, leaving her to wonder if Sibyl was even alive. Even if she was, she was beyond reach now.

Maura was truly alone.

Cain thought he could follow Rory? That was cute and all, but that was the one nice thing about her curse: She could see him coming.

And it was Cain. She'd caught a glimpse of his hand, along with her pink hair, and doubted anyone else had hands that big, especially not with those same scars.

She stopped in her tracks and turned to face him. She saw nothing. "I know you're there. You might as well come out."

This section of the street was dark. There wasn't any traffic this late. The bars and nightclubs had long since closed. Dawn was still hours away. People were mostly asleep, giving her a bit of a reprieve from her suddenly hyperactive visions. She could still see what they saw, but at least it was the calm, quiet black of the inside of eyelids.

Cain stepped around the corner. He seemed even bigger than he'd been before, looming like some kind of giant. He was imposing, his body giving off ragged, desperate vibrations that called to her. If she hadn't seen him save her life with her own eyes, she would be running right now.

But she wasn't running. In fact, the urge to inch closer was nearly overwhelming. She remembered how it felt to be surrounded by his strength, to have the visions disappear, leaving her floating in peaceful serenity. It would be so easy to cross the distance and fling herself at him—beg him to make her problems and fear go away, just for a little while.

If she'd been a weaker person, that's what she would have done. But weakness like that wasn't a part of her makeup. It had been burned out of her DNA before birth, preparing her for a life that was harder than most.

She knew fear. She knew pain. Those things were as familiar as old friends. It was her neediness that freaked her out—her desire to get closer to a man she didn't dare trust.

What if she found the person who stopped her visions and she couldn't trust them, either? What if she never found a cure?

She couldn't go there now. That place was a dark, scary one best left behind a locked door of nice, solid denial. She couldn't possibly face both her deepest fears and Cain at the same time.

The wind ruffled his dark hair. His feet were braced apart, planted firmly on the pavement. He kept his hands at his sides, but it wasn't a lazy stance. She had the distinct impression that he could have his invisible sword in hand in an instant if necessary.

"How did you know I was there? I didn't make a sound."

She ignored his question. "What do you want?"

"You need to come with me. We're going to take you somewhere safe."

"Thanks, but no thanks." She turned and walked toward where her car was parked. It was still a few blocks away, but the chances of her running into the person who blocked her visions were getting slimmer by the moment. Time to cut her losses and head home before the city woke up and she was too blind to drive.

"Please don't make me stop you," he said from behind her, much closer than he'd been a minute ago. "I really don't want to touch you again."

A spurt of adrenaline hurried her stride. She wasn't going to give him the satisfaction of running away. Power walking away didn't count as a cowardly act. As far as she was concerned, power walking in public was an act of bravery whenever it was done. "Wow. Way to make a girl feel good."

"You know what I mean."

She did, but that didn't mean she'd admit it. "I'm not asking you anymore. Leave me alone."

"Or what?"

He had to go and ask, making her struggle for a good answer. "You saw my gun."

"Empty."

"I could have more bullets."

"You would have used them on the demons."

Good point.

He glided past her and stopped right in front of her, barring her path. Rory had to skid to a stop to keep from running into his wide chest.

She craned her head back to look him in the eye. Her

body lit up with a giddy response to his nearness. Nerve endings danced a little jig, and tingling heat spread out over her skin.

His effect on her pissed her off, giving her the spurt of anger she needed to get her head on straight. "What the fuck do you think you're doing?"

His expression was solemn, almost regretful. "Saving your life. Again."

"Did I ask you to?"

His mouth twisted like he'd just bit into a lemon. "What kind of dishonorable asshole makes a woman ask for such a thing?"

Even in the darkness she could see his eyes roaming her face, like he was searching for something important. A crazy part of her really wanted him to find whatever it was he was looking for.

Proof she was one step closer to that inevitable insanity conclusion.

She took a long step back. "I'm going to make this clear enough that even you can understand it. I'm not going anywhere with you. Ever. You're wasting your time. Go away and don't come back."

He flinched. It was barely even a movement, more of a tightening of the fine muscles in his face, but she saw it anyway.

And it made her feel like shit.

Damn it. This would be so much easier if he didn't have feelings for her to hurt.

She pulled in a deep breath. "I'm sorry. I don't mean to be a bitch, but this following me around thing is a bit stalkerish and creepy."

"How else am I to protect you from demons if I'm not nearby?"

That was not the kind of question Rory had any practice answering. "You . . . don't?"

"I can't leave you to die. We need you too much."

"I'm not the kind of person anyone needs. Really. I've got parts that don't work right, my blood is dangerous, and I'm kind of a flake."

"A flake of what?"

"Flaky. As in you can't depend on me. I can't even tell you how many jobs I've lost."

"Because of your visions?"

"How the hell do you know about those?"

"You can't trust a Sanguinar."

"You mean Hope. She tricked me into telling her what she wanted to know and then she went and told you? Great."

He nodded. "She's not as bad as some. She only told me because she's worried about you."

"I'm a big girl."

One side of his mouth lifted in a grin. "Hardly."

No one was big compared to him. Rory had no trouble believing he was an alien, because humans weren't built like that. Or maybe it was his presence that made him loom large—blocking out the existence of everything around him.

She squared her shoulders. "I mean I can protect myself."

"Like you did earlier tonight?"

"You can't prove that demon was going to eat my face if you hadn't shown up."

"I don't feel the need to prove anything."

"Then why are you arguing with me?"

"Because the alternatives are to sling you over my shoulder or render you unconscious. Both of those require me to touch you, which I'd rather not do."

Again with the ego blow. This guy had the world's deadliest aim when it came to that tender spot. "Does it really hurt you that much to touch me?"

"Only when I stop."

Oh. Well. That was different. "When you touched me,

my visions went away," she admitted before she could control her flapping mouth.

His whole demeanor changed in a heartbeat. His eyes darkened and without moving, he was somehow closer than he'd been a second ago. She saw his throat move as he swallowed, and felt the heat of his body wrap around her.

She shivered in reaction, and she was sure he saw it. He was the only man she'd ever met who she felt was looking at her, rather than skimming the surface. She'd always wondered what that would be like, but now that she was facing the brunt of his unwavering attention, she found it was too much for her to take. He made her squirm, made deep, needy parts of her wake up and howl.

"I stopped your suffering?" he asked, as if the answer was important to his very survival.

She didn't understand his odd reaction, but her mouth was too dry to ask him about it. Instead, her chin went up, and he must have taken that as a nod.

"If I touched you now, do you think it would drive your visions away again?"

She did. She couldn't say the words, but deep down she knew that if she so much as brushed his hand with hers, she'd be free.

At least for a moment.

"You make me want to take risks," he whispered. "You make me forget the danger." His hand hovered near her cheek, so close she swore she could feel sparks of static electricity arcing between them.

Why wasn't she running? Why wasn't she even backing away? This was the part where she was supposed to back away and deliver some kind of cutting quip. Instead, she felt herself sway on her feet, leaning toward him.

Even being this close felt good. Waves of heat swept

out of him, driving away the wind. She couldn't smell the dirt of the city, or lingering exhaust fumes. All she could smell was his skin and the leather of his jacket. The combination went to her head, making it spin.

His lips parted, and a warm current of air swirled up into the night.

He had a nice mouth. Not girlie, but full enough to be soft. Wherever he kissed her.

She was not thinking about letting this stranger kiss her. Was she?

Rory licked her lips and felt her breathing speed. His nostrils flared, and she swore his head dipped down a fraction of an inch before he stopped.

His pupils were huge, and there was a flush of color in his cheeks that hadn't been there a moment ago. "You should back away."

Back away? That wasn't what she wanted. Getting closer would have been nice, though. She could wiggle up against him and soak up his heat. He could strip the barrage of visions from her, along with some of her clothes.

Oh, yeah. She was definitely thinking about letting him kiss her. And then some.

His deep, gravelly voice was so quiet she could barely hear it over her own thudding heart. "I'm not strong enough to stop."

He made that sound like it was a bad thing when every cell in her body was doing a little happy dance at the idea of him not stopping.

She didn't move. She couldn't.

"If you don't move away, I'm going to touch you, Rory." His words rumbled out, vibrating against her skin.

Her eyes slid shut so she could focus on the feeling. There was no moving away for her now. Not anymore. Whatever he did to her was potent and intoxicating, driving away all rational thought. She didn't even care that she hadn't wanted this only a moment ago. She wanted it now. Bad.

His hand brushed her hair, barely tugging the pink strands.

It wasn't enough. Not even close.

She tilted her head up to look at him. Her mouth was only inches from his. All she had to do was go up on tiptoe and she could kiss him.

This was so insane—so completely off-the-charts bonkers—that she didn't even feel like herself anymore. There was some primal urge way deep down inside of her, driving her forward, demanding that she take what was hers.

She tried to remember that he wasn't hers, but logic wasn't rating high on her scale of things to care about right now. Her whole body was humming. She could hear whispered urges inside her skull and feel them radiating out of her skin.

His necklace pulsed with color, drawing her gaze. It was way too pretty for him to wear. It would look so much better on her, tucked close to her skin.

"I want it," she whispered.

She reached for it, needing to feel its texture against her fingertip.

Cain was there one minute, and the next, he was simply gone. Rory blinked, her whole body swaying in discord. He was several feet away, breathing hard, his limbs vibrating with tension.

Disorientation swarmed in her head, along with narrow, dim sights that were not her own. Ceilings, walls, alarm clocks. The visions were coming from people sleeping nearby.

Normally, Rory never had to fight against what people saw when they slept. And now they were coming to her stronger than ever.

She closed her eyes, but that only made it worse. The visions were clearer, glaring at her in vibrant defiance.

She saw some woman's knees as she sat on the toilet. A man pulled a bottle of water from the fridge.

"Rory?" came Cain's deep voice.

The sound of it calmed her enough for her to remember to breathe.

"I need to go." Now, while she could still see well enough to drive, before the city woke up and she was trapped here to suffer all day.

She took three steps and ran into a brick wall she hadn't seen.

"You're not going anywhere like this. Let me help."

"Don't touch me. Don't even get near me. Every time you do it gets worse."

"Fine. I won't touch you. Just stop moving before you walk out into a street."

Rory stopped. This crazy vision steroid thing he did to her would fade. It had before. It would again.

"Logan. I need your help," she heard Cain say, presumably into his phone.

She crouched low to the ground, putting a bit more distance between her and those living in the upper floors of any nearby apartment buildings.

"It's not that close to dawn," he said. "Fine, then send Hope. She needs our help."

He was talking about Rory. She was still pissed at Hope for tricking her like she had. Now everyone knew about Rory's visions, which was exactly what she'd been trying to avoid her entire life. "I'll be fine. I just need to get to my car."

"You're not getting behind a wheel when you can't even see to walk."

"I need to get away from people." If there were no people around, there were no eyeballs around to shove images into her brain.

"Will that help?" asked Cain.

"Yes."

"I'm taking her to a Gerai house," he told whoever was on the phone. "Joseph can send someone to pick her up."

Rory didn't know what a Gerai house was, and she truly didn't care. "I'll be fine in a minute. I'll be even better if you leave."

"Are you going to come quietly, or not?"

"Not. I told you I'll be fine." And she really hoped it wasn't a lie.

"I'm sorry about this," he said, regret hanging in his voice like an executioner's axe.

"About what?" She opened her eyes and stood. The visions were blocking most of her sight, but she saw enough to witness his big body approaching.

He moved too fast to be real. Too fast for her to even pull in a full breath to scream. His wide palm pressed hot against her forehead, and said, "Sleep."

Rory did.

Chapter 6

Cain caught Rory as she crumpled. The metallic sting of drawing in enough power to make her sleep still burned his hand, but the rest of his pain was blissfully absent.

He held her in his arms and caressed her cheek as he'd been dying to do before. She was even softer than he'd remembered, her skin warm and smooth under his rough fingertips.

As much as he would have loved to linger over her, there wasn't time. She wouldn't sleep long, and when she woke, he wanted her to be as far away from people as possible. If that's what helped mute her painful visions, then that's what he'd do.

The walk back to the shelter seemed to pass in a blink of time. Her ridiculously pink head was cradled against him so that her forehead was pressed to his neck. The smell of something sweet filled his nostrils, and he kept breathing it in, trying to identify the intoxicating scent. It reminded him of spring, the way it used to smell centuries ago.

He made sure her skin never left contact with his. The blast of agony he suffered whenever he stopped touching her was not something he wanted to face until absolutely necessary. It was as consuming as it was incapacitating. Night was still upon them and demons roamed free. He wasn't sure he'd be able to fight if the pain hit him again. He wasn't sure he'd even be able to stand. The thought of dropping her made him careful, not that touching her was any hardship.

The soft brush of her breath over his skin made every muscle in his body tighten in anticipation and longing. She made him want things he refused to name. She gave him hope where he'd thought none could be found, and while that was a gift, it was also a curse. Hope was good only while it lasted, while there was still some question as to the future.

But how much question could there be when she clearly didn't like him, when she couldn't wait to be rid of him?

And yet she'd nearly touched his luceria. She'd said she wanted it.

Of course she had no idea what she was getting herself into. There was no way she could know.

The fact that he'd almost chosen not to stop her showed just how far he'd slid from the man he'd once been.

Cain knocked on the shelter door and Hope let him in, panic straining her voice. "What happened?"

"She's just sleeping. I couldn't let her run away."

"You did this to her?"

Cain carried her back toward the safe room. "I had to. She left me no choice."

"Oh, man. She is going to be furious when she wakes up."

"As long as she's still alive, she can be as mad as she wants."

Logan sat bent over the small demon carcass with a scalpel in his hand. He looked up as Cain entered and rose from his seat.

"She's fine," said Cain, preempting any more concern.

He went to lay Rory on the gurney, but there was a

black smudge of demon blood staining the sheets. No way was he laying her on that.

Instead, he settled into a chair and leaned back so she was resting comfortably against his chest, holding her close so she wouldn't slip off. Her forehead was tucked against his neck, and he could feel streamers of energy sliding out of him, reaching for her, sinking into her skin wherever they touched. There was a heady kind of magic in the exchange—one he didn't allow himself to think about for long. That minute transfer of energy was too close to the way it was supposed to be with a woman—his partner. He'd never felt it before like this—not even with Jackie—and he had a feeling he could get used to it way too fast.

Maybe he already had.

Cain guessed that the longer he touched her, the more the separation would hurt, but right now he couldn't bring himself to care. He liked this blissful lack of pain—this tiny glimpse of what should have been—and he would use any excuse he could find to stay like this for as long as possible. It would end too soon no matter what he did, and that pain would be waiting for him, ready to pounce.

Logan stared at him for a moment, his pretty head tilted to one side, studying Cain.

"What?" demanded Cain.

"Nothing," said Logan in a way that clearly meant something else. "We have no need to worry about her being poisoned."

Relief swept through him, and he felt something in his chest unclench. "That's good news."

Rory shifted on his lap. Her hand slid up until the tips of her fingers were touching the skin above his collar, mere inches from his luceria.

He caught himself holding his breath and had to make a conscious effort to let it out.

"There is, however, some bad news," said Logan.

"What?" Cain choked out.

"This creature contained no poison glands that I could detect, but it did have this strange bit of anatomy attached to its barbs."

"What was it?"

"A type of bladder, but it was empty. And its barbs were hollow. I believe that it is meant to collect fluid. Like blood."

Slow, feral anger began to simmer in Cain's gut. "You think that thing that stung her took her blood?"

"I'd have to have a live specimen to be sure, but that seems a reasonable assumption."

Some demon out there had Rory's blood? Cain couldn't let that stand. "I'll track it down and kill it. And I'll bring you back a live one to study."

He began to move, but Rory let out a small whimper as if the motion had disturbed her.

Cain went still, his need to see her content and his need to rescue her blood warring within him.

"How will you find it?" asked Hope.

"I don't know. I just will." The task was a simple one. He wouldn't fail.

Logan spun his chair around to face them. "Perhaps I could detect the scent of her blood within one of the creatures, but it's too close to dawn for me to go out hunting."

"Fine, then I'll go kill them all." As soon as he could bring himself to let Rory go. "But one of you needs to take her out of the city. She said that being around a lot of people makes her visions worse."

Hope looked down at her friend. "I can take her."

"No," said Logan, his voice harsh and final. "It's too dangerous. What if the purpose of taking her blood is to use it to track her?"

"It will be daylight. The demons can't follow her during the day."

"No, but they can use Dorjan," said Logan, speaking

of the brainwashed human servants the Synestryn used to do their bidding. "And there's no way of knowing what the Synestryn will do with her blood. They could use it to control her. She could attack you."

Hope paled and took a step nearer to Logan. "That's ridiculous."

No, it wasn't, and Cain couldn't ask Hope to risk herself like that. Despite her growing power and strength, she wasn't a Theronai. She wasn't a warrior.

The way Rory would be if she chose to take a man's luceria.

Until that happened, Cain was going to see to it that she was well protected. "I'll have Joseph send some men to take her to Dabyr. Then I'll go hunt down these barbed creatures. You two have already helped enough."

"She's not going to hurt me," said Hope.

Rory's fingers clenched around his shirt, and she let out a groggy whisper. "Don't let me hurt her."

She tried to sit up, but Cain kept his grip firm so she wouldn't accidentally stop touching him. If she did, he'd likely thrash around and dump her onto the hard floor, or worse yet, land on top of her and crush her.

The thought of being atop her for a different, more pleasurable reason hit him from out of nowhere. He could almost see her pink hair splayed out across white sheets, her face draped in shadows and shaped by pleasure as he pushed them both toward a bright, shimmering release.

In an instant, his mouth went dry, his throat constricting hard enough to cut off his air. His cock swelled, and he barely shifted fast enough to hide his shameful lack of control from her. Lusting after a helpless woman was disgraceful, and yet he couldn't seem to find enough honor to let that stop him. Everything about her called out to him in a siren song meant to tear down his willpower. Even that ridiculous pink hair was growing on him.

Hope gave Logan a hard, irritated look. "See what

you've done? Now you've got her worried for no good reason."

"There is good reason, love. You were already attacked by a Dorjan once. I will not let you risk yourself again. Not even for Rory. Not when Cain is capable of seeing to her care."

Fury darkened Hope's face and she loomed over Logan, her voice quiet and shaking. "You don't get to tell me what to do or who to help."

Logan rose to his feet, his usual grace gone in the face of his own anger. "So you'd risk your life for something another can do just as easily?"

"It's my life to risk."

"And what of me? Where do you think I would be without you? You are my world, and like it or not, you are now responsible for my life as well."

Their argument was beginning to escalate, and Cain could feel Rory growing more upset by the moment, her slender body going tense in his arms.

"Is he right?" asked Rory, her voice too quiet to travel beyond his ears alone. "Could I hurt her?"

Cain couldn't lie to her, not when she sounded so vulnerable and afraid—so trusting of him. "It's possible."

"Then help me get me out of here. Please."

"I can help her," said Hope. "Even if things go wrong, I'm getting stronger every day. I can protect myself."

"You haven't been a part of our world long enough to know just how wrong things can go," said Logan.

This was not the kind of lovers' argument Cain wanted to witness. It was a private affair, and he wanted to help keep it that way.

He stood up and left the room with Rory in his arms. He kicked the door shut behind him, muting sounds of their increasingly heated argument.

When he got to the kitchen, he paused long enough to ask, "Are you feeling okay?"

"Yeah. You can put me down now."

Cain grudgingly eased her to the floor, holding her hand and making sure she was steady on her feet. She swayed, and her eyes didn't seem to focus on any one thing. He wasn't sure if that was from grogginess, or if her visions had come back despite his touch.

"I'm fine. You can let go."

Shame burned in his cheeks. "I'm afraid I can't. Not if you want me in any shape to drive."

She nodded, her head wobbly, and laced her fingers through his. "I'd kill us right now if I got behind the wheel, but I really want to leave. If I did anything to hurt Hope, I'd never forgive myself."

Cain knew all too well how horrible hurting another felt. He couldn't stand the thought of Rory suffering through such guilt. "I won't let that happen."

He led her outside to his truck. Rory crawled in, moving over so he could get in behind the wheel. He kept his grip on her fingers tight so they didn't accidentally slip away. Not that that was any hardship. He liked the feeling of her delicate fingers laced through his, the warmth of her skin, and the trembling streamers of energy vibrating between them. It was all he could do to focus on operating the vehicle safely.

Cain drove out of the city toward Dabyr, pleased that she was on her way to where she belonged. He hadn't wanted to be the one to take her, but he was counting this as a victory nonetheless.

Until she went stiff beside him and cast him a glare so acidic he could feel it against the side of his face. "You knocked me out," she said as if just now remembering. "I was going to leave and you knocked me out."

Cain blew out a breath and accepted his incoming scolding. "I sent you to sleep. You left me no choice."

"Yeah? Well, you've left *me* no choice. Pull the fuck over."

"Why?"

"Because in about ten seconds I'm letting go of your

hand, and I'd rather not die in a fiery crash and spill my blood everywhere so the monsters find us and eat our corpses."

Ronan preferred the role of hunter to prey.

He could smell the fetid stench of demons tracking him, hear their skittering hearts racing. There were more than a dozen of them following along behind him. He couldn't very well let them follow him to the human couple whose sick, blooded son he needed to heal.

Ronan led them away from his destination and found a quiet, dark loading dock at the back of a vacant warehouse. There were no prying eyes here—no reason for him to waste his precious, dwindling stores of magic on shielding what he was about to do from sight of humans.

The cold air seeped through his leather trench coat, into his bones. The chill slowed his reflexes and made his joints ache with the need for warmth.

He was on his own out here—the way he preferred. Despite the fact that a Theronai's blade would be handy right about now, his job was simpler when he had to make no explanations to another for his actions.

Project Lullaby needed him, and his dedication to saving his race had to be absolute.

Ronan drew his sword and turned to face the oncoming threat. His gaze cut through the darkness, latching on to the first demon brave enough to show itself.

It was small, but he knew better than to let that make him overconfident. Even the tiniest demon could kill a man just as dead as a giant one could. The only difference was that he had a chance at defeating something so small without exhausting his dwindling power.

The demon's thick insectoid tail was curved up over its back, with three long barbs gleaming from the tip. It moved fast, low to the ground, its claws making only the faintest sound along the cold asphalt. A pale green glow spilled from its six eyes as it neared Ronan.

In the distance more of the things appeared, their eyes lighting with hunger and excitement. He heard the fluttering of their hearts speed with anticipation as they scrambled to reach him.

Ronan counted twenty before the first one got close enough for him to strike. He speared it with the tip of his sword and flung it against a wall hard enough to make it splatter. By the time he turned back around, another three of the things were at his feet.

He kicked two away and stomped on a third.

More flooded close, and Ronan had no choice but to jump back onto the thin ledge of concrete left outside the closed dock door.

The demons crawled up the wall, not even slowing.

Ronan no longer had the luxury of options. His sword was no good against so many of the things. He was going to have to dip into his reserves.

He gathered power from his cells, feeling it tingle along his limbs as a faint blue light seeped from his skin. His fingertips blazed like blue flame as the energy coalesced into a searing disk.

Ronan slammed that power down on the horde at his feet, ordering the disk to roll over the demons and crush them as it passed.

The small creatures screamed as they died. Only a few escaped, cowering in the shadows nearby.

His flesh felt like it was sagging on his bones. Every breath was labored, every beat of his heart an effort. A deep chill sank into him, shaking him from the inside out, whispering to him that he was never going to be warm again.

He leaned against the door, letting it support his weight while he caught his breath.

Three of the demons remained, inching closer as if sensing his weakness.

Through a sheer effort of will, Ronan lifted his sword just as the first demon charged.

He sliced through it, more by accident than skill, but by the time he'd recovered from the swing, one of the demons had crawled up his leg and shoved its barbs into his thigh. The other one seemed to be going for his groin.

Not in this lifetime.

Ronan plucked it off, and as soon as his skin touched it, he felt a wave of malignant compulsion seeping from the thing. The power of that compulsion was so strong, it shocked Ronan to stillness.

The demon that had stung him jumped off and scurried away. There was no sign of poison in his blood, which was odd, but what was even more important was figuring out who was controlling these things. They weren't simply demons out looking for food. They were under orders, and whoever had given those orders was the real threat.

Ronan kept a firm hold on the demon's tail while he reached into its puny mind, searching for answers. There were no real thoughts inside the thing, only instincts and the most basic of emotions.

It was sent to hunt him. It knew his scent as well as that of several others. Its orders were to collect blood and bring it back to the one who'd compelled it to hunt. There was no hint of why the blood was needed, no trace of rational thought beyond its mission.

But there was something there—a whisper of power running through it, controlling it.

Ronan reached for that power. He studied it, memorized it as he would a scent. It was vile and reeked of malignance. Vengeance.

The Synestryn that had sent these demons out was powerful and looking for revenge on very specific targets. And now it had Ronan's blood.

Chapter 7

Rory's head was still foggy, but her anger was helping her wake up faster than any double espresso ever could.

Cain's fingers tightened between hers, and the firmer contact made those warm tingles soak into her even faster.

His voice was low and calm. "I'm not pulling over. You're being unreasonable."

"No. Unreasonable would be pulling my hand away before giving you fair warning. I think I'm being a saint under the circumstances."

He didn't pull over. The sky was beginning to lighten with the first hint of dawn, and as they sped down the highway, she could see traffic picking up in the opposite direction as it flowed into the city.

"I'm not stopping. Not until I get you to Dabyr."

"I don't know who or what that is, but I'm not going anywhere with someone who would rather knock me out than accept my decision to leave."

"You'll be safe at Dabyr. It's well protected, and the walls keep out most hostile magic. There are people there who may be able to help your visions disappear."

As tempting as that was, it had to be too good to be true. "How?"

"The same way I help you, but more . . . permanent."

"How permanent?" She wasn't sure if she could survive having her visions go away only to return again. At least now she had hope to cling to. If the visions came back . . .

"That would be your decision."

"You make it sound simple," she said.

"I promise it's anything but simple." He didn't expand on that, and his silence was thick and heavy, telling her that he was done discussing it.

Rory should have pushed the issue of forcing him to pull over, but her fear held her back. She was so close to the city, she knew that as soon as she stopped touching him, her visions would inundate her. Thousands of sights would flood her head, leaving her blind and stumbling along the highway—not a good position to be in. "Are there many people there?"

"About five hundred or so."

"How big is this neighborhood?"

"It's not a neighborhood, it's more of a compound. There are some smaller structures, but most of Dabyr is one big building."

She groaned at the thought. "Five hundred people under one roof? You've just described my version of hell."

"It's lovely. You'll like it."

"Like it? How would you like to have the things that five hundred people see shoved into your brain all at once, setting your eyeballs on fire? How do you think those people will feel knowing that I can't help but invade their privacy? Or will you keep that a secret and use me as some kind of spy?"

The truck slowed and he moved into the right lane. "I hadn't considered that going there would hurt you. My only thought was to keep you safe."

"Yeah, well, I'm safe at home. Just take me back to my car and we'll forget we ever met each other." As soon as she uttered the words, she knew how ridiculous they were. Cain was not a man easily forgotten. Not his size, or his power, or his lethal ability with that invisible sword. Not the way his skin felt as it brushed hers. Even now, after several minutes to get used to his touch, she still felt every strand of electric warmth as it slid into her, wrapping around her spine and making her tingle all the way down to her toes.

"Where is your home?" he asked.

"You really think I'm going to tell you that?"

"If that's where you want to go, then that's where I'll take you. If you tell me where to go, that is."

She needed her car, but if she could at least get home before the city woke up and bombarded her with visions, that would be better than nothing. She'd find another way to get her car back.

"If I tell you, how do I know you won't come back after you drop me off and bother me? I like my privacy."

"I suppose that's a chance you're going to have to take," he said. "If it's any comfort, I plan to go kill the demon that stole your blood. I'll be too busy to bother you."

That thought drove all others out of her in a single instant. As pissed as she should have been at him, fear over him facing more demons and whatever was going to happen to her now made that anger pale in comparison. "What will that thing do with my blood?"

"We don't know. And I don't plan for you to find out the hard way. I'll kill it first."

"How do you even know where it went?"

"I don't, but I've hunted down plenty of demons in my lifetime. And if I can't locate its nest, Logan will be able to help."

"How?"

"He's smelled your blood. He should be able to track that scent back to the demon."

Rory let her head fall against the seat in overwhelming defeat. "I don't understand any of this. I don't know how Logan can smell my blood. I don't know why the demons want it. I don't know why your touch blocks my visions or how it can make me feel like this. All I know is that I want to live my life in peace, without monsters hunting me all the time."

"That's all any of us want, Rory. But you and I aren't like humans. We don't get that kind of life."

She was human, albeit a fucked-up version of one, and no one could persuade her otherwise. But there was another question his comment brought up, one she could barely stand to ask. If it hadn't been for the curiosity that was burning a hole in her brain, making all logical thought dribble out, she would have stayed silent. "What kind of life *do* you have?"

He didn't say anything for several seconds. His jaw was tense and a vein pulsed in his temple. He really was a handsome man in a barbaric kind of way—not at all like the type of guy she normally went for, all artistic and flimsy—but that was part of his appeal. She'd made so many bad choices in the past, it was comforting to be sitting next to a guy so utterly *different*.

Rory would have been willing to bet Nana's house that the man didn't have a single flimsy spot on his entire body.

He pulled in a deep breath that expanded his thick chest even further. "There are two kinds of Theronai: those who are joined as they were meant to be, and those that aren't."

"And which are you?"

He glanced at their twined fingers, and she swore she could feel a sense of sadness and loss radiating out of his touch.

"I'm like most of my kind. We live a long time. We hunt and kill demons. We protect humans and each other, and try not to think too hard about the things that we can never have."

"Sounds like a pile of suck."

His mouth twitched. "It's a life filled with honor, duty and purpose. It's more than many ever have."

It was more than Rory had, which was disgustingly pathetic. Ever since she'd lost Nana, *she'd* been lost. The only friendships she could manage were long-distance ones—people online she'd never meet in person for fear of what she might see through their eyes. They helped fill the void, but there were still gaping holes Rory knew would never be whole. She was twenty-five and hadn't been able to go to a normal school or hold down a job or keep a boyfriend for more than a few days—at least not one who wasn't planning to hand her over to a demon in exchange for drugs.

She'd stopped dreaming about a future years ago. The only thing that drove her was her quest to find the person who made her visions go away. It was her white whale, her reason for getting up in the morning.

Now she was holding the hand of a man who blocked her visions, and as nice as that was, it wasn't enough. It was hollow. Worse than that, it allowed her to see just how empty her life had become. How worthless.

Once her visions were gone, then what? What would get her out of bed then?

She had no answer, which made a whole writhing mass of fear spring to life in her stomach. She wasn't the type of person who panicked, but she could feel that now, cutting at the edges of her confidence, wearing it away, bit by bit.

Her visions had defined her life. She couldn't live with them, but she wasn't sure she could live without them, either.

Rory didn't know how to calm her fears. She didn't even know if it was possible. What she did know was that the man she'd pitied only a few moments ago for his crappy life had a better life than she did, and if she didn't start taking some chances, she was never going to be able to make something of herself.

"Head south at the next exit," she told him.

"You're going to let me take you home?"

"Looks like."

She was quiet for a long time, only speaking to give him directions to Nana's house out in the country. "These people you said might be able to help me? Would they be willing to come see me or meet me somewhere—somewhere without a lot of people around?"

"The men would swim entire oceans to meet you."

That sounded a little over the top and left her confused. "But not the women?"

"The women can't help you. That's not the way it works."

"Then how does it work?"

"Our kind—Theronai—were created to work in pairs. One man, one woman."

"You don't know I'm your kind."

"I do. Your ring-shaped birthmark proves it."

Outrage slammed into her, and if he hadn't had a firm hold on her fingers, she would have pulled away in shock. "You looked at my ass when I was asleep?"

A slow smile pulled at his mouth. "No, but now I know you have the mark. No denying it."

"You tricked me."

He shrugged and she felt the powerful movement all the way up her arm. "Denial will get you nowhere. It could even kill you, which is something I can't allow. We all have to face reality, and yours isn't going to change just because you don't like it."

"You say that like you know my life better than I do."

"Not your past, maybe, but I know your future."

She grunted in amusement. "So you can see the future, can you?"

"Only yours."

"Fine. Then spill. What does my grand future hold?"

"Power. More than you can imagine. Purpose, too. Your life will be filled with fear and danger, but also love.

Undying, unyielding love and devotion from a man who would put your safety and happiness above all else, except, perhaps, that of your children."

Rory laughed at the ludicrous image he painted. "You know, back when I used to think about having kids, I always thought my visions would come in handy. I'd know what they were up to all the time. No sneaking cookies before dinner or cutting their own hair without me knowing."

"You say that as if you no longer think about having children."

"I don't. How can I care for someone else when sometimes I can't even walk without running into walls?"

"I'm certain that you will learn to control your visions."

"Oh. I see. You're certain. Well, that makes it true then, huh?"

"Every female Theronai has a special gift. These visions are yours, and once you're connected to your mate and have access to his power, you'll be able to use that power to control them."

"And the winner of today's Too Good To Be True contest is . . ."

"I'm serious, Rory. I've seen this kind of thing before. You have no idea how much power awaits you once you connect yourself to the right man."

"And just how do I find this right man?"

"I'll send some men to you."

"And I'm supposed to trust your judgment?"

"It's not a judgment call. There will be no question. His luceria will react to your presence. It will vibrate and change color."

That sounded kinda kinky. "Luceria?"

"The ring and necklace our kind wear."

"Oh. Not at all what I was thinking." She looked at his left hand, which was clamped around the steering wheel.

Purple and pink swirls danced madly along its iridescent surface. "Yours is doing that."

"Yes."

"Is that why the visions go away when I touch you?"

"I believe so."

"So why can't you be the one to take the visions away?"

"I'm not right for you. You'll have to make a promise to this man—one that will demand trust."

"You're saying you're not trustworthy?"

Cain shifted in his seat, his jaw bunching. "You clearly don't trust me."

"Yeah. Knocking me out like that was definitely a big black mark in the Don't Trust column."

He snorted, dismissing her statement. "That was nothing. And for the record, I'd do it again if I thought it would keep you safe."

"We'll call that strike two."

"Call it what you want. It doesn't matter. Our path together will end as soon as I'm sure you're safe."

Rory didn't like that thought, but she was sure it was only because his touch brought her so much relief and pleasure. Once he was gone, he'd take that with him, and she'd be alone in her hollow little life, hiding from the blindingly bright world.

She sat in silence while they rumbled down the gravel road leading to Nan's house. "What kind of promise?" she asked him.

"That's your decision, but whatever you promise will be binding, so choose your words carefully."

"You know this doesn't make any sense, right?"

He pulled in a deep breath as if seeking patience. "Your chosen man will vow to protect you, even if it costs him his own life. Then you will give him a promise in return. Something like vowing to stay with him until the end of time."

"Whoa. That's a hell of a promise."

"It doesn't have to be that. You could choose to stay with him for one single night, though it's doubtful that would give you enough time to learn to control the power you'll have access to."

"What kind of power?"

"You know those sparks sinking into you wherever we touch?"

"Oh, yeah. I definitely know those."

"They're like single snowflakes inside an avalanche. As your trust and connection to your partner grow, so will the flow of power. Your job will be to learn to control it and mold it to perform the task you choose."

"Can I use it to dust my house?"

He let out a long sigh. "I'm explaining this badly. It will be much easier if you let me show you."

"How?"

"I don't have much ability, but there are a few things I can do."

"Like knock me out."

"Yes, like that. I can also touch your mind if you let me."

"Uh."

"I've done it before with others," he hurried to say. "We frequently have to remove the memories of humans who are attacked by Synestryn so that they can continue to live normal lives."

"You want to remove my memories?"

"No. But I could show you mine—let you see what I've seen. Then you'll know the kind of power you'll possess."

"Will it hurt?"

"No. I'll be gentle. Go slowly so that there is no pain."

Once again, her mind went off the rails into the gutter. Maybe it was these warm tremors of magic soaking into her that were filling her mind with inappropriateness. Maybe it was simply the man himself, big and strong, saving her life and turning her into a wilting, vapid mess.

But whatever it was, Cain was potent, going to her head, weaving through her thoughts and sending her off on naughty little tangents that had her thighs clenching.

She hadn't been with a man in a long time. Matt hadn't done more than kiss her, a gift for which she was thankful every day. Letting him trade her for drugs was bad enough without having slept with him.

And she'd never been with someone like Cain, all lethal grace, dripping with testosterone. She shouldn't have even been thinking about him like that. She knew better. Her taste in men was about as good as a ten-year-old boy's fashion sense. She would only end up naked, embarrassed and wondering what the hell had happened.

"Is this really necessary?" she asked.

"It depends on whether or not you want to be informed or ignorant before you're asked to make what could possibly be the biggest decision of your life."

"Gee. No pressure."

"This isn't a game, Rory. I'm trying to help you."

She could tell that. His earnestness was obvious in his tone, and she really did want to be rid of these visions permanently. If this was a way to make that happen, she had to at least do everything in her power to learn more.

"Okay," she told him. "I've had a long and intimate relationship with bad decisions. I think it's time we broke up."

"A wise choice."

"Assuming it's not a bad decision to let you do this thing in the first place."

"It's perfectly safe. I'd never do anything to harm you."

She believed him. That made her a fool, but at least she was staying true to form.

Maura hurried down the street, her head tucked low to ward off the cold wind. The suitcase in her hand was too light, reminding her of just how little she had. A few items of clothing, a few toiletries donated by humans. Those things wouldn't sustain her for long.

Maybe it was time to go home. Take her punishment. Let the Sentinels exact their revenge.

It was no less than she deserved.

Then again, neither was the cold chill in her bones, the empty churning in her stomach and the fear that constantly walked at her side.

If the Synestryn found her, she knew she wouldn't survive. Her value to them as an ally was gone. The only thing they'd want from her now was the blood and meat her body offered. Or worse yet, a vessel for their spawn.

Maura refused to end her life that way. Even she, with all her vast sins, deserved more than that.

She rounded a corner, walking in no specific direction. All she knew was that if Cain saw her, he would be honor-bound to take her into custody. With her powers gone, she had no way to defend herself.

Her focus was so tightly turned inward, she didn't notice the trio of men ahead of her until she was upon them.

The street here was dark. The nearby buildings were run-down, their windows more often boarded over with wood than filled with glass. Neglect and decay lingered here, and if she were seeking out Synestryn nesting grounds, this would be the kind of place she would look.

But as she lifted her head, she realized that the danger to her here now was not of the demon kind, but human.

The men barred her path, their faces shadowed by hoods and hats.

"Where you goin', pretty lady?" asked the tall one in the center.

Maura straightened her spine and used the same voice she'd used to command armies of demons. "Step aside and let me pass."

Two of them broke into laughter. The third stared at her, leering. "He asked you a question."

Fear clamored in her stomach, so familiar and yet so unwelcome. She tried to hide the quake in her voice. "And I issued you an order."

He reached out and slapped her. It happened so fast, she barely had time to register what had taken place. By the time her head swung back to center, the violent ache radiated through her jaw.

No one had ever struck her before. She was so stunned by the mere thought that someone would dare touch her that she simply stood there, holding her slack jaw.

"Answer the question," said the tall one.

Maura had killed better men than these. She'd watched their struggles weaken as the blood was drained from their bodies, as the meat was stripped from their bones. She'd never once felt fear standing over them, and refused to show any now.

She lowered her hand and straightened her shoulders, staring the man right in the eyes. "Where I go is no concern of yours."

The tall man spoke again, still grinning. "Listen to miss fancy pants. Maybe you wouldn't be so uppity with those pants around your ankles and my cock in your cunt."

Revulsion swarmed over her, choking the air from her lungs. She'd seen violence. Rape. But never had she feared it would happen to her. None of the demons dared touch her. Everyone who touched her died screaming in pain.

At least they had until the night she'd shed her child's body and become a woman. Since then her powers had failed her, leaving her weak and defenseless.

That had never been more evident to her than it was now, and that weakness disgusted her.

Even as a grown woman she was no match for the strength of three men—human or otherwise. Her only choice was to run.

Maura swung her suitcase up, slamming the one on

the right in the face. Blood sprayed from his nose, and she darted around him, taking off as fast as she could.

She made it three steps before a weight hit her back and shoved her to the ground. Her chin hit the concrete, stunning her for a moment. Wetness cooled on her skin. By the time she recovered her wits, she was on her back, with the man's hands ripping her jeans open.

Fear trembled through her, taking hold of her body. She kicked and clawed and screamed, struggling to push the man aside.

His friends came to his aid, taking control of her arms. There was nothing she could do. She was trapped. Helpless.

Anger exploded in her chest, shoving a scream from her lungs. That furious cry echoed off the surrounding walls, mocking her as it came back to her ears, weaker and weaker each time. She tried to fight, but nothing she did freed her body from these men. They were going to do what they were going to do, and there was nothing she could do to stop them.

But when they were done, she would seek them out. She would find human weapons and make sure that each of them paid for what they did to her now. Revenge would be her domain, just as fear had always been. She would not allow that part of her to die along with everything else.

The man on her left pulled away from his death grip on her arms, staring at his hands in horror. A scream ripped from his lips and blood poured from his fingers.

The man on her right stumbled back, blood raining from his eyes.

The man on top of her leaned back, his screams adding to the discordant chorus of his friends'. His blood splashed across her face and ran into her hair.

Maura shoved him aside and pushed to her feet, wiping her eyes. The trio of men clutched their heads, their screams quieting only as they died.

She stared at her hands. They were bright red with blood. It was such an odd sight, she stood there in shock. Usually the blood was black. She hadn't killed a human or Sentinel in a long time.

She hadn't meant to kill these men now, but she was glad they were dead. She rejoiced in their suffering.

Didn't she?

Maura was shaking too hard to know what she felt. Relief, rage, fear—it all bundled together too tight for her to make sense of it. But there was one thing she did know for sure: Her powers were back. She could kill with a mere touch. That kind of power didn't belong among the Sentinels. Hers was the power of evil and pain. The power of a soulless being with no hope for redemption.

She wiped her hands on the jacket of the man who'd intended to rape her. Then she emptied their wallets, picked up her suitcase and walked away. She didn't know where she was going, but she knew where she *wasn't* going, and for now, that was enough.

Chapter 8

Raygh locked his latest acquisition back in her cell. She wouldn't regain consciousness for hours, if she did at all. He should have been more careful with her, but his hunger had been too great, overshadowed only by his anger.

The Sentinels had taken what was his, killed his sons, and those crimes had to be punished.

This system of caves that had previously belonged to his son was damp and cramped—not at all like those at the center of his own holdings—but he had to be here, close to where the crimes had been committed so that he could find those to blame.

Water trickled down the walls, and the smell of human filth burned his nostrils. At least he wouldn't have to be here long. Already his minions were roaming the nearby city, scouring it for traces of those he sought.

One of those minions nudged his foot to gain his attention, and he allowed it to crawl up his leg. A barb on the curved tail of the thing was caked with dried blood—blood that smelled of power. The bulbous sac below the trio of barbs was bulging with that blood.

This creature's hunt had been successful.

Raygh twisted the tail from the demon, ignoring its scream of pain, and punctured the engorged sac with his teeth. Blood, sweet and powerful flowed over his tongue—a rare treat he hadn't tasted in far too long—the blood of a Sanguinar.

"Did you find one?" asked Canaranth, the stringy, weak-willed servant that had previously belonged to another Synestryn lord.

Like Raygh's beloved son Murak, Canaranth had been gifted with a deceptively human appearance. His pale skin had a pinkish tint, rather than the gray cast so many of their kind had. And his eyes—nearly black, with perfectly round pupils—showed small slivers of human coloring. He could mingle with the cattle, pretending to be one of them, coaxing them ever closer so that Raygh could pick off the ones of his choosing.

Like the girl lying in the locked cell.

"There are still more samples to collect," said Raygh. "I want to find every Sentinel and human who helped kill my sons. I won't rest until they've all paid for what they took from me."

"Another swarm of scouts has returned. None of them were successful."

"Send them out again."

"It's nearly dawn."

"I don't care. They can find shelter from the sun or burn to ash for their incompetence. I want them out there, searching."

"Yes, my lord," said Canaranth, bowing low, his human eyes downcast.

"Have you been able to locate any of the women that were taken from us?"

"No, my lord. The Sentinels have kept them well hidden. We do have an ally who may help."

"You speak of the spy your previous master Zillah had within the walls of Dabyr?"

"Yes, my lord. A Sanguinar who served us in exchange for blood."

"Will he bring to me the blood of those I seek?"

"No, my lord. Zillah had a blood bond with him and could have compelled him to act, but without that—"

"Cut this Sanguinar off from all contact. Starve him. Make him question if we will ever provide for him again. Perhaps when he becomes hungry enough he will be more cooperative."

"Yes, my lord." Canaranth bowed again and backed out of the room. Not once did he turn his back on Raygh.

If his human genetics hadn't gotten the best of him, maybe there was hope for the sniveling servant yet.

Rory's house was not at all what Cain had expected. It was an old-fashioned, stone, two-story farmhouse, with a big wraparound porch complete with a swaying swing. A bright spray of mums flanked either side of the steps. A few large trees dotted the grassy acreage near the house, and thicker, old growth forest insulated the area from any nearby neighbors.

"It's nice," he said. "Isolated."

"That's the only thing that keeps me sane, I think. I don't suffer from the visions here, except when the mailman or someone comes by."

"So you live alone?"

She nodded, her lips tightening in grief. "Since Nana died last year, yeah."

"I'm sorry."

She shrugged as she unlocked the door and turned on the lights. He could tell by the subtle tension in her fingers that her nonchalance was simply for show. The loss of her grandmother had been a great one.

The place was cozy, filled with framed photos and handmade needlework. A brightly colored yarn blanket was tossed over the back of the couch, and several cross-stitched pictures hung on the walls. The dining room table was cluttered with papers, and an outdated desktop computer sat in the middle of the chaos.

"Forgive the mess. I wasn't expecting company."

"I won't stay long. Just until sunrise. You should be safe then, so long as you keep your doors locked."

"No one knows where I live. I'll be fine."

"You can't trust that to be true anymore. That demon took your blood. Synestryn could use it to find you." Or worse. If a powerful demon got her blood, they could use it to control her. He couldn't bring himself to scare her by mentioning it. If that happened, there would be nothing she could do to prevent it. The best protection was binding her to one of the men so they would sense if a compulsion hit her. At least then she could be incapacitated so no one would be hurt.

"But not during the day, right?"

"Synestryn are less powerful during the day. And I'll make sure that there is at least one warrior here before sundown."

"Are you sure sending people here is a good idea?"

"You want to control your visions, don't you?"

"Of course I do."

"Then let me show you what you need to know so that you can choose the right man."

Rory hesitated for a moment, biting her lip. Her indecision made her look younger and more vulnerable than the fierce, aggressive side of her he'd seen earlier. It also made him ache to reassure her in whatever way he could, even if it meant lying to her—something he would have normally found repulsive.

More of the man he'd been had clearly died. Iain—a Theronai who had gone through this same torment—had warned him that it would happen, that little bits of himself would simply disappear. He wouldn't even know they were gone until it was too late. At least Cain still had enough of himself left to mourn for what he'd lost.

Rather than dwelling on that, he set his focus on Rory. The sight of her soothed him, lending him comfort and a sense of calm he so desperately needed. He only wished he could offer her the same.

Her dark eyes met his and she gave him a small nod.

Relief swelled in Cain's chest, and only then did he realize that he'd been preparing to force her to see what he wanted her to see. Her agreement had saved him from yet another black mark on his soul.

Before she could change her mind, he backed her toward the couch until her legs bumped it. He cradled her head in his hands and slid his thumbs over her eyes to shut them. Her pink hair brushed over the back of his fingers, silky and warm.

It would have been so easy to kiss her right now. A single shift of his wrists would tilt her head back to the perfect angle. Her lips were already parted. He could have a taste of her before she could even pull in the breath to tell him to stop.

Her tongue wet her lips in a nervous gesture, but his body took it as an invitation he felt tingle all the way to the base of his spine.

He hadn't been with a woman in a long, long time. Not since he'd taken over Sibyl's care centuries ago. Several of the Theronai claimed that sex eased their pain, but Cain's pain had been bearable right up until the day his ward had walked away.

He'd been so lonely since then. His best friends had been killed. Many of his other friends had recently found their mates and were living happily together. Some of them were expecting children—a gift none of them had ever expected to receive.

Jackie had wanted a child. Cain had bargained with a Sanguinar for the ability to give her one only to find out that it wasn't to be. She was pregnant with Iain's baby now, a fact that gave Cain great joy, and jealousy so feral he could no longer speak to the man who had once been his friend. Iain would see Cain's jealousy, and after what the other man had been through, it wasn't fair to steal even a sliver of his newfound joy.

It was better for Cain to keep his distance and forget

all about the hope he'd once felt when looking at another man's woman.

And yet now, holding Rory so close, that hope tried to bubble up again and trick him into believing things that could not be. Jackie had seen Cain's inadequacy. She'd known that he'd failed to keep Sibyl safe—that his weakness had allowed her to be stolen from them. If he stayed with Rory long, she would see his failures as well.

It was better not to hope at all than to witness hope's death.

Rory stood before him, compliant in his grasp. Her trust in him was as humbling as it was frightening. She was too vulnerable to trust the wrong man. Part of him wanted to stay close and make sure she picked the right man, but the other side of him knew that he had no right to judge his brothers. As far as he knew, he was closer to turning than any of them. That made him the worst judge of all.

But preparing her for what was to come—this was something he could do. He would show her what she needed to know and leave all judgment calls to her. This was her life. It had to be her decision. If he could arm her with knowledge, then she would at least be equipped to choose her own path.

That thought eased him and gave him the mental quiet he needed to complete his task.

"Just relax," he said, his voice a low rumble between them. "Let me in."

Cain eased into her mind slowly, using every bit of skill he'd learned over the centuries to keep from hurting her. He'd slipped into another's thoughts many times before to remove memories, but never had he done so to show someone something from his own life.

Sliding inside her like this was easy. Peaceful. The urge to search through her memories tugged at him, but he resisted. She would belong to another man soon. Invading her mind more than necessary was too close to cheating on one of his brothers for his peace of mind.

Besides, the less he knew her, the easier it would be to walk away in a few minutes. There was a goodness within her that shone too brightly for him to think he wouldn't bask in it if he allowed himself the pleasure. It was better to do the job and get back to reality as soon as possible.

Cain raced through his most recent battles—the ones he'd fought alongside Gilda and Angus. Their deaths still haunted him, but he felt better knowing their memories lived on inside of him, as they would now also do inside of Rory.

It took only moments to find what he wanted—a skirmish small enough so as not to frighten or confuse Rory, but one where Gilda had wielded her power openly. He wanted Rory to see what she would become, not fear it.

Cain let the memory play through his mind, slowing it down to show fire spilling from Gilda's fingertips. It consumed a demon in a matter of seconds. Light burst from her, arching up to shield her husband's head a heartbeat before another demon jumped down from the trees. Its claws scraped against the barrier, sending up pale sparks.

The rest of the memory slid by, and when the fight was over, Gilda laid her hands on a wounded human, and three gaping claw marks healed shut in the space of a few moments. The red streaks of poison faded from his skin, and his eyes opened, shining with gratitude.

"Wow," breathed Rory. "That is so freaking cool."

He could hear her voice and her thoughts at the same time, and it felt . . . right. He didn't want to leave her, which was enough warning to tell him he'd nearly crossed a line.

Cain slipped out of her mind, and the moment he left her, that gaping loneliness opened up inside of him again. Something dark and terrified expanded beneath his skin, spreading out to steal his warmth. It left him shaking and oddly vulnerable.

She stared up at him, her dark eyes wide. "That was amazing. You really think I can do stuff like that?"

He had to swallow twice before he could speak, and when he did, his voice was rough and strained. "I know you can."

Her hands were on his chest, and he could feel his lifemark—the living image of a tree imbedded in his skin—swaying beneath his shirt, toward her touch. He'd never cursed a bit of fabric more in his life than he did his shirt for its mere existence.

"Can you show me more?" she asked, eagerness lifting her voice.

He wanted to. He could have happily spent the entire day within her thoughts, but it wasn't right. In fact, touching her like this was also not right.

Cain let go of her face and took her hand in his. "I need to make some calls, get some men on the road to come see you."

She let out a reluctant sigh. "Yeah. I need to work, anyway."

"Work?"

"I have to eat, don't I?"

"What do you do?"

"Day trader."

"You mean like the stock market?"

"Yep. Just like that. I'm not rich, but I make a decent living and I don't have to be around anyone. It's boring, but it works."

Cain could no longer find a reason to delay, no matter how hard he tried. "I need to release you now."

"I figured. I could use a bit of alone time anyway. I'm not used to having someone around for so long, you know?"

"Hold still. Hopefully this won't hurt you now that there are no people around." But it was going to hurt him like hell.

"What about you?" she asked.

"I'll be fine. As long as I keep breathing, don't touch me, okay?"

"What do you mean? Is there a chance you'll quit breathing?"

He hated to make her worry. "I'll be fine."

Cain sat so he wouldn't fall down and make a fool of himself again. Slowly, with great care, he let go of her hand. As soon as the tip of her finger left his, pain slammed into him, wringing the breath from his body. Every muscle inside of him went tight and hard, straining against the force of so much agony. A feral growl burst out of him as he fought to breathe. Little, stuttering breaths filled his lungs, but it wasn't nearly enough oxygen to keep him going. The edges of his vision faded into gray mist. The couch beneath him rattled against the floor. He tried to regain some kind of control, but it was no use. He couldn't fight it. There was too much agony to fight. So he did the only thing he could do—he gave in and let the darkness have him.

Rory freaked.

Cain was shaking like he was having a seizure, and his skin had gone pasty white. Veins stood out in his neck, and the necklace he wore seemed to have gone still and dead. All color had vanished, but at least she could see his heart beating in the band's shiny surface.

She clenched her fingers together to keep from reaching for him. His big body thrashed on her couch until it bumped against the wall, and then he went still.

His chest rose and fell fast with his labored breathing. Sweat dotted his forehead, but she didn't dare touch him enough to take off his leather jacket for fear she'd make a bad situation worse.

She stared at him for several long minutes, aching with indecision. He seemed to be through the worst of it, but she could still sense his pain, as if it were coming off of him in palpable waves.

She didn't know how to help him. She wasn't like the woman she'd seen in his memories. She had no power.

And that pissed her off.

He'd said that power would be hers once she met the right magical guy, and while all of that had the ring of truth to it, she felt as though something was off. He'd purposefully left something out.

As Rory tried to figure out what that omission might be, she occupied herself with work. But no matter what she did to distract herself, her gaze kept sliding back to Cain. He was sprawled on her grandma's dainty yellow couch, this thick arms and legs hanging off. He looked completely uncomfortable, but she didn't dare try to adjust his body.

She could see through his eyes intermittently, but it wasn't as intrusive as usual. His eyes were mostly closed, and the silent darkness trickling from him was calming. As long as she could see that darkness, she knew he was still alive.

Minutes ticked by slowly. She was too distracted to accomplish much. She read e-mail, chatted with one of her online friends, saying nothing about the recent, gargantuan developments in her life.

Lunchtime came and went, and Cain didn't so much as shift positions as she heated and ate a frozen meal.

Finally, after struggling with herself for too long, she gave into the urge to stare at him.

He really was a fine-looking man, carved from stark angles and hard planes. Even in his sleep she could see the smooth ridges of muscles along his chest where his jacket gaped open. His dark hair fell carelessly across his forehead, tempting her to brush it back. Stubble shadowed his jaw, but it was a good look for him, making the thought of beard burn more appealing than she'd ever thought possible.

She really wanted to touch him. The effort to resist was all but consuming her willpower.

His luceria had reacted to her, just as he'd said it would for those men who could offer her the kind of power the woman in Cain's memories had. Even now, simply reaching close to him, letting her fingers hover an inch from his skin, she could feel energy tingling just out of reach. The closer she got, the more the colors danced inside his ring and necklace.

So pretty.

Rory stared for a long time until her eyes burned from not blinking. She'd never seen anything like it before, and the urge to slip that necklace on and see how it would look on her was nearly overwhelming.

She should have been afraid of the unknown, but it just wasn't in her. As many horrible things as she'd seen—as much as she hated having monsters haunting her every move—she craved more knowledge. There were things she'd learned about in the last few hours she hadn't even known existed. How many more things could a man like Cain show her?

He'd said he wasn't right for her, but he'd never said why. And it wasn't like she was going to promise any man more than a few days. A trial run to see if she even liked having access to that kind of power. For all she knew it would hurt or make her itch uncontrollably or turn her skin orange.

As trapped as she was out here all alone, she craved new experiences. And being able to wield magic was definitely that.

Excitement hummed through her, vibrating under her skin.

What harm could there possibly be in giving it a shot? Cain seemed like a decent guy, if a little barbaric. He certainly hadn't hurt her, though he'd had ample opportunity. In fact, he seemed so earnest in wanting to help her. Surely he wouldn't mind if she practiced with him first before giving others a test drive.

Patches of sunlight slid across the carpet as Rory sat there in indecision. Nana's clocked ticked away, counting the seconds. The heater switched on and off again. The ice maker dumped out another batch of ice in the freezer.

Her instincts were pounding inside of her, chanting, *take it, take it.*

She wanted to listen. She wanted to know what it felt like to have that pretty necklace lie close to her skin. It belonged to her. She wasn't sure how she knew that, but she did.

Rory moved closer and stood over him. His pulse beat beneath the iridescent band, strong and steady. Her own heart pounded twice as fast as she undid the tangle of chokers and chains around her neck. They landed in a shiny pile on the carpet, discarded and forgotten.

She knelt beside him, driven to get closer. She couldn't see any latch or closure, so she used the tip of her fingernail to carefully lift it up so she could slide it around without touching him. The instant her fingers gripped the slippery surface, it came loose in her hand.

His body's heat clung to the necklace, sinking into her skin. It was smooth, heavy. The ends were blunt, as if they'd been sliced. She wasn't sure how she was going to fasten it, but the thing was buzzing with magic, and her instincts were listening.

Rory moved her hair and slid the band around her neck. As soon as she did, the ends snapped shut with an audible click.

Cain's eyes opened as if someone had stabbed him. He jolted upright, and his gaze zeroed in on her throat. A look of intense, desperate longing covered his face, and he rose to his feet in a fluidly graceful movement.

He stared down to where she knelt beside the couch. He was silent and so serious she started to wonder if she'd made a mistake.

"I'm sorry," she whispered.

"It's too late for that," he said, his stare fierce and determined.

He stripped his jacket off and tossed it aside. A second later, his shirt was gone, too, and he stood there, his bare chest consuming every speck of her attention.

His body was beautiful, eliciting a deep, primal response from places inside of her she didn't even know she had. Thick layers of muscle bulged on his big frame. Without his clothes, she could see that the width of his shoulders was not due to any kind of padding or tailor's tricks. It was all him.

She wanted it to be all hers—to let her hands roam over him, lingering over every smooth ridge and hollow. Even thinking about touching him was enough to make her hands sweat and shake.

A giant tree tattoo covered his chest, its bare branches reaching up over his shoulder. With every deep breath, the limbs swayed, making it look alive. Whoever had put this on him was a true artist.

Like a woman in a trance, she rose to her feet. Her finger settled against the tree, and she was shocked to feel the smooth heat of his skin rather than rough tree bark. She traced one branch, watching the others move like they were trying to get closer to her.

Cain drew in a deep breath and his whole body shuddered.

Rory looked up at his face, trying to gauge his reaction. "I'm sorry. I forgot I wasn't supposed to touch you."

But she wasn't going to stop now. His skin felt too good against her hand. Warmth slid up her arm and encircled her throat where his necklace lay. It seeped into her, making muscles that had been tense for way too long unclench.

A languid, sleepy heat suffused her. It felt like sunlight in winter—precious and so welcome, she didn't even think to question it.

Rory felt his muscles shift under her palm, heard the rasp of metal on metal.

He drew his sword.

She should have been afraid. Somewhere in the rational part of her brain warnings were going off, but she felt too good to listen to them.

Cain moved her hand from where it rested over his heart and used the sword to cut himself.

The horror of seeing his blood drip down his skin shook her out of her stupor. "What the hell are you doing?"

"My life for yours, Rory."

"What?"

"You took my luceria. I question the wisdom of your choice, but you made it. Without force or compulsion. There's no turning back now."

Chapter 9

Cain couldn't think straight. The hope he'd been trying to fight off since meeting Rory had won. It exploded inside of him, shouting in celebration.

Rory had taken his luceria. He didn't understand why she'd done such a thing, but the deed was done. Her recklessness had backed her into this corner, and Cain had dreamed of this moment for too long to control his deep, visceral reaction to her choice.

She stood before him, quivering, representing everything he'd ever wanted. He wanted to push her—to demand she hurry and finish tying herself to him. But he'd seen enough of her now to know that his Rory did not like to be pushed.

This moment was as important to her as it was to him, and while his mind was still reeling from the implications of her actions, he had to give her room to do as she willed.

"Give me your vow," he said, his voice so rough he barely recognized it.

"I don't know what to say."

"I can't tell you. It has to be your decision alone." Because if he gave her any advice, it would be selfish, tying her to him permanently so they'd have forever to work out their differences—whatever they may be.

"How long does it take to learn to use magic like that woman you showed me?"

"Years. Decades."

He wanted more time than that, but he'd take what she chose to give. And he'd use that time to prove to her that he was worthy of her, despite his past failures. For her he'd find a way to be a better man.

She swallowed, and the movement brought his eyes back to the luceria around her throat. It was too big for her still. The vow was not yet complete and the magic that would bond them not yet invoked.

"That's a long time."

"Not really. Not when you live as long as we do."

He could see skepticism flash in her dark eyes. She still didn't believe him about who and what she was, but she would. Eventually, she would see that he'd never lie to her about such things.

Her lips parted, and Cain held his breath, everything inside of him coiled tight in anticipation of her vow. "Wait. Before you say what you're going to say, you need to know that what comes next can be frightening. You'll see a vision of . . . something. I don't know what, but I don't want you to be scared by whatever you see. Nothing can hurt you, okay?"

She nodded. "You don't need to worry about me."

He collected a drop of blood on his finger and touched it to the necklace.

She didn't get it yet, but she would. Eventually she'd learn that he would always worry about her—at least for as much time as he had left. She was part of him now. The rest of the binding ceremony was a formality. A vital one, certainly, but her decision to take his luceria was the catalyst that had changed the shape of his life forever. She'd given him hope for a future that was otherwise bleak and desolate, and for that, he would never be able to thank her enough.

Rory pulled in a deep breath. "I will stay with you

long enough to find the person or thing that I've been looking for—the one that makes my visions go away."

Cain's hope shriveled and died, just as it had when Jackie had chosen Iain. A woman as determined as Rory would find her savior within a few weeks. Perhaps even a few days.

She hadn't saved his life. She'd found a way to end it sooner.

He knew better than to let hope get the best of him, and despite his warnings to the contrary, he'd let himself get pulled into the fantasy.

At least she'd saved him from spending his last days in pain. He tried to take solace in that, but could find none.

He couldn't hide his disappointment and grief. He knew she'd see it on his face, and he didn't want to burden her with his selfish wishes.

Cain turned away to hide his expression and an instant later, a vision slammed into him.

He saw Rory as a child, perhaps five or six years old. Her hair had been a pale blond then, but her dark eyes and the curve of her upper lip were unmistakable. She sat in this very house, at the same dining room table that still perched in the same spot. An older woman—her nana—sat with her, her aging body drooping with grief and guilt.

"Your mama is gone, honey. The drugs have taken her. She's not coming back."

"Mama always comes back. She said so."

"Not this time, Rory. It's just you and me now."

And that statement had proven to be true. Cain saw a string of events, and while there were fleeting glimpses of others, the only constant at Rory's side was her grandmother. She didn't go to school with the other kids. She played alone. As she grew, that loneliness hung on her, weighing her down with sadness. And then that sadness disappeared and in its place was anger, rebellion. Her hair changed color. Her clothing became revealing and chaotic. She'd pierced her nose, her eyebrow, her belly button. Each new piercing brought a deeper frown to her nana's face.

Then something happened. The visions slowed to show Rory sitting at the same table in the same chair where she'd always sat. Tears streamed down her face, making her heavy makeup run in black rivulets.

Nana was gone. Dead. Cain could feel Rory's grief as clearly as if it had been his own.

She was truly alone now.

Time sped again, and several of the piercings disappeared. The slutty clothing became less revealing and more defensive. The colorful hair remained, but began to grow out to its natural blond. Rory worked a lot, spending hours and hours at her computer.

Her life was a string of quiet isolation, marked occasionally by brief trips into the city to search for a way to rid herself of her visions.

Finally, the story the luceria had chosen to show him was over, but he didn't know what he was supposed to take from it. The confusing jumble of images had to have some meaning, but he wasn't sure what it was.

The only thing he could think was that the man she was supposed to be with—the one she would eventually find—would have known what the luceria was trying to say. The fact that Cain couldn't figure it out only strengthened his conclusion that Rory wasn't truly meant to be his. This situation they were in now was simply a passing mistake on her part—one she'd correct as soon as she found her true partner.

Ronan rarely dreamed. It was better that way. Safer. But today, his usual control over such things had slipped while the sun hovered high in the sky, muting his limited powers.

A dream had sucked him in, weaving around him in grim despair.

Everything was dark, tinted with helpless defeat. His hunger was consuming, driving him to hunt for even one drop of sustenance, but there was none to be had.

The streets were empty. Human homes sat vacant and hollow, their doors ripped from hinges as a sign that others had passed this way before him. Ronan's wasted body ached as he forced his legs to move.

The stench of decay and filth hung in the air, so thick it created a cold fog around his feet. It sucked the heat from his skin and forced his weary heart to beat faster, restoring what little warmth it could.

There were no more people to be found—no more blood. The only blood that remained was the tainted poison flowing in the veins of Synestryn.

And that of his own kind.

The dream shifted and Ronan faced his friend, Tynan. They'd shared their lives for millennia, hunting side by side, working to ensure the survival of their race by protecting the strongest human bloodlines.

Their efforts had failed, and all that remained was ash, rot and hunger.

Tynan was as hungry as Ronan was. His flesh hung on his bones, loose and empty. His face, once beautiful, was now the face of death—as gaunt as a skeleton and burning with the sickly tint of infection.

His eyes glowed, flaring with a weak flicker of light. "One of us must die."

Ronan nodded, even that small effort nearly too much for him to maintain. He tried to tell Tynan to take his blood and end his suffering, but the ravening beast within him—the one driven by hunger and instinct took over.

Ronan lunged for his lifelong friend and ripped his head backward until his neck nearly broke. Tynan's skin parted easily for Ronan's fangs. His friend's blood filled his mouth, too weak to do more than ease his growling hunger.

Tynan's pulse slowed. Ronan ordered his body to stop, but his mouth kept moving. He sucked down great gulps of blood until his friend's heart stuttered, and then finally, inevitably, stopped.

Ronan held Tynan's corpse in his hands and knew that he'd just killed the last creature on earth that had loved him. He'd just destroyed the last being he could ever love. And now the world was not only devoid of food, it was also empty of friendship and love. Forever. Ronan's greed had destroyed all that was good, and in doing so, he'd slain hope.

His hunger returned, worse than before. This time, there was no way to appease it. He was going to die of starvation. Alone.

Ronan woke, sweat pouring from his body. He was shivering, his muscles so tight he could barely breathe. The cellar of the Gerai house where he slept seemed to close in around him, suffocating him.

He forced himself to take slow, even breaths while the shivering terror passed.

That nightmare hadn't been natural. There was a taint of malevolent magic about it—a dark Synestryn stain Ronan recognized only now that he was awake.

A tendril of power hovered nearby, reaching up from the earth.

Furious that some creature dared invade his mind, Ronan grabbed that tendril and shoved his consciousness back through it, following it to its source.

Deep within the earth a Synestryn lay hidden, sending out twisted threads of power. As soon as Ronan felt the fetid confines of the demon's mind, he reeled back in revulsion. Rotted, stinking decay clung to the creature's thoughts, each one pulsing with the staccato beat of hatred and revenge. There was little sense to be made of such chaos, but Ronan could feel the power this demon wielded. He was stronger than most—stronger than

Ronan could ever hope to be given the dwindling supplies of Athanasian blood lingering on the planet.

The demon sensed him immediately, and tried to snag him, pulling him farther inside the decaying constructs of its mind. Ronan dodged the attempt, but he was clumsy, and the effort left him weak. There was no time to linger and figure out what this demon had planned. Ronan had to escape now, before he no longer could.

With a hard thrust of power, he shoved himself out of the Synestryn's mind. Searing hot claws raked across the inside of Ronan's skull, making him cry out in pain. He landed in his own body, panting and shaking. His head throbbed, and blood leaked from his nose.

He was nearly too weak to breathe, much less move and clean the blood from his skin. He didn't know how strong the wards on this Gerai house were, and whether or not they'd keep the scent of his blood contained. Even though he rested in the darkness of the locked basement, there were no guarantees that he would not be found here as soon as the sun set.

Ronan tried to sit up, but his body refused to obey his commands. Even his pitiful attempts to wipe the blood away had done little more than spread it across his face. He needed help, but all of his brothers were sleeping and suffering through their own daylight weakness.

Ronan felt the demon poking at the edges of his mind, as if seeking a way in. He went still, reserving every bit of strength he had as he concentrated on keeping the creature from invading his thoughts.

It was stronger than he was. It was hungry and violent, battering itself against Ronan's defenses in an effort to break through.

Instincts warned him that if he let down his guard, his mind would never again be the same. Touching such darkness would leave its mark, permanently.

Ronan began to sweat under the strain of protecting himself. He could no longer feel the diseased touch of the demon, but that didn't mean it was gone. Some instinct told Ronan that he was no longer alone.

With slow, painful care, he retrieved his phone from his pocket and sent out a call for help. For blood. If someone didn't come soon he wouldn't survive the day, but at least they'd know where to find his body.

Chapter 10

Rory was used to visions, but what she was seeing now was way more than that. There were sounds and smells to accompany the sights she witnessed, as well as a low vibration of emotion coming from those she saw.

Cain had said not to be afraid, and that was the only thing that kept her from freaking out.

She stood in a bedroom she didn't recognize. It was dark, but somehow, she was still able to see. Cain lay asleep in a big bed, his body sprawled beneath a sheet. There had been lots more leaves on his tattoo then, which meant he must have had some removed.

Something about that conclusion was wrong, but she didn't waste time questioning it. Not when she saw the huge, furry monster slinking across his carpet.

Rory screamed at him in warning, but he didn't so much as twitch. The monster came closer, moving as silent as a thought. She tried to pick up a book and throw it, but her hand passed through, reminding her that this was all a vision, albeit a fucked-up one.

The monster pushed itself upright, standing at least eight feet tall. It pounced on the bed, digging its claws into Cain's chest.

He woke on a bellow of pain and rage. His fist slammed into the monster's jaw, but it did little good.

"Sibyl!" he shouted. "Run!"

The word was barely out of his mouth when the demon picked him up and slammed him headfirst into a wall. He bounced off, hit the floor and didn't move again.

But the demon didn't stop. It dug its claws into Cain's unconscious body and flung him across the room. Blood sprayed over the bedding. A lamp toppled and shattered.

Over and over, the demon tossed him about, slowing only to slide its blistered tongue over Cain's bloody body before each vicious attack. Then suddenly, the monster's muzzle lifted as if it had heard something. It dashed off through the door, leaving Cain in a puddle of blood and broken glass.

The whole thing had taken only seconds, and in that time, Rory had grown cold and nauseated. She'd been helpless to stop the demon, forced to witness the brutal display of violence and power.

People rushed into the room and went to work healing his injuries. She wanted to stay and make sure that he was safe, but the vision shoved her out of the room into a different one. This one was filled with frills and pastel pink. A child-sized bed sat under a canopy near the shattered window. The covers were streaming through the ragged opening as if someone had ripped the child from her bed.

A porcelain doll sat on the floor, its glassy eyes staring at the ceiling. There were no signs of a struggle here. No blood. No toppled furniture. Only the broken window and empty bed.

Rory felt like there was something here she was supposed to see, but she had no idea what it was. Her fear for Cain was still pounding through her, making it hard to concentrate. She knew he was alive and well—he'd told her not to be afraid, but that was easier said than done.

She forced herself to take a step, and then another, scanning the room for whatever it was she needed to see so that this blasted vision would end. The tiny table and chairs, set with a china tea service held no interest. The looming bookshelves were stuffed full of textbooks and stories way too adult for this room's occupant. Sitting on one of the lower shelves, lovingly framed in silver, was a single photo.

Rory bent down to look at it. Cain was there, smiling so big his fatherly pride shone through all the way to his eyes. On his lap sat a little blond girl with the cutest ringlet curls Rory had ever seen. Her cheeks were round and pink, and her blue eyes were the same color as a cloudless summer sky. She wore no smile on her face, only a lonely, haunted look, as if some vital person was missing from the photo.

Once again the vision shifted and Cain stood in the same bedroom alone. The air in here was different now. Heavier, darker. Grief and guilt hung on him, bowing his shoulders with their weight. Tears hovered in his eyes, but did not fall. He made a slow circle around the room, touching things here and there, as if each one held some importance or precious memory. As he came across the photo, he picked it up, his hands shaking visibly. He cradled the image with a kind of reverence reserved for priceless, irreplaceable things.

His obvious pain and grief burrowed into Rory, filling her with the need to make it stop. He'd lost his little girl, but Rory could think of no way to bring back the dead. She'd lost Nana, but this was different. Nana had been ready to go. It had been her time. The girl in that photo could not have been more than eight or nine. There was nothing natural about her death.

Rory stepped forward to wrap her arms around him, only to find herself standing in her own living room once again. The sun had begun to set, leaving a golden glow over her familiar surroundings.

Cain stood in front of her, filling her line of sight. There were no hints of weakness about him now—only the solid, unyielding strength she'd come to recognize. But now she saw something she hadn't seen before, or maybe she simply hadn't recognized it. Sadness hovered over him, shadowing his eyes. Once again, the urge to rid him of his pain crashed into her, sending her into a tailspin.

Rory wasn't used to feeling such things. She hadn't been around people enough to even know how to see what made them tick, much less patch up whatever damage had been done to them.

All she knew was that the man standing before her now was the same one she'd met last night, but she could no longer see him in the same light. He wasn't simply some crazy stranger who turned her on and made her visions go away. He was . . . real. He hurt, he grieved, he bled. Cain was such a formidable-looking man that it had been easy for her to assume he had no weakness.

And yet she'd seen exactly how grief-stricken and devastated he could be.

"You had a daughter."

Cain's face crumpled for a moment before he regained his composure. Sadness poured out of him, chafing against her skin. His voice was a low, quiet rumble, like distant thunder. "She was my ward, but she'd been with me for a long, long time."

"But she was only a child."

His words came out slow and unsteady, as if each one had been ripped from a place down deep, leaving a ragged bleeding hole in his chest. "Sibyl was more than a child, and while she was not mine by birth, she was my greatest joy." His lips pressed together as if he was trying to hold back words he didn't want to say. "She was cursed to appear as a child even though her mind was anything but. Her small size and weakness made her vulnerable. She needed me." He said those last words as if Sibyl had given him some kind of gift—as if her need for Cain was something precious to him, rather than a burden, and now that need was gone.

Rory remembered the way he cradled the photo, anguish twisting his features. There had been guilt there, too. Based on what she'd seen—the demon attack, the broken window and empty, child-sized bed, Cain's torment and guilt—she knew how the story ended. "I'm so sorry you lost her."

"It was my fault. Had I been more careful, she never would have walked away. But I failed her, and now she rarely calls or writes."

"She's alive? I saw the broken window, saw that she was gone."

Cain nodded as he pushed out a rough sigh. "So that's what the luceria chose to show you, is it? My failure?"

"Failure? Hardly. I saw a monster attack you in your sleep." Even now the memory of that vision had the power to make her fingers and toes go cold with fear.

His mouth tightened in frustration. "The night Sibyl was taken, I didn't even hear the Synestryn coming for her. My only job was to ensure her safety, and I failed. It's no wonder she left."

"I'm sure she'll come back."

He sounded doubtful. "She left me for a reason. She grew up and needed to become the woman she was born to be. Sibyl was always smarter than I was. She knew that if she stayed with me I would stifle her. After centuries of being trapped inside that small, vulnerable body, unable to take care of herself, when she finally grew up, she needed to spread her wings and fly—go somewhere where no one treated her as a child."

"Where did she go?"

"Africa. We have a stronghold there that was attacked a few months ago, and she went to help them rebuild. And maybe to find a man who can give her the kind of power she needs to prove to herself that she's no longer weak."

"You don't sound too happy about the idea."

"I don't like the thought of men pawing at her, especially when I'm not there to force their good behavior."

"Is that what they'll do? Paw at her?"

Cain's shoulder twitched in a slight shrug. "It's unfair of me to think such things, but I can't seem to help it. All I can do is try not to think about it."

Rory wasn't exactly helping him on that front. Time for a change of subject—anything to rid him of that guilt that robbed his eyes of their usual brightness. She hated seeing his pain, and the idea of distracting him from it was a compelling temptation.

He hadn't looked at her since she'd come out on the other side of those visions. His gaze went past her, focusing on the wall behind her, or the floor, as if he was ashamed. It struck her that she missed the way he looked at her, seeing beyond the superficial. Part of her reveled in it, but the rest of her was freaked out that he'd completely ignored her armor. His scrutiny was usually too intense, but now that it was gone, she missed his directness.

Rory stepped away from him, putting some distance between them. A flash of someone browning hamburger in a pan shoved its way in her head, shocking her. Her neighbors were too far away for her to pick up on what they saw, and yet the image of Mrs. Wittle's gnarled hands was unmistakable.

She swayed in shock, gripping the back of a dining chair to steady herself.

"Are you okay?" asked Cain.

He took a step toward her, but she held up her hand to hold him off. "Fine. Just not used to all of this magic junk."

He stayed where he stood, but she could feel him looking at her again, *seeing* her. She tried not to squirm, but there wasn't a thing she could do about the blast of tingling heat that cascaded down her body in a slow, lingering caress.

"I'm sorry you had to suffer through the vision. I never would have asked you to witness that part of my life. Why the luceria chose to show you that is a mystery."

"The luceria chose . . . ? You make it sound like the thing has a mind of its own. It's just a piece of jewelry."

"It's much more than that." His gaze lingered at her neck, and she saw the faintest flickering of hope light his green eyes. "It has the power to change lives, to bind people together irrevocably."

"So does a wedding ring, but it's still just a piece of jewelry."

Cain glided toward her, his body moving too smoothly for his size. She wanted to retreat, but her pride held her in place and forced her chin up to meet his advance.

"Can a wedding ring do this?" he asked.

A second later, Rory felt a shimmering curtain of energy streak down from her throat, caressing her skin as it went. Her nipples beaded up, and a shiver of pleasure shook her all the way to her bones. It felt too good, and she was unable to stop the audible moan that fell from her lips. She sagged under the weight of so much sensation, not caring whether or not she landed on the floor in a sloppy pile of quivering delight.

Cain's hands gripped her arms to hold her upright. She swayed toward him, drawn by a magnetic force she was too weak to resist. Her forehead hit his bare chest, and she swore she could hear the creak of branches moving along his skin. He radiated living heat. His scent filled her head, warm and delicious—familiar, though she couldn't put her finger on what it was about him that made her feel like she *knew* him.

With so much naked male skin at her disposal, she had to resist the crazy need to press her lips to his chest. Kissing him seemed like the height of stupidity, and yet she couldn't think of anything else at the moment, not when her whole body was trembling in the wake of whatever he'd just done.

"What was that?" she finally managed to ask.

"My power, flowing into you through the luceria—a small pulse of it meant to show you what's to come."

Rory's knees went soft, and she steadied herself, pressing her hands against his hot, naked chest. "If that was small, I won't survive anything bigger."

His voice was rough, deep with a hint of amusement. "Perhaps not at first, but soon you'll be able to take much, much more. As much as you need."

She wasn't sure if he'd chosen his words to paint vivid, arousing images of the two of them, bodies entwined, but her pesky imagination was running wild, like some drunk frat girl. "What would I need it for?"

"To find the person who stops your visions. That is what you want, isn't it?"

Visions were the last thing on her mind right now. She couldn't think straight so close to a man like him. He made her too hot and achy to concentrate while simultaneously drenching her in thrilling, heady excitement. She wanted things she had no words for—things that sparked to life within her chest, tiny and quivering with possibility.

"Yeah," she said, hating the vapid, breathless quality of her voice. "That's what I want."

His body shifted slightly, the movement so minute she could hardly feel it. Even so, his entire demeanor changed. He held her tighter, nearly lifting her from her feet. A fervent energy spilled out of him, and his voice dipped low, coming out in an almost inaudible whisper. "You don't have to find this person. We could work together to find a way to block the visions. With my power at your disposal, there's nothing the two of us can't do together."

Oh, man. Not fair. He was intoxicating her with his sexy voice, with his touch, with his scent. His entire presence wrapped around her and held her captive, making her yearn for things she knew better than to want.

She'd been so lonely since Nana had died. His companionship was a welcome respite from the daily grind, like a patch of sunlight in an endless sea of cold fog. She wanted to snuggle right in and take what he was so eager to give her, but nothing this good could be true. His eyes made promises that no one person could ever be powerful enough to fulfill.

"But you said I had to word my promise to you carefully. If I don't find the person who stops my visions, then what happens?"

His finger traced the necklace she now wore. It jumped in response to his touch, shivering and humming against her skin. "My luceria stays fixed around your neck."

"For how long?"

"You know the answer to that."

She did. She felt the knowledge shimmering inside her mind—like some dormant, forgotten memory suddenly sparked to life. "Forever."

He nodded, his throat working as he swallowed hard.

"You don't even know me. Not really. How can the idea of us having this weird, magical connection not freak you out? For all you know, I'm a serial killer."

"The luceria would have shown me that had it been true. It didn't. I saw other things, though."

"Are you saying that this necklace showed you something from my life?"

"That is the way it works. I show you mine. You show me yours."

In an embarrassingly swift rush, her mind went to a naughty little place where the two of them were naked and pressed together as close as two people could get. It was a silly, immature thing for her to imagine, but she couldn't stop herself from feeling a giddy rush of girlish excitement all the same.

"What did you see?" she asked, looking at her toes because she was too afraid to see any hints of mockery on his face.

"Bits of your life. Your grandmother. Your isolation." He tipped her chin up with his finger. "It doesn't have to be like that now. You're not alone anymore."

Tears burned her eyes as a wave of unwanted emotions swept over her. She was ashamed of her weakness, embarrassed by her affliction and the loneliness it caused. But mostly, she was relieved to be able to be this close to another person again. She hadn't been able to see through Nana's eyes for some reason, and Cain was like that, too—at least when she touched him. He made her feel normal, rather than like the fucked-up freak show she really was.

With him, it was easy to pretend that everything really was going to be okay, and that her life wouldn't be a constant struggle to keep the visions away.

And that was the problem. With him it was pretend. Not real. Not permanent.

Sure, he said pretty words about forever, but that wasn't the way the real world worked. Sooner or later she'd piss him off, or he'd irritate her and they'd go their separate ways. And that was assuming he didn't simply grow bored with her. A man built like him could have any woman he wanted. Sooner or later, that woman would walk into his life and leave Rory looking like a dirty, wet sponge by comparison.

"I need to finish what I started," she told him. "I will find the person who makes my visions go away and figure out how they do it. Hope said that it might be as simple as finding a magic ring or something."

That little spark of hope that had lit his green eyes was snuffed out. He nodded and let his hands drop to his sides, leaving a cold wedge of air between them. "If you want to find this person, then it's time you learned to use my power."

"How is that going to help?"

"Because you may be able to use magic to aid your search."

"Really?"

"Really. And even if you can't use it in that way, you need to learn how to protect yourself."

"I have a gun. I know how to use it."

"That will do little good against most demons."

One part of Rory thrilled at the idea of learning how to use magic, but the more reasonable side of her was cautious. Having something that cool in her life and losing it was too hard. She'd already lost too much, and maybe in this case it was better to never know what she was missing. "I think I'll pass on the magic stuff. But thanks anyway."

His mouth opened in shocked silence, then closed again. His dark brows dipped low and his jaw bulged with frustrated anger. "You're going to *pass?* That's not how this works, Rory."

"Who says? Is there some kind of manual or something you've failed to share with me?"

"Of course not."

"Good. Then it's settled."

"Are you saying that you would rather remain tied to me for eternity? Because that's what will happen if you never find this person you're seeking. I told you to word your vow carefully. The words you chose tie you to me until you've found the one who makes your visions go away. Your words. Not mine."

Rory took a long step back, needing some space to think. Cain loomed too large, overpowering her with his mere presence. She was too aware of him, and it was taking up a portion of her brain that she really needed free to work on an escape clause.

Mrs. Wittle's gnarled hands shoved their way back into Rory's head as she added pasta to a pot of boiling water.

The old lady's home was half a mile away. Rory had never been able to see through the eyes of someone that far away before. And it scared her.

Cain's low, gravelly rumble cut through her fear just enough to keep her steady. "What just happened?" he asked.

She didn't want to answer that question—not even to herself. If her visions were getting worse, she wasn't sure what she would do. She'd no longer be able to drive or see her computer screen. How would she take care of herself if she couldn't earn money or go buy groceries?

Rory swallowed down her fear and tipped her head back to look him in the eye. She wouldn't let him know she was afraid. She'd faced bigger problems than this and survived. This would just be one more. "Tell me exactly what I'll be able to do with all this magic bullshit."

He winced at her wording. "Many things. Where your skills lie is still a question, but chances are you'll be able to defend yourself at the very least."

Rory remembered the woman Cain had shown her from his memories—the one who had used some kind of invisible shield to stand in the way of attack. "What about finding people? How do I use magic for that?"

Cain shook his head. "I don't know. I can have you talk to Andra. She's a Theronai and has the ability to find lost children. Perhaps she could give you some pointers."

Okay. That was a good start. "What about offense? Am I going to be able to sling fire around like that chick you showed me?"

"It's likely. You should learn to defend yourself first, though, don't you think?"

"Boooring. I'd much rather blow shit up. If you show me how to do that, then we're on."

He stood there for a long minute, staring at her. "If that's what you want to learn, then I will do my best to show you. Outside."

"Good idea. If I lost Nana's house, I'd have nowhere to go."

"That's not true," said Cain as he stepped closer, filling her sight. "You're family now, and we look out for our own."

The throb of emotion that lodged in her throat was completely unexpected. She blinked fast to hide her tears, unsure as to why his simple statement had caught her so off guard.

Maybe she'd been alone for too long. She couldn't remember the last time she'd spent this much time with anyone—definitely not since Nana had died. Even Matt had been too grating on her senses for her to be around him for long.

"I do better on my own," she told him, but the wavering in her voice made it sound like a petulant lie.

"Too bad. Those days are over."

"You don't get to tell me what to do."

"I'm not trying to. I'm simply pointing out a fact. You and I are joined now. Even when we're separated, I'll still be able to feel you, to hear you if you call for me."

"Yeah, right. How?"

She was pushing him. So far he'd been pretty easygoing, but she could see the way she strained his control—the way she made the veins in his temples pound, and the tendons in his neck stand out. She was grating on his nerves, the way she did with everyone sooner or later.

He reached for her, his movement so smooth and fast, she didn't even think to dodge.

"Like this." His hands cupped the sides of her face, hot and too big for her to have a prayer of escaping. The rough patches along his palms reminded her just how capable he was with that sword, and how much stronger he was than her. That strength was under control now, but if she kept pushing him, he might not remember to be so gentle.

A second later she felt him slide inside her mind, and her worries of his physical strength evaporated.

Basking in his presence was like standing naked under a warm sun, making her feel exposed and caressed all at the same time. He was too intense to look at directly, and yet she was drawn to him, wanting to get closer to his heat.

"Can you feel me?" he asked, and she heard the words echo within her thoughts.

"Kinda hard not to."

"You don't have to be afraid."

"I'm not," she said automatically, even though it was a lie. All of this was so new and strange, it terrified and delighted her.

"You can't hide anything from me like this."

Which made her wonder if it worked both ways. What if he was hiding the knowledge she needed to find the cure for her visions? She could feel how important it was to him that she'd taken his luceria—that it helped him in some way. What if he didn't want her to give it back?

Rory wasn't sure how to find the information, but as soon as the desire to look for it bloomed into reality, she found that searching through his thoughts was as easy as searching through her own. Sure, the walls here were different—harder and darker—but the space was basically the same. Navigating it was intuitive, as if she'd been here before.

"What are you doing?" he asked.

"Hush. I'm busy."

She spun through the data in his head, seeking out knowledge of magic and its uses. She found memory after memory of things he'd seen other women do, as well as a few men. Battle, healing, creation of magical devices—it all swam together in a blur of information. She sensed leads here, and maybe some ideas she could try, but as he said, there was no definitive knowledge of how to solve her problem.

As Rory was leaving, pulling herself out of his mind, she felt something brush against her, so bright with hope and yearning that it nearly burned. She wasn't sure what it was, but curiosity had always been one of her flaws.

She went back to that place, seeking out the raging energy of it. She thought she might get burned if she touched it again, but instead, she was drawn in, compelled to slide inside the thought or memory or whatever it was.

There was a man there, possibly even more beautiful than Logan. He injected something into Cain that burned like acid, but Cain had felt only hope and a sense of joy as glittering and fragile as a crystal snowflake.

"What did he do to you? Were you sick?" As she asked the questions, she sped through his mind toward the answer.

A pretty woman stood there, her gray eyes brimming with happiness. Around her neck was a shimmering, golden band—a luceria like the one Rory now wore. This woman smiled up at Cain, her hand splayed over her stomach in a gesture of maternal joy.

Rory had thought Cain said that his daughter wasn't his by birth, but the feeling she had now was unmistakable. The child that woman carried was his.

As Rory watched, the edges of the thought wobbled, crumbling away. The woman's hand fell. Her smile faded. The hope and happiness this image created withered and died. And then, an instant later, the woman reappeared as she had been before, vibrant and glowing with eagerness. The whole cycle played out, over and over.

It was then that Rory realized what it was she'd stumbled upon. It wasn't a memory, but some kind of dream. A wish. This image was something that Cain had wanted. Badly.

"It doesn't matter now," he said. "She's with another man. A good man."

Rory felt him trying to push her away, and she didn't like it. "You wanted her to have your baby. That's why you got that injection."

He pushed harder, making her head throb with the strain of staying where she was.

"As I said, it doesn't matter."

Only it did. It mattered a lot to him.

With one final shove from Cain, Rory landed firmly back within her own mind. Her physical body was shaking and exhausted, as if she'd just run a marathon. Cain was panting with effort, his face red and his body quivering with tension.

His hands slid down to her shoulders, holding her steady. "Why did you fight me?"

"Why did you try to shove me out? You were the one who wanted the mind-meld thing to happen. Not me."

"It was a mistake to let you see that. I'm sorry."

Fatigue bored down on her, but she refused to let him see her weakness. "That whole brain-bending thing is messed up. All this magic stuff. Memory surfing."

His green gaze darkened as his pupils expanded. "Being in your thoughts is easy. Peaceful."

Oh, crap. She hadn't considered that it would be reciprocal. "What did you see?"

"Less than you, I imagine."

"No deep, dark secrets?"

"My desire to have a child isn't a secret. I simply thought that it might freak you out."

"Why? It's not like it was me you were picturing as your baby mama. So what if you're pining after some woman? I don't really care."

Only she did. She had no reason to care, but she liked having Cain's attention to herself. Sure, eventually he'd get in the way and drive her bonkers, but right now, it was nice having him around. Not that she'd ever tell him that.

He let go of her and took her coat off the back of the chair where she'd left it. Once again, he closed up shop, leaving her wondering what was going on inside his head.

As the urge hit her, she felt a fluttering presence brush her mind, as if she'd simply reached out and found it. For one fleeting second, she felt a faint hint of something dark and sad, but then it was gone as fast as it came, leaving her wondering if she'd imagined it.

He draped her coat over her shoulders. "Come on. There's not much time until sundown. We should go outside and see what you can do."

Rory was far more intuitive than he'd given her credit for. She'd simply walked right into his thoughts as if she owned the place and dug up his deepest, most private fantasies.

Cain had wanted Jackie to be his. She'd offered him a union, but things had not gone as either one of them had anticipated. Jackie had ended up with Iain, and the child they were now expecting was Iain's.

Jackie had given him a few precious hours of hope—of dreaming of what his life could have been like with a wife and child to cherish—and the loss of that hope had nearly killed him.

He refused to make the same mistake with Rory. She'd been very clear that their union was to be temporary. He had to accept that and not get sucked into some pretty fairy tale.

Why not? asked a little, hidden part of himself. Why not enjoy the fantasy while he had the chance? Rory would be leaving him soon, and when she did, his chances of having found another woman to keep him alive were slim. He was going to die in the end. Why not enjoy the ride while he could?

He'd been given the serum to restore his fertility. All he had to do was seduce Rory and let nature take its course. Whether or not he died, at least there would be a chance that some part of him would live on.

But could he really use her like that? Was that the kind of man he was?

Cain wasn't sure anymore. At one time, he would have been appalled by the idea, but a lot had happened since then. His lifemark had yet to be restored. His soul was still in jeopardy. Sibyl was gone. A cure for the infertility of their men had been found. And now here was Rory, so tempting and sweet.

Giving in would be easy. Now that they were connected, seducing her would be simple. All he had to do was invade her fantasies and find out what she liked, what turned her on.

Even the thought of doing so made his cock swell.

"Are you coming?" she asked. She was at the door, looking over her spiked, chain-clad shoulder at him. Her pink hair stood out in brilliant contrast against the black leather. Below that, her jeans clung in a loving hug around her ass and thighs. She was rounded in all the right places, making his hands clench with the need for just one long, lingering touch.

Oh, yeah. Seducing her would be no hardship at all. And maybe, just maybe, if he made her feel good enough, she'd think twice about ditching him once her visions were gone.

His people needed him. Humans needed him. It was his duty to live for as long as he could—to fight as long as he could—and if he had to tie Rory to him to make that happen, then who was to say that it wasn't the right thing to do?

Something about that line of thought bothered him, but he pushed it aside,

"Be out in a minute." He went into the bathroom to wash the dried flakes of blood from his chest down the drain. As he pulled his shirt back on and settled his jacket on his shoulders, the beginnings of a seduction strategy sprang to life.

Rory wasn't going to stand a chance.

Chapter 11

Rory didn't wait for Cain to catch up with her. She'd seen a myriad of images in his mind—things that other women could do. The basic concept was there, too. All she had to do was put it all together and make things happen.

The luceria around her neck hummed with eagerness. She could practically see the tiny thread of invisible power stretching between her and Cain. Like a shimmering strand of spider silk blown by the wind, it vibrated, drawing her attention. At the end of that thread she sensed a trickle of power. Barely discernible and flickering, she grabbed hold of it, feeling it fill her. It shoved her fatigue away as it passed, fading into the earth.

Below her feet, dry grass crackled and swayed, bending away from her in a perfect circle.

A vision of Mrs. Wittle slapped against her, showing her a plate of spaghetti and a gnarled hand winding a strand of pasta around a fork. This sight was stronger than the previous ones, lasting longer and blocking out the sight of all else. Usually it took at least a dozen visions superimposed on one another to blind Rory, but usually they weren't so clear and solid, either.

A moment later, the vision shifted until she was

blinded by the sight of herself standing out in her back yard, huddled against the cold.

Cain. That was what he saw, and based on the way she was growing larger, he was getting closer.

His hand settled on her arm, and her own eyes started calling the shots again.

"Are you okay? You were just standing there."

She waved it off as unimportant, rather than let her growing fear take over. "Just concentrating."

"I felt a little tug on my power a second ago. You figured that out fast."

"Comes from years of being self-taught. I couldn't exactly go to regular school with the whole vision thing. Too easy to cheat."

"Can you do it again?"

"Sure."

"Offense or defense?"

She gave him a level stare. "What do you think?"

He grinned and pointed to a dead clump of weeds at the base of the clothesline post. "Try to set it on fire."

"Really? We're jumping straight to fire?"

"Don't tell me you're afraid of it."

"Of course not. Don't be an idiot. I only meant that there's got to be something before that."

"Like what?"

"I don't know. Levitating a leaf or something."

"How is that going to kill a demon? You're the one who was all in favor of going on the offense. Well, here's your chance to *blow shit up*, as you put it."

He grabbed her hips and turned her to face the target. He stood at her back, his body right up against hers, all hot and hard.

Yeah, right. Concentrating now was going to be impossible.

"Care to give a girl a little space?" she asked.

"You don't need space. You need power. And I'm going to give it to you."

He reached around her body, wrapping his left hand around her neck. His iridescent ring clicked in place, locking against the matching necklace, and the instant it did, Rory's whole body came alive.

She could feel everything. The sway of each individual hair as the wind swept past. The warm brush of Cain's breath near her ear. The tightening of tiny muscles along her skin as goose bumps hit her hard. The blast furnace of heat sinking into her back, battling the chill in the air.

Energy pulsed through her body, making it swell and throb. A tingling ripple of power gathered in her belly, coiling tight with silent purpose.

Cain lifted her hand toward the little clump of weeds. "My power is yours now. Tell it what to do. Make it obey."

His words made her feel powerful, filling her with confidence. She could do this. Right now, she felt like she could do anything.

A bright bolt of sparks shot from her hand, igniting the weeds in a flash of flame and smoke. A giddy sense of elation exploded in her chest, screaming of victory. It shoved her up off the ground in an excited jump only to find that when she landed, her knees no longer worked.

Cain caught her around the waist and pulled her back against his solid chest. She could feel his heart beating slow and steady, while the frantic little organ in her chest tried to flutter away.

"You did it," he said. The low rumble sank into her, easing some of the frenetic nervousness racing through her.

"I did it." Her words came out in weary pants, humiliating her.

"It's okay," he told her, as if sensing her anxiety. "It's supposed to be tiring at first."

"I'm not a pitiful weakling." And to prove it, she forced her legs to take her weight and found another target, this time a few yards farther away.

"You don't have to do this."

She did. She had to be sure the first time wasn't just a fluke.

Rory sucked in a deep breath. Cain's hands were at her waist as if he expected her to fall over. Without his ring touching her luceria, it was harder to tap into his power. She could feel it there, shimmering like a distant sea, but couldn't quite reach it.

"Focus on the luceria." His deep voice rumbled into her. She could feel it all along her back, distracting her for a moment.

Rory focused. She tuned herself in to the skin that lay just beneath the band. It seemed to heat and buzz, as if excited.

"Reach through it," he said. "Find the narrow ribbon that connects us."

She found it. She wasn't sure how, but she could practically see it, and it was glowing like the filament in a lightbulb. But instead of burning her when she touched it, the ribbon jumped and seethed with anticipation.

"Just like that." Cain's mouth was right by her ear now. His lips brushed her skin, wringing a shiver from her. "You have it. Now tug on that ribbon. Pull it into yourself."

Yes. That was what she wanted to do—let it become a part of her, let it fill her up.

Instincts took over, and Rory needed no further instruction. She drew that strand of energy into her body. It heated her skin and heightened her senses. She could smell Cain, so hot and delicious. She could feel his body cradling hers in a protective embrace. She could hear the beat of his heart, in time with her own. As the power inside of her grew, she recognized Cain's strength and intensity shining through. It was a part of him, and now it was a part of her.

She didn't want to let it go. She wanted to hold on to it forever so it could keep her warm.

"You have to let it go," he said, as if he'd seen her intent. "It's dangerous for you to try to hold on."

"I like it. I want it." She didn't care if she sounded petulant. She had to make him understand that she needed this.

His tone was calm, reassuring. "I'll give you more. Whatever you want. Just let go."

The coil of energy inside of her continued to grow, thickening as she pulled more into herself. And as it grew, it began to push against her insides, making her feel too full.

"Let it go, Rory."

He was right. This was too much. She couldn't hold it all, no matter how much she wanted it.

She tried to lift her hand as she had before, but she couldn't move. Her arms were too heavy, too weak.

Cain whispered soothing words across her mind. He was right there with her, holding her body and her mind. She didn't know how that could be, but she didn't have the strength to ask. She simply accepted it as one more strange mystery to add to the pile.

His fingers wrapped around her wrist, holding her carefully, as if she might break. "I've got you. Let it go."

Rory did. She shoved out the giant coil of power she'd collected, letting it spring out at her target. Heat blasted her face as a blob of fire hit and burst like a watermelon filled with explosives. Weeds and dirt spewed up in a geyser. As the flash of light faded, she could see a small crater left dug into the cold ground. Little fires ringed the area as weeds burned.

A sense of elation filled her, only to be swept away by the grueling weight of fatigue. Her legs seemed to evaporate, but Cain's grip on her body held her up.

Without that power glowing inside of her, she felt cold and empty, as if something vital was missing. For a moment, she considered pulling just a little into herself, but she wasn't sure how smart that was. Control had never been one of her strengths, and what if she got sucked back into that high? She didn't think she was strong enough for another round of magical whack-a-mole right now.

"You did well," said Cain. "As soon as you catch your breath, we'll try something else—perhaps something on the defensive side."

Rory wasn't sure how much more she could do in one day, but she'd be damned if she let him know that. If the women in his memories could sling magic around all day, so could she.

Right after she found the strength to support her own weight again.

He lowered her to the ground, settling her on his lap. She would have complained, but the fact was he made a great chair—all warm and scented like her darkest fantasies. She leaned back against his arm, letting him keep the cold chill of the ground away from her ass.

"How long does it take to get good at this?"

"Depends," he said. "Every woman is different. Some take to it faster than others. Some struggle with certain things. There's no way to know until you try."

The sky was still bright as the late-afternoon sun tried to break through the clouds hovering above in gray bands. The wind pushed them along at a quick clip, giving Rory a touch of vertigo. She closed her eyes to block out the sight, but it made her only that much more aware of just how cozy she'd gotten with Cain.

She hadn't known him long enough to be this comfortable with him, and yet part of her felt like she'd known him forever—likely some by-product of being inside his head or having him in hers.

As her breathing steadied, she started feeling more like herself again. More in control and less exhausted. She opened her eyes so she could look at Cain to tell him she was ready to try again, but her words died on her lips as she caught sight of him.

He was watching her, but it was more than a simple act. There was something predatory in his eyes, some kind of silent intent, as if he'd made a decision involving her. Something important. Desire darkened his eyes and lingered around his mouth. His lips were parted and her whole body shifted with every one of his breaths.

She hadn't noticed before, but there was a faint scar parting his hair just above his left temple. She'd witnessed him throwing himself into the path of danger before, but seeing the scar gave her a sick sense of fear, reminding her that he could be hurt, too. He wasn't as invincible as he appeared.

For one ridiculous moment, she wanted to protect him—to stand by his side and blow up the demons before they could lay a claw on him. Her protecting a man like him was such a ludicrous idea, she was sure it was proof that she really needed a reality check.

His finger traced over her forehead and down her cheek. It came to rest at her throat, where his luceria lay close to her skin. As he stroked the band, she swore she could feel his touch running along her spine as well, pulling another shiver from her.

"It suits you."

"Your necklace?"

His gaze hit her again, and this time, that dark, masculine hunger was far brighter. "My power. You like having it inside you. It makes you feel good."

She couldn't deny that. In fact, she was aching for more right now, even as exhausted as she was. "It's not supposed to be like that?"

"Oh, no. It's perfect. I simply hadn't expected it. I thought you'd resist using me—that it would make you feel weaker somehow."

She tried not to snort in amusement, but she couldn't help it. "Yeah, 'cause I'm so tough lounging in your lap like this, shaking and too flimsy to stand. Besides, it's just temporary. If I have to use you for a few days in order to stop these visions, then that's just a blow my pride is going to have to take."

His smiled faltered, and his hand covered her neck, splaying wide. The magical jewelry connected again, and she was flooded with a rush of energy, like she'd just mainlined some Red Bull.

"Better?" he asked.

It was more than merely better. Tingling clusters of heat and light spread out through her limbs. Fatigue fell away. She felt buoyant. She swore her body even lifted an inch off his lap.

Cain held her down, feeding more power into her until she didn't think she could hold anymore.

"Stop. It's too much."

The flow of energy stopped, and Cain's hand slid down to rest above her breasts. Her jacket was open in front, giving her no insulation from the heat of his touch. His fingertips hit bare flesh, sliding in small circles as if he enjoyed the texture of her skin.

Rory's nipples tightened until her breasts ached. She should have moved his hand off of her, but it felt too good. Every one of his fingers was giving off happy little streamers that wove through her, knocking her stupid.

She didn't let men she barely knew touch her like this, and yet if he tried to move his hand, she would have grabbed it and put it right back where it belonged, just above her heart.

The wacky urge to kiss him unfurled in her chest. He had a nice mouth, and as she watched, a knowing grin lifted the corners.

"You're in my head, aren't you?"

"Maybe a little. I only meant to help you channel my power, but I find I like seeing what makes you tick."

There was no heat in her words, despite her intention to scold him. "It's an invasion of privacy."

"For a human, perhaps. For our kind, it's the way things are meant to be."

Turnabout was fair play. If he was going to be nosy, she could be, too. She wasn't sure exactly how all of this worked, but her instincts had been pretty good up to this point, so she followed them.

"So you won't mind if I—" Speaking became impossible as she succeeded in her task, sinking into his thoughts, hitting a wall of need so hard she was sure she'd break apart upon it.

Desire, potent and seething, boiled below his calm surface. He hid it well, but now that she was facing it, she wasn't sure how that had been possible.

Images of the two of them together swirled through his mind, teasing her as they danced around. Shadows hid their bodies, but the action was clear. He wanted her, and the idea was so shocking, she found it hard to breathe.

She was prettier through his eyes, with a sultry kind of sex appeal she'd never seen in herself before. She was a dork, not some kind of exotic goddess the way he seemed to think. Her eyes weren't nearly that big, her skin not even close to that luminous. As much as she liked the way he saw her, it wasn't real. It wasn't true.

As she watched Cain's fantasies, her body began to heat, and a flush spread out over her skin. Her clothes felt too small. An empty, needy ache coalesced in her belly as every feminine part of her perked up in interest.

His vision-self bent to kiss her neck, and she swore she could feel the soft brush of his mouth on her real throat—the one that was not nearly so long and elegant as this fake Rory. But fake or not, watching his dark head work its way down as he layered kisses on her too-luminous skin was intoxicating. Tempting.

A moment later, the lovely images vanished, and she found herself being pushed away from his mind. She fought it, but was too weak from flinging magic around to fight him.

"You weren't supposed to see that," he said.

"Oh, I see how it is. You get to barge into my head, but yours is off-limits?"

"No, but there's no point in subjecting you to my lack of control. Is there?"

Lack of control? That's what he thought that was?

Her voice was a bit breathless, her mouth dry from what she'd seen. "What's that supposed to mean?"

"Once you find your savior, we'll part ways—in a few days, maybe a few weeks." His arm shifted. Muscles hardened at her back, and she was lifted closer to him. Almost close enough to reach his mouth. "The things I want to do to you will take far longer than that. Why taste something rare if you know you're only going to want more?"

Oh. Well. She hadn't thought of it quite like that. She opened her mouth to respond, but not a single coherent thought came to mind. He'd robbed her of every one of them with the way his eyes lingered on her mouth as if dying for a taste.

The low, quivering heat in her belly was all in favor of giving it a shot. For however long she could have him. "You might not like me as much as you think."

"Or perhaps I'd like you more. I haven't been with anyone in a long, long time. It may take me a while to work my extended celibacy out of my system."

That sounded like the most delightful of challenges to her. "Okay."

"Is that an offer, Rory?"

She wanted it to be—she wanted to feel just a fraction of what those naughty thoughts of his made her feel—but the huge lag between her brain and her mouth was causing problems. All that came out was a noncommittal squeak.

His head bent over hers, his lips only an inch away from her mouth. And then he stopped. "I couldn't slow you down like that," he said. "You have your savior to find. We should probably get going."

A second later, his mouth was gone and his hot expression froze over, as if they hadn't just been talking about ending his extended celibacy. With her.

Cain's pants buzzed, and she realized that his phone was vibrating. For a second, she thought it was some new kind of magic meant to rob her of her last few remaining brain cells. Everything was so messed up, she hadn't expected something as mundane as a cell phone.

Cain answered the call. Rory wanted to step away from him and give him some privacy, but her legs weren't cooperating. The sexy images, as well as playing with magic left her shaken and her knees way too weak to go for a stroll.

She heard the muted voice of another man on the line. Cain's body straightened, and he shifted from relaxed to red alert in seconds. "I can be there by sundown . . . No, it's my debt to repay. I made a vow."

The other man spoke again, briefly, and then Cain hung up. "I have to go. It's an emergency."

She didn't want him to leave, which was ludicrous. A few hours ago, she hadn't even wanted him to know where she lived, and now she was having a freak-out festival over this?

Apparently, all this magical crap caused brain damage.

Rory put on a nonchalant air of indifference. She refused to let him know that anything he did affected her—leaving or otherwise. "No problem. I'll call a cab to take me into the city to get my car. You can call me if you want to meet up later."

He didn't move a muscle, and yet he seemed to grow bigger, scarier. His arm at her back tightened, and she could feel his fingers curl at her hip. "If? You clearly still don't understand the situation between us."

"Kinda hard to understand something when no one's bothering to explain it to me."

Cain drew in a long breath and let it out slowly. His

chest expanded to monumental proportions, and Rory couldn't help but want to dig her fingers in just to feel all those muscles flex beneath his skin.

So yummy. But she was not nearly woman enough to eat him up. No way. A man like him was too much for her to handle. She'd been with only a couple of guys, and both of them were like children by comparison—all small and stringy. She was not a strong enough woman to withstand the kind of lover Cain would be—especially not after a long time of abstinence.

Though how he'd managed to go more than a week without some woman attacking him was a mystery.

"You're right," he said. "I should be more patient with you."

If he was any more patient, her panties were going to combust. "Just tell me what's going on."

"I need to leave now—someone is in danger. I'd like it very much if you'd come with me."

He would? A small girly part of her did a giddy little dance. "Why?"

"Because you'll be safe at my side."

Some of that giddiness lost its shine, deflating her. "I can take care of myself."

"I'm not suggesting you're weak, but you have to admit that not being able to stand on your own has its disadvantages. Especially if the demons find you. And if I leave, you have no car, no way to escape if you need to."

That sounded like a perfect formula for a bad day.

Rory pushed herself to her feet and stepped back well out of his reach. Maybe if she put more distance between them, her brain would start working right again.

Her legs trembled, but held her up, which was all she was asking of them right now.

She'd thought that if she was no longer touching him that her normally adequate brain would start working right again. Instead, she was able to see him better from this distance, which gave him a completely unfair advantage.

She closed her eyes to block out the sight, and Mrs. Wittle's gnarled hands appeared out of nowhere as she dunked a tea bag in hot water.

Maybe getting out of here was a good idea. She could get her car back and things could go back to normal. Seeing visions at home was just too weird for her to handle. At least when she left her house, she expected to be invaded by the sights. Having it happen here was too . . . intrusive.

"Okay," she said. "Let's go. But on the way, you're going to tell me everything you know about how all this magic stuff works."

"Whatever you want to know. All you have to do is ask."

"Let's start with where we're going."

Cain stood up in one smooth, beautiful movement and brushed the dead grass from his jeans. "To save a vampire's life."

Chapter 12

Cain drove as fast as he dared. He was racing against the sun, and if he didn't make it to Ronan before dark, the Sanguinar wasn't likely to survive.

Cain's promise to Logan to give Ronan his blood pushed Cain to hurry, filling the back of his mind with a searing sense of urgency. Beside him, Rory reloaded her gun.

"How far away is your vampire buddy?" she asked.

He glanced in the rearview mirror at the setting sun now touching the horizon. "Too far, I fear."

"Stop it with the vague answers. Be specific."

If specific was what she wanted, he would give it to her—anything to keep her at his side where he could ensure her safety. His plans for seduction, his playing hard to get, was working on his feisty Rory, just as he'd hoped. Perhaps it was devious of him to use her own stubbornness against her, but his life was at stake. He found he couldn't help himself. And even if it hadn't been, the prize of feeling her body glide naked against his was more than enough to compel him.

Cain cleared his throat and tried not to sound like his cock was so hard it ached. "Ronan is lying in the basement of a Gerai house about twenty miles from here. He's too weak to move, and he's bled, which means that once the sun goes down—"

"The demons will come to chow down. Got it." She tucked her gun in her purse. "What's a Gerai house?"

"Blooded humans—those who are descendants of an ancient, magical race—sometimes agree to help us Sentinels. One of the things they do is keep homes stocked with food and supplies and ensure that we have places to go when we need to rest or heal."

"Like safe houses."

"Exactly."

She was quiet for a moment, and it took Cain a healthy dose of willpower to keep from reaching through the link the luceria created in order to see what it was she was thinking. Eventually, she might welcome him into her head, but Rory wasn't the most trusting woman he'd ever met. And she was armed.

"You know, if you would have told me last night that I'd be going on a rescue mission with a sword-wielding warrior to save a vampire, I wouldn't have believed it."

"And now?"

"Completely plausible. How crazy is that?"

"Another day on the job for me." *For us,* he wanted to say, but held his tongue. She'd made it clear where her boundaries were, and Hope's warning was not lost on him. *Push her and she'll push back. Hard.*

He didn't want that. In fact, what he wanted was to be right back where they'd been a little while ago, with her hands on his chest and her lips close enough to touch. If she'd so much as glance down at the time, she would have seen just how much she affected him—how the mere idea of her lips on his skin made him rock hard.

But she hadn't looked down, and she was taking their rescue mission, as she called it, in stride.

Rory was certainly an adaptable creature. She rolled with the punches, which was something he was sure would serve her well in the days ahead. Maybe sooner.

Her body tightened up, and he could feel a spurt of frustration trickling through the luceria. That feeling had come from her, but Cain absorbed it and let it become part of him, marveling at how their connection was growing so fast so soon. "What's wrong?"

She shifted in her seat and smoothed her pink hair behind her ears. "Just a bit of mental channel surfing. Nothing to worry about."

"We're not near any populated areas." In fact, they were even farther out than her house was, even more isolated. There was no traffic around—no one in sight.

"Yeah. Normally it's not a problem. Too bad normal isn't on the menu lately." Her voice was clipped with irritation, but that didn't bother him nearly as much as the small tremor of fear he felt seeping out of her.

"Talk to me. Tell me what's going on. Maybe I can help."

"I'm probably just tired. I kinda missed getting any sleep last night."

Her need hit him hard as he realized he had been neglecting his duty to see to her health. Not that he could simply order her to bed like a child. She'd be as likely to shoot him as she would be to obey a command of his, no matter how much she agreed with it. She was the most contrary woman he'd ever met, and yet that made her only that much more interesting to him.

So rather than risk a bullet, he kept his mouth shut about her needing to take a nap. Later, when the danger to Ronan was over, then he'd see that she rested. There were several ways he could wear her out, some of them more enticing than others.

"It's more than that," he said, keeping his lust clear of his voice. "You're afraid."

Her spine went rigid, and her tone dripped with indignation. "We are going to meet a vampire. Most sane people would be a little apprehensive about that, don't you think?"

He cast a quick glance in her direction. Her skin was pale, and he could see a fine trembling in her fingers as they toyed with the strap of her purse. No matter how indignant she sounded, she couldn't fool him. "The visions are getting worse, aren't they?"

"Yeah," she whispered, as if saying it too loud would make the situation worse. "I had a couple at home, too. That has never happened before—at least not with my neighbors. They're too far away. Or they *were*."

But no longer. "Try to stay calm, okay? Whatever is going on is probably just a temporary problem caused by you taking my luceria. You could be inadvertently using my power to amplify your ability."

Sarcasm sharpened her tone. "Right. 'Cause I know so much about all this magical bullshit. I wouldn't even know where to start using your power to amplify anything."

"You know more than you think. Otherwise, how would you have known to take my luceria? I didn't even tell you it was possible. You simply knew."

"That was different. I saw it and wanted it. It was a selfish, impulsive thing to do, and look where it got me."

Cain covered her hand with his, wishing he knew how to ease her frustration. He hadn't been around a lot of people in the last few centuries. Most of his time had been spent with Sibyl, and Rory was nothing like Sibyl. Rory was fiercer, more independent. He wasn't sure what to say to make her feel better, no matter how loudly the need to ease her clamored inside of him.

"It's going to be okay," he told her, wincing at the lame inadequacy of his words.

She went still beneath his hand. Even her trembling quieted. "How do you do that?"

"What?"

"Whenever you touch me, the visions go away."

"It's not something I'm doing purposefully."

Her pink head fell back against the seat in frustration. "I don't suppose you've got some magical, vision-blocking ring stashed somewhere, do you?"

"Sorry."

"It's okay. I'll survive. I always do."

There was something more to her words than what lay on the surface. Cain could feel a jagged vibration of fear buzzing through their link. With it came a chaotic flurry of images of dark water and terror. They were gone before he could blink, but the greasy remnants of her fear remained.

He wanted to delve deeper and seek out the source of that fear, but didn't dare distract himself like that while driving.

"Did something happen to you?" he asked. His voice was rougher than he'd intended, more forceful.

"Lots of things have happened to me. That's life." She turned away from him to stare out the side window. Her fingers slipped out from under his hand, and she crossed her arms over her chest. "How close are we?"

The distance she'd shoved between them echoed with a hollow chill. Cain felt it all the way to his bones until he was aching with the need to feel her warmth again.

If it hadn't been for her very loud body language and the neon KEEP OUT sign it painted, he might have reached for her again. But as it stood, all he could think to offer her was the small amount of privacy the cab of his truck could allow.

The last two miles of their trip seemed to take forever. He wanted to touch her thoughts and search for a way to make her relax, but he didn't dare—not when he was behind the wheel and so new to their partnership. The kind of concentration he'd need to make contact was more than he could spare. And even if he had, it would have felt like a violation—an encroachment on her wishes to be alone.

So Cain let it drop, feeling useless and restless. By the time he pulled up into the driveway of the Gerai house, all he could think about was getting this chore done and finding a nice, quiet place to sit her down and work through some things. Or perhaps lay her down. That had its own lovely set of possibilities as well.

There was no way to know how long their partnership would last. And even if it was only for a few days, they needed some ground rules. Namely, she needed to stop shutting him out. If he didn't know what was going on, he couldn't help her.

Then again, if her quest to find the person who stopped her visions failed, then she'd be tied to Cain indefinitely. He could spend the rest of his life touching her as often as possible, driving away her visions. She would need him. He would once again have purpose. And Rory.

Before that thought began to grow and fill his mind, he crushed it, refusing to even entertain the idea of sabotaging her wishes like that. She wanted a cure. Freedom. Forcing himself into her life, making her need him, was only going to grate against her independence. That was not the kind of man he was—or at least not the kind of man he wanted to be.

And if he *was* that kind of man, he didn't deserve Rory.

With his path firmly in mind, he got out of his truck just as the last sliver of the sun was visible above the horizon. Rory was a few steps in front of him, and he saw her falter as she neared.

"What?" he asked.

"Nothing new. There's definitely someone in there. There are spots of blood on his pillow."

Cain sped up, anxious to have that blood burned away before full dark fell. Synestryn would be drawn to the scent of it, and with Rory here, he didn't want to take any unnecessary risks.

He found Ronan on a cot in the unfinished basement. The small, high windows had been blacked out with thick layers of paint. Several utilitarian shelves lined the walls, stocked with clothing and canned goods. A washer and dryer sat in one corner, next to a small bathroom. The cement floors gave off a damp chill.

Ronan hardly twitched as Cain hurried down the wooden steps. His gaunt frame lay in listless stillness as Cain approached. Only Ronan's eyes moved, tracking Cain as he came closer.

Rory was behind him, hovering at the top of the stairway. He could feel a little tickle of curiosity coming from her, along with a healthy dose of caution.

"Can you please start a fire?" he asked her. He wasn't keen on letting her watch what was about to happen. Chances were Ronan wasn't going to like an audience, either.

"Sure. No problem."

Ronan's eyes glowed with pale blue light. His lips peeled back from his teeth in hunger. Skin sagged on his frame, and traces of blood left dark patches on his deathly white face.

Cain stripped out of his jacket as he came near. The look in Ronan's eyes was not one of calm intellect. There was only instinct there—a quivering, animalistic hunger that Cain had seen before. Ronan was nearly dead, famished, and that made him dangerous.

"I'm here to feed you," said Cain. He extended his left arm, keeping his right hand on the hilt of his sword.

In a move too fast for Cain to track, Ronan grabbed his wrist and jerked it to his mouth. Sharp teeth split Cain's skin, and a heavy, ravenous gulping sound echoed in the space. After a couple of minutes, he felt his body begin to weaken. A dizzy lethargy spun in his head, and his legs felt too heavy.

"Stop," he said. "You've taken enough."

Ronan didn't stop. Cain pulled on his arm, but Ronan held on tight, his strength fueled by Cain's powerful blood.

He tugged hard, eliciting a growl of warning from Ronan.

A moment later, Cain was on the floor, though he couldn't remember how he got there. His need to sleep was nearly overpowering—a compulsion from Ronan, no doubt—and Rory was upstairs, unprotected. With the blood Ronan had spilled, it was only a matter of time before they had company of the Synestryn kind. And if he passed out, there wasn't a thing he could do to protect Rory from the demons.

Or from Ronan.

Raygh felt the moment his prey slipped the noose. The Sanguinar tethered to him had fed, giving him the strength he needed to shove a wall between them.

Not that it mattered. Raygh already knew where the Sanguinar was. He couldn't hide now—not from the minions Raygh had crawling all over the countryside.

Another swarm was nearby, waiting for the last rays of daylight to fade before they moved. One of them had the blood of one of those he sought, and as soon as it came home, another of his prey would be within his grasp. This one a woman.

Raygh had something special in store for her—something that made him squirm with anticipation.

He reached out for those under his control who were near the lost Sanguinar. Most of the lesser demons were still asleep, but a few were awake and ready to do his bidding. As soon as he touched the searing, alien minds of his Handlers, he gave them instructions for tonight's work. The Sanguinar was close. They would have no trouble rooting him out and bringing him back to face the punishment he deserved.

He'd been present at the death of at least one of Raygh's sons. For that, he was going to suffer.

The second Rory saw through the vampire's eyes, she knew that Cain was in trouble. His body was crumpled on the floor, his thick arm reaching all the way back to the vampire's mouth.

Cain didn't look good. He was too pale, and there was a drooping kind of fatigue hanging over him, as if he were too weak to sit up straight.

That wasn't like him at all. He normally radiated strength, which meant that whatever was going on down there wasn't normal.

She raced down the steps and saw the vampire hunched over Cain's arm. His sword was out, but it hung loose in his grip, as if it were too heavy to lift.

"What the hell are you doing?" she demanded.

The vampire looked up at her then. His pale blue eyes flared wide with excitement, and a watery light brightened his gaze. As she watched, his throat moved as he drank more of Cain's blood.

Shock, disgust and fear all rose up into a tangled knot that lodged in her throat. She tried to tell him that he was killing Cain, but she couldn't seem to shove the words out. But she had to do something. Fast.

Rory had always struggled with impulsiveness. Her Nana had told her over and over that it was going to get her hurt one of these days.

Well, apparently that day had arrived.

She charged the vampire, her fists balled up tight. She wasn't sure exactly what was going to happen until her knuckles connected with the side of his pretty head. She landed a solid blow on his temple that was hard enough to knock his mouth away from Cain's arm. Blood seeped from the wounds.

The vampire rose to his feet, anger and hunger making the gaunt angles of his face stand out in stark detail.

Rory shoved him back away from Cain and lifted her fists. "Want to go another round, pretty boy?"

He stared at her in shock for a moment. A frown creased his brow, and he gave his head a little shake. Suddenly, the pale blue light in his eyes winked out and he lifted his hands in surrender. "I'm sorry. I lost my head there for a moment."

He moved toward Cain, but Rory shifted to block his path. "Stay back."

"I need to heal his wounds and restore some of what I took from him."

"Yeah, I don't think so. You've done enough."

"It's okay, Rory," said Cain from behind her. "Ronan is himself again."

"Who the fuck was he a minute ago, then? 'Cause I'd like to kick that asshole in the junk."

"You have every reason to be suspicious, but I assure you that I'm no longer out of control. I also promise that if we don't get all this blood cleaned up, demons will find us soon."

There was that.

Cain pushed himself to his feet. The look he gave Rory was a combination of pride and humiliation. "Thank you for stepping in."

"Yes," said Ronan. "I'm sorry you had to interfere, but I'm glad you were here to do so."

"So what the hell was that all about?" she asked.

"I was hungry. Cain fed me."

Blood. The word went unspoken, but it hovered there, in the cool, damp air, painfully obvious.

"Is the fire going?" asked Cain. He still looked pale and shaky, but at least he was on his feet, which was a big improvement.

"Yeah. Someone had already laid in the logs and stuff. I just had to light the kindling."

"Good. We need to burn away all traces of blood." Cain started to strip the bloody pillowcase from the pillow, but Rory stopped him.

"I'll do that," she said, taking the pillow away from Cain. "You sit down before you fall over, and put some pressure on your wrist." She pointed her finger at Ronan. "And you keep your teeth to yourself."

He was way too pretty to be trusted. In fact, he reminded her of Logan, with his perfect features and his sleek, streamlined muscles. His dark hair fell over his forehead, and there was a bit of stubble riding his jaw—just enough to accentuate the perfect little indent in his chin.

Ronan's gaze lingered at her throat for a minute, and she saw what he saw flash in her mind, complete with the pretty, pulsing, shimmering band around her neck. It was darker than it had been before, with more purple than pink running through it.

"Don't even think about her blood," rumbled Cain in warning. "She's off-limits."

"Of course," said Ronan, but his tone made it sound more like the answer to a challenge than acceptance. "May I see to your wrist?"

Cain held his arm up, but he wasn't looking at Ronan. His gaze was fixed on Rory, making her squirm. There was something different in his expression now—a kind of new awareness, as if he were seeing her in a different light.

Ronan pressed his fingers against the teeth marks in Cain's wrist, and a second later, his skin was whole again, with only a few smears of blood to prove anything had ever happened.

"Wow. That's handy," said Rory.

"My debt is paid now," said Cain. "Tell Logan that the next time you talk to him."

Ronan gave Cain a formal little bow of his head. "Of course. And thank you for coming."

"We're not out of the woods yet. You still have blood on your face. We need the place cleansed of all scents. Rory is new to her power, and I won't put her at risk."

"You know, the way you guys talk about me like I'm

not here is irritating as hell." She grabbed the bloody fabric and marched upstairs to burn it. When she turned around, Cain was standing there, a bloody washcloth in his hand.

He added it to the flames, and she could see that his hand was shaking. "I'm sorry about that—about talking past you, about making you see Ronan lose control."

"Why aren't you more freaked out by it?"

Cain lifted one shoulder in a shrug. "We're all weak sometimes. Ronan can't help what he is any more than I can. I know what it's like to feel out of control. Rubbing his nose in his mistake will only make his life harder. And I assure you, it's hard enough."

"And what about your life? You're shaking, your skin is pale, and you look a little unsteady on your feet. If demons smell the blood and come here, you're not going to be in any shape to swing that big ol' sword around."

"I'll manage. I've been weaker than this before and survived."

"She's right," said Ronan from the stairway. "Rory's life is precious. You need to be able to keep her safe." The blood was washed off his face, leaving him even more beautiful than before.

She turned to face him, irritation grating along her nerves. "Rory has a gun. She can keep herself safe."

Ronan had the balls to smile at her. "You are delightful. Have we met before?"

"No." She was fairly sure she would have remembered a man like him if she'd so much as seen him walk down the street.

"You smell . . . familiar."

"Smell?" She turned to Cain in humiliated horror. "Do I smell?"

"You smell lovely," said Cain, his voice so rough with desire she had to press her thighs together around a pulse of raw need.

Ronan took a step closer. "I'm certain we've met before. Your scent . . ." His eyes widened in recognition and flared pale blue. He turned to Cain, his voice harsh with urgency. "Get her out of here."

"What is it?" asked Cain.

"The Synestryn lord who left me weakened and bleeding—it sent out these scorpion-like creatures to hunt down certain people. That's why she smelled familiar. Rory's scent was one that it was seeking, and recently found."

"You mean those things with the three barbs sticking out of their tails?" asked Rory.

"Yes. Have you seen them?"

"One of them stung her last night," said Cain.

"So the Synestryn has her blood now."

"What for? Why does some demon want my blood?"

"To connect to you. To hunt you. To . . ." He trailed off, and reached for her.

Rory stepped out of the way even as Cain shoved his body between them.

Ronan cast a look of irritation at Cain, and leaned around his shoulder. "Have you had any nightmares since you were stung?"

"No."

"She hasn't slept except for a few minutes of rest I forced on her," said Cain.

Ronan went back to ignoring her and told Cain, "Guard her sleep. That demon found me while I slept. It could be because I connected to the mind of one of its minions, but it could also be something the Synestryn can do with the blood they took."

"Did one of them get your blood, too?" asked Rory.

"Yes. And the nightmare . . . let's just say you don't want to face what this particular Synestryn has in store."

"No sleeping. Got it."

Cain turned around, concern tightening his brows. "You have to sleep sometime."

"So do you, Cain. Now that I've taken so much of

your blood." Ronan's hand gripped the back of Cain's neck, and he swayed on his feet.

Ronan sagged a bit, looking thinner than he had a moment ago. His eyes flared bright, and then the light died out like a flame starved of oxygen.

Cain grabbed Ronan's arms and eased him down to the couch. "There was no need for that."

"Yes, there was. You know how rare women like Rory are. We can't lose her. You have to be able to keep her safe."

"I have a gun," Rory nearly shouted. "None of you seem to hear me when I say that."

Cain spared her only a brief glance. "Guns won't work—not unless you blow off their heads."

"I can do that," she said with more confidence than she felt.

Outside, a piercing howl split the twilight.

Rory's shoulders shot up by her ears as a knot of fear coiled tight along her spine. "Is that what I think it is?"

Cain looked at her, but his expression was anything but comforting. Rage twitched around his mouth, and his eyes were narrowed with determination. "Demons," he confirmed.

Ronan was panting a little as he spoke. "You should go now. Get her away from here. I'll stay here and draw them away."

From the pained look on Cain's face, that was clearly a bad idea. At least it was for Ronan.

"He's not going to be safe here alone, is he?" asked Rory.

"Not in this condition."

"I'll be fine," said Ronan.

"We can't leave him alone, can we?" she asked, ignoring Ronan's protestations with a little stab of satisfaction. See how he liked being treated as if he were invisible.

"He's a healer. We need him."

Ronan pushed to his feet. "I'm strong enough to drive."

Rory didn't see how. He was paler than before, since he'd touched Cain. He looked all frail, like an old man, even if his face was a thing of beauty. "You said this demon had access to your brain. What if he tries something and makes you crash?"

"I'll resist."

"How?" asked Cain. "Unless you take more blood."

"You can't spare any more. It was shameful of me to take as much as I did."

Another howl rose, this time much, much closer.

From out of nowhere, Rory was hit by the need to fight. It burned in her, so bright and fierce she felt like she'd explode if she didn't let it out. She grabbed her gun from her purse and made a beeline for the front door.

Cain grabbed her by the arm to stop her. "Where are you going?"

"To kill me some demons. Obviously. You two are too busy yammering to do the job yourself. Someone's got to."

Ronan tilted his head to the side as he studied her. "That creature that haunted my dreams. I sense its presence in her—its malevolent taint. This has got to be some sort of compulsion," he said. "Perhaps to drive her out into the night so that she's easier to find."

She ripped free of Cain's grasp. "Oh, I'm easy to find, all right. Let the fuckers come get me."

She started for the door, only to have Cain grab her around the waist and stop her progress. "Not tonight. There will be other nights to fight. Tonight, we run."

"I am not a coward," she snarled at him, working to pry his thick arm away from her body.

It was no use. Her legs were off of the floor, giving her no leverage.

Cain dropped her on the couch, following her down to cage her body with his. His face was taut with tension, his voice low and earnest. "The demons have your blood. They can make you do things. The power I fed you earlier is only temporary, and once it fades, you'll be weak. You need to calm down."

Rory was not that easy to control. She was no one's puppet—demon or otherwise. She wanted to kill. Needed it. No one was going to stand in her way. Not even Cain.

"There's no time for this," said Ronan. "We must leave."

Synestryn howled again, and this time it was much closer. She could no longer stop herself. She had to get out there.

Power circled her throat. All she had to do was figure out how to shape it so that she could get Cain to back off and let her pass.

"Rory," he said, his tone a warning. "I can feel that. What are you doing?"

Energy leapt into her, eager to do her bidding. It wasn't nearly as exhausting as it had been before. In fact, she was sure that the flow of power into her was faster now. Thicker.

She gathered it up and used it to strengthen her limbs. With one hard shove, Cain was tossed backward and out of her way. She bounced up and sprinted for the door, her legs fueled by the magic flowing into her.

Rory made it outside. The door behind her bounced hard on its hinges. Cold air hit her face, scented with something dark and musky.

Demons.

She bared her teeth and started to sprint in their direction, but a second later, she was tossed sideways by a hot, heavy battering ram.

Cain's bulk pinned her to the ground. His mouth was tight with anger, his eyes bright with fear.

She fought his hold, driven to find those demons. She needed to make their blood flow—to set them on fire and watch them burn. Why could Cain not understand that? He was supposed to want the same thing.

No matter what she did, she couldn't find enough strength to slip his grasp. Even the power that had been at her fingertips before seemed to sputter and fail as she reached for it.

Cain cupped her chin in one hand. She felt him shove his way into her mind, his determination burning so bright she could no longer see her own thoughts through the glare.

His deep voice settled over her. "Calm down."

She couldn't. She had to get up and fight.

Another hand appeared from over her head. The fingers were long and skinny, almost feminine—not at all like Cain's. The hand settled on her forehead, cold and unwanted. Pain sliced through her skull, making her cry out. Ronan's face hovered over her, flat and without mercy.

Her vision started to go gray. Her limbs began to buzz with the beginnings of numbness. A weak lethargy fell over her like a warm blanket. She tried to fight it, but she was pulled down, sucked into the silent black of sleep. The last thing she saw was Cain's expression of anguished regret as he said, "I'm sorry."

Chapter 13

Cain couldn't stay and fight. Not now. The Synestryn would have to wait for another time when he didn't have an unconscious woman and a weak Sanguinar to protect. When he wasn't weak himself.

Ronan got behind the wheel of his van. Cain didn't wait for an invitation to come along. He simply picked Rory up and climbed into the back, furious at what Ronan had done.

"Go," ordered Cain. His voice came out as a growl of anger.

Ronan took off down the gravel driveway. "I didn't hurt her."

"You weren't exactly gentle, either."

"I had to knock her out. You saw how rabid she'd become. She was willing to do whatever it took to go after those demons—no matter who she had to go through to make it happen. It was the right choice."

"Yeah. I'm sure she'll see it that way when she wakes up." And the fact that Cain had held her in place for Ronan to subdue was not going to sit well with her.

Cain tried not to care if she was angry at him. As long as she stayed out of danger, she could be as mad as she liked. But that was a lie. He was trying to connect to her, to tie her to him. Letting Ronan hurt her wasn't exactly the way to win her over.

"Shall I head for Dabyr?"

That would have been Cain's first choice, but they would never find the person who blocked her visions from behind those walls. And so many people around would hurt her. If he tried to lock her up there, he knew she'd find a way to escape, and there were too many humans around to get hurt.

She'd already proven that she was willing to use his power against him. He'd felt her intent as clearly as if it had been his own. What if she used his power against the humans as well? She could easily kill someone. He couldn't let that happen. He couldn't force her to live with the guilt that kind of mistake would create.

"She was definitely compelled to act. I could feel the power of it spreading through her as I touched her mind." Cain caught Ronan's gaze in the rearview mirror. "Can you free her?"

"It's possible, but the creature I touched was strong."

"So is she. If anyone can shake this off, she can."

"I'll need more blood—more than you can give. I'm currently too weak to do much. And some of that blood will need to be hers. There's no way around that."

Every protective instinct in Cain stood up and roared in defiance, but he knew the stakes. He knew Ronan wouldn't hurt her. At least no more than he had to.

As angry as he was at what Ronan had done, Cain knew it had been the right choice. His hesitation could have cost them Rory's life had Ronan not acted when he did.

And that wasn't the only thing men like Ronan had done for him. The Sanguinar had restored Cain's fertility. They'd given him something he'd never thought he'd have again. And with that gift of hope, they'd earned his trust. At least more than he'd given them in the past.

"I'll put out the call," said Cain. "I'll make sure you get what you need."

"Do I head east toward the closest Gerai house?"

"No. South. Toward her house. I think she'll feel better if she's at home when she wakes. It's not far."

Ronan drove while Cain split his attention between Rory and the surrounding landscape. He saw no signs of demons, but he knew they were out there. The demons were always out there.

By the time Ronan pulled into Rory's driveway, Paul and Andra were already there, waiting. Paul's sword was out, his gaze on the line of trees skirting Rory's property. Andra's long body was propped up against the white porch, watching Paul. As the van pulled in, Andra galloped down the steps, her combat boots kicking up little clouds of dust as the stairs bounced under her feet. Paul stayed put, watching her back.

She pulled the van door open. Moonlight gleamed off her leather coat and her blue eyes went straight to Rory. "She okay?"

"She will be," said Cain. "Thanks for coming."

Andra gave a nonchalant shrug. "We were nearby, and tonight's fun really hasn't gotten started yet."

Despite her comment, Cain thought she looked tired, worn thin and desolate. There were circles under her eyes, and sadness lurking along her mouth.

Then again, Andra's baby sister, Tori, was in bad shape after a decade in the hands of the Synestryn. They'd fed her their blood, tortured and raped her. That was more than enough to fuck up anyone. She'd recently left Earth in the hopes that a powerful woman on another world would find some way to clean the Synestryn poison from Tori's blood, and with it the homicidal rage she suffered.

That was months ago, and no one had heard from Tori since. It was no wonder Andra looked like she'd had more than her fair share of sleepless nights.

Ronan glided up to Andra's side, a strange excitement crinkling the corners of his eyes. "How are you?"

She gave him a brief glance and uttered a distracted, "Fine."

"Let's get inside," said Paul.

Andra nodded at her husband. "I'll put up some defenses."

Paul shot her a worried look. "Don't push yourself, okay?"

"I'm fine."

She wasn't, but Paul was obviously aware of that.

Cain carried Rory inside. Ronan held the door. Paul cradled Andra's neck in his hand and a faint blue light seeped over the house. Cain could see it shimmering over the windows, warping the view outside.

"That should hide us for a while," she said as she shut the door.

Cain laid Rory on her bed, arranging her so she looked comfortable.

Paul stood in the bedroom doorway, watching. "What happened?"

"A Synestryn took her blood and compelled her to run toward combat. Ronan thinks he can help, but he's low on juice. I've given all I can."

Paul nodded, his face impassive. "I'll take care of it."

"Thanks."

Paul's gaze hit the luceria around Rory's neck. "Congratulations."

A little spurt of excitement shot through Cain as he stared at her. The colors in the luceria had darkened, streaming with a deep amethyst purple. "Don't be too hasty with the congratulations. We'll see how long she stays by my side."

"You're a good man. I'm sure she'll see that."

Cain couldn't look at his friend as he admitted, "I'm not the man I used to be. And she knows what happened the night Sibyl was taken. Hell, tonight I couldn't even do the right thing and render her unconscious so she wouldn't go and hurt herself. What woman wants to tie herself for eternity to a man who keeps screwing up?"

"You're too hard on yourself. And if she isn't smart enough to see through to the man you really are, she doesn't deserve you."

Cain snorted. "No big deal, I'll just go out and find the next compatible female Theronai on the streets."

"How close are you?" asked Paul.

Cain didn't need to ask for clarification. He knew exactly what the other man meant. "I was down to two leaves when I found her."

Paul winced in sympathy. "What did she promise?"

"To stick with me until she finds the person who blocks these visions she has. They're debilitating, but seem to go away when I touch her. Then they come right back with a vengeance."

"So you're not the person, then?"

"No. Whoever it is, they are able to help her from some distance. Rory's never even seen them as far as I know. She thinks it might be some kind of magical device."

"Gilda had a fairly comprehensive list of items. I'll call Joseph and ask him to have someone look for it. Maybe we'll get lucky."

"I know I should be busting my ass to help Rory cure her visions, but I can't say I'm enthusiastic about her vow being fulfilled."

"Right. Of course. I understand. No calling Joseph."

Paul turned on his heel and left. Cain sat there for a long moment, staring down at Rory's sweet face. Her dark makeup was a smeared mess around her eyes, and there was a red mark on her forehead that looked suspiciously like the outline of Ronan's fingers.

Cain smoothed his hand over the mark, wishing he could wipe it away.

If he'd been a little faster the night he'd met her, she

never would have been stabbed by the demon. Her blood would be safe, and she would be awake and as feisty as ever. Instead, she was locked in an unnatural sleep, possibly with those nightmares Ronan had warned them about.

As much as Cain wished there had been something he could do, he wasn't that powerful. All he could do was make sure Ronan got what he needed to help her.

No, that was wrong. There was something else he could do—something he knew he *should* do.

Cain dialed Joseph, but the leader of the Theronai did not answer his phone. Cain left a message, telling Joseph to find Gilda's list of magical artifacts and search for one that could help Rory. With that chore done, he eased her out of her spiked leather coat and tugged off her shoes to make her more comfortable. He pulled the blankets up to her chin and went to figure out just how much blood it was going to take to fix his precious Rory.

In the living room, Paul was already rolling down his sleeve after feeding Ronan. A flush of color stained the Sanguinar's cheeks, and a faint glow lit his eyes.

"Is that enough?" asked Cain.

Ronan shook his head. "It was all I dared take from Paul. He needs to be able to fight."

"Take my blood," offered Andra.

"No," clipped Paul.

Cain should have been right there with his brother, defending Andra's blood, but he couldn't do it. If the choice was a small sacrifice from Andra to save Rory suffering, it was an easy one to make.

Paul took Andra's hand in his. "You're too tired. You haven't been sleeping or eating. It's not safe."

Ronan stayed where he was, his body still. Excitement and hunger shone in his eyes, but he made no moves to take what he so clearly wanted. "If not Andra, then you will need to call someone else. Not a Gerai, either. I will need more power than that if I'm to fight this demon."

Andra gave her husband a hard look. "I'm doing this. I can't help Tori right now. At least this way, I'll be helping someone."

Paul shook his head. "I don't think it's a good— "

"I need this, Paul. Please don't fight me."

He let out a long sigh, but gave a grudging nod. He looked at Ronan, warning clear on his face. "Don't push it."

Ronan had lied, but for all the right reasons. He could hear the heartbeat of Andra's child and needed to reassure himself it was safe. The strain of Andra's grief was weighing her down, exhausting her. It was obvious in her listlessness and the heavy fatigue riding her features. That strain wasn't good for the child she carried, which meant it was his duty to do what he could to rid her of it.

And the only way to do that was by having access to her. And her blood.

Paul was overprotective of his wife, and the only person who could have swayed his decision was Andra herself.

The setup had been too perfect for Ronan to resist, so he'd woven the lie, refusing to feel even a moment's guilt. Every Theronai child was a gift, and Andra needed to be strong right now to ensure that child was healthy.

Ronan didn't dare go for the woman's throat. Instead, he held out his hand for hers, and bent over her wrist. Hot, potent power flowed into him, clouding his thoughts for a moment. The baby was a boy, and the strength of that little life was shocking. It seeped into Ronan, filling him with a giddy sense of hope. He knew he wouldn't have long before Paul intervened, so Ronan gathered his wits and moved past sensation into pure intellect.

Weariness pounded through her with every beat of her heart. Grief. Guilt. Loneliness for her baby sister. All of it swirled together into a tight knot he wasn't sure he could loosen. He was inundated with input, with emotions so raw and ragged they were nearly overwhelming.

Using a burst of power fueled by Andra's rich blood, Ronan went straight for the source of her anguish—her baby sister—and laid a muting veil over it. The fix wouldn't last long—only a few days—but it would give her time to rest and regain her strength before those deep, searing feelings of guilt and loss came back to haunt her.

Ronan sought out the new life, needing to reassure himself it was safe. As he did, he felt a curious stand of magic winding through her.

Someone had altered her, and based on the familiar feel of it, Ronan was sure that either Logan or Tynan was to blame. Or thank, depending.

Whatever had been done to her, she was fine. The baby was fine. And taking more blood would not be good for either of them. If her emotions interfered with the safety of the child, then he was sure that Paul would not stand in the way of Ronan doing what needed to be done.

With a thought, Ronan closed her wounds. He sat back on the couch, feeling a wide grin stretch his face.

"What?" asked Paul, his hand on his sword.

He didn't know. There was no way he could know. Andra didn't even know.

Ronan considered not telling them, but there seemed no point in waiting. Good news might be just the thing for them right now—something to help them through these trying times.

He looked at Andra, who sat calm and still. A soft, sleepy look tugged at her eyelids. "You're pregnant."

She blinked slowly, as if not understanding his words.

Paul's body went still in shock. "What? Are you sure?"

"I am."

Andra looked up at her husband. There was no accusation in her eyes, only faint curiosity. "How? I thought you couldn't get me pregnant."

"I was with you when you found out Nika was pregnant. I've been with you as you watched her over the past few months. I felt what you did." He sat down beside Andra and took her hands in his. "You know I would do anything for you. Give you anything you wanted. And you wanted this. I bargained with Tynan for the serum."

Andra's words were slow and halting, tinged with guilt. "I didn't want you to know how I felt. The timing was bad. The war . . ."

Paul gave her a lopsided grin. "To hell with the war and the timing. Our child will grow up with Nika's. I'd say that's all that matters."

"Your son," said Ronan.

A smile quivered on Andra's lips. Tears flooded her eyes. "Our son."

Ronan saw Cain leave the room in a rush he tried to hide. The Theronai disappeared into the kitchen. Ronan decided it was his time to leave the couple alone to absorb the news as well. He had a call to make. Tynan was going to be overjoyed.

Cain was happy for his friends, but he knew he wouldn't be able to hide his jealousy over their news. Staying would have given his selfish feelings away, ruining what was an otherwise beautiful moment.

He wasn't hungry, but he hadn't eaten in hours. Neither had Rory. And Paul and Andra had both given blood. They all needed food, whether or not they wanted it, so Cain made himself busy in the kitchen, whipping up some pancakes and eggs.

The faint blue light of Andra's shield was still shimmering over the window, reassuring Cain that Rory was safe to rest. But once that shield went down, they needed to be ready to move.

Cain needed a plan.

Ronan slipped silently into the kitchen just as Cain was flipping the last batch of pancakes. He glanced at the Sanguinar. "Hungry?"

"I am. Will you wake Rory?"

"You said she shouldn't sleep. That the dreams would screw with her head."

"I believe Andra's shield will keep the Synestryn out. I can't sense him right now."

"Then maybe she should stay asleep while she can."

"That's your call." Ronan started a pot of coffee.

"Any ideas on how we're going to find that demon?"

"It's a Synestryn lord—like Murak."

"Who nearly killed us."

"Indeed. In fact, I got the distinct impression that the two of them were related."

Cain slid the pancakes onto the growing mound. "Great. Strength runs in the family."

"This demon is angry. Filled with the need for vengeance."

"Can you find it?"

"I think so. And if not, I'm certain it can find me."

Cain sighed. "I don't like it. We can't risk Andra, and even if Rory wasn't being mind-fucked, she's not strong enough yet."

"So we call in the others. Helen and Drake. Perhaps Liam and Dakota."

"Dakota isn't exactly a veteran yet, either."

Ronan poured some coffee and offered it to Cain. "No, but she is powerful."

Cain had heard rumors of the Defender who had a talent with electricity, but he had yet to see her in action. "I think our safest bet is to go back to Dabyr."

"You think Rory will go quietly?"

"No. I'm not sure how much I care at this point. My job is to keep her safe."

"Forever," said Ronan.

"What?"

"Your job is to keep her safe forever. If she walks away from you because you were an overbearing ass, how will you ensure her safety then? You have to think long term. Tie her to you now with a bit of indulgence and you will be rewarded with a lifetime together." Ronan's gaze met Cain's. "Perhaps also children of your own."

Cain shoved away from the stove, anger driving the air from his chest. "You had no right to go snooping around in my head."

"I do what I must to protect the survival of my race. Just as you will."

"I can't risk her getting hurt just to trick her into caring about me."

"Who said anything about tricking her? You're a good man. You want to give her what she wants. And she wants to stop her visions."

"If that happens, then she's free to go."

"Only if your vow is fulfilled."

"I don't understand. You're not making any sense."

"You're not looking at this objectively. Her vow will be fulfilled only if she finds the person who stops her visions, right?"

"Right."

"So what if she never finds them?"

"I've already thought of that, much to my shame. I won't tie her to me that way. I won't leave her to suffer just so that I can get what I want."

"There are other ways she could lose the visions. If she grows strong enough, she could block them herself. Had you considered that?"

Cain hadn't, which proved that Ronan was right. Cain wasn't being objective.

"See," said Ronan, sounding smugly pleased with himself. "Everyone gets what they want. Rory's visions go away and you get a family."

Leave it to a Sanguinar to tie everything up and dangle it right where Cain had no choice but to long for it. "It doesn't seem right. It seems . . . sneaky."

"Perhaps a bit, but ask yourself what you'd be willing to do for a child of your own."

"You've been in my head. You know the answer to that."

"Tynan's already given you the serum, has he not?"

"He has, but that doesn't mean I'm going to do anything about it." Despite how much time he'd spent fanaticizing about it.

"Rory wants you. I've seen that delightful truth lurking in your memories."

"Me. Not a baby. There's a big difference."

"So what will you do? Resist your desire for her? Resort to human methods of birth control?"

"If I have to, yes."

Something in Ronan's expression shifted from genial to scheming. The look faded so fast, Cain wasn't even sure he'd seen it.

Paul stuck his head in the kitchen. "Andra and I are leaving. I'm taking her back to Dabyr where it's safe."

Cain's instant denial of their decision died a swift death. Of course they had to leave. They had a child to protect now. Cain would have done no differently.

However, that didn't stop him from worrying about what would happen to Rory now. He questioned his ability to keep her safe without their help. All he had was his sword, and that wasn't nearly good enough for her.

"Are you sure it's safe to leave now? You could wait until dawn."

Paul shook his head. "If I wait, she may change her mind about letting me take her home. I've worn her down, and I'm getting her away from you while the getting's good. No offense, but knowing some Synestryn lord has your blood and can find you is just too much of a risk."

"I understand," said Cain.

Paul gave him a relieved nod. "Andra says her shield

will hold for another hour or two. That will buy you some time."

Ronan set his coffee down. "I'll see if I can find some way to obscure the blood connection to Rory."

"What about you?" asked Cain.

"I'm much more capable of protecting my mind from invasion than Rory is. I'll be fine."

Cain wasn't so sure. "If you're too weak—"

"I won't be. Now go and wake her. I want this done before Andra's defenses fail."

Paul gave Cain a grim, apologetic look. "I'm sorry to ditch you like this."

"You're doing the right thing."

Ronan pushed Paul out of the doorway, shooing him. "Cain can handle his woman. You need to do the same. Go."

Cain was fairly sure that Rory wasn't the type of woman anyone simply *handled*, but he said nothing and went to do what he could to keep her alive for one more night.

Chapter 14

Joseph stood in the doorway of his friends' suite, letting his grief hit him head-on. There was no other way to face something like this. As far as he knew, no one had come here since Angus and Gilda had died. Their rooms were just as they'd left them.

An old book sat open on the coffee table. There was a glass in the sink. One of Gilda's gray cloaks lay over the back of a recliner. Angus's boots stood by the front door.

Despite all these little signs of life, the suite was empty. Hollow. It echoed of loss and desolation, mocking what could have been.

As the leader of the Theronai, Joseph should have come here long ago to clean out his friends' home. But every time the thought crossed his mind, something pressing would come up, allowing him to put off the sad chore for a while longer.

Now that "something pressing" had forced his hand. A new female of their kind had been found, and she was in need. Joseph couldn't allow anything to come before that, no matter how much he wished to avoid more grief.

With a heavy sigh, he went to the spare bedroom they'd used as a library. Shelves lined the walls. In the center of the room was a small, antique desk that, based on its size, had to have been used by Gilda alone.

Joseph leaned over the desk and saw a leather-bound notebook filled with her elegant, scrawling script. As he began to read, he heard her voice in his head, lilting with her Celtic heritage.

This was a journal of some kind, recounting the events leading up to her last days. She'd been worried, upset. Angus had been angry with her for a reason she didn't state.

The longer he read, the more he felt like an intruder. He had no reason to pry into her private thoughts. All he needed was her book listing the magical artifacts she'd catalogued over the centuries.

Joseph went through the drawers, finding nothing of importance. He scanned the shelves, searching past the mass-produced titles to those that were older, and made by hand. He opened each one, pausing at those containing handwritten passages. As the stack of books he'd rejected grew, he heard a tentative knock on the doorframe.

Lyka stood there, looking like sunshine incarnate. His pounding headache eased, and some of the weight of grief he'd felt since coming here seemed to lighten. Something deep in Joseph's chest lurched toward her, desperate to be closer.

He didn't move an inch. Every time he'd approached her, she'd fled. This time he would hold his ground and hope that she stayed for more than a few seconds. He really needed her to stay, to ease him, just for a minute or two.

"Lyka. What's wrong? Are you okay?"

As usual, her lean body was covered by soft, clinging clothing that revealed as much as it hid. He'd never seen her arms or legs bare, even when they'd been hit by a sweltering heat wave. She crossed her arms over her chest, tucking her hands out of sight. "Yeah. Fine."

"Why are you here? Not that you're not welcome, of course," he hurried to add. "I just mean that it's unexpected."

She stared at the walls, the carpet—anywhere but at him. "I was told I could find you here. Miss Mabel said I'd need to get your permission."

"For what?"

"It's probably a bad time. You've got a lot on your mind, I'm sure. I'll just go."

"No, please. I could use a bit of a distraction. Go ahead."

She pulled in a deep breath like she was about to jump off a high dive. "I want to work with the kids—teach a class."

Lyka was a Slayer, held here to ensure her brother Andreas maintained the truce between his people and Joseph's. In return, Joseph had sent one of his own people, and there wasn't a day that went by that he didn't wonder how Carmen was doing. The few reports he got via e-mail were sent from one of Andreas's men. Joseph never got to speak directly to Carmen, just as Lyka was never allowed to speak with her family. It was the only way to prevent suspicion of her being sent here as a spy.

The idea that Lyka was starting to fit in here unknotted a tension right between his shoulder blades. He hated thinking that she suffered, that she was lonely. Her wanting to lend a hand was a good sign.

"Sure," he said, hoping he sounded happy about the idea without giving too much away. Lyka was prickly, and he worried that if she thought she was making him happy, she'd stop. Even if she suffered because of the decision. "You'll have to be supervised. You understand."

"I understand I'm your enemy. You don't want me brainwashing your kids or luring them to my suite so I can toss them in my oven for dinner."

That ridiculous image pulled a smile from somewhere deep down. "We're not enemies anymore, remember?"

She lifted her shoulders in a shrug, but it only emphasized how vulnerable she was here. She hadn't let any of the Sentinels get close to her. She played with the kids when she thought he wasn't looking, but truth be known, whenever Lyka was around, Joseph was always looking. He couldn't help himself.

"So, do I have your permission?"

He nodded. "Pick one of the teachers to supervise. Come by my office later and let me know who you chose."

She frowned as if confused. "That easy?"

"What did you expect? Some kind of torture session?"

She stared at him for a long time, her pale yellow eyes fixed on his face. "I never know what to expect in this place."

"You're fitting in just fine."

"I don't want to fit in. I want to go home."

Joseph felt a sympathetic wave of homesickness for her. "I know. Soon, I hope our people will trust each other enough to move past this. But until then, I'm glad you're here. So are the kids."

A ghost of a smile lit her eyes. "I like them. They're . . . uncomplicated."

"And they like you, too. I'm sure they'll love your class."

She was silent for a moment, but didn't leave as he'd expected. Finally, after she gave him the delightful opportunity to stare for a while, she said, "Thank you, Joseph."

"For what?"

"Not being the self-important asshole my grandfather said you were."

"Uh, thanks."

"What are you doing here, anyway?" she asked.

"I'm looking for a ledger Gilda kept of magical artifacts."

Lyka whistled. "Serious treasure."

"Not as serious as the artifacts themselves, but I'm hoping it will give me the information I need."

"You won't find it in here."

"Why not?"

"This is the first place you looked, right?"

"Yes," he said.

"That's why. If I had something that valuable, I wouldn't stick it in my office. I'd hide it—stow it somewhere no one would look."

She had a point.

"Like?" he asked.

"Secret compartment. Hidden safe. A tampon box."

Joseph grinned at the thought of Gilda doing such a thing. "Care to help me look?"

A flash of excitement fluttered across her face before it died. "You don't want to trust me with something like that."

"It's less precious to me than those human children and I'm trusting you with them."

"With a witness."

"And I'm here now to serve as your witness in our search."

Her breathing sped, and he swore he saw her eyes darken before she looked away. "No, thanks. I don't want to start any rumors."

"Don't worry. Everyone knows you can't stand to be around me."

"Not that kind of rumor. I was thinking more along the lines of stealing secret information for my people."

"You wouldn't do that."

"You don't know me well enough to say what I would or wouldn't do."

Joseph stepped closer before he could stop himself. Her whole body went tense and she backed up until she hit the hallway wall.

He stopped in his tracks and shoved out a rough sigh of frustration. "I'm not going to hurt you, Lyka. You don't have to be afraid of me."

Her jaw thrust out in defiance. "I'll leave a note on

your desk as soon as I find someone brave enough to keep an eye on me."

With that, she turned and fled, leaving him alone once again. His headache came back with a vengeance, and a familiar knot twisted along his spine. Lyka had given him an amusing distraction, but she was gone now, and he needed to get back to work.

Maybe if he hurried, he'd be there when she came by his office.

The thought gave him a heady rush, and quickened his pace. After another few minutes of scouring the suite, he found a box tucked beneath a pile of frilly underwear and lingerie he would have preferred never to have seen.

Inside that box was the book he'd been looking for along with a thick envelope. The outside of the envelope was labeled with Gilda's handwriting, its intent unmistakable.

My Death Wish

Honor required that Joseph do whatever he could to uphold Gilda's dying wish, so with grief lodged in his throat, he opened the envelope. Inside was a list of valuable items located in her suite. All of them were to be put in the hands of whoever led the Theronai—namely Joseph.

There were also several letters inside the envelope, each one labeled with a different name. The instructions indicated that those sealed letters were to be delivered, and if the intended recipients were dead, Joseph was to burn them.

There was one for each of Gilda's daughters, plus Angus, Helen and Tynan.

The urge to open and read them burned in his gut, but Joseph shoved his curiosity away. Gilda hadn't always been the easiest person to live with, but she had always put the needs of the Sentinels above her own desires.

Joseph could learn a lot from her.

He tucked everything back into the box. Later, he

would return and clean out their suite himself. Until then, he would lock it up tight and make sure one of the cameras was pointed at the door and monitored twenty-four/seven. There were far too many potential surprises in here, and he didn't want anyone stumbling upon something they shouldn't.

On his way back to his office, he took a detour to the Sanguinar wing, to Tynan's suite. The sooner these letters were delivered, the better.

Though how he was going to deliver Maura's letter to her, he had no idea. She'd long ago turned on her own people and gone to live with the Synestryn. They'd had only rare glimpses of her over the years, including the night Angus and Gilda had died.

Maura had been there. She'd helped kill her parents. The memories living within Angus's sword had shown Joseph that much. They'd also shown him the breadth of a parent's love, which had humbled him and angered him all at the same time.

Maura's parents had forgiven her for turning against them, but Joseph couldn't bring himself to do the same. She was their enemy. She deserved to die.

Tynan opened the door of his suite, looking more tired and harried than usual. His hair was a bit long, and a growth of beard shadowed his gaunt jaw. Fatigue rimmed his icy blue eyes, which lit with hunger as soon as he saw Joseph at the door.

He handed the Sanguinar the letter. "I found this in Gilda's room. Her death wish was for you to have it."

Tynan's eyes narrowed with suspicion as he took the letter and opened it. Joseph stayed where he was, not even trying to hide his curiosity as to what it contained.

As Tynan's gaze scanned the page, a look of shock began to take over his pretty face. He gripped the door frame as if to steady himself, and the letter began to flutter in his hand.

Joseph waited while the man read it again from the

top, as if unable to believe what he saw. When Tynan was done, he looked at Joseph, shell-shocked.

"What?" asked Joseph.

"I need you to do something for me."

If it had something to do with Gilda's death wish, Joseph's honor compelled him to agree. "Sure. Name it."

"Gilda's wish was for me to distribute a cure for Theronai sterility across the planet. Without asking for payment in blood. If I manufacture it, can you distribute it and get the men to take it?"

Joseph's mind was reeling. "You're going to *give* it away? No blood price?"

"That was her wish. I feel obligated to fulfill it."

"Yeah, okay. If that's what she wanted, I'm sure the men will comply."

"She wanted them all to accept the cure, Joseph. That means everyone. No exceptions."

Something was off here, but Joseph couldn't put his finger on what it was. Perhaps it was simply that Tynan was upset about all the blood he was going to miss out on because of what Gilda had done. The Sanguinar had poured months of time and energy into a cure, and he'd nearly killed himself finding it. And while Joseph would uphold Gilda's wish, that didn't mean that he couldn't offer Tynan payment.

"You can have my blood."

"Even though Gilda asked me to give the cure away?"

Joseph shrugged. "She was looking out for us, but it's my job to look out for you, too. I'm sure some of the men will see things my way."

Tynan nodded, sagging in gratitude. "I thank you. I have a lot of work to do if I'm to manufacture enough serum for all of the Theronai across the earth."

"Can I offer any help?"

"I could use a small team of Gerai, as well as supplies: syringes, vials, packing material."

"Whatever you need. Just send me a list." And as

much as Joseph disliked the idea of giving Tynan access to his blood—of risking weakness and allowing Tynan the chance to screw with his head—he lifted his arm in offering.

Tynan's eyes flared with internal light for a second. "I will give you the serum first. So no one can say I forced you to offer your blood."

"Fair enough."

The Sanguinar stepped aside to let Joseph in. "Have a seat. This won't take long."

Tynan escaped to his lab with the excuse of fetching a dose of the fertility serum.

Not that he needed it.

As he'd suspected, it hadn't been his cure that had given the Theronai back their ability to reproduce. Gilda had done that. Somehow.

It couldn't be a coincidence that her death had immediately preceded the recent pregnancies. Not if what she'd stated in her letter was true—and Tynan had no reason to believe otherwise.

Gilda had sterilized the men. Centuries ago, on the night her last son had died. Grief had driven her mad with rage, and in a moment of fury—in her desire to never go through the trauma of watching another one of her children die in battle—her magic had spread over the planet, leaving every Theronai male infertile. Only then could she be sure that no more children would be born to her.

She hadn't meant to do it. She'd meant only to sterilize Angus, but the power of her emotions had been too great, tossing her magic out of control.

It wasn't the Synestryn that had robbed them of their ability to have children. It had been Gilda.

All those months of effort and magic that Tynan had expended were wasted. He wasn't powerful enough to reverse what Gilda had done.

Her letter had explained how she'd tried and failed to unravel what she'd wrought. Apparently she'd either found a solution, or her death had been it.

Either way, the damage was done. All male Theronai were likely fertile now, and it was only a matter of time before they figured out that it wasn't Tynan's doing. Not only would he be accused of trying to deceive them, it wouldn't take long before others began looking into what had happened. Maybe some of them would believe that the Synestryn magic they'd thought it was would wear off, but not everyone would. Someone would start hunting for the truth, and eventually they'd find it.

If the Theronai learned what Gilda had done, her entire life's work would become suspect. Her honor would be shattered.

The Theronai needed their honor. It kept them strong and held them together despite the pain they faced. Without their honor, many of them would lose faith, lose hope. Their souls would decay faster, and good men would die—men on whom Tynan's people depended for survival.

He would not let that happen. Whatever it took, no matter how many lies he had to tell or people he had to deceive, he would protect Gilda's secret.

He fired up a Bunsen burner and torched her letter until only ash remained.

Chapter 15

Rory woke on a bubble of rage. It surged inside her, thrashing against her ribs as if seeking to bust out. A ferocious scream erupted from her lips, only to be silenced by thick, hot fingers.

"Shh. You're okay now." A low, rumbling voice that stroked over her like sun-warmed silk.

Cain.

She wasn't okay. She'd wanted to kill, to feel blood run between her fingers and dig her teeth into flesh and bone.

So fucking disgusting.

Rory forced her heavy eyelids open and saw that she was in her own bed. The familiar sight eased some of the lingering ick and fear, but not nearly as much as seeing Cain sitting on her bed, close enough to touch.

The image of her pale face smeared with super-whore eye makeup and tangled pink hair popped into her head. Superimposed on that was the sight of long, beautiful male fingers texting from a phone. The vision was so strong, she knew someone had to be nearby.

She didn't even try to stop herself from touching Cain. She simply reached out and grabbed his hand, letting the warm frisson of pleasure he gave her wriggle through her arm and into her chest. Her quickened breathing slowed, and her rapid heartbeat began to seek out the pace of his, mirroring the slow, steady rhythm.

The visions disappeared, leaving her in relative peace.

"How do you feel?"

She swallowed to ease her dry throat. "Better. Less homicidal maniac-y."

He offered her a steaming cup of coffee. "Good. I brought you food."

She took the coffee, but refused to let go of his hand. He didn't seem to mind too much. Or maybe he was just being nice.

Her neediness grated on her raw nerves, but she still felt weak and brittle from whatever it was that had happened to her earlier.

She took a sip, letting the hot liquid ease her dry throat. "Care to tell me how I got here?"

"What do you remember?" he asked.

"Wanting to kill you."

He cringed openly.

Nothing like a dose of blunt truth to drive a man away. "If it's any consolation, I pretty much wanted to kill everyone. I'm an equal opportunity lunatic."

"You're not a lunatic. The demon that took your blood was using it against you, controlling you. Those feelings were his. Not yours."

"So I'm not a homicidal lunatic, but I let one in my brain? That's really not a whole lot better."

"Ronan thinks he can help."

Thinks? Great.

She ignored her spurt of fear and glanced out the window. A faint bluish light hung over the glass, like a layer of moonlit water. "What's that?"

"Andra put up a shield to keep the Synestryn away."

It must have worked, because there was no trace of that fetid rage in her head anymore. "Andra? Isn't that the woman who can find lost kids?"

"It is."

Rory sat the coffee down, tossing back the covers. "I need to talk to her."

Cain's fingers tightened on hers, stopping her. "She's already gone."

Disappointment bore down on her, shoving a sigh of frustration from her lungs. "But I was going to ask her how she does it."

"I talked to her before she left. I asked for you. She told me everything she could think of and she said to give you her cell number if you have any questions."

"So? How does she do it?"

Cain grabbed a plate of food from her dresser and held it out. "I'll tell you while you eat."

She caught a whiff of maple syrup and was sold. "Did you make this?"

"I did."

"You cook, too? You know that's not playing fair, right?"

"What?"

"Gorgeous men are supposed to be deeply flawed and relatively helpless. You're neither, which gives you an unfair advantage over the entire man-loving population."

A slow, warm wave of pleasure rippled out of him at her statement. It felt so good, she wondered if she should compliment him again to see if she could get another heady dose of yum.

His grunt was hinted with a touch of amusement. "I may not be helpless, but I assure you that my flaws run deep enough."

She took a bite of food, which made her stomach wake up with a vengeance. "Pancakes make up for a lot of bad stuff, but then again, my taste in men is less than stellar. So what the hell do I know? The last guy I trusted sold me to demons for drugs."

His face flushed red with anger. "He . . . what?"

She kept eating, wishing she'd shoved her mouth too

full of food to talk. "No big deal. He got eaten, so the joke's on him."

She still had nightmares about those two days spent in the flooded basement swimming with monsters, but as long as she could joke about it, it couldn't scare her nearly as much.

That was her theory, and she was sticking to it.

"So spill. What did Andra say?"

It took Cain a moment to regain his composure enough to speak. She was sure he was going to blow a gasket or something. Every few seconds, she felt a shard of fury slip out of him. She wasn't sure how the whole magic stuff worked, but if she just stopped thinking and let herself go on instinct, the signals coming from him were much easier to decrypt.

He was worried about her. He was pissed as hell that someone had hurt her. He felt guilty that he was sitting here. But most of all, he was determined to fix something. She didn't know what that was, but woe be to any who stood in that man's way.

"Andra says she follows a trail of emotion. She goes to where the child was taken and tries to put herself in their place. Usually, the kids who are taken are terrified, and she said she can see that as a kind of faint, misty trail of light."

Rory's throat closed around that last bite, nearly choking her with fear. She shoved the half-empty plate at Cain and scrambled from the bed.

"What?" he asked, concern tightening his brow.

"There's no way I'm going back to the last place where my visions disappeared. And even if I could stomach the idea of going back to that flooded building, I wouldn't know where to begin with finding a trail of emotion. I have no clue who this person is, or what they might have been feeling."

"Fear is a good guess."

"What if it was one of those drugged-up humans?

They certainly weren't afraid. Most of them were too stoned out of their heads to be feeling much of anything."

"Euphoria, then? There's got to be something. I think you owe it to yourself to go back and try."

Instant, ferocious denial swelled inside her. "You don't know what you're asking. You weren't there. You have no idea what it was like."

He stroked her temple with one finger, but that was all it took to give her a thin thread of calm to grasp on to.

"I won't make you do anything you don't want to do. If you like, we'll forget all about it. Whatever you want."

If she walked away now, he'd be stuck with her, and while she was sure the idea didn't bother him much now, eventually it would. She never kept people around for long. And as much as she wanted to lie to herself and pretend it was the visions that drove them away, she knew better. She grated on people. She rubbed them the wrong way. Sooner or later, Cain would feel the same, and before that happened, she needed to work with him to fulfill her end of the bargain, because working with him after he was tired of her was going to hurt.

"No. You're right. This is something I need to do."

He frowned at her, and she felt a slight pressure behind her eyes and a soothing presence. "You don't have to be afraid. I'll be right there with you."

Her spine went straight out of habit more than anything. "I'm not afraid. But I'm also not stupid. That building where Krag died has got to be crawling with monsters."

"You mean the facility where Logan and Hope were held prisoner?"

"Yeah. They weren't the only ones."

"We cleaned it out. Demolished it. There's nothing left but dirt and ash."

"So it's safe?"

"As we could make it."

"Then we should go there." Before she lost her nerve and decided to hide under her bed for the rest of her life.

"We'll go, but Ronan needs to check you out first."

"I feel fine."

Cain waved toward the window. "Because of Andra's protection. Once you go past her defenses, all bets are off."

She groaned in dismay and got off the bed. She couldn't quite bring herself to let go of Cain's hand, because she knew visions lurked beyond his touch. "If I'm going to have some vampire playing brain surgeon, I'm going to do it after a nice hot shower."

"There's really no time for—"

She got right in his face, which was much easier to do with him sitting on the bed. "Listen, Cain. My whole world is a pile of suck and desolation right now. I at least deserve clean hair."

He gave her a solemn nod. "Whatever you need. I won't stand in your way."

He was so fucking patient with her, so *kind*. All she'd done so far was use him, and he'd been with her every step of the way, right there, unwavering and solid, as if she could throw anything at him, and he could take it.

She wasn't used to men like that. Usually they used her. And she hated it. Now she was doing the same thing to Cain, and it was only a matter of time before he caught on.

Assuming he hadn't already.

Maybe he was wired differently. Maybe it was part of his old-school charm to be so . . . indulgent with her.

Rory wasn't sure, but whatever it was, he was wrapping her up, bit by bit, tying her to him in ways she hadn't even known were possible.

Even now, as she stripped and stepped into the shower, she could feel his concern for her traveling through the link between them. She could see through his eyes that he stood outside the bathroom door, staring at it.

A heavy pulse of desire hit her hard, making her grip the wall to stay on her feet. Her thighs clenched together, and suddenly her senses went bionic. She could feel every drop of water cascading over her body, drenching her with wet heat. The smell of her soap swirled in the air on thick tendrils of steam. Even the rainy, white noise of the water hitting the tub was louder.

She stared at the white wall, but all she saw was what Cain saw. His huge hand splayed over the wooden door, his fingers clenching as if he could reach through if he tried hard enough.

And just like that, she wanted him in here with her, all slick and naked.

A man as strong as him would have no trouble propping her against the wall and holding her there while he thrust deep. The question was whether a woman like her would be able to keep up. She'd had only two lovers, and neither one had been enough for her to wish for a third. Until now.

Her sexual experience was a pitiful drop in a rusty bucket.

A familiar presence wove through her thoughts, stroking against the most intimate parts of her. Desires, dreams, fantasies. Cain slipped in between all of them, lingering as if he had all the time in the world.

What she wouldn't give to find out just what patience like that could do to her in bed. She didn't know if she'd survive it, but she knew she was more than willing to give it a try.

Whatever you want.

The words hadn't been meant as any kind of seduction, but they felt that way now. She could think of a whole mountain of things she wanted, and every one of them started with him walking through the bathroom door.

She found her connection to him, the humming heat encircling her neck. His essence thrummed in that link, tempting her.

All of this magical stuff was new to her, but parts of her seemed to instinctively know what to do. She had only to think of letting him feel what she did, and she could sense the reverberation of her emotions rippling between them. She let him feel her desire, let him feel what it did to her when she imagined him touching her.

Rory's hands slid over her body, showing him what she liked most—what made her breath catch in her chest, and what made her whimper in pleasure.

His hand tightened into a fist against the door. She swore she felt his cock harden and throb, though she had no idea how that could happen. His lust was rougher than hers, but no less demanding. The jagged edges of it cut at her, making her ache to bring him relief.

Whatever you want.

She tried to show him what she wanted, but her inexperience left the fantasy flat and colorless. Cain grabbed hold of it, layering on color and texture, sounds and scents, until the picture he painted was vivid and glowing with promise.

His hands roamed her slick curves. He wrapped his body around her, trapping her under the hot spray. The cage of his naked arms and chest was one she reveled in, letting her fingers stroke and pet until he was shaking with tension.

His mouth found hers, so hot and hungry, her head spun from lack of oxygen. Not that she cared. As long as he didn't stop, she was happy to let him do whatever he wanted.

He kissed his way down her neck, over her collarbone. His erection lay hard and heavy against her belly. His pulse pounded there, and she wanted to feel that beat inside of her more than she wanted her next breath.

Cain didn't let her rush. Any other man would have been inside of her by now.

She was ready for him, slick and hollow and needy. She was hovering on the edge, so close to coming she knew it would take only one stroke to send her flying. But that stroke did not come. Not with a man as patient as Cain.

The fantasy played on, sucking her along for the ride. In her mind she saw him reach for the bathroom door knob. His fist tightened around it. Tendons in his arm shifted to turn the knob.

He was going to walk through the door. The real man, in the flesh. She was going to get everything she wanted, whether or not she could handle it.

A second later, Ronan's pretty face appeared, looming large in her vision. He'd interrupted Cain—stopped him from opening the door.

The fantasy collapsed. Rory was left shaking and desperately needy, shivering under a stream of cooling water.

Outside the door, she could hear the two men talking. She could see both of their faces, their mouths moving. The actual words were lost to her, but the tone of the conversation was clear enough.

Time for Rory to get out of the shower and face her demons. Literally.

Chapter 16

It had been a long time since Cain had wanted to kill one of his allies, but Ronan was asking for it. He had to have known what was going on. Cain's galloping heartbeat should have given him away if nothing else.

As the grip of lust loosened and Cain began thinking like a rational creature again, he realized that he owed Ronan a debt of thanks.

A man sworn to protect his lady did not have shower sex while the last of the magical protection she had faded.

Behind the door that had taunted him with its mere existence, he heard the water turn off. Rory would be stepping out of the shower now, all pink and dripping wet.

She'd shown him what she looked like, sharing her perception of herself through their link. He knew exactly what shade of dusky pink her nipples were, and that her natural hair color was a pale ash blond. What he didn't know was how her nipples tasted, or how those wet, blond curls would feel under his fingertips.

Cain had never needed to know anything more in his life than the need to learn the answer to those compelling mysteries.

"I conferred with Tynan and Logan," said Ronan.

"They both agree that there are two options for dealing with the blood link the demon has on us."

Cain had a hard time tracking the conversation. His mind was still firmly back in that shower with Rory, wondering how long he could hold out before pinning her against the wall as her fantasy demanded.

The bathroom door opened at his back. He felt the wet caress of steam curl around him. It was scented with soap and hot, damp skin. Rory's skin.

Cain turned, unable to stop himself.

She wore only a towel wrapped around her breasts. Her face was scrubbed free of makeup, showing off the rich, dark brown of her eyes. She'd removed her multiple earrings, leaving his luceria the only jewelry left on her body. A deep flush of arousal painted her cheeks. Water droplets clung to her skin.

The mental image of him licking away each drop as he peeled away the towel plowed into him.

Her lips parted on a silent breath, and her nipples tightened against the thin towel.

One little tug and he'd be able to see for himself if her body was as beautiful as he'd seen through her eyes.

Behind him, Ronan cleared his throat. "Are you going to decide?"

"Decide what?" asked Cain, unwilling to take his eyes off of her for even a second. Opportunities to soak in such a rare sight did not come by often, even for men who lived as long as Cain had.

"Which approach we take to deal with the demon that has Rory's blood."

"Maybe Rory would like to decide herself," she said. "After she puts some pants on."

She brushed past them and shut the door to her bedroom.

"She doesn't like me very much, does she?" asked Ronan.

"You don't respect her. You treat her as if she's an idiot."

"She's new to our world, to her power. It seems reasonable that she would defer to you in important matters."

That made Cain laugh, releasing a bubble of sexual frustration and tension. "Defer to me? Really? Have you met Rory?"

Ronan frowned, but it made him look pensive and artistic. "I don't know her as well as you do, clearly, but—"

"But nothing. Women like Rory don't defer to anyone. She's like Gilda. If you're lucky, you get to voice your opinion before she decides to ignore it."

"Stupid. Dangerous and stupid."

"You never would have said that to Gilda's face. At least not twice."

Ronan nodded, a grimace of self-deprecation thinning his lips. "That is true. Though I doubt anyone could replace Gilda."

Grief caught in Cain's throat, surprising him with its ferocity.

Rory stepped out of her bedroom as she finished pulling a shirt down over her bare stomach. Her movements were rushed, her eyes plagued with worry. Those dark brown eyes met his. "Are you okay?"

She'd felt his grief. Already their connection was deeper than he would have thought possible in such a short time.

He was awestruck by it for a moment, unable to speak. Since Jackie had chosen Iain, he'd given up on the idea of finding a woman like Rory. He still wasn't sure whether to believe she was real. Or that he'd get to keep her.

"We were discussing an old friend, lost to us now," said Ronan. "No need to worry."

Her cheeks turned as pink as her hair, and she stammered. "Sorry. Didn't mean to butt in."

"You weren't," Cain hurried to tell her.

A pink lock of wet hair clung to her cheek. Without thinking, he smoothed it back in place.

Her skin was hot and damp, reminding him all too keenly of the shower fantasy they'd shared. Not that it was a sight he'd soon forget. She'd shown him how she liked to be touched, which spots were the most sensitive. That was not the kind of knowledge he would carelessly toss aside.

Tie her to you with pleasure.

The stray thought caught him off guard. His mouth went dry, and he had to force his hand to fall by his side so he wouldn't wrap it around the nape of her neck and pull her in for a kiss. Then, finally, he'd know just how she tasted.

Ronan cleared his throat. "So. About those options?"

"Options?" asked Rory, a bit breathless.

"For getting that Synestryn lord out of your head."

Right. That.

Cain crossed his arms over his chest and stepped away. He couldn't even look at her without losing every strand of concentration he had. She touched him too deeply, rocking him down to his core.

"What are they?" he asked.

Ronan had the good sense to address Rory directly. "I can sever the connection, which while the more permanent option, is also the more dangerous one. Or I can mask it, giving us enough time to track down this demon and slay it."

"Sever it," she said, without hesitation.

Cain suffered through a spike of fear before he got himself back under control. "Wait a minute. I think you need more details than that." He looked at Ronan. "How dangerous? What are the risks?"

"Death, for one."

"I'm okay with that," she said. "I'm not okay with toting a demon around as some kind of brain buddy for the rest of my life."

"I'm *not* okay with it," said Cain. "Your life is far too valuable to toss away."

"My life. My choice."

Ronan held up his hand for their attention. "I'm not done. Death is not the only risk. There's also brain damage."

Rory went stiff and a little trickle of fear slid between them. "Yeah, I'm not a fan of that."

"It's still better than the worst possible side effect."

She groaned. "I'm not sure I want to know."

"I'm certain you don't. But I will not proceed unless you're aware of the risks."

Cain couldn't stand it anymore. He couldn't simply stand here, pretending like she wasn't suffering. He *felt* her. He couldn't ignore her distress.

He threaded his fingers through hers. They were cold and trembling, bringing out every protective instinct he'd ever birthed. If he could, he would have tucked her away somewhere safe, but that was not an option. Not with Rory.

"What's the worst-case scenario?" Cain asked.

"I fail utterly, and you will be trapped indefinitely within the Synestryn's mind, unable to escape. You would essentially become part of the demon."

She stopped breathing as a palpable wave of fear rushed through her, straight through the luceria into Cain. He gritted his teeth, suffering through the emotion alongside her.

Her voice shook harder than her fingers. "I'm not letting that happen."

"On that, we're agreed," said Cain as he pulled her up against his side. She fit perfectly under his arm, like a piece of himself that he'd been missing all his life.

Ronan nodded once. "Good. Then I shall mask the beast and show you how to defend yourself against it, giving us enough time to find and destroy it."

"Do you know where it is?" she asked.

Ronan's pale blue gaze hit the carpet, as if he was hiding something. "I believe I can find it."

Something was off here. Cain was sure of it. "What aren't you telling us?"

The Sanguinar's mouth flattened into a thin line of acceptance. "This creature is strong. Frighteningly so. The closer to it we get, the more power over us it will hold. And it's not alone. I sensed connections to hundreds of demons. They bow to its will."

"So we're not simply fighting one demon, we're going after an army."

"I believe so, though it could be that the creature simply wanted me to believe that."

"No," said Rory. She scooted tighter against Cain's side and gripped his hand as if seeking comfort. "Ronan is right. Any demon that is strong enough to make us believe it has an army is probably strong enough to actually have one."

Cain gathered a warm strand of comfort and sent it streaming through their link. He was amazed by how easily he'd learned to use their connection—as if he'd been born knowing how.

Tears gathered along her lower eyelids for a moment before she blinked them away.

In that moment, with fear bleaching her skin and her slender body trembling against his, he felt filled with a sense of purpose. It swelled in his chest, making him feel stronger, faster. Invincible.

For Rory he would do anything—find a way to give her whatever she needed. She may not stay with him forever, but for now, she was his, and it was his duty—his joy—to provide for her.

He squared his shoulders as determination buoyed him. "If this beast has an army, then I will build one as well."

A hot, bubbling feeling spread over his chest, tingling as it passed. His lifemark swayed like mad, as if tossed around by a fierce wind.

Rory looked at him in shock, like she'd felt it, too. Maybe she had. Or maybe she was reacting to his declaration.

She put her hand on his chest, and his heart leapt at the contact. "Are armies easy to come by in your crazy corner of the world?"

"No, they are not," said Ronan. "There are only a few bound couples available to help."

"They'll come." Cain was certain they would. "I'll call Joseph and have him coordinate a meeting."

A fierce rush of eagerness flooded through the luceria. Beside him, Rory seemed to vibrate with anticipation. "And in the meantime, Ronan can scrub my brain. After that, target practice."

"Target practice?" Cain asked.

"If I'm marching into war, I'd better at least know what kind of gun I'm carrying, don't you think? I wasn't so hot with fire. But I should be good at something useful."

He couldn't bring himself to tell her that it could take years for her to grow comfortable with her abilities. She needed to believe she could do this, and because she needed it, so did he.

"Are we agreed?" asked Ronan.

Rory and Cain said, "Yes," in unison.

"Good, then it's time to see what this creature has done to your mind. Before Andra's shields fail."

"Go downstairs," Cain told Ronan. "I want a minute alone with Rory."

Ronan left. Cain pulled Rory into her bedroom and shut the door.

"What?" she asked, suspicion narrowing her eyes.

"I wanted to prepare you for what's going to happen. I don't like the idea of you being scared or unpleasantly surprised."

"Okay. Just do it quick, because now I'm even more freaked out."

"He's going to drink your blood."

"Uh. No, he's not."

Cain cupped her shoulders in his hands. "There's no other way. But you should know that I'll be right there. I won't let him take too much or do anything else to hurt you."

"He's going to be fucking around with my head. How will you even know what he's doing?"

Without the heavy mask of eye makeup, she looked more vulnerable. She *was* vulnerable. She just didn't always acknowledge it. He'd taken his cues from her, assuming she was okay with everything that had been piled atop her over the past few hours. But there was no way she could be okay with that large a burden.

"If you allow it, I'll slide inside your head as I have before. I'll be as close to you as I can, monitoring everything that Ronan does."

"If I allow it? I demand it. I don't trust him. I'm sure he's a good guy and all, but I don't trust anyone when it comes to psychic brain surgery."

But she trusted Cain—at least enough to *demand* that he monitor Ronan's actions.

That was a gift Cain hadn't expected, and it lifted him up on another heady wave of renewed purpose.

Again that strange, bubbling feeling spread across his chest. Only this time, he was sure Rory felt it, because she shoved his shirt up, baring his lifemark.

New, tiny buds now lined the branches of the tree. A few of them had unfurled to reveal pale, shiny green leaves.

He knew it was supposed to happen, but it was still hard to believe. The sight left him shaken and so grateful he was unable to speak past the knot in his throat.

Rory had saved him. Her connection to him had renewed his lifemark, driving away all traces of pain and decay.

Cain was reborn, and it was Rory who had given him new life. At least for now.

"Whoa. How the hell . . . ?" Rory ran her finger along his skin, making his abdomen clench with delight.

His voice was thick with emotion and quiet with reverence. "You did that. You took my luceria and gave me a second chance."

Her fingers trembled across his chest, gliding up until she'd reached his heart. She looked up at him with gratitude shining in her dark eyes. "I've never done anything that cool in my life. It makes me wonder what other cool stuff I might be able to do."

"Whatever you want, Rory. I'm certain that you will be a force of nature."

"Like that woman you showed me from your memories?"

"Yes. Just like that."

She was quiet for a moment. "Thank you, Cain."

"For what?" He had done nothing, when she had given him everything.

"For making me believe I don't completely suck. For showing me that magic is real."

He'd hardly shown her anything—just a single drop in an ocean. "You haven't seen anything yet."

If she gave him a few centuries, he'd show her the world.

She went up on tiptoe and kissed him lightly on the mouth. It was over so fast, he hadn't even gotten over his shock before it was over.

His mouth tingled, and watered for more, but he stood there, frozen, sure that if he so much as twitched, he'd simply drive her back to the bed and spend the rest of the night claiming her body as his own private playground.

The longer he stood there, the darker her cheeks became, flushed with embarrassment. "Sorry. I just wanted to know what it was like to kiss you. In case things with Ronan go bad."

Finally, his sputtering brain caught up with what had

just happened. She'd kissed him because she thought she might die. Because she wanted that before her life ended.

Cain wouldn't let anything bad happen to her, but he couldn't fault her for being afraid. He was as well. Only his certain knowledge that he would find a way to keep her safe—whatever the cost—kept him steady.

"You still don't know what it's like to kiss me," he finally managed to say.

"What?"

"That wasn't a real kiss." He gripped her hips to hold her still while he closed the gap between their bodies. "This is a real kiss."

He lowered his mouth to hers. Slowly, this time savoring the moment that his lips touched hers. A tingling shock so gentle it was almost a caress lingered between them. He tilted his head slightly, willing her to open her lips and let him in. He needed to taste her, to commit all of her to memory so that he could always find this moment in his thoughts.

The intoxicating scent of her skin spun around him, the air heated by the growing inferno in his body. Desire rained down, pelting him with the need for more.

Her lips parted on a soft sigh of surrender. The rougher side of him—the one that had fought and conquered for centuries—rose up in ferocious excitement. It wanted to stake a claim—to take what it wanted and never let go.

Cain shut it down before things could get out of control, but that need was burning there, ready to break free if he presented even the slightest crack in his willpower.

Rory's mouth became demanding, her tongue gliding along the inside of his lips, dipping to tease him. She pushed him back. He let her, willing to go wherever she wanted so long as he didn't have to lift his mouth from hers.

He hit the wall hard enough to send something to his left crashing to the floor. He didn't care what.

Rory's fingers gripped his head, her nails leaving the most delicious little stinging bites in his scalp. He lifted her up, propping her ass in one hand so she could more easily reach him. But now that his hand was full of hot, curvy flesh, his world went a little sideways.

His body throbbed with lust, each beat of his heart working in a futile effort to cool his skin. It did no good. The press of her breasts against his chest, the sweet heat of her mouth on his, the aggressive little growls she let out—it all crashed together, rendering him senseless.

He had to have more. All of her. Strip her down, lay her out, fill her up until there was no more room between them for anything other than pleasure. That's what she deserved.

A hard knock sounded on the door. "Everything okay?" asked Ronan. "I heard glass breaking."

Go away, was what Cain wanted to say, but he couldn't stand to pull his mouth away from hers for even a second.

Ronan knocked again. "We really need to get on with this. Andra's shield won't last forever."

Shit. Ronan was right.

Cain hated to admit it, but he couldn't risk Rory's safety—not even for the pleasure of kissing her.

He lowered her to the ground, disengaging their bodies. She stared at him in challenge, her dark, shiny lips parted in a speedy pant. "I'm not done with you yet," she said.

His cock jerked toward her in demand. "Good to know."

"When Ronan is done, you and I are coming right back here. And you're going to give me what I want."

"And what is that, Rory?" he asked, cursing himself for tempting fate like that.

She stroked his erection through his jeans, nearly making him come apart. "I want you naked, in my bed. In my body."

Cain shuddered at the image she painted, unable to deny her. "Anything you want. As soon as it's safe."

He hadn't intended it to be a vow, but the weight of his words settled over him, sealing him to his commitment.

"Now I'm not so afraid."

"Why is that?"

A sexy grin curled her mouth, nearly bringing Cain to his knees. "Because there's no way I'm dying now—not with you as the prize for surviving."

Chapter 17

Connal woke up ravenous. He'd sent repeated calls for help to his contacts among the Synestryn, leaving messages in all of the locations he'd previously used, but no responses had been forthcoming. As the days passed, he grew weaker.

None of the Gerai blood he'd taken over the past few weeks seemed to ease his hunger. The only time he'd felt sated in the past year had been when he'd fed from the woman that Zillah had impregnated—Beth, the woman who had been stolen from Zillah and now lived here at Dabyr with her sister.

She had been taken as a child and raised in the caves. She'd been fed demon blood—her body altered so she could bear half-Synestryn children. Beth's child had died before it was born. But Ella's had lived. She'd lied and said that her child was human—that she'd been pregnant before she'd been taken by the Synestryn—but Connal could sense the lie running through the little boy's veins. He wasn't sure why no one else could.

Maybe because Connal had been altered in some small way, too.

He'd fed from Beth, and the child growing inside of her had enough of its father's power to weaken Connal's control. He'd been made to do things, to turn on his allies in exchange for the only food that made the pangs of starvation ease.

And now that food was here, living under the same roof as him, tempting him with her proximity.

Connal had been avoiding her for months for fear that she'd recognize him and reveal what he'd done. He'd tried to assuage his guilt by telling her that her blood was the key to her rescue, but he'd never dreamed that his decision would put him in this situation.

Knowing she could ease his hunger, but keeping his distance was killing him. No matter how much blood he took, he still remembered the dark power lacing her cells, filling him and making him strong, the way he was meant to be.

He could no longer hold back. He had to feed. From her. Now.

He'd catch her alone and wipe her mind of the event. She'd never even know he'd found her. He'd be sated and able to stay away. At least for a while.

Connal pulled the hood of a sweatshirt onto his head. Cameras were everywhere in the compound, and there was no sense in taking any chances. He'd already been caught on camera once, disabling the security devices along the outer walls so others could break in. His face hadn't been visible, and no one knew that it had been him, but he was a cautious man. Only starvation forced him to take chances now.

He knew where Beth lived. He'd watched her from a distance as she'd shared meals with her sister or the other human women here. She was trying to move on with her life. She was still so young. With luck, she would live a long, long time, providing Connal with the blood he needed to survive for years to come.

It was late. Many of the humans were in their quarters, preparing for bed. As he passed through the dining hall, he spotted Beth's sister sweeping floors.

Everyone pitched in to keep Dabyr running. And if Ella was here, chances were good that Beth was alone.

Perfect.

Connal kept his head down as he hurried to her suite. He knocked on the door, and she opened it a crack.

He didn't wait to give her time to recognize him. He simply pushed into the room and shut the door behind him, taking control of her body as he went.

In one corner of the living room was a playpen. Sitting inside was Ella's son, far too large for his age. He realized then that he hadn't seen the boy around since his birth, even when the women were present.

They were hiding him, covering up his parentage.

Good. That gave Connal potential leverage to use against Beth, should the need arise.

Her eyes flared wide with recognition. "You," she breathed as she began to tremble.

Connal could hear her heart racing, hear the blood speed through her veins. His mouth watered in response, his stomach twisting with ravenous hunger.

He should have slowed down and eased her fears or at least subdued her mind so that she would relax, but he found the idea of wasting even one more second too much for his willpower.

He grabbed her up and craned her neck back, sinking his fangs deep. Blood poured over his tongue, drowning it in power. She was stronger now. Well fed, well rested. She was no longer taxed by the burden of growing a life inside of her.

Connal had never experienced anything like it before. The dark taint flowing through her—the one that made her capable of bearing Synestryn young—wove around his cells, fueling them like nothing else ever had.

The thought gave him pause. There had been a time when tainted blood would have burned his mouth and twisted his stomach. But that time had passed. Whatever Zillah had done to him by slowly feeding him her blood over the years as they altered her, it had changed him as well.

"Please," she gasped as her heart raced faster.

He was taking too much, but he couldn't stop. He needed more. All of her.

Her heart fluttered. Her limbs went weak. The useless blows she'd landed on his back and arms had slowed. Then they stopped.

So did her heart. The last sputtering beats sent a faint trickle of blood into his mouth. He sucked on her, needing more, but there was no more left to take.

He'd killed her. Drained her dry.

Connal dropped her and stumbled back in shock. Her body sprawled, pale and lifeless on the floor. There wasn't even enough blood in her for the ragged wounds on her neck to bleed.

It was then that he was hit with the implications of what he'd done.

Once her body was found, any Sanguinar would be able to detect his hand in this. He couldn't replace her blood.

But there was one thing he could do.

Connal grabbed a knife from the kitchen, carried her to the bathroom, and laid her body in the tub. He closed the wounds at her throat and wrapped her limp, cold hand around the knife. He sliced a few hesitation marks into her skin, followed by a long gash running right along her vein. He turned on the shower and pointed it at the open cut in her arm. A few pitiful drops of blood joined the water, swirling down the drain.

By the time anyone found her, it would all be washed away, but at least it would appear as if she'd done the exsanguination herself. He hoped.

He turned to leave and saw the child down the hallway, still safely in his playpen. As Connal cleaned up all signs of his presence and left the suite, the child stared at him with black eyes filled with accusation.

Maybe it was a trick of the mind, but Connal was almost certain the child understood what had just happened. If he'd been old enough to speak, Connal would have had to kill him as well. As it was, he would keep Connal's secret, if only because he was unable to do otherwise.

As soon as the heat of that scorching kiss with Cain had faded, dread began to set in.

Rory didn't want to do this—she didn't want a vampire drinking her blood. Even worse, she didn't want him in her head. Letting Ronan see behind the curtain felt too much like some kind of betrayal. That was something she shared with Cain, not some bloodsucking Sanguinar.

Still, she was in trouble and Ronan was the one who could fix it. If that meant stripping down naked and sacrificing live chickens under a full moon, then that's what she'd do to be rid of the demon's control.

Cain hovered nearby, his thick arms crossed over his chest. Seeing him there, looking like nothing in the world could hurt him, gave her a precious moment of peace. His presence was reassuring—a looming reminder that he was on her side.

"So what happens now?" she asked Ronan.

"I take some of your blood to strengthen me and create a link between us. After that, I'll find the demon's presence and try to mask it."

"And that will make it so the thing can't control me anymore?"

"That is my hope."

"What are my chances?"

Cain surged forward, only to grind to a halt a second later. She saw a flash of herself through his eyes, hating how small and vulnerable she looked huddled on the couch. Her hair was damp, lying limp around her face. She wore no makeup to hide how pale she was. Even her tucked-in posture screamed she was scared shitless.

Fuck that. She was tired of being afraid. The sooner she got this over with, the better.

"Never mind," she hastily added. "I don't want to know."

Ronan patted her hand, his skin cool to the touch and not at all comforting. "Everything is going to be fine."

Cain let out a rumbling growl. "Just do it. She doesn't want you to linger."

Before Rory could respond or even register what was happening, she saw a light flare in Ronan's eyes—unnatural, internal light spilling from within. Her wrist was at his mouth, and a fleeting pain came and went so fast she questioned if it had ever happened.

Lethargy collapsed in over her, giving her no time to fear its approach. One minute she was awake, and the next, she had fallen into a gray, groggy state where nothing could touch her: She floated there, weightless and without feeling, as if her body had dissipated into smoke.

An alien presence wedged its way into her mind, forcing her acceptance. A headache spiked behind her eyes, shoving her up toward the surface of wakefulness.

This presence wasn't like Cain, who had slipped in, winding through her thoughts as if he belonged there. This one was harsher, colder—not the same frigid, screaming demand as the demon had been, but just as unwelcome.

"Don't fight me," she heard Ronan say. He was too close. His words echoed in her ears and inside her skull, bouncing off the jagged tension between her eyes.

Get out.

She didn't want him here. He didn't belong.

"I must be here."

Get out.

He didn't leave and she couldn't shove him away. Panic slithered up her spine, lodging itself in her throat. She couldn't breathe.

A second presence in her mind woke up, as if sensing her weakness. It sank in through a crack, expanding like smoke to twine around her thoughts. It was icy and furious, seething with caustic hatred, dripping with malice.

"That's the demon," said Ronan. "You must let me in to fight him."

Get out!

The demon didn't listen. It grew, uncoiling until it was huge and looming.

Cain! She tried to shout the word, but no sound came out, only an empty, gaping silence.

"I'm here." His voice settled over her like a warm blanket. A second later, he was with her. Inside her. She recognized the humming power that flowed through him.

Rory clung to him, not caring if it made her look weak. She didn't understand this mental landscape or how so many creatures could fit here with her. All she knew was that everyone wanted something from her—everyone but Cain.

"Let Ronan help you," he said.

I don't know how.

"I'll show you."

He'd done this before. He knew exactly what he was doing, arrowing in on her intent to shield herself. As he wrapped himself around it, she felt the barrier crumble.

Full-blown panic pounded at her to stop him. He was going to destroy her.

"Trust me." His presence swelled, its power so huge and bright it was like staring at the sun, blinding her.

Whatever he was doing was going to kill her. She didn't know how he couldn't see that.

"I will never hurt you."

If she hadn't been intertwined with him, she might have scoffed, but she felt his resolve reverberate down to his very soul. She wasn't sure how she knew it was so, but the feeling was as unmistakable as it was potent.

Rory let go, trusting Cain to have her back. She was floundering and ignorant of all this magical crap. Cain wasn't. And if what he was doing killed her, at least she wouldn't be alone when she went. It was more than she'd expected from her life.

She was overcome, completely defeated, but Cain was here with her, cradling her close and making her believe he really did care. That it would all be okay.

With a rumble that shook her to her bones, the barrier she'd created crumbled to ash. The demon was behind it, teeth bared, claws extended, looming huge over Ronan, who was also there.

"Perfect." She heard Ronan's voice praise her, lilting low and soft. "Just relax and let go."

She'd already let go of everything she had. There was nothing left to give him.

Ronan swelled and grew, his form expanding to dwarf the demon. Rory cringed back from the pair only to feel Cain's soothing presence there to cushion her.

A hissing, ultraviolet light spewed out of Ronan's mouth, hitting the demon. It jerked back in pain only to lunge forward in defiance. Ronan grabbed the beast between two huge hands and crushed it. Behind the demon a metal box appeared.

He shoved the creature back toward the gaping doorway, his intent to cage it clear. The demon lashed out, slicing through Ronan's skin. More ultraviolet light bled from the wounds, giving the demon nowhere to hide from the burning light.

It cowered and screamed as Ronan crammed it into the box that was far too small to contain it. Bones cracked and scales scraped over the metal like fingernails on a chalkboard, but Ronan kept pushing until the demon was fully inside. He slammed the door shut and it fused closed, as if the metal had been instantly welded in place.

A second later, Rory jolted awake as if she'd been

doused in iced coffee. She shot upright, nearly bashing Cain's chin with her forehead.

"Easy," he said as he took control of her shoulders to keep her from flailing and taking out his eye.

Ronan was slumped on the floor by the couch where she lay. His head was bent, his shoulders heaving with rapid, heavy breaths.

"Are you okay?" she asked.

"Give him a minute," said Cain. "What he did was incredibly difficult."

It hadn't been a picnic for her, either, but at least she didn't feel as bad as Ronan looked.

Cain's hand slid over her shoulder until it cupped her neck. The tingling heat calmed her down, feeling oddly familiar and grounding. She hadn't had his touch in her life for long, but she knew it now to the point that she was certain that if blindfolded, she would know his hand on her skin out of a thousand different men.

"How do you feel?" he asked.

"Fine. Freaked, but okay. Did it work?"

Ronan gave a weak nod. "For now."

Cain's fingers curled at the nape of her neck. The luceria jumped toward him in excitement, as if it, too, recognized his touch.

"Andra's shield went down just as Ronan started. Had he not acted fast, you would have been back where you were before, fighting to get outside."

"I'm glad it didn't turn out that way. Thanks, Ronan."

He lifted his head, and his face was starkly pale and gaunt, like a starving prisoner of war. Deep, bruised grooves were etched beneath his eyes, and his whole body appeared almost skeletal.

She couldn't hold back her shocked gasp. "What the hell?"

"I will be fine. I must go and feed. The demon still lurks within me, and I must not be too weak to fight it."

Cain nodded. "We will head back to Dabyr."

Ronan gave a weak shake of his head. "You cannot go there."

"Why not?"

"The Synestryn lurking within Rory will not stay contained for long. The only way to free her is to find it and kill it. If you take her back to Dabyr, she could draw it there."

"Isn't that the place where you said hundreds of people lived?"

Cain didn't have to say anything. She could see the truth in his frustration. "We can't stay here."

"Sounds like we can't stay anywhere. Ronan said we need to go hunting."

"I'm not taking you to hunt a powerful demon that may or may not have some control over your actions."

Ronan pushed to his feet, wobbling slightly. She didn't know how he was going to drive in this condition.

Rory remembered what Cain had done for Ronan in that basement—how he'd fed him blood. That's what the vampire needed now. And after what he'd just done for her, it seemed that a small donation was the least she could do.

"You can have some of my blood," she offered.

Cain's body vibrated with instant tension. "No."

Ronan's eyes brightened with an eerie, silvery light. He was completely still, staring at her like she'd just handed him something too good to be true.

"Why not?" she asked.

"He's too hungry. He'll lose control and take too much, leaving you weak and vulnerable."

"I would be careful, maintain control."

Rory glared at Cain for thinking he had any say in what she did with her own blood. "If he goes too far, you can thwack him in the head. Until then, let him have a snack. Poor man's about to fall over."

Cain's mouth went flat and hard, not at all like it had been when he'd kissed her. "I'll call some Gerai to come and donate."

Ronan swallowed hard. He was breathing too fast, and his pulse fluttered in his temple. "It would take ten of them to give me what she could."

Rory went to where Ronan stood and lifted her arm in offering. Her gaze stayed fixed on Cain, daring him to try to stop her.

Ronan grabbed her wrist. She felt that fleeting pain again, gone before it could even register. A sleepy calm filled her, washing away all traces of anger she'd felt a moment ago.

"That's enough," barked Cain. One hand was at his belt, gripping his invisible sword, like he thought he may need to use it.

Ronan's cool mouth grudgingly left her skin. She looked at her wrist for signs of damage and saw nothing but a slight pink flush. "I'm fine. Stop glowering."

"I don't glower," said Cain.

A slight smile lifted Ronan's pretty mouth. "She's right, you know." He looked better now than he had a moment ago. Still flimsy, but no longer like he was at death's door.

Cain growled.

Rory opened her mouth to say something, but she stalled out as a vision hit her hard. She saw the outside of Nana's house in the distance. In the foreground were several rust-colored, furry monsters charging closer. A length of delicate silver chain flicked through the air, over and over, snapping at the backs of the demons to spur them on. Little tufts of fur caught fire wherever the chain touched.

And then another angle appeared, along with another fiery chain. And another.

Fear sprang up through her bones, driving a yelp from

her lips. An instant later, she felt Cain touch her thoughts, seeking the source of her terror.

She showed him what she saw and watched as those images were superimposed upon the sight of him pulling his sword.

"Handlers," he said. "Moving in fast."

Chapter 18

Cain pushed Rory toward the back door. The Handlers were approaching from the front, cutting off their escape.

Ronan had already started moving, taking Rory by the arm. "We have to get to my van. We'll never outrun them on foot."

"What are they?" asked Rory.

There was no time for detailed explanations—for laying out their strengths and weaknesses. All of his focus now had to be on getting them out of the house alive. So, he settled for, "Deadly."

Before they reached the kitchen, the front wall of her house began to smoke. A thin, silver chain—the whips the Handlers used—cut right through the wall. Glass shattered, and a heartbeat later, three of the Handlers' pets crashed into her living room. The burned-out holes that had once been their eyes angled toward Rory and Ronan.

"The exit is blocked," said Ronan.

Cain looked over Ronan's shoulder and saw flames licking up along the wooden door.

Rory's voice was squeaky with fear. "We're trapped."

"No, we're not." Cain kicked the table over, sending her computer and papers flying. He shoved it with his boot, sliding it a few feet forward as he closed the distance.

A Handler appeared behind its pets, a red-hot poker in its spindly hand. The chain extending from its whip sizzled and sparked as it flew through the air, burning through yet another section of wall.

The thing's oddly jointed legs bent backward as it came closer. It was the pale color of deep-sea creatures, and delicate for one of the Synestryn. Cutting it down would be easy. Getting close enough to do so was the hard part. One single touch of that whip would cook flesh down to the bone.

But before Cain could even reach the Handler, he had to get through the smaller demons it controlled.

He charged, keeping track of the reach of the Handler's whip. Centuries of fighting guided his sword as he lopped off paws and snouts. The demons screamed and snapped, but every inch he gained, he shoved the table toward them, keeping the barrier in place.

He was making good ground, but it wasn't fast enough. The whole front wall of Rory's house was consumed by fire. Thick black smoke poured along the ceiling, billowing out in a choking cloud.

Even with his attention on the task at hand, Cain still felt Rory's keen sense of loss as she watched her childhood home go up in flames. The fear and grief plowing through her were nearly overwhelming. He tried to offer some sense of comfort, but his attention was already split too many ways. He wasn't used to being connected to her. He wasn't used to the additional emotional input. As he continued to fight, it was becoming hard to tell where she stopped and he began. His attacks became sloppy as the onslaught continued. He tried to get a grip, but Rory was such a potent force. She could not be ignored.

Cain's sword dipped too low, missing its mark. One of the furry demons lunged over the table and clamped on to his left arm.

Pain shot through him as the teeth dug deep. His bone snapped. A searing cold swept through him as poison entered his bloodstream.

"No!" shouted Rory, fear and fury resonating in her voice.

A second later, the demon's teeth ripped free. It flew across the room, into the wall of flames. Cain had no idea if it had been Rory or Ronan who'd freed him.

Another demon snarled and bounded toward him. Cain kept fighting. Rory was behind him, and he couldn't let any of these things get past.

His shoulder was consumed by frigid agony as the poison crept over his skin. His eyelids became heavy, and his vision spun for a second. Only instinct allowed him to lift his sword in time to stop the next set of jaws from reaching him.

"We need a way out," called Ronan.

Cain tried to tell him that he was working on it, but there was no air to spare for words. Every ounce of effort was going into staying on his feet.

He was completely on the defensive now, making no ground toward the gaping hole in the front wall.

Rory was right. They weren't going to make it. He wasn't strong enough to hold all the demons back—not now that he was poisoned and bleeding. More demons would smell the blood and come. It was only a matter of time.

"Like fucking hell," snarled Rory.

A huge wash of power gushed out of him as she drew it into herself. The side wall of her house burst open. Wooden splinters and glass spewed out onto the lawn. The explosion was deafening. The rush of cold air solidified in his lungs.

A strong hand grabbed him by the arm and bodily hauled him out of the house. They dropped down three feet, and by the time they hit the ground, there were demons chomping at their heels.

A Handler's whip whizzed by Cain's ear. The smell of burned hair gagged him, but he kept moving.

Ronan had one hand on Cain's arm and another on Rory's. His face was furrowed in determination, his eyes burning bright.

Cain's vision faltered, tunneling out so that everything looked too far away. His whole back was numb with cold, and it was sinking into his legs fast. A few more seconds was all he had until he was no longer able to run.

Rory brushed his mind, her ferocity so brilliant he couldn't help but be drawn to it. He felt her pull on his power, and blue light splashed out, protecting their flank.

Cain stumbled, but Ronan kept him on his feet. The black van appeared as a speck in the distance. Ronan's arm reached out, looking freakishly long. The door slid open. Cain was pushed inside, headfirst. He had no choice but to tumble where he was sent.

Numbness inched up his neck. The van's engine started.

"Go," said Rory, her voice shaking with strain. "I don't know how long I can hold them off."

Cain's body lurched to the side as the van sloshed over the gravel road. A body collided with his, and he knew instantly that it was Rory. He tried to open his mouth to ask her if she was okay, but it wasn't working. He couldn't move.

"He's bleeding bad," she said.

Ronan's voice was calm. "There is duct tape in the blue box."

Cain heard the sound of tape ripping, but he couldn't feel what she was doing. All he could see was a faint, distant blob of blurry shadows he thought had to be her.

"Don't you dare die on me, Cain," she growled at him. "Not you, too."

He wanted to ask her what she meant by that, but it was no use. His body shut down and he slipped away.

* * *

"It *wasn't* suicide," said Ella, her face stained with tears. "My sister would never have killed herself—not now that we were finally free."

Joseph stared at the weeping woman, his heart breaking for her. She'd already been through so much, and now this.

Nicholas and Tynan were in the bathroom where Beth's body had been found, trying to determine cause of death. It all seemed pretty cut-and-dried to Joseph—dead, bloodless woman in the tub with her wrist slashed—but if Ella needed them to be thorough, then that's what they'd be. Whatever he could do to ease her in her time of need.

"When was the last time you saw her?" he asked.

"Right before I went to work. She was watching my son. She was happy. Playing with him."

"Where is the boy now?"

"Lyka came and took him to her suite to spend the night there. I didn't want him to see me like this."

The mention of Lyka's name got Joseph's attention, making him wish he could spend the night in her suite, too, but he shoved his own interests aside to deal with the matter at hand. "And you had no sign that she was depressed or upset?"

Ella dabbed at her eyes with a soggy tissue. "I told you. She was happy. We were safe here—or so I thought."

"What do you mean by that?" he asked.

"I mean that someone had to have done this to her. She did *not* kill herself."

Joseph nodded and cupped her shoulder in what he hoped was a gesture of comfort. He was all ragged nerves and exhaustion these days, and he wasn't sure he even remembered what comfort looked like. "Okay. We'll look into it. We won't assume anything. In the meantime, I need you to stay somewhere else. Can you spend the night in a friend's suite?"

Ella nodded. "Yeah. I'm sure Lyka will let me stay, and she's already got all of the baby's things."

"Do you want me to walk you there?" He wanted her to say yes so he could catch a glimpse of Lyka, but he could tell before he finished the question that Ella was going to turn him down.

"No, it's only a few doors down. What I want from you is to find out who did this."

Joseph nodded, biting back the promise that formed behind his lips. There were no guarantees that they'd find anyone, and even fewer that there was anyone *to* find. Beth had been in those caves a long time—much longer than Ella had. She didn't know what Beth had been through. From all accounts, Ella had already been pregnant when she'd been taken into the demon caves. She couldn't have known what it was like to suffer the way that Beth had.

Chances were that Beth had simply been hiding her depression from her sister to save her the pain. If so, she was a troubled woman, but a good one. For that reason alone, he would treat her death with the care and attention it deserved.

Ella left, and Joseph went to join the two men in the bathroom. The space was big enough for all of them, but Beth's body took up a lot of room all the same. Her faded presence hung there like an empty spot in the air, sucking out all chances of happiness.

"What do you think?" he asked.

Tynan set the woman's hand on her stomach and stood. "She has been drained of blood."

"I see that. She cut herself open from the elbow to her wrist."

"No," said Tynan. "If she'd done that, there would have been more pooling of blood in her limbs when her heart became too weak to pump it out. Gravity would have held some inside of her body."

"And there would have been more staining on her

clothes," added Nicholas. "The water was hot. Would have set the blood. Plus, her head isn't wet. I think it would have been hard to turn the shower on without at least getting hit a little before she laid back."

"So it wasn't suicide," said Joseph on a sigh. "She was killed."

"Drained," said Tynan again.

And then the meaning of his word kicked in, slamming Joseph in the gut. "This was one of the Sanguinar?"

Tynan nodded gravely. "I believe so. Someone became too desperate, too hungry."

"We need to find him. Now."

"That won't be a problem," said Tynan.

"Why not?"

"Her blood still held the taint of Synestryn. I was working to filter it out, but there was little I could do for her. She wasn't as bad off as Tori was, but any of my kind who drank this much from her will be desperately ill. There will probably be signs of blisters on their mouth as well, since they wouldn't have been able to heal themselves with her blood."

Joseph looked at Nicholas's scarred face. "Close the gate. We're on lockdown. No one leaves until I say so."

"I'm on it," said Nicholas, and he left.

"You," Joseph said to Tynan, "gather every Sanguinar and check them out. Find who did this and bring him to me. Understood?"

Tynan nodded. "Of course. But please, I beg you to keep this between us. If the humans think we're out to hurt them . . ."

"I won't say anything until we've found our killer. But you find him tonight, Tynan. I'm not letting another human under my care die like this."

Tynan started to leave, but Joseph stopped him. "Can you fix her arm—just the skin. I don't want her sister remembering her like this."

Tynan ran his finger along the woman's skin, knitting

it shut. It left a bluish line that wasn't quite right, but it was better than the gaping flesh that had been there before.

After Tynan left, Joseph stripped the wet clothes from Beth and left them in the tub. He picked her up and carried her into the nearest bedroom, where he dressed her in something bright and cheerful. After he was done, he arranged her body so she looked comfortable, and covered her with a blanket.

Tomorrow they would bury her and burn her clothes and bedding to make sure no traces of blood remained behind. Tonight, Beth would lie in a real bed one last time before they returned her to the earth, where she'd spent far too many years of her young life.

Pain burrowed behind his eyes, throbbing as it worked its way down his spine. He tried to ignore it, but when things like this happened—when he failed in his duties to protect the humans under his care—the pain was always worse. It was like it knew when he was weakest.

Joseph left the suite to crawl into his shower and wash away the grief and loss the last few hours had left on him. His shoulders bowed. He felt older, weaker. As he passed Lyka's suite, his feet slowed as he lingered outside of her door.

Seeing her always made him feel better—distracted him from the pain—and right now he would have given nearly anything to feel even a little better. But Ella needed comfort more than Joseph did, so he kept walking.

Chapter 19

Rory's hands kept slipping on Cain's blood. There was so much of it. The duct tape was coated and slick, making it impossible for her to tear off strips.

She used her teeth, and tasted something vile. Her tongue went instantly numb. She didn't even hesitate to turn her head and spit the horrible substance from her mouth.

Ronan cast a quick glance over his shoulder at her. "Don't you dare swallow that. He's poisoned."

Eww. He didn't need to tell her twice. She wiped her tongue on her sleeve as she settled for wrapping Cain's arm without tearing the tape.

She didn't know how he was still alive after all the blood he'd lost, but she could feel his presence dangling at the other end of the luceria, keeping her from freaking out.

Ronan spoke into his phone. "We need help. . . . Three Handlers and at least eight or nine demons. . . . Cain's been poisoned. I'm going to need blood."

Rory had just started adding another layer of tape to the first, insufficient one when Ronan said, "Come take the wheel. I need to tend him."

"Where do I go?"

He went through a few screens on his phone, sparing

only an occasional glance at the deserted road. "GPS will lead you to a Gerai house. There's a tracking device in the van, so they'll be able to see where we're headed."

They did an awkward maneuver that put her behind the wheel. She gripped it tight, and sought out Cain's weak presence. She gathered it close, trying to reassure him that he was going to make it.

Rory had lost too many people in her life. She'd just started caring about Cain. It wasn't fair that she'd lose him, too. Not now. Not so soon.

Then again, maybe it would be better if she didn't grow any more attached to him. A man like Cain would be too easy to sink into and let herself be carried away on pretty wings of trust—trust that he'd return her affection. Trust that he'd survive.

No one could promise her that, not even someone as powerful as Cain.

And if she hadn't believed that before, she did now. He bled just like anyone else. That meant he could die just like anyone else.

She didn't realize she was pulling away from that faint, familiar essence of his until she felt him lurch for her. She'd been sliding back into herself, cutting him off as if he were already dead.

Here he was dying and she was abandoning him, just to save herself a little pain.

So fucking selfish.

Rory slipped back to where she'd been, offering a silent apology. She wasn't sure if he could understand her or not, but for now it was all she could do. The closer to civilization she got, the more she had to concentrate on seeing the road rather than what others saw.

"I'm not going to be able to go much longer," she warned Ronan. "My visions are getting too thick, and I won't be able to see through them."

Ronan didn't answer. She glanced in the rearview mirror and saw him bent over Cain's body. He was stripped to the waist, and so pale she hardly recognized him. Only the lifelike image of the tree seemed familiar.

Someone nearby opened their fridge, and the blinding light seared her eyeballs. She hissed and held the wheel straight, hoping that kept them on the road. The van slowed without her foot on the gas. She felt the looser ridge of gravel at the edge, and eased the van back to the left.

Finally, the vision passed and her eyes adjusted again to the darkness. It dawned on her that she'd been driving without the lights, using Cain's power to allow her to see.

She was getting way too accustomed to having access to magic. It came easily to her. All she had to do was listen to her instincts and things happened. Just like magic.

Cain groaned in pain, and she took that as a good sign.

"How's it going back there?"

A cold blast of air sucked the heat from the van. Ronan sent Cain's bloody tape-covered clothes out the window. "He'll live. Assuming we don't run into demons before help arrives."

"I could hold them off again. Like I did before."

"Yes, but for how long? Dawn is hours away."

A trio of visions shoved their way into her brain all at once, blinding her with their intensity.

"Don't slow down," said Ronan. "There are still traces of blood on us."

"Can't help it. I can't see a damn thing."

"Let me."

They did the awkward tango, switching places, only this time it was harder with her unable to see much of anything. As the visions cleared, she saw that Ronan was in bad shape again. Pale, gaunt, shaking. She wanted to offer him her blood—he had saved Cain after all—but she worried about it leaving her too weak to keep them safe.

"I'll be fine," he said, as if he'd heard her thoughts. "I've lived through much worse than this. Go back there and clean off as much blood as you can."

Rory went back to Cain's side and found a package of baby wipes in the blue box. She pulled out a wad of them and started scrubbing the drying blood from his skin. It was hard to stay focused on the task at hand with so much naked male flesh on display, but her flashing visions kept cutting into her enjoyment, reminding her to get the damn job done. Finally, she splayed her left hand over his tree tattoo to drive the visions away.

Heat trickled out of her. She actually felt her hand warm and vibrate against his skin. The branches of the tree swayed, tickling her palm.

She ran her finger along the mark, marveling over the magic he housed. Tingling ribbons of heat wove their way up her arm, wrapping tightly around her. Tying her to him.

Rory pulled back. She didn't want to be tied to him. His job was too dangerous. He took too many risks.

For her.

Cain's eyes opened. A dark green sliver of color showed between his lids. Yearning filled his gaze, but she couldn't figure out what it was he wanted.

And she really wasn't sure it was something she wanted to give.

His hand fumbled toward her, reaching for her. She couldn't deny him the simple comfort of human contact, so she took his hand in hers.

He pressed her fingers over his heart. Need shimmered through the luceria. Desire, too, but his need went deeper than that. It cried out for beautiful, dangerous things—things that had the power to rip her soul from her body and stomp it into a pulpy slush. Without even trying, she could see the things he wanted. Secret, hidden things that he didn't dare even admit to himself.

Rory felt herself being pulled into his need—the

things he'd denied himself for years. Centuries. They were shiny, filled with hope and purpose, so bright she couldn't look directly at them for fear of blinding herself.

What she couldn't see scared her, but not nearly as much as what she felt. Those bright hopes swirled around her, as if she were their center, as if without her, those precious, glimmering things would all fly away into oblivion. He needed her to need him.

She couldn't be anyone's center. It was too much to ask.

Rory pried her fingers out from under his and grabbed up another thick pile of baby wipes. She distracted herself by scrubbing away more smears of blood, being careful not to touch his skin. The visions came back with a vengeance, but she was used to those. She could stand those.

She couldn't stand the desire that had tumbled out of Cain, or how he saw her as the sun around which his hopes revolved. She couldn't need him like that—it would destroy her to depend on anyone the way he clearly wanted her to do. She couldn't be the one to provide him with the sense of purpose he needed to keep going.

It would be kinder of her to keep her distance. Cain was a good man. If she couldn't give him what he needed, the least he deserved was her letting him down gently.

When Cain woke fully, he was in a bed. His clothes were gone, but his sword was propped close at hand, fitted with a new leather belt. He saw no signs of danger, but something was definitely wrong.

He got up and found a robe draped over a chair. It was barely big enough to cover him, but a sense of urgency drove him not to care about his lack of modesty. His body was weak and wobbly. Thirst grated along his throat.

He recognized the feeling as the aftermath of Sanguinar healing, so that didn't disturb him, but something was off.

Rory.

He reached out through their link only to find a hard wall blocking his path.

Terrified that something had happened to her, he stumbled from the room and down the hall. The sight of her ridiculously pink hair made him sag with relief.

"Rory, are you okay?"

She was at the front window, holding the curtains back as she peered out at the sunrise. At the sound of her name, she spun around. Her dark gaze slid over his body. She took a step toward him as if compelled, but stopped short. Her gaze hit the floor and stayed there. "I'm fine. How are you feeling?"

"Thirsty. What happened?"

She walked into the kitchen and pulled a glass from the cabinet. "A team of Gerai came. They gave Ronan enough blood to heal you, carried you to bed and then cleaned up the mess. The whole thing took only minutes. They're very efficient."

"Where's Ronan?"

She filled the glass and set it on the counter near him, rather than handing it to him, as if she didn't want to risk any accidental contact. "In the basement, sleeping."

The water eased the burning in his throat, but did nothing to get rid of the nagging sense that something was wrong. She was acting strange. Cold.

And then it hit him. She'd lost her home. It had gone up in flames, along with all of her grandmother's handmade things, their family photos—precious, irreplaceable things.

"I'm so sorry about your home, Rory." He reached to put a comforting hand on her shoulder, but she jerked away.

"Don't. I'm fine. It was just a house."

"No, it was your home. Your grandmother's home. It was a place of happy memories and safety."

A hollow, bitter bark of laughter erupted from her mouth. "Yeah, well, not last night, it wasn't."

Cain ached to ease her grief, but she clearly didn't want physical contact. Once again, he prodded the connection the luceria offered, hoping for another way to lend her comfort. Instead, he was met with a cold, blank wall keeping him out.

"We can rebuild your home if you like," he offered. "I realize it will never replace the things you lost, but at least you'll have a place of your own."

She turned her back on him, shaking her head so that her pink hair swayed over her shoulders. "That was never my place. It was always Nana's, and it was the last thing I had of hers that made me feel like she was still with me. I was surrounded by her there—the things she'd made, the way she smelled." She paused, and when she spoke again, there was a catch of sorrow in her throat. "That house made me feel like she could still hug me. Now it's gone, and nothing you can do will ever bring that back, so don't bother."

Cain could no longer stand to give her space, not when she was suffering such a deep loss. His need to protect her—even from her grief—drove him forward. His bare feet were silent on the floor. He gave her no warning of his intent, but as he approached, she became stiff, as if she knew he was there.

Her visions. Of course.

He slipped his arms around her waist, ready to face whatever fury she wanted to unleash.

She spun around inside his embrace, shoving against his chest. "Let me go."

"No. If your grandmother can no longer hug you, then I will."

Now that he was close, he could see the signs of her grief etched under her eyes and around her mouth. She'd been crying, and the remnants of those tears threatened to spill over now. He knew that if he witnessed her weakness, it would only make her more resistant and prickly.

He tucked her head under his chin and let her hide

her face against his chest. The barrier she'd shoved between them trembled, though he couldn't tell if it was from the force of her emotions, or if her resolve to keep him out was weakening.

"You're not alone, Rory."

Her voice was small and uncertain. "Everyone is alone. Everyone dies. I'm so tired of being crushed when it happens."

"Things appear bleak now, but it won't always be this way. Days will pass. You will heal."

"Yeah, just in time to get kicked in the gut again when the next person I care about dies. I'm sorry, Cain, but it's just not worth it. I'm done caring."

She didn't mean that. It was her grief talking. But nothing he could say would clear away the pain and give her room to see the truth. Only time could do that.

Cain stroked her hair, reveling in the feel of her pressed against him like this. She was safe, and for a few horrible moments, he had been sure that they were all going to die. He'd been sure that he'd failed her the way he'd failed Sibyl, that he'd broken his vow to keep her safe.

He'd been given a second chance, and it was one he would not squander.

She was no longer resisting his touch. Her body leaned into his, and her hands gripped his robe, rather than pushing him away.

It was a start.

Cain slid his fingers through her hair, massaging the tension along the back of her scalp and neck. "Perhaps you should get some sleep."

He felt the slight shake of her head at his chest. "I feel like I'll never sleep again. Those demons were all sorts of fucked up. And seeing you hurt like that, seeing Ronan barely able to get down the steps on his own . . . There's just way too much shit in my head for me to close my eyes and watch it all play out again."

Cain pressed against the barrier between them, feeling it bulge and wobble. "I could help you sleep."

"Yeah. I'm aware. Don't you dare."

"Okay." He found her chin and tipped her head up so she'd look at him. "But I need to do something to help you. How will I know what you need if you keep me out?"

"I don't want you in my head anymore."

"That's not true. I felt how much you liked it before. You can't lie to me."

"Before was before. This is now."

"Nothing has changed," he said.

"Wrong. Everything is different now. I have a Synestryn locked in my head, ready to spring out like a demonic jack-in-the-box. I'm homeless. I apparently have nowhere to hide from the visions, no matter how far away from others I go. They only go away when you touch me, and we can't exactly go around holding hands all the time." She let out a long sigh. "I need some space to figure out how to deal with all of this on my own. Whenever you slip inside my thoughts, it makes it hard to remember that you won't always be around. That's why you have to stay out."

"Who says I won't always be around?"

"Oh, gee, I don't know. The universe? How the hell should I know? I don't make the rules, I just suffer because of them."

"I've lived for centuries. If you were going to take a chance on anyone, I'd say I'm a fairly safe bet."

"How can you say that when you nearly died *only hours ago*?"

"That wasn't as bad as it looked. I've been through worse."

"The night Sibyl was taken. Don't remind me." She shuddered before getting a grip on herself. She stepped back, out of his embrace and looked up at him with determination burning in her dark eyes. "The point is, I'm done with the fear and worry. I'm moving on."

Cain went still, dread pooling in his chest. "What do you mean, *moving on*?"

"I talked to Ronan. He said that without me, or someone like me, you'll die. I won't be the cause of that, but I also won't hang around, waiting for it to happen. I don't want to be there when it does. So I'm taking off."

Anger coalesced in a slow, burning coil that tightened around him with every breath. "You're leaving me?"

"I'll wear your necklace. Ronan said that will keep you alive, even if I'm on the other side of the planet. But I need my space."

He could barely shove the words out through his growing fury. "To do what?"

"Don't get mad at me," she snapped. "I'm doing the right thing here. I'm getting away from the demon where it can't control me so easily. And I'm not letting you die."

"But you're not willing to stay by my side, either. You're not willing to become what you were meant to be."

She blinked fast, and her gaze slid around as if she could no longer see. "There are no rules saying I have to cling to your side like some kind of infatuated schoolgirl. Ronan said this will work. I'm sorry if you don't like it."

"Who will keep you safe?"

"I will. I've got some power now. I'll use it if I have to."

"Where will you go? How will you even get around if your visions are worse?" Just to prove his point, he grabbed her hand, knowing it would make her visions fade again.

Her mouth flattened in frustration and her words came out with a growling edge. "I'll manage. Blind people do it all the time."

"I see. So you'd rather be blind and struggling on your own than allowing me to fulfill my vow."

Her shoulders inched up toward her ears. "I'm sorry, Cain, but I really don't give a fuck about your vows."

"None of them? Not even my promise to kiss you again? Do you remember that one, Rory?"

He could tell she did by the way her gaze snapped to his mouth. She jerked her hand away from his touch, and he was sure she'd done it to intentionally blind herself. "That was before last night's eye-opening events. I've changed my mind."

"That's not the way it works. When we make a promise, we are bound to it, compelled to fulfill it. Whether it's keeping you safe or kissing you as you'd asked, my choice to act is dictated in that moment."

"So what does that mean? You have to kiss me to fulfill the promise?"

"That was what you demanded of me."

She thrust her chin up. "Fine, then kiss me and be done with it."

"What about the other vow? My life for yours, Rory. Even if I kiss you, that vow will still tie us together. I can't protect you if I'm not nearby."

"Sounds to me like you did that last night—you nearly died getting us out of there."

"Yes, but intent matters as much as the words. My intent was to protect your life no matter what, even if it means forfeiting my own. Not only once, but for as long as I live."

She swallowed hard, her voice growing weak. "Your vow. Your problem."

"And what about yours? What was your intent when you and I were in each other's arms in your bedroom? Were you only asking me for a peck on the cheek?"

He knew she hadn't been. She'd been asking for much, much more. And he'd been more than willing to give her whatever she wanted. Even now, he could feel the need to pull her close and finish what they'd started. Only his concern for her state of mind held him back. But as time passed, the compulsion to fulfill his vow would increase until he could think of nothing else.

She stared at him for a long time, indecision wrinkling

her forehead. "If we do what I asked of you, it's going to make it so much harder for me to walk away."

"I'm okay with that. I don't want you to leave. It's not safe." There was more to it than that, but he dared not even admit that to himself, much less her. With her talk of leaving, he had to do what he could to protect himself. No one else would, apparently.

"I can't stay with you, Cain." There was no heat in her voice this time, only a sadness that ran so deep, he wondered how it didn't split her in two.

Once again he tried to break through the barrier she'd erected. It was weaker than it had been, so thin, he could feel her presence gliding just on the other side. He needed to feel that again, to wrap himself in her very essence and revel in the goodness that shone out from her soul.

She was hurting so much right now. If only he could break through, he knew he could ease her.

Cain needed that. Instincts and his desire to make her happy drove him on, forcing him to prod more heavily at the barrier.

"What are you doing?" she asked.

"My job. You've seen through me the way things are supposed to be between us. You may not believe that you could ever want that, but I do. I've seen the power and joy that comes from what you and I could have. And I'm willing to fight for it. For you."

The barrier shattered. Rory gasped and swayed. Cain grabbed her arms as he dove through their link, letting all that she was surround him.

Fear screamed through her, so loud it nearly brought him to his knees. She was terrified of leaving, of being blind and on her own, but that fear paled in comparison to her worry that he would die. Right after she'd grown to love him.

The idea that she even thought she could love him was

a heady, intoxicating thrill. It was more than he expected, no matter how much he'd secretly hoped that it was possible. She'd seen his failings, his mistakes. She'd seen how he'd let Sibyl be taken, and yet she held none of that against him. All of her thoughts were of protecting herself from his inevitable death.

She'd pictured the possible scenarios over and over, in an array of bloody, violent ends. It was jarring to witness his own death, but the emotions surrounding the events were what shocked him the most. She already grieved for him on some level. Which meant that she'd already come to care for him on some level.

Cain let that hope buoy him up and fill him with a renewed strength of purpose. She couldn't walk around with this kind of fear clawing at her insides. It would weaken her, make her hesitate. It could even get her killed.

He would not allow that to happen. His vow to protect her gave him the permission he needed to help her. If she was angry at what he was about to do, so be it.

She hated feeling afraid, so he took control of her fears, of each bloody event and changed them, showing her another possibility. When the claws of countless demons tore him apart, he showed her an image of her power shielding him from the blows. When poison riddled his body, he let her see herself driving it from his veins. When fire charred his flesh, he made her watch as she called a torrent of rain to fall over the flames, dousing them before they could so much as singe his hair. With each defeat, he gave her victory, and with each victory, he felt her swell and strengthen.

Finally, when the last of her bloody nightmares was destroyed, he let go of her thoughts. He couldn't bring himself to leave her completely for fear that she'd block him out again. And because he liked lingering within her too much.

She stared up at him, her dark eyes huge with disbelief. "You really see me like that?"

"I do."

Her mouth quivered as if she were seeking the right words. "No one has ever seen me like that before—strong, capable. No one has ever really seen me at all. Not since Nana."

"I see you. Inside and out."

"And you still want me to hang around?"

The words that tickled the end of his tongue were desperate, needy things. He wanted so much from her—things he didn't dare ask for. He'd been so lost before he'd met her, empty of hope. And now he was filled with it, with purpose. He knew she wouldn't understand how he felt. She wasn't raised as one of them. She wasn't taught what to expect of their bond, or how it was designed to function. How both of them needed that connection, how they were made for it.

All of those things would make him sound like some kind of desperate, groveling weakling, and he didn't want her to see that in him. She loathed weakness in herself, and he assumed the dislike would carry through to him as well.

So instead of pouring out his deepest, darkest desires, he simply said, "I do."

Rory's hand settled on the side of his face as she stared into his eyes. He could feel sparks igniting beneath the pad of each finger. The slight trembling of her hand made his protective instincts roil beneath the surface. He fought them, holding perfectly still so as not to scare her away. She was teetering on the brink of a decision, and as much as he wanted to tip the balance, he didn't dare. There was no guarantee of which way she'd fall.

Her feet slid closer to his, nudging his bare toes. The scent of her skin curled around him, forcing him to combat his visceral reaction to her nearness. The tips of her breasts brushed across his chest, and it was all he could do not to strip out of the robe to feel her more fully.

Even through the thick terry cloth and her clothing, he could still feel her hardened nipples graze over him.

A pretty pink flush swept over her face, but he couldn't tell if it was embarrassment or arousal. The need to know dug at him, driving him to seek out what she was feeling.

A hint of anxiety. Curiosity. Excitement.

Desire.

It was a fluttering, fragile wisp of a feeling, but it grew brighter as she continued to stare.

Her gaze dropped to his mouth. She wet her lips with her tongue. The memory of their kiss flared bright in her mind, casting a blinding light over everything else.

Her fingers tightened on his skin. She lifted up on tiptoe, bringing her mouth closer to his.

Lust thrummed through him, but that was nothing new when Rory was near. He was unable to stop his cock from swelling, but that didn't mean he'd do anything about it. He was a patient man. He could wait as long as it took for his skittish little Rory to make up her mind.

A moment later, he felt her decision shift and solidify, taking on the rigid shape of determination.

Cain needed no further encouragement. Her decision was made. She wanted this. She wanted *him*.

He lowered his head, meeting her mouth halfway. The first contact drove the breath from his chest as searing sensations lanced through him, pinning him in place. Her lips parted on a sigh, and he wasted no time taking advantage of the opportunity to taste her again.

Fire and sugar. Sweet and hot. She went to his head, ridding him of the need to think. There was no space between them for worry or fear or guilt, only the heady swirl of complete and total rightness.

This was how things were supposed to be, and everything Theronai inside of him stood up and roared in victory.

Her mouth was fierce and demanding against his. Her

fingers slipped under the robe, parting it. Her hands went seeking beneath the fabric, shoving it open as she went.

He wore nothing beneath it but his need for her, which was rampant and obvious. His erection jutted up between them, throbbing in an effort to get closer. Her hands wrapped around him, shoving out a hiss of pleasure from between his teeth.

No woman had touched him like this for centuries, and even then he wasn't sure that any woman had ever touched him the way Rory did—like she knew just what he liked and how to give it to him.

There was no hesitation in her grip, no timidity. She stroked his length, spreading the slick heat that welled up from him.

Cain covered her hands to stop her before he came. She went still and stared at him with a witchy little grin.

The look in her eyes was a dare. A challenge. And Cain was more than up for it.

He tugged her hands away and pushed them behind her back where she could no longer reach him. With one hand, he held her wrists there, which thrust her breasts out at him. Her stiff little nipples taunted him, and he no longer had the willpower to hold himself back.

Cain drew circles over her breast with one finger while he watched her face. The link between them pulsed with impatience as he came closer and closer to her nipple. The supple fabric of her shirt molded to her skin, denying him the contact he craved. It was all he could do not to shove her shirt up to feel her naked skin fill his palm. Her pupils dilated, and she bared her teeth at him, tugging at his grip as if she could actually break free.

Of course if she really wanted to get away, all she had to do was use his power to shove him into a wall. The fact that she hadn't done that yet spurred him on and gave him great satisfaction. Though not nearly as much as he planned to give her.

His finger slid over her nipple and she sucked in a sharp breath. Her head fell back, putting the luceria on display. Dark, rich amethyst purples swam below the surface, swirling like they'd been stirred. Her pulse pounded in her throat, and a heavy flush spread over her skin.

The added heat heightened her scent, making it hard for Cain to think straight. He needed to slide inside her and fuse them together even tighter. The luceria wasn't enough. Even with that, she could walk away. He needed more—to bind them together in a way she'd never be able to break.

A child. That was a bond she wouldn't be able to deny. Even more, it was what Cain wanted. What he'd always wanted.

He stared down at her, knowing that if he went any farther, he wasn't going to care what *she* wanted. The gift she'd given him—the hope for survival and some kind of future—was too precious for him to throw away with trickery and betrayal.

His hand covered her breast. The cotton of her shirt was so hot he wondered how it didn't simply ignite. Her nipple stabbed eagerly against his palm. Her eyes were closed, and a look of abandon covered her face.

Opening his mouth and shoving out words was one of the hardest things he'd ever had to do. "We need to stop."

Her eyes opened, revealing confusion and a foggy layer of lust. "What? Why?"

Words were beyond him. Desire was too heavy in his veins, depriving him of the oxygen he needed to speak. So instead, he formed a single, coherent thought and sent it flying through their link.

He showed her the two of them together, naked and in the throes of climax. The image morphed to her, with her belly rounded with their child; then of her holding that baby in her arms, rocking it to sleep as it suckled at her breast.

Rory's body shook as the image dissipated. She stared

at him in silence for so long, he was sure that she had to be disgusted by his near loss of control. He was fertile once again, and with that hope came responsibilities. Responsibilities he'd failed to attend by finding some human means of birth control.

"Is that all that's stopping you?" she said, her voice faint and rough around the edges.

"It's enough, isn't it? Unless you want a—"

"No. I don't. But it's okay. I'm protected." With her words, she sent him her own set of thoughts—her fears that her monthly bleeding would bring the demons, her worry for her grandmother, her trip to the doctor to get pills that would stop her cycle.

She was on birth control.

"Good enough?" she asked. "Because I really don't want to stop."

His erection hadn't dissipated one iota. It didn't control him, but it certainly was trying.

He nodded, unable to find the breath to speak.

Rory gave him a smile that promised heaven. "Good."

Chapter 20

Rory was shaken. The things that Cain had shown her had thrown her for a loop. It wasn't just the idea of having a baby that freaked her out, it was how she'd felt when she'd watched those images play out inside her mind. Before, the concept was this distant, alien thing that would never happen to her—something she'd thought about only in the vaguest sense, the way she thought about traveling the world or going to the moon.

Now the idea seemed . . . possible.

Maybe it was just Cain's emotions rubbing off on her. She really didn't know. What she did know was that if she stopped and thought about it too long, she might forget the way things were. She was dangerous. People around her died. As tempting as the idea of having a child one day might be, it wasn't in the cards.

Right now, all she needed to know was that Cain was ready and willing to drive away all of the unsettling thoughts that came to haunt her.

The man had a way of making her forget to think.

Before his brain started working again, finding some impossible reason for them to stop, she decided to take things into her own hands.

Rory stepped out of his grip and stripped off her shirt. She dropped it on the kitchen floor and started walking as she undid her bra. She felt him behind her as she hit the first step. His imposing bulk had its own gravitational pull on her. The only reason she was able to walk away now was because she knew he would follow.

Her bra landed on the banister. She caught a fleeting sight of herself through his eyes—of her bare back and swaying hips as she walked away.

One of her shoes tumbled down the steps. The other hit the bedroom door as she kicked it off. By the time she reached the bed, her jeans were open and on their way down her thighs.

Cain grabbed her waist from behind. His hands were hot on her skin, his fingers clenching as he pulled her back against his body. The hard ridge of his erection pulsed against her bare skin, making her groan with need. He pinned her in place with an arm across her hips while his hand slid over her belly, her ribs, and finally he cupped her breast. She looked down, enthralled by the sight of his huge hand covering her. As she watched, he slid his fingers over her skin until just the bare tips were stroking and plucking at her nipple.

A jolt of pleasure arced from his fingers to her center. She felt a rush of heat between her thighs, felt herself grow wet.

Cain's chest vibrated with a low growl of approval. His cock jerked toward her, throbbing in time with his heart.

Her thighs were trapped together by her jeans. Cain slipped a single finger along her slick folds, barely brushing her clit as he gently pinched her nipple.

A wash of tingling electric sensations shot through her, bouncing around along her insides until she was sure she had to be glowing from within. Her head was too heavy to support. She let it fall back against his shoulder, simply enjoying the way he learned her body.

His lips found her throat. He kissed her, his mouth hot and open, his tongue swirling over her skin in a way that made her shiver in reaction.

Rory wanted to touch him, too, so she reached back and gripped his head in her hands. It wasn't enough. She needed to kiss him, too, and watch his face so she could learn how to please him the way he pleased her.

She found the strength to turn in his grasp, nearly falling over as her jeans tripped her up. The bed was right behind her now, so she sat down to get rid of the offending garment, only to be completely waylaid by the sight of his glorious cock thrusting out at her.

Her mouth watered. She reached for him, gripping him in both hands. Hot, velvet skin sucked her in, tempting her beyond reason. His scent curled around her, making her dizzy. She closed her eyes and took the tip of his erection in her mouth.

His body clenched and he let out a hiss of pleasure. His taste went to her head. She needed more—all he had to give.

Cain's fingers cradled her head. Rory felt his self-control tremble through him, saw his abdomen clench as his fingers tightened against her scalp. He was close to losing control. She wasn't sure how she knew, but the idea gave her a heady rush of power, and a naughty little jolt of satisfaction.

She wanted to make him go wild—to drive him out of his mind with pleasure. Before she could, her mind blazed with a vivid image of her laid out on the bed, her body completely open as he worked the tip of his thick cock inside of her. The sight was so erotic, so compelling, she trembled with need.

Cain had done that to her. She felt his presence hovering in her mind, gauging her pleasure, feeding her his. She wasn't sure how he'd done it, but there was no room in her head to study the technique right now. Thought was beyond her. Only feelings were strong enough to make it through the lust-filled maze of her mind.

He lifted her away from his body and laid her back on

the bed. His dark green gaze dared her to fight him—to stop him from taking what he wanted.

He pulled her jeans off her legs, and gripped her ankles in his hands as he came over her. His wide body blocked out the sight of everything else. He'd shed his robe, leaving himself gloriously naked. She drank in the sight of smooth skin layered over dense muscles. The tree along his chest swayed, its branches now fuzzy and green with new leaves. The roots of the tree spread down toward his groin and over his left hip.

Before their time was over, she was going to trace every one of those roots and branches with her tongue.

Cain kissed her calf, the inside of her knee, spreading her legs wide as he eased his body between them. The hot trail left by his tongue cooled as he worked his way toward her pussy. Every inch of her skin tingled in anticipation as his mouth settled over her, kissing her.

She arched off the bed, making a desperate, mewling sound she never would have thought herself capable of making. It vibrated with pleasure and need, stringing her tighter as Cain simply did as he pleased. He made her feel what he wanted her to feel, sucking and licking until she was no longer in control of her own reactions.

A tiny spark of heat leapt from his tongue, and Rory's whole world went up in a blinding flash of light and sensation. The climax exploded from her core, shoving the air from her lungs and all rational thought from her mind. She was suspended in a wave of pleasure, held in place by Cain's strong hands.

As the cataclysm eased, as she struggled to catch her breath, Cain began working a single finger into her body. As sensitive as she was, as slick as she was, the penetration was nearly too much to stand. She tilted his head up to get his attention so she could tell him to slow down, but the look on his face made the words dry up and blow away.

His skin was dark with lust. Sweat lined his brow. His mouth was wet. Determination ruled his features.

"Too much," she managed to get out between gasps for air.

"If you can't take my fingers, you'll never be able to take my cock. You do want that, don't you?"

Oh, yeah. She'd never wanted anything more in her life. Thankfully, she didn't have to say the words. He seemed to understand her silence.

Cain gave her a dark grin. "Good. Now lie back and relax."

Relaxing was out of the question, but his finger moved inside of her, sliding deeper, and she no longer needed a breather. A trickle of desire flowed into her, sharpening her own until it clawed at her for more.

He'd done that to her—fed her some of his lust—and she was right back to where she'd been a few minutes ago, clamoring with the need to come.

Rory watched as his dark head lowered once more and his mouth worked magic between her thighs. As he eased a second finger inside of her, the stinging stretch pulled her tighter. All it took was one gentle suckling kiss against her clit and she flew to pieces.

The force of her orgasm left her blind, but she couldn't find the space to care. Tears slid along her temples, and her voice shimmered in a breathy scream she couldn't keep contained. As each searing wave slammed into her, Cain pushed her higher, using his lips and tongue and fingers to draw out her pleasure until she was boneless and limp.

His satisfaction pulsed through their link. Even as wrung out as she was, his own sharp need still had the power to make her need more, demand more.

Her pussy was still fluttering from her orgasm when she felt the blunt tip of his cock press against her opening.

She opened her eyes, and saw his body blocking out all else. There was the faintest hint of apology in his eyes—something she didn't understand. Instinctively, she went searching for the explanation.

As she glided through their link, she hit a wall of lust so hot and jagged, she was sure it would tear her apart. Instantly, the edges blunted, as he shielded her from his raging need, but it was too late for that. His need was hers now, and her body responded with an answering rush of arousal.

New, prickling sensations spread out over her skin as her body stretched to accept him. It was too much, and yet not enough. She wasn't sure she'd ever get enough of a man like him.

Before that thought could douse her enjoyment, she shoved it away and pulled him closer.

The damp heat of his skin against hers sang through her. The feel of his muscles shifting, vibrating as he restrained himself, struck some kind of chord deep inside. As much as he wanted her—as much as he was dying to bury himself within her body—he still held back, moving slow and careful so he wouldn't hurt her.

As wet as she was, she didn't think that was going to happen. Her body was clamoring to be filled, eager to feel every inch of him buried within her. Nothing he'd done had caused her pain. Her only discomfort came from feeling how desperately he fought himself.

Rory wanted him to enjoy this as much as she did.

With that thought in mind, she yanked a surge of strength into herself and pulled his hips toward her. His erection thrust deep. The intense stretch, along with his shocked growl of pleasure, was enough to toss her into a sudden, choppy climax. She bounced around, trapped inside pure sensation as her body fragmented.

When she finally settled enough to make sense of the world, she found that Cain had gathered her wrists in his hand and pinned them above her head. He balanced over her, his muscles bulging as he held himself up.

His jaw was clenched tight. The cords in his neck stood out. He didn't move.

She felt his heartbeat inside her—the throbbing, thick

heat of his cock wedged deep within. Her body was a jumbled mess of feelings and emotions too intense and heavy for her to examine. There was a faint wisp of anger flickering out of him, but she couldn't tell if it was aimed at her for taking what she wanted, or at himself for letting her.

"Are you hurt?" he asked, the gravelly sound of his voice vibrating her nipples deliciously.

"I don't get off on pain."

"Good. Because I could never hurt you—not even if you begged for it."

"Are you going to make me beg now?"

"No. Whatever you want, it's yours."

"I want you to stop holding back. I'm not fragile. I won't break. I want the real you—all of you."

Something in his expression shifted, going darker. The tension she'd seen in him before seemed to drain away. A small, wicked smile tugged at his mouth. "Then open up, Rory. I'm going to give you everything."

She wasn't sure what he'd meant until she felt the luceria vibrate around her throat. An instant later, a flood of images and sensations flowed into her, rocking her down to her soul. She saw the two of them together, naked and locked together in positions she hadn't even imagined. She felt his heated lust lash across her like plumes of fire, leaving every inch of her skin glowing and flushed. His fantasies and hopes and dreams all funneled into her, filling her with the need to see each one of them come true.

She wasn't just with him, she existed inside of him, their two minds woven together in a way she could hardly believe possible, even as she felt it.

And then he started to move. His cock slid out of her, leaving a hollow ache behind. She opened her mouth to scream at him to come back, but there was no need. He was already surging forward again, giving her exactly what she needed, as if he'd felt her need as keenly as she had his.

Maybe he had. She wasn't sure. She didn't care. The physical sensations, piled onto the things he did to her mind, were almost too much to stand. She no longer had any control over her actions. Her hands went where they wanted. Her mouth sought out his, desperate for his taste. Her hips arched up to accept him into her body, over and over again.

This was more than sex. It was the fusion of two people, two souls. More meaningful than the physical pleasure it brought, she felt the experience change her—altering her on a fundamental level in a way she'd never be able to undo.

But with ecstasy like this, she couldn't bring herself to care.

Cain drove her higher, both with his touch as well as with his thoughts. He hid nothing from her, forcing her to feel everything he did, down to the coiling buildup of his impending orgasm. Rory's body responded in kind, answering to his call, bulging with her own growing pressure.

His mouth ate at hers, drinking in her breathless cries. She would have been embarrassed by how loud she was being had she not felt how much it turned Cain on. He liked her loss of control, the proof of her enjoyment. But it wasn't enough. He wanted all of her. Forever.

And right now, tied to him like this, glowing with so much glorious sensation she could barely contain it, she wanted that, too. Reality didn't matter in this space. No bad things could reach her here. She knew there was some reason why forever should bother her, but she couldn't remember what it was. If he wanted this forever, she was more than happy to give it to him.

His presence in her mind seemed to swell and brighten. She felt a change come over him—a kind of feral intensity that hadn't been there before. His gliding pace began to speed, drawing her attention back to her body.

Pleasure rained over her, pulsed through her. Cain

surrounded her with his heat and strength, driving her higher with every slick thrust. Words spilled from his mouth into hers. She couldn't understand them. She didn't even care that she couldn't. The pressure inside of her was too much now. She was never going to survive its release.

He gathered her close, curled around her body and sent a tingling surge of sensation tumbling out of his skin. Wherever they touched, her nerve endings came alive, sending crazy, rioting signals up her spine.

It was too much. She couldn't hold it all. A hard, ferocious climax ripped out of her in a soundless scream. Cain's cock plunged deep and he came, rocking in shallow, urgent thrusts as his semen filled her. Each pulse of heat spilling into her drove her higher until she could no longer breathe.

Rory let go of everything. It was the only way to survive the intensity of this storm. She let it buffet her about, accepting what came, too weak to fight anything he made her feel.

Slowly, her abdomen relaxed enough for her to find a shallow breath. The blotchy spots in her eyes shrank, allowing her to see Cain.

He was draped over her, limp and spent. He covered her completely, like a living blanket, but so much hotter. Sweat shone on his body, making his golden skin glow.

She kissed his shoulder, licking the salt from his skin. His scent, his taste, they were part of her now—the knowledge buried so deep she was sure she would never forget.

They were still joined—their bodies, their minds. Even now, exhausted and spent, Cain was still with her, giving her what she'd asked of him. Gentle, softer images of them together overcame the more fiery, passionate ones. She saw them holding each other, laughing.

He'd already shown her what a bonded pair of Theronai could do—how they could fight and hold back the demons. But now he showed her a different side. Years spent growing closer. Multiple lifetimes to joke and play. Yes, their lives were dangerous, but that wasn't all they had. There was a closeness there that Rory had never considered—a familiarity forged from centuries of partnership.

As she let him feed these images into her, a deep yearning began to take shape. She wanted this. She wanted this closeness, this unity. Which only made reality that much harder to face.

People around her died. Cain would, too, unless she beat him to it. Knowing that others could have what he'd just showed her only made real life that much more stark and bleak by comparison.

The longer she stayed with him, the easier it was going to be to forget the way things really were—the promise she'd made after Nana had bled out. Rory's life was not destined to be like the pretty fairy tales he showed her. No matter how much either of them might wish otherwise.

Her life was already shaped by her actions, by who and what she was. She had no intention of abandoning Cain to die, but he had to find someone else—someone brave enough to take risks and earn the happily ever after he'd shown her. She wasn't strong enough to play such a high-stakes game of chance.

Cain rolled aside, frustration making his movements jerky. "You're going to run away now, aren't you?"

"I'm just going to the bathroom."

"To hide from me."

He wasn't supposed to know that part. It made her feel like a coward, which she hated.

She got up and grabbed the bathrobe from where he'd dropped it on the floor. "I need a little space, Cain. That was too . . . intense."

"You loved it. You can't lie to me. I was there, *inside* you."

"Believe me. I remember."

He sat up as she slipped the robe over her body. Everything about him was so appealing. His size, his looks. His soul. She wanted to wrap herself up in him and hold him close—let him keep all of life's bullshit away.

But that wasn't the way things worked. She was a big girl who knew the score. She couldn't afford for sex to be anything more than just that.

A mocking, snarky laugh welled up from her gut, but she clamped her lips shut to hold it in. That had been a hell of a lot more than sex.

A fact that Rory was now going to ignore.

Cain thought he'd almost had her. He'd let her have all of him, as she'd asked, holding back nothing. He'd bared himself to her, body and soul.

And she'd walked away.

He hadn't thought that anything could have hurt as much as losing Sibyl, but he'd been wrong. Rory's rejection was just as bad—reminding him of all the reasons why he'd been a fool for letting her get that close.

The damage was done now. He couldn't turn back time. He refused to make her forget. She'd made up her mind, and he was going to have to find a way to accept it.

The only thing he could think to do now was find the demon that Ronan had subdued and kill it so that there was no chance of it ever controlling her actions again.

At least that was something real and solid—a purpose he could focus on so that he didn't have to think about what had just happened.

The shower turned on behind the closed door. She was in there right now, washing away all traces of him from her skin. The notion bothered him more than it should have. Or maybe it was his own need to cling to the scent she'd left on him that made him feel that way. Their partnership was far too lopsided. She had all the control, all the power. All he could do was flounder in the aftermath of her choices.

He couldn't change her vow. He refused to force her to stay with him. Ronan's chat with her had informed her that she didn't even need to be close to him for him to survive. If she walked away, no guilt necessary.

Fuck that.

Cain was no doormat. He was tired of watching the people he cared about walk away. He was a fighter by nature, and if his survival meant he had to fight a little dirty, then so be it. Rory held his future in her hands, and he'd be damned if he'd let her crush it.

One way or another, he was going to find a way to get through that pink head of hers.

Chapter 21

Ronan waited until the sun was high before he dared reach out for the Synestryn lord who had stolen his blood. The connection between them was weak now, as was the demon that had forged it. Like Ronan, its powers dwindled during the day, sapping its strength.

Carefully and slowly, he slipped along the thread of blood and power that bound them, seeping into the demon's mind by the tiniest drops. This contact was not about control, or about trying to rid Ronan's mind of the foul presence that infected him. He didn't make so much as a ripple as he passed, seeking out information only.

The demon's sleep shifted as it began to wake. Ronan held still, letting vile thoughts and memories flow around him like sewage. As each one touched him, he let it seep in, granting him information.

The pain this creature had caused was a fetid, rotting cancer in Ronan's mind. He didn't dare fight it, but not judging the evil acts was much, much harder. Each moment of revulsion, each second of accusation forced the demon into wakefulness.

There was little time left—only seconds before the beast woke and realized what Ronan was doing. Before it was too late and the demon snagged him and sucked him in, Ronan drifted back out of the festering decay of the creature's thoughts and back into the cool, dark confines of his own mind.

The familiar space comforted him. It helped wash away the repulsive horror of what he'd seen.

Ronan lay still in the blackness of the basement, slowly sifting through the information that he'd gathered. Most of it was useless sludge that he discarded before it could take root and grow. But there were details that he'd collected—things that had been at the forefront of the demon's thoughts.

Of Raygh's thoughts.

This demon had a name. It fancied itself as some kind of king. As powerful as it was, Ronan was certain that lesser demons were quick to obey.

Like the Handlers that Raygh had sent. They were powerful creatures in their own right, but had chosen to answer to Raygh for some reason Ronan could not fathom.

That was interesting, but not nearly as important as the other information that Ronan had learned.

Raygh had two sons. Both of them had been killed, and now he was seeking out all of those who had been present at the time of his sons' deaths. That's what those barb-tailed creatures were about. They were gathering blood, giving Raygh a way to track his prey and control them.

And thanks to Ronan's time in the festering slime of the demon's mind, he knew exactly who Raygh was going after. Ronan had smelled them all before—both human and Sentinel.

Rory and Cain were among them, as well as Iain, Jackie, Hope, Logan, Drake, Helen, the human child Autumn, and Beth—the woman Ronan had pulled from a cave a few months ago. All of them needed to be warned, and those who were tucked safely behind the walls of Dabyr needed to remain there.

Ronan tried to lift his hand to pull his phone from his pocket, but he was too weak. In a few hours, when the sun lowered, he would be able to warn the others, but until then, his sole job was to maintain the barrier that he'd erected in his own mind—similar to the one he'd designed for Rory, but not nearly as strong. She had no idea what she was facing. Ronan did. There was only so much power he could expend, and his options were one weaker shield or two weak ones.

The choice had been simple. The demon and he were a matched set. Both of them were stronger by night, both of them lived on blood. The only difference was, Ronan was careful of his food, while Raygh cared little for those from which he fed. They were vessels. Empty husks to be tossed aside when he was finished with them.

That lack of hunger made Raygh stronger, but Ronan had something else on his side. Years of needing that which he could not have had given him an iron will. He controlled himself, and that was why, no matter how well fed the demon was, it would never get past Ronan's defenses.

He was no thing's puppet.

By the time Rory got out of the shower, Cain was dressed and waiting for her, wearing a do-not-fuck-with-me look on his face.

She eyed his jacket and the keys dangling from his thick fingers. "I guess we're leaving?"

"I'm leaving. You stay here with Ronan. You'll be safe here."

"Safe? Are you kidding me?"

"As safe as you'll be anywhere. We can't go to Dabyr with that demon in your head, which means I need to go kill it."

"Just like that. Do you even know where it is?"

"Nope. But it's got to be close to where you lost it. The more distance between you and it, the harder it would be for it to control you."

She didn't want him to go. She wanted someone else

to go and kill the bad guy. Not Cain. She wasn't ready to lose him—especially not when he was risking his life for her. "This is insane. You can't just go out there alone and hunt for demons."

"Why not? I do it all the time. Just another day at the office."

"Yeah, if your office is filled with poisonous teeth and claws."

He shoved the keys in his pocket and zipped up his jacket. "I should have left you a note. Just pretend that's what I did."

He started to walk away, but she grabbed his arm. "Really? That's how it's going to be?"

"I have no idea what you're talking about."

"Yes, you do. You're mad at me, so you're going to punish me by making me worry."

His brows drew together, and she swore she felt his arm vibrate with anger under the leather. "You've seen me, Rory. All the way through. You know me. Do you really think I'm that petty?"

"I wouldn't have thought so until right now, seeing you ready to go."

His eye twitched. "I could have left without saying good-bye."

"Wouldn't be the first time that's happened to me. I'm a big girl. I can deal." She pretended like it didn't hurt that he was going to walk away. She didn't want to give him the satisfaction of knowing that he'd hit the mark.

Rory turned her back and went to pick up her clothes. He'd gathered them from where she'd tossed them through the house and laid them on the bed. It was a thoughtful thing for a man to do when he was otherwise trying to hurt her.

"I wasn't trying to hurt you," he said, his voice dipping low.

She tugged at the luceria, cursing its existence. "Stupid fucking necklace."

"Would you rather I go and find the person who can make it fall from your throat?" he asked.

Rory sagged onto the bed, gripping her clothes against her chest. There was too much going on inside of her—too many emotions, too much stress. "What I want hardly seems to matter."

He stepped closer, his big, booted feet coming into view. "It matters to me."

"Does it?" She tipped her head back to look him in the eye. "You keep pushing me to be like those women in your memories, but I'm not like them."

"I know that now. I won't make that same mistake again."

"So where does that leave me? I still have a demon trapped in my brain, and a magical necklace trapped around my throat. If I take it off, you die."

"Eventually. The colors in the luceria have not yet solidified. We still have time."

"You forget that you threw yourself wide open to me. I know how slim the chances are that you'll find another woman compatible with your power before your soul dies. I'm not the kind of person who can walk away from that."

"I don't want or need your pity."

Her voice lifted in frustration. "It's not pity. It's human fucking decency."

"You're not human." His face was impassive. He'd blocked off the link between them, giving her no idea how he felt.

Until now, she hadn't realized just how easily she'd come to accept that connection to him as a kind of additional sense, something she took for granted, like her sight. Now that the connection was gone, she felt . . . lonely.

"You know what I mean," she said.

"Apparently not. You're the one who wants to walk away from our partnership. You asked for space, and now that I'm trying to give it to you, you're angry. Just tell me what you want me to do."

She had no answers. The things she wanted were not things he could give her. She wanted guarantees—a promise that he wouldn't die and leave her floundering the way she had when Mom had died, when Nana had died. She couldn't go through that again.

But she couldn't stand to let him walk away either, knowing that he would be so much safer with her at his side—with her power there to take out anything that tried to hurt him. She wasn't very strong yet, but she was stronger now than she had been a few hours ago. The time she'd spent in his arms had somehow widened their connection, allowing the space for more energy to flow through. She could feel it humming there, churning with anticipation for her to make use of it.

Strength hovered at her fingertips, making her crave it. She was tired of being a victim, tired of being scared to get so much as a paper cut. Cain made her stronger and gave her a fighting chance. She was pretty sure that was the best deal she was going to get in this lifetime.

"Take me with you," she said. "Show me how to fight."

He stared at her for a long time, and she wished he would let her take a peek behind the curtain, just for a second. She didn't like being on the outside like this—like everyone else—alone and wondering what was going on in his head.

Finally, without any hint of how he felt, he said, "Get dressed. I won't wait long."

Chapter 22

Cain knew that he was manipulating Rory, and that it was wrong, but he couldn't make himself stop. He knew how much she hated feeling weak. Her strength and independence meant everything to her, and yet here he was, tempting her with one in order to rob her of the other.

He tried to assuage his guilt by telling himself that it was his duty to keep fighting, and he could only continue to do so if Rory stayed at his side. But while factually correct, his efforts to tie her to him were still a type of deception. And if he let down his guard and allowed her to peer into his thoughts, she would see it, glaring with guilt.

So he did the only thing he could think to do: he kept his mind closed to her and took her outside, in the field behind the Gerai house.

"What are we doing?" she asked.

"You said you wanted to learn how to fight."

"I do, but I need a real fight—nothing huge or overwhelming, but more than an evil clump of weeds."

"You really think I'm going to purposefully drag you into battle when you've barely learned anything? It's bad enough that you were subjected to it accidentally."

"I'll learn on the fly. I think fast on my feet. I never

would have survived two days locked in a basement full of monsters if that weren't the case."

He couldn't stop the growl that emanated from his chest at the picture she painted.

"It's no big deal. Not my idea of a primo vacation spot or anything, but let's just say that it proved to me that I'm at my best when the shit hits the fan."

"I'd rather not prove your theory wrong the hard way."

She let out a weary sigh. "So you're not taking me to really fight. I'm stuck with defeating evil weeds?"

"For now. When I'm sure you're ready, then we'll move up the food chain. Maybe defeat a malevolent bush."

"And just hope that the demon-in-the-box stays put." She propped her hand on her hip, bringing his attention to the deep curve of her waist.

Cain knew just how that skin felt under his hand, against his tongue. His mouth watered with the memory, making him wish he could march her back up to bed and keep her there for a year or two.

"I will kill the demon, but you're not ready for that kind of fight. Not yet."

"And what if we run out of time?"

"Then I will subdue you."

"Before I managed to kill you first with my magical firepower?"

He shrugged, refusing to let her see how much he hated letting that creature linger within her. "If you kill me, you'll have no more power. You'll be as much of a threat as any normal human woman would be."

"Clearly, you've never heard of PMS or you'd be more afraid."

"I'm not taking you into combat until you prove you're ready."

"Fine. Test me."

Before she had time to sense what he was doing, Cain

drew his sword and sent it swinging toward her head. He had no intention of hurting her, but she wouldn't know that. Just before he slowed the blow, a hot blue dome of light spilled down over her body. His sword skittered off the shield, throwing him off balance.

"Good."

She grinned, and her dark eyes twinkled with excitement. "Easy. Try again."

He kicked his leg out, sweeping her ankles. She began to fall, but it turned into a gravity-defying spin that landed her on her feet a few yards away.

Cain nodded his approval. "Your self-defense is decent, but there's only so much I can do to you without risking damage. What I really need to know is how much firepower you have."

"Give me something to destroy. A target—any target."

He pointed toward the eastern edge of the clearing to where a dead tree leaned precariously to one side. "There. That tree."

She pushed her chin in the air and started walking toward it. Cain grabbed her arm.

"No. From here."

Her confident posture wobbled, but her jaw took on a defiant stance. "If I do it, will you take me with you to go hunt the demon?"

"Depends."

"On?"

"Whether or not you're still standing. You're no good in a fight if I have to carry you."

She pulled her arm away and gave him a hard stare. "No one has needed to carry me since I was a child. At least not until the night I met you."

"Are you saying I made you weak?" Cain sent a bubble of energy through the luceria, reminding her that without him, she would have no power.

She shivered, but hid it quickly. Once again her jaw

was tight with defiance, forcing her words through gritted teeth. "I'm not weak."

"Prove it."

He felt a sucking rush of power flow out of him with so much force it shook his frame. As the transfer occurred, a flicker of her emotions appeared, churning just beyond reach. She was furious that he doubted her. Terrified that she would fail. Determined to prove her strength.

A ragged scream poured from her mouth. Her fingers extended toward the tree as if she were throwing something at it. A second later, a whoosh of flames engulfed the trunk, turning it to ash within seconds.

Rory fell to her knees. Cain panicked and reached for her, but she jerked away. "Don't."

She panted there on the cold ground, holding herself up with her hands. Her body swayed, and it was all he could do not to reach out and steady her.

Slowly, she pushed herself to her feet. She stumbled to the side, but caught her balance before he was forced to grab her.

Her feet were braced apart. Her skin was ghostly pale. Both of her hands burned bright red with smudges of soot at the tips. She glared at him, daring him to make the wrong move.

"There," she said. "Now let's go."

Cain hated himself for what he was about to do, but if she refused to acknowledge her limits, then it was his duty to force her to hit them. Hard.

"Sure," he said. "Let's get in the car."

He started walking, and it took every bit of willpower he possessed not to turn around and help. He was halfway back to the house when he heard her hit the ground.

Cain stopped. He knew he should keep walking and prove to her that she wasn't as tough as she thought, but he couldn't leave her lying there or force her to crawl like some kind of beast. She needed him, and whether or not she accepted that fact, it was still a fact. Just like he needed her.

He turned and saw her trying to regain her feet. Her pink hair whipped around her face with the wind, giving him fleeting glimpses of her pained defeat.

He stopped in front of her. She stared at his boots, her arms shaking so hard he wasn't sure how she held herself up. She wouldn't lift her gaze any higher, as if she was embarrassed.

Cain crouched by her side, and tucked her hair behind her ear to keep it out of her eyes. Tears glittered there but did not fall—apparently held back by sheer will. Her bottom lip was wedged between her teeth so tightly he feared she'd draw blood.

He said nothing as he waited there, warring with himself over whether or not to touch her. The next move was hers, and it was not one he could make for her.

"Fire is hard," she finally said.

"Looks like."

"I really suck at this, don't I?"

"Is that what you think?"

"I saw those women in your memories. I saw what they can do. They could go all day and hardly break a sweat. I burn down one dead tree and I'm about to fall over."

"So what do you want to do now?"

"You think I should quit, don't you?" Her voice was as cold and biting as the wind. "You think I should just sit around and wait for the big, manly men to save me."

"You know me. You've been inside my thoughts. Is that really what you think I think?"

Her gaze met his, and he saw fear lurking there. And shame. "No," she admitted. "I saw the things you want from me."

"And?"

"They're not the kind of things a weakling princess in need of a rescue would do."

"Which brings us back to my previous question. What do you want to do now?"

She bared her teeth at him, and damn if it didn't turn him on, just a little. "I want to be strong enough to fight, Cain. I want to get up off this freezing fucking ground and blow the hell out of some demons."

He stood. "So get up."

"Don't you think I would if I was able?"

"You are able. You just can't do it alone. Ask for my help."

"Fuck you."

He shrugged, and pulled a muscle trying to make it look nonchalant when every instinct inside of him was screaming for him to act. He didn't like her down there, looking weak and helpless. He knew she had to be cold, and that grated against every instinct he had to care for her well-being. But this was important. If she refused to lean on him, it would get her killed.

His voice was as rough as frozen gravel. "Fine. Stay there."

"You're really going to make me ask?"

"I've helped you before without you having to ask, but I need to know if you're even capable of asking."

"I don't need you," she growled. "I don't need anyone."

He ached for her and everything she'd lost. His own losses had made him angry as well, but he hadn't given up on others. Not like she had. Rory was so alone in this world—so alone she couldn't even see any other way to be.

"Everyone needs someone. There's no shame in that," he told her.

"Says the man standing on his own two feet."

"Only because of your quick thinking back at your house. If those demons hadn't had your shield to slow them down, we'd all be dead."

"Or worse," she said, shivering in revulsion.

"Or worse," he agreed.

"So you owe me?"

"If you want to keep score."

She was quiet for a moment, and when she spoke, her voice was so faint the wind nearly stole it from him. "I'm cashing in, then. Help me up."

It wasn't what he was hoping for, but at least he was getting her off the cold ground. That alone was a huge relief.

Cain pulled her to her feet. Her whole body was trembling visibly. She wasn't going to be able to stand, but he didn't dare grate against her independence by picking her up. Instead, he eased her body against his, propping her up while he slid his arm around her body and cupped the back of her neck.

The two parts of the luceria connected with a spark. It cascaded through him, leaving a warm path as it went. He pushed a trickle of power into her, replenishing her strength. The fix was temporary, and he didn't dare go so far as to make her feel completely recovered for fear of her pushing herself, but for now, it was enough that she could walk.

Rory stared up at him, her dark eyes searching his face for something he wished he understood. He wanted her to be happy, to fit into their world. He wanted her to accept him as her own before their time together was over.

He'd come a long way since the night he'd met her, when he was still angry at the world for stealing from him—stealing Sibyl and Jackie, killing Gilda and Angus. His pain had heightened his anger, blinding him to anything resembling a future.

But he could see one now. And the thought of losing it before he'd ever really touched it scared the hell out of him.

Rory gave him hope—the most powerful sustenance known to man—but she also had the ability to crush that hope with as little as a few careless words. As much as Cain wanted to believe, he was afraid. He'd already lost so much. If he let himself fall for her, the risks were too high.

Still, every time he touched her, every time he looked into her eyes, he saw his future stretching out before him, like some brilliant, golden pathway. And then in the next second it was gone—a mere trick of the eyes.

Her fingers curled against his arms as her weight shifted to her own feet. She no longer needed him to stand, but she hadn't pulled away. She stared at his mouth, and her lips parted as if remembering his kiss.

Just like that, he needed to kiss her again. The desire hit him from out of nowhere, making him shake with the force of the compulsion.

He realized in that moment that he'd never get enough of her. It didn't matter that he'd bedded her less than an hour ago. It didn't matter that she refused to depend on him, insulting his ability to do his job. It didn't even matter that she had the power to end his life. He was drawn to her in a way that defied reason and went all the way into madness. She was part of him now—in his blood. Perhaps if he'd abstained he could have gone on with his life never knowing what he'd be missing. But that option was long gone, leaving only his need to get as close to her as possible.

She didn't want that. The kind of connection he craved terrified her. It made her dependent on him—something he was certain she would never choose to be.

He didn't want to scare her or force her to change who she was simply because it was what *he* wanted. If his dreams hurt her, then how could he continue to want them?

He couldn't. He wouldn't. His only choice was to either change what he wanted, or let her go. And he couldn't let her go.

So rather than forcing her to accept his unwanted advances, he kept the mental link between them tightly closed as he bent to kiss her. No fleeting thoughts of what he wanted from her would leak through. No secret desires would be put on display for her to see and be made uncomfortable. He would hide that part of himself from her, giving her only so much as she asked for. And in doing so, he would also protect the small kernel of himself that remained untouched by her.

That was what was keeping the colors in the luceria fluid. He hadn't given himself to her completely. And so long as he held firm in that, he could go on fighting again once she found her blasted savior.

Rory's lips were tentative against his. Her fingers tightened on his leather jacket, and she went up on tiptoe to meet him, but she was holding back, too.

The need to reach inside her thoughts and find the cause of her hesitation was nearly overwhelming. Only centuries of practicing self-control allowed him to stay true to his decision.

Heat built between their bodies. Sparks of tingling power tumbled out of him to caress her skin wherever they touched. He couldn't stop that from happening, any more than he could stop the throbbing swell of his cock.

Rory felt it, too. Her hips did this delightful little swivel, grinding against him in a way that sucked the air from his lungs. She opened her mouth on a sweet moan of approval, and Cain took advantage of the opportunity to deepen their kiss.

She tasted like hot, spun sugar and wild temptation. He drank her in, reveling in the scent of her skin and the heat sliding out of her. She became pliant in his arms, writhing like flames and burning away his good intentions.

His limbs resonated with eager need. He felt her push against his thoughts, seeking entrance, but held firm. If he let down his guard, he knew he'd be lost. Having her inside of him like that was too intoxicating. It made him lose his head.

Her mouth quested down his neck, her tongue playing along the skin where the luceria used to sit. Searing tendrils of raw sensation jolted through him, falling in an erotic jumble at the base of his spine. She slipped her fingers under his jacket and shirt, until her bare hands were splayed over his heart. His lifemark swayed in response to her touch. His whole body clenched from a punch of lust.

Against his will, his hips surged toward her. He felt a small tug of power leave him, and a second later, she bared her teeth and ripped his shirt open down the front.

Cain almost grinned at her ferocity, but his lips were too tightly twisted with desire. He stood there, watching her mouth move over his chest, not even daring to breathe for fear she'd stop. The branches of his lifemark whipped around wildly, shocking him with the sight. But not even that riotous display could compete with that sweet, pink head moving down his body with clear intent.

If he let her go any farther, she'd be on the cold ground again, and that was not something he could stand.

"Inside," he grated out, proud that he was able to form that single, coherent word.

She looked up at him, her dark eyes huge with desire. Her mouth was shiny and wet, swollen and tempting as sin. Her skin was flushed a dark pink. "No. Here. Now."

She went for his belt, and there was nothing he could have done to stop her. His hands barely functioned. His whole body was sputtering with the few gasps of air he'd given it.

The leather tongue of his belt flipped free of the buckle. The weight of his sword tugged at it. His cock bulged shamelessly at his fly, twitching with the need to get closer to her.

Rory rubbed him through the denim before opening

his zipper. The metallic hiss was lost on the wind. She tugged down the fabric, baring him to the chill air. A drop of wetness spilled from the tip of his erection, completely beyond his control. She saw it and held his gaze while she licked it away.

Cain nearly came just watching her. He clamped down on the urge, every muscle in his body trembling from the effort. Her hot mouth closed over him, her dark eyes daring him to stop her.

She was such a challenge. A delightful, sinfully sexy challenge. One he was going to meet head-on. If he let her get the upper hand, his fiery Rory would overwhelm and destroy him without even trying. He had to maintain some level of control, because the only alternative was to give himself away completely.

That he would not do.

Cain lifted her up from her crouch and kissed her. It wasn't soft and gentle. It was a battle for conquest and air. He nipped at her lips, sucked the bottom one into his mouth to hold her attention. His hands snuck under her shirt to cup the full weight of her breasts. She groaned into his mouth and arched against his hands, wordlessly asking for more.

Continuing on was the last thing he should have done, and yet he was driven by her irresistible force to give her what she wanted.

She shed her jacket, and a moment later, her shirt flew away on the wind. He was sure she had to be cold, but all that greeted him was hot, flushed skin. Her nipples were tight little buds, thrusting upward in silent invitation.

Cain bent down to warm her with his mouth, drawing a high cry of pleasure from her lips. Everywhere he touched was soft, hot, supple. Even the sting of her fingernails digging into his scalp to hold his head in place was its own kind of gentle pain. It sent electric streamers of need coursing through him, pounding at him to strip her naked and plunge inside her sweet depths.

His fingers went for her waistband, only to find that she'd done the job herself. Her jeans were gaping open, her hand inside her panties, stroking herself. A momentary spike of jealousy made him growl. *He* wanted to be the one to please her. He wanted *his* fingers sliding in her pussy and over her clit, making her breath catch in needy gasps.

As selfish as that desire was, he couldn't deny it. Not now when his blood was scorching his veins in hard pulses that roared in his ears. Later he'd get a grip on his selfish urges, but right now, it was all he could do not to throw her on the frigid ground and shove himself inside of her.

Cain pulled her clinging jeans down her thighs. She bent over to help him, their fingers tangling together in haste. As soon as she was bare, his whole body stalled out as he stared at her.

Sunlight clung to her skin, draping it with golden highlights. The blond curls covering her sex were darker where her arousal had dampened them. He knew what she'd taste like if he laid her down and feasted on her, but he couldn't tolerate the thought of her lying naked on the cold ground, even with his body to warm her from above.

Instead, he spread out his jacket and laid back on it, pulling her over him. She straddled his body, her knees cushioned by the leather. Her breasts hit his bare chest, causing a sheet of lightning to zing through him into her.

She pulled in a shocked breath and let it out as a ragged groan. Cain gripped her hair to hold her so he could kiss her again, needing her mouth too much to find the words to demand her cooperation.

The wet heat of her sex ground against his abdomen. His cock jerked and twitched behind her, throbbing and dripping with need. She reached behind her and took him in her hand, stroking him just the way he liked. He didn't have to tell her how. He wasn't tied to her mind. She simply knew what he needed, somehow.

She lifted up, aligned their bodies and sank down, taking the tip of his erection inside of her. The clinging, slick fire of her pussy welcomed him in. He watched as she stretched to accept the invasion, marveling over how erotic it was to see their bodies merge. With every slow thrust of her hips, more of his cock disappeared inside of her, only to emerge with her excitement shining on it.

There were no shadows to hide anything. No darkness to cover them. Everything was on display, making it burn with the keen edge of reality.

This truly wasn't a dream. Too good to be true, certainly, but still so real he had no choice but to believe it.

Rory met his gaze. Her lips were parted, her eyes dark and slumberous. She prodded at his thoughts, but Cain had kept the barrier in place, refusing her entrance.

That unity had freaked her out before, and he was not about to make the same mistake twice. Not even if it felt like she was asking for it. This was purely physical, and if that wasn't enough for him, then he deserved no more.

Her hands settled on his chest and she leaned forward, giving him a kiss so hot he knew she'd scorched the ground beneath them. Bright dots filled his vision, and an orgasm careened toward him out of the blue.

He held back, but his control wouldn't last long. And when he came, she was going to be right there with him, pleasure roaring through her.

He sat up and assumed control of her hips, holding her still while he filled her. She took all of him, shaking in his arms as he fit them together perfectly. Her lids were at half-mast, her pink lips parted as she panted wildly.

Once again he felt her brush across his mind as if seeking entrance. It would have been so easy to give in and open the gates. Heaven knew he wanted her there with him. But down that path lay disaster. He couldn't really remember why, but the lingering impressions left behind by his decision were strong enough to rein him in.

Her head fell back, displaying her neck and the dark amethyst luceria gracing those slim, delicate lines. For now she truly was his, and while the connection might have been temporary and fleeting, it felt real.

He couldn't keep his mouth off of her. The taste of her skin was addictive, and the nibbling, sucking kisses he gave her, left behind the marks of possession. His tongue caught the edge of the luceria, and her whole body clenched, squeezing him inside and out.

"Do that again," she said, her words breathless and demanding.

Cain did, and this time, he recognized the gentle fluttering of her impending orgasm.

Yes. That was what he wanted. What he needed. Giving her pleasure gave him a heady sense of satisfaction he'd never found anywhere else.

He urged her hips to move faster atop him, pulling her down on each stroke so that they were joined as deeply as they could be. The urge to also join their thoughts hit him hard, but he ignored it and focused on the physical—the scent of her arousal, the pretty flush of her skin, the increasingly loud cries filling the cold air.

She began to tremble. Her muscles tightened. The pitch of her voice rose and her fingers dug into his shoulders.

Cain cupped the nape of her neck in his palm, connecting the parts of the luceria. Energy flowed from the ground into him, then into her. It lifted her hair, creating a pink halo around her head. Sparks cascaded from the strands, sinking back into the ground from where they came. With each beat of his heart, power pulsed into her. And with each pulse came a tightening of her body.

Pleasure swirled through him, growing huge and blindingly bright as it consumed his vision. He felt her quivering at the edge of ecstasy and knew he was going to fall right over with her.

Her nipples tightened and dragged over his chest, making his lifemark respond in a frenzied flurry of rioting branches. Her pussy clenched around him, and he knew he was a goner. Holding back was impossible. There was simply too much pleasure to bear—too much perfection to be found in her arms.

Her mouth opened on a scream of completion, and Cain covered her lips with his to drink it down. He fused them together as the first frenzied wave hit him. Sparks spewed from her hair. He heard them crackling in the air. The taste of her cries swept over his tongue, and deep within her body, the first pulse of his release broke free.

Rory's hips wiggled madly and her sex hugged him tight, clenching as her orgasm swept through her. He poured himself into her, filling her with hard spurts of semen. The pleasure was endless, and yet over far too soon. He held her close while the storm passed.

She drooped in his arms, resting her head on his shoulder as she caught her breath. He petted her back and stroked her hair, unwilling to let her go. His heart thundered in his ears and his heart was racing, but he was content and completely blissed out, hovering in that moment when the world's problems could not break through.

As the cold wind passed over them and the sweat cooled their bodies, Rory began to shiver. Cain found the closest article of clothing he could and draped it over her naked back. It was his shirt—the one she'd ripped open.

He grinned at the memory of her ferocity, even as it made his softening cock twitch with a little thrill. He liked that she wasn't shy about taking what she wanted from him, and the thought of when she might next make demands had his deflating erection swiftly reversing course.

They couldn't stay out here like this no matter how much he wanted to make her come again. The sun was hanging low in the sky. It wasn't safe to be out here. And it was too cold now that there was no longer a lust-fueled inferno pouring off of his body.

He stood and set her on her feet. She held on to him as she gained her balance, her gaze fixed on his.

"What?" he finally asked, as it became clear that something was on her mind.

She gave him the slightest shake of her head. "Nothing. We should get moving. It's cold."

He helped her gather her clothes, offering her his ruined shirt to clean away the wet mess he'd left between her thighs.

"Sorry about ripping your shirt," she said, a sheepish grin on her mouth.

"No, you're not. You liked it."

"Maybe a little. I've never torn a man's clothes off before." She pulled her panties and jeans on, covering the most tempting ass he'd ever seen.

He pulled his own jeans on and buckled his sword in place. "Feel free to do it again whenever you like."

Her smile brightened his whole world and warmed him all the way to his bones. It struck him in that moment that he could love her if she let him. Part of him already did, maybe, though to admit it would make him too vulnerable. Once the colors in the luceria solidified, he wouldn't survive without their bond, and the last thing he wanted was to tie her to him with guilt.

No, it was his duty to her to make sure that didn't happen. She deserved a choice that wasn't swayed by her feeling responsible for his life. So he'd hold his heart closed, his thoughts tight, and do his best not to fall in love with her.

Rory felt . . . cheated. The sex had been great—that man nearly blew the top of her head off making her come that hard—but it wasn't like before. Cain had held back, and she didn't like it. She liked feeling what he did, knowing what turned him on and how her touch drove him crazy. She liked the intimacy of their connection and knowing that he'd never shared that with any other woman before. That he was holding out on her now pissed her off and made her feel insecure, which pissed her off even more.

The sun was low on the horizon, giving each blade of dead grass a long shadow. They headed back toward the house, him all shirtless and beautiful under his gaping leather jacket.

Given the chance, she'd gladly rip another shirt from his body and see where it took them. But now was not the time for that. Now was the time for reality, for impending danger and tough decisions.

Reality sucked donkey dick.

Rory wanted to hold his hand or put her arm in his—anything to connect them—but he was too far away, his gaze watchful on their surroundings as if expecting trouble. It made her nervous, driving away the languid heat of their erotic interlude.

"What happens to me if we find the person who blocks my visions before we kill the demon in my head?"

"I can only guess."

"So guess."

He spared her a quick glance before he hurried ahead and opened the back door for her. "If you're not able to pull on my power to defend yourself, then there's no end to the damage the demon could do. He could simply haunt your dreams, tormenting you for fun, or he could use your body against your will, wreaking untold havoc."

"How long do I have before Ronan's cage fails?"

"Years. Hours. There's no way to know."

She slipped past him, dragging in the scent of his bare chest and leather jacket as she went. So yummy. It went to her head and rolled around there, derailing her train of thought for a second. "So until we kill it, I'm a ticking time bomb to everyone around me."

"Yes."

At least he didn't bother to lie.

"Including you," she guessed.

"Better me than someone weaker."

That was just like him to think of it in those terms—like his safety was an afterthought.

She turned to face him. "It would kill me if I hurt you. We need to find that demon."

"Ronan may know where he is, or be able to locate him. He'll wake soon now. I think we should wait for him."

"Is he a walking time bomb, too? I mean, he's got the same demon in his brain, right?"

"Yes, but his mental control is better than yours."

"Because I'm a woman?"

"No, because you're a Theronai. Sanguinar have abilities that exceed ours. I meant no insult."

Too bad. A nice, screaming fight would have gone a long way toward easing her growing tension.

"You need to rest while you can."

"I feel fine," she said.

"For now. The power I fed into you will fade soon, leaving you just as weak as you were before. You really don't want that to happen at the wrong time, do you?"

"No. But if I go to sleep, I'm afraid you'll leave."

Cain shook his head. "I won't leave you alone right now. Until that demon is dead, you're at risk. And if Ronan comes with me, then you'll have to come, too. Unless you'd rather I call someone else?"

She didn't want anyone else around. Even now, she could see the fleeting images of a couple in the distance as they sat down to dinner. Once Ronan was up, she'd start getting feedback from him, too. Even Cain fed her visions once in a while. The only thing that stopped it all was his touch, and she really doubted that whoever he'd send to take his place as her guardian would have the same soothing effect.

"I'm going with you," she said.

"Then you should sleep."

"Can't. Too wired. But I'll lie on the couch and rest until we go."

He followed her into the living room, and the next thing she knew, she felt his presence brush her mind, sending her into sleep.

Her last conscious thought was that she was going to have a long talk with him about boundaries when she woke up.

Chapter 23

Joseph looked up from his desk as Tynan walked in shortly after sunset. Anger vibrated through the Sanguinar's lean frame. "None of my people show any signs of having taken the dead woman's blood."

"I thought you were sure she was drained."

"I was. I am."

"What about the blisters? I've seen the effects your efforts to filter Tori's blood left on you. Those would be really hard to miss."

"I missed nothing. Every Sanguinar who was inside the walls of Dabyr at the time of Beth's murder has been accounted for. I saw no signs on any of them."

"So where does that leave us? Could a Dorjan have drained Beth of blood?"

Tynan shook his head and eased himself into a chair as if sitting too fast might make him shatter. "I didn't want to raise suspicions, so I was careful in my investigation. I could, however, question them more thoroughly."

"You mean search their memories," guessed Joseph.

"Yes." The single word spoke volumes of his disgust for the idea.

Joseph sighed and called Nicholas, who had spent the last several hours searching through security camera footage. "Any leads?"

"Yeah. Just found something—something you're going to want to see."

"In my office. Tynan is here, too."

"Good. Maybe he can shed some light."

Joseph hung up and asked Tynan, "What about the sleeping Sanguinar? Is there any chance one of them woke up for a midnight snack?"

"I checked the sleeping vaults. All were there. None showed any signs of tainted blood." The way he said it, with a weary hesitation in his voice told Joseph there was something else to say.

"But . . . ?"

"But two more of my people are near death. I hadn't realized how frail they'd become. I need to go hunting for them. The blood available here is simply not enough."

"You can't leave. No one can leave until we find who killed Beth."

"Can I at least request one of the Sanguinar in the field come home, then?"

"Of course. And I can give you some more blood to tide them over until help arrives. It's not like I'm headed into battle anytime soon." No matter how much he hated stagnating behind this desk.

"Thank you, Joseph. Your generosity will not be forgotten."

Joseph knew a thing or two about desperation. And while he didn't trust all of the Sanguinar, Tynan had proven himself willing to sacrifice for Joseph's race over and over recently. A little donation was the least he could do.

Nicholas walked into the office, a laptop clutched in his hands and a furious glare on his scarred face. He plunked it down on Joseph's desk, aligning it so that both Tynan and Joseph could see. "I caught some video footage of someone walking into Beth's suite."

"Who was it?" Joseph demanded.

"No clue. But check this out." Nicholas brought up a split image. On the left was the photo of the man who had sabotaged the cameras a few months ago, allowing Dabyr's walls to be breached. The traitor who'd done that had yet to be found.

On the right was another image of a man. Like in the older image, all that was visible was the back of a head that was cloaked by a hooded sweatshirt. There was not even a glimpse of his face, as if he knew how to avoid the cameras.

Both men were wearing the same brown sweatshirt.

"The traitor is the one who killed Beth," said Nicholas.

Joseph fell silent in shock, unwilling to voice the truth that hung so glaring and obvious in front of them.

"It was one of my people," whispered Tynan. "A Sanguinar is our traitor."

Nicholas's hand settled on his sword. Joseph doubted the man even realized the silent threat.

"We don't know that for sure," said Joseph, hoping to defuse the situation before it got out of hand. "That's only a guess."

"No," said Tynan, gliding to his feet. "You do not understand blood the way I do. I'm telling you that Beth was forcefully drained. If the man in these images is the same, then it is one of my own."

"I ran the photos through a program, comparing height and proportions. Everything was the same except the man who went to Beth's door was quite a bit thinner than the one who disabled the cameras. Much thinner than the man who walked out of her suite."

Tynan's body shook with rage. "He was desperate for blood. Starving."

"How many Sanguinar are under our roof?" asked Joseph.

"Dozens," said Nicholas.

"Most of whom are sleeping," added Tynan.

Joseph gave Tynan a level stare. "You know what I'm going to ask you to do, don't you?"

Tynan nodded. "I will question them directly."

"If they resist?" asked Nicholas.

"I would like to say that I would subdue them, but I'm far too weak for that. I'm afraid I'm going to need backup."

Nicholas nodded. "Sure. Whatever you need, man."

The hair along Joseph's arms lifted in awareness the second before Lyka appeared in his open doorway. Just seeing her sent a surge of relief washing through him, cooling the searing, furious corners of his soul.

Her golden gaze swept over the gathering, and she came to a rocking halt. "Sorry. I didn't mean to interrupt."

Joseph wanted to tell her to come in, but he knew better than to waste his breath. If she was here, it wasn't because she wanted to see him. In fact, the paleness of her complexion and fine tremor running through her fingers told him that the visit wasn't for fun.

"It's okay," he said. "Do you need something?"

She looked at the other men gathered and her lips went tight and flat, as if she was trying to hold back what she'd come here to say.

Joseph knew better than to send his witnesses away, but the chance to be alone with her, even if she hovered well out of reach, was too much for him to resist. He looked at Tynan. "Go do what you need to do. Nicholas will back you up."

The men left. Lyka stayed in the doorway, gripping the frame so tight it drove the blood from her slender fingertips. "I don't know how to say this."

"Say what?"

"I'm not even sure you'll believe me."

"Just say it. Whatever it is. Then we'll go from there."

"I've been babysitting Ella's son Ethan for a while

now, taking care of him while she worked. She asked if she could stay in my suite for a few days. I told her I'd be happy to have her, that I'd be happy to watch the baby whenever she needed. She's dealing with so much right now, you know?" Her chest heaved with emotion, and for a second, Joseph was completely distracted from his duties by the sight. The swell of her breasts was emphasized by the clinging sweater she wore.

"Are you okay?" he asked, resisting the urge to take even one step toward her. He couldn't stand the thought of her fleeing. He needed her here for some reason he couldn't name, calming his nerves and easing his nearly constant headache.

"I don't know, Joseph. This is all so fucked up."

The sound of his name on her tongue made him shiver. He didn't even try to hide it. There simply wasn't enough strength left in him to preserve his pride. He had too much left to do before he could rest, and all of his energy had to go into finding this traitor before he killed again.

"Just tell me what's going on," he urged. "Let me try to help."

She nodded. "Ella finally cried herself to sleep a few hours ago. Ethan was fussy, so I sat down to rock him." She paused and pulled in a deep breath. "He . . . showed me something."

"What? I don't understand."

"Neither did I at first. Ethan has always been a little strange—so sober and quiet. And he's grown so fast."

Warning bells went off in Joseph's head. Small details all clicked together with an audible snap. Ella had been found in Synestryn hands. She'd said she hadn't been there long—that she'd been pregnant when they'd taken her, but what if she'd lied? Joseph hadn't seen Ethan at the day-care facility—not even when both Beth and Ella were working. In fact, he hadn't seen the baby since he was born.

Ella hadn't wanted the Sanguinar to help her through labor. She'd had the child in her suite, without medical help. Joseph hadn't known her intent to go through labor alone, but even if he had, he wouldn't have questioned it. Why would she want to trust a Sanguinar who would take her blood when she'd just escaped demons who had fed from her?

Unless she wasn't sure of the child she carried—wasn't sure if it was human or something else. Like its father.

One other half-Synestryn child had been born recently and survived. He was being raised by a Gerai family, well away from Dabyr. Few people even knew he existed, and even fewer knew how different he was from a human baby. He, too, had grown too fast. He, too, had been able to touch the minds of others, showing them things he'd seen.

"What did he show you, Lyka?"

She swallowed twice, and then squared her shoulders. "He saw Beth's murder. He saw who did it. That's what he showed me."

This time, Joseph was unable to keep himself from approaching her. Only the sudden coiled tension radiating through her—as if she were poised to flee—made him stop in his tracks.

His voice came out cold and hard enough to make her flinch. "Who was it?"

"One of the Sanguinar. The one with the baby face and grass green eyes. I think his name is Connor."

Joseph knew exactly who she was talking about. "Connal."

Dread pooled in his stomach. A killing rage suffused his limbs. His sword was drawn before he'd realized what he'd done.

Lyka's eyes had grown huge with fear. She hugged the frame of the door, making herself as small a target as possible.

"Stay here," he barked, pissed that she'd even think she could be his target. "Close the blinds and lock the door behind me."

"Why?"

"Because you're a witness to murder."

"Ethan was the witness, not me."

"Yes, but he has no words. You do. Stay here while I go deal with this."

"What are you going to do?" she asked.

"First, I'm going to get Ethan to show me what he showed you. And then I'm going to execute a Sanguinar."

Connal knew from Tynan's not-so-subtle snooping that he had discovered that Beth's death was not suicide. He was looking for signs of tainted blood—even going so far as to check the sleeping vaults of their own kind.

There wasn't much time before Connal's act was discovered. The compound had been locked down, but he'd compelled one of the human security guards to open the gate for him later, when he was ready to leave.

And he had to leave. There was no choice but to go. He would be discovered. Tynan's next act would be to scour the memories of those here and pull the truth from Connal's mind. As strong as he was with Beth's blood flowing through him, he wasn't strong enough to thwart Tynan's efforts. Of all of them, Tynan was the strongest, even when he was weak.

Connal's mind raced for some kind of plan. He'd already collected his things and stowed them in his van. But where would he go? There was nowhere he could run that they would not find him.

Unless he turned to the Synestryn. They'd already fed him—albeit for a price. Maybe they would shelter him as well. They would no doubt demand payment for that, too, but it had to be better than what the Theronai would do to him if he was caught.

What Connal needed was leverage. Tribute. The only thing the Synestryn cared about was food, vessels for their progeny, and access to the Gate.

He wasn't strong enough to move a Sentinel stone, and he didn't have the time to create a way in through the walls. But what he did have was access to one of their offspring. And its mother. Ella had lived through birthing one of the Synestryn young. She could do it again. That had to be worth the price of admission and the protection the demons could give him.

Connal suffered only a moment's hesitation at the thought of trading two lives for his own. Perhaps there had been a time when that would have bothered him more, but that time was past. He'd been backed into a corner, and like the animal he was, he would react accordingly.

He sensed Ella inside Lyka's suite. He didn't bother to knock on the door. He simply barged in. The child stared at him in accusation, so Connal sent him to sleep. The mother was already asleep, but he urged her to drift deeper into its clutches. He flopped Ella over one shoulder and scooped up the child in the other arm. The power he used to mask his presence was precious, but the loss necessary if he was to get out of here with his tribute in tow.

No one saw him as he rushed to his van. A couple of particularly sensitive humans frowned in confusion as he passed, but that was all. He stowed both Ella and Ethan in the back of his van, and drove out of the garage.

Just as he'd commanded, the human guard opened the gate, allowing him passage. Connal was certain the human would do the rest of his job as he'd been compelled to do.

Now all Connal had to do was reach safety before the sun rose. And he knew just where to go.

Chapter 24

Ronan was shaking with effort when he woke. The Synestryn lord's hold on him was growing stronger. Ronan wasn't sure how much longer he'd be able to maintain control. As it was, it took him several long minutes to shove back the swelling rage and need to kill that pulsed through his veins.

He needed to feed. He was weak from fighting, weak from keeping the demon at bay.

The smell of food drove him upstairs. Rory lay sleeping on the couch, her pink hair spread out across the leather arm. Her pulse beat in her neck, so steady and strong it made Ronan's mouth water.

He glided toward her, seeing the light from his eyes spilling over her in an icy glare. He knelt by her side and lifted her toward his mouth.

The hiss of steel being drawn stopped Ronan cold.

"Bad idea," said Cain from behind him.

Rage surged through Ronan, combining with hunger until there was no room left for rational thought. "I need," was all he could spit out.

"Need someone else's blood. She's off-limits."

Cain didn't understand hunger. Not truly. He knew pain, but not weakness—not the grinding need for something he was constantly denied.

Just one drink. That's all he needed to keep him going so he could seek out another source of sustenance. He would be careful. Gentle.

Ronan lowered his head. The cold prick of steel burned at the nape of his neck.

"Back off, Ronan. That demon is fucking with your head. This isn't you."

It was him. The real him. Shivering and weak with hunger, craving something so rare that the fleeting bits he got were barely enough to keep him going—more like teasing hints meant to torture him with what he could never have.

But he understood Cain's quiet threat. He believed it. Theronai males were unreasonable when it came to the blood of their women.

Ronan set Rory down and turned to face Cain. "I'm too weak to hunt. The demon within me . . ."

Cain sheathed his sword and rolled up his sleeve. "Take only what you need to go hunt. Not a drop more. I need to be strong enough to fight."

Ronan took what he was offered. Cain's power flowed into him, fueling his mind enough for the fog of blood-lust to dissipate. As soon as he was able, he pulled away from the larger man, closing his wounds.

"I must leave now," said Ronan, being careful not to look at the temptation Rory posed, lying there like an offering.

Cain nodded. "We're hunting for the demon tonight. Call if you want to join us. I know you want him dead as much as I do."

Ronan wasn't so sure. As much as he *should* have wanted the demon dead, part of him was growing fond of the dark presence crouched in his thoughts. He knew that wasn't right—that he shouldn't feel that way—but there was nothing he could do to stop it.

The longer Raygh was in his head, the more familiar they became. Maybe if he just stopped fighting, it wouldn't be so bad. Raygh had power. Oceans of it. He was rarely hungry, and when he was, he took his fill.

What would it be like to be sated? Truly full?

Ronan had no idea, but if Raygh could help him find out, then perhaps he wasn't completely evil.

Cain watched Ronan go, knowing the man was running out of time. Having been near the end himself, he knew what that looked like. The desperation and fear. The realization that time was not an endless river flowing past, but a shallow kiddie pool too small to hold all the things he really wanted to do with his life.

And there had been something else in Ronan's eyes that had bothered Cain. A kind of acceptance. Almost submission. The Sanguinar hadn't even fought him for more blood.

Whatever was going on, it wasn't good. And while Cain was a long way from trusting anyone the way he had Gilda and Angus, he actually liked working with Ronan. He wasn't all creepy and mysterious like so many of the Sanguinar. He was more pragmatic, and that was something Cain respected.

The last thing he wanted was for Ronan to lose his battle with the demon and go crazy. Because if that happened, Cain worried that he might actually have to use his sword on the man, rather than merely threaten to use it.

Rory still hadn't moved. He'd helped her to sleep. He was sure she'd be angry about that, but he knew what she'd face if she didn't take care of her body. He'd fought by Gilda's and Angus's sides for enough centuries to know how it worked, and he'd rather Rory be angry than to have her simply run out of steam at a dangerous time.

He would have liked nothing more than to stay here and watch her sleep, but there wasn't time for that. The longer that demon roamed the earth, the more threat he posed. And while he would have preferred to tuck her away somewhere safe, that wasn't going to work. Not only was there no place he could take her without risking the inhabitants of Dabyr, he also didn't trust anyone else to protect her the way he would—down to his last breath.

So, Cain tucked her in the car, buckled the seat belt, and hit the road.

He drove toward the system of caves closest to where Rory had first had her control ripped away by the demon. There were no guarantees that this was the place, but it was as good a guess as any.

Maybe once Ronan fed he'd have some better ideas about where to look.

The vehicle the Gerai had left for Cain's use was smaller than he liked. His head kept bumping the headliner as they bounced along the country road. His shoulder brushed Rory's every few minutes. Her scent filled the confined space, tempting him with memories of what they'd shared.

He would have rather spent the rest of the night lying with her, coaxing as much pleasure from her body as she could stand, but that was a dream for men whose mates accepted them. Rory wanted his power, and she'd even wanted his body, but she didn't want him—at least not in the way that really counted.

Still, if the power he gave her drew her to him, then that was the lure he'd use. He refused to give up on her. There was too much at stake.

As they drew closer to a small town, she began to shift in her seat and make little whimpering sounds of discomfort.

Her visions. They seemed to be growing stronger if the tension vibrating through her was any indication. Every time a car passed them, her whole body jerked in her sleep. Finally, Cain took her hand in his, hoping his touch would make it stop.

A car in the opposite lane swerved to miss some roadkill, and Cain had to swerve off the road to avoid collision. He'd instinctively put both hands on the wheel, and in doing so, he'd stopped touching Rory.

She came awake with a start, and he could feel the clammy pulses of shock buffeting their link.

"Where are we?" she asked after a few seconds. Her voice was low and sexy with the remnants of sleep.

"Heading east, to where you first felt the demon's presence."

She opened the bottle of water sitting between them and drank deeply. "I think we're getting closer."

"How can you tell?"

"That cage Ronan built? I feel it rattling now."

Oh, hell, no. If the beast got loose, there wouldn't be a thing Cain could do to stop it. There would be nothing physical for him to kill. She would become the threat, and no matter who was pulling her strings, he knew he wouldn't be able to strike her down. The best he could do was knock her out, and he wasn't even sure that would work.

Cain pulled over on the side of the road. There was little traffic, but enough that it rocked this little toy car as it passed.

"What are you doing?" she asked.

He pulled out his phone. "Calling for backup. I think it's a bad idea for you to go after this demon. I'll call for someone else to guard you while I hunt for it."

"What? I'm not sitting around with some babysitter. I'm not afraid, you know."

"Yeah? Well, I am. I'm scared as hell that Ronan's cage will fail and you'll lose control again."

"So? If that happens, knock me out. It worked last time."

"I'm not taking any chances. The demon has to die, but you don't have to come with me. I'll find someone who will be willing to guard you with his life." Morgan, perhaps. Or Nicholas. Both men were fierce, noble warriors. Both would come if Cain asked.

What if one of them was the man she was looking for—the savior who freed her from her visions? What if she was compatible with one of them?

Cain couldn't let that sway him. He hesitated for only a second before he sent out a text asking for help.

"Whoa. Just hold the fuck on. I'm the one with the demon-in-a-box. Not you."

"Yes, but your safety is my responsibility."

From the way her face turned a mottled, angry red, he was guessing that was the wrong thing to say.

Her eye twitched. "I haven't been anyone's responsibility in a long time. I'm a grown woman and I *will* make my own choices. Especially when it comes down to deciding what to do to evict the prick in my head."

This was going to end badly, and yet he couldn't think of a single reasonable thing he could say to refute her. She was an adult. It was her head the demon inhabited. The longer they argued about it, the more danger there was of the beast breaking free.

Nicholas's texted reply came back fast. *Dabyr on lockdown. No one can leave. Will come as soon as possible.*

Lockdown? texted Cain.

Long story.

Are any warriors nearby who can help?

Only Ronan.

Looked like they were on their own.

Cain managed to keep his voice calm despite the churning need to scream her into submission. "What do you want to do?"

"Find the fucker. Kill it."

"You make it sound simple. I assure you it's not. Especially if Ronan's protections are failing."

She stared at him, her dark gaze hard. A flicker of insecurity made her chin wobble, but it was gone before he could be sure he'd seen it.

"Then how is it?" she asked. "Tell me what to expect.

Show me like you did before." She thrust her chin out at him, as if daring him. "Go ahead. I can take it. Whatever scary things we'll see, whatever nasty hordes we'll face . . . I can take it."

Maybe she could. Maybe she was as tough as she thought she was. But he didn't want to put any of that in her head. He wanted her life to be safe and happy and filled with clean, beautiful things. Not demons and monsters and the remnants of ravaged children. He'd seen enough of those things for both of them. He needed her life to be better.

Just as he'd tried to make it better for Sibyl. He'd fought her every attempt to play a role in the war. The few times he'd been forced to take her into danger, it had nearly killed him. And the night she was stolen . . . Cain still had nightmares.

He'd wrapped Sibyl up tighter, forcing her to stay safe, and the first chance she'd had to leave, she'd taken it.

What if Rory did the same thing?

That was his mistake. All this time he'd been trying to keep Rory out of danger. But if she was to be a true partner—the way he wanted her to be—she couldn't sit behind and wait for him to come home from battle. She had to be by his side, fighting and killing and facing all the horror associated with those acts.

In that moment he realized that shutting himself off as he had was not doing her any favors. Sure, it might prolong his life, but it could just as easily cost hers. She didn't know what to expect, and the only way she could was to either live through it—which they didn't have time for—or for him to show her what he'd lived through.

Cain's job was to keep her safe, and the best way to do that was to teach her how to stay alive in combat. Because if she chose to stay with him, war would be her life from now on. It wouldn't be a safe place filled with clean, beautiful things. It would be scary and dangerous and dark.

But he needed her. And the world needed her, too, even if it didn't know it.

The car rocked as a truck sped past them. She was still staring, waiting for her answer.

Once he did this, he wouldn't be able to undo it. His skills with removing memories weren't that good, and he wouldn't risk damaging her.

"Be sure, Rory. Once you see these things, they can't be unseen."

"I've already had my share of nightmarish memories. A few more is no big deal."

"You had two horrible days in captivity, and a few fleeting encounters. I have centuries of battles in my head."

"If you can take it, I can take it. Besides, think of all the strategy and tactics you know, all the information you've collected."

"You're sure?" he asked, hoping for a reprieve.

"I'm sure."

Cain nodded and cupped her face in his hands. Feeling her skin against his again eased some of the raging terror stampeding through him. He still hated this, but at least it was easier to face when he was touching her.

He gathered up the things he'd seen, the battles he'd fought, the demons he'd killed. He collected it all together in a growing ball of images and sensory details. The barrier he'd built between them dissipated like smoke in the wind, letting a roar of pure thought flow out of him.

Rory jerked and made a choking sound. Her body went tense, and her eyes rolled back in her head. A silent scream ripped through her, but she didn't try to fight him. She didn't try to stop the torrent of information. She accepted it into herself, without judgment for the things he'd done or hadn't done.

His failures blazed in blinding detail as they bubbled

from the depths of his memory, but Rory absorbed them, too, unfazed by his countless mistakes.

Slowly, as the memories flickered and died like a flame starved of oxygen, she drew in a long, sucking breath. "Wow."

Cain studied her face, certain he'd see disgust or at least disappointment cross her features. Instead, what he saw was sheer awe.

"You really *are* old," she said.

A rusty laugh broke free of his chest. "That's all you've got to say? I show you my life's work and that's it?"

"Yeah, sure, there were monsters and junk. But damn, Cain. You've held up well, all things considered."

"You're not afraid? You're not upset?"

"I'm completely blown away. You've been through some awful stuff—lots more than me. Kinda makes me feel safe."

Shock rattled him. That was the last thing he'd thought she'd say. "Safe?"

"Yeah. I mean, look at all the crazy shit you've survived. With you on my side, I'm invincible."

"Hardly. And don't you dare go getting cocky on me. That's a good way to get us both killed."

Her eyes went wide and she gripped his arms hard enough to leave bruises. The color leached from her skin and her whole body began to shake.

"What is it?" he asked.

"The demon. It . . . figured out what just happened. It knows what's in my head now—all that information you showed me, how you fight, what you know, where you live."

"What about it?"

"The demon wants to see it, too."

Chapter 25

Rory tried to get a grip, but panic was coursing through her, piling on top of the crazy collage of memories Cain had put in her head. She wanted to play it cool, to pretend that what he'd done hadn't rocked her all the way to her foundation. Making light of what she'd seen had helped dispel some of the lingering fear and pain left behind. But she couldn't be flippant about the demon. Not when she felt how close it was to breaking free.

"I think we need to find Ronan," she said. "I'm not sure how much longer his box is going to hold."

Cain was already dialing his phone before she finished speaking. "We need to meet." He listened for a moment. "Yes, we're close. We will be there."

Cain pulled back onto the road.

Rory was hit with a barrage of images as a cluster of cars passed. She closed her eyes and tried not to let the bright flicker coming at her make her puke. People were walking, driving, watching TVs. It all slammed together, clashing in discordant, nauseating chaos. She gripped Cain's hand, not caring that it made her look weak. She couldn't fight the visions, too. Not now. It was taking all of her concentration to hold together the shaking walls of the cage Ronan had constructed.

As her skin met his, visual peace settled over her, making her slump with relief. Now that one set of stimuli was gone, she felt the jarring rattle of the demon in her head. As soon as she noticed the thing searching for a way out, it stopped. She could feel its sinister intent, but the specifics of what it was trying to do were lost to her. It wanted to break free, but there was more to it than that—more even than its desire for the knowledge Cain had given her. She just wasn't sure what it was.

The one thing she did know was that it was close to busting out of the cage Ronan had formed, and if that happened, there wouldn't be a thing she could do to stop it from hijacking her body. With Cain this close, she had no doubt he'd be her first casualty.

The woman was getting closer. Raygh could feel her drawing near, bringing with her both information and blood. He wanted to shove himself into her mind and force her to come to him, but he restrained himself, biding his time. Breaking out of the cage the Sanguinar used to protect the woman's mind would take too much effort. Weaken him.

Eventually, she would be his to punish. He would take from her the knowledge the Theronai warrior had given her, and then use what was left of her to quench his thirst for vengeance. She'd been there when Krag had died. She'd allowed it to happen, mocked him. That was not something he could let go unanswered, no matter how enticing the knowledge she carried within her was.

None of his minions had managed to find more blood for him. It was as if all of his targets had disappeared into hiding, out of his reach.

The idea infuriated Raygh, making him wish for something to kill.

Canaranth entered the throne chamber with two male Slayers in tow. Both were bone thin, filthy and covered in festering bite marks. Fever burned in their eyes, barely visible beneath a wild mass of tangled hair.

Zillah had kept this potent stash of blood a secret, locked away in the deepest recesses of these caves. It wasn't until Raygh had taken over the other Synestryn's holdings that he'd made the delightful discovery.

The Slayers had been kept in relative submission through years of hunger and fatigue. Zillah had been careful to keep them alive, but only barely—only enough to produce more blood to replace that which he'd drained. Still, even after years of captivity, the blood flowing through them was a powerful cocktail.

No wonder Zillah had been in such robust health when he'd been sentenced.

"Bring them closer," ordered Raygh.

Canaranth shoved the Slayers forward. They were naked, clothed only in dirt, dried blood and scars. Their chins tipped up in defiance, and their eyes promised retribution. Too bad neither one would live long enough to fulfill such promises.

Raygh touched the forehead of the first man. Violent thoughts filled his head. There was little sense to be made of what Raygh saw—no useful information. The man's lean muscles clenched as he strained against the rope holding his wrists behind his back. He bared his teeth, letting out a low growl of warning.

How adorable.

Raygh shoved his head back and bit his throat, sucking down huge gulps of hot power. It took only seconds to empty the Slayer of blood, at which time, Raygh let him fall to the ground.

With a thought, he gave the surrounding demons permission to feast on the remains, which were quickly dragged off in the jaws of dozens of his minions.

Raygh turned to the second man. There was no hint of fear in him, not even after having seen what had just happened to his kin.

He shoved the other man's head back, but Canaranth's words stopped him. "You're going to kill him, too?"

Raygh regarded the human-looking creature, questioning whether his usefulness was worth him daring to speak his mind. "Why should I not?"

"The blood of a Slayer is powerful. Zillah lived off of these few men for years. If you kill them all, then they can no longer feed us."

"So, go out and bring me more." Raygh needed more blood, more power. He had to be strong enough to break through the chains that bound him in place, preventing him from bringing to him what was his.

"More? But we lost hundreds of our own collecting these few men."

"Our own? You mean mine."

Canaranth bowed his head. "Of course, my lord. I meant no disrespect."

"Then perhaps you should not question my actions. If I want to drain every Slayer on the planet, then that is my right. And it is your duty to make it possible."

"Yes, my lord."

Raygh twisted the Slayer's head to the side and bit deep. His body spasmed, then went limp as death fell over him.

Raygh cast the body aside. "Now go and fetch me another Slayer from our pens. I need more blood."

Just a little more blood, and he was sure he'd have the power to break through the last, dwindling defenses that kept him from the minds of his prey. Before sunrise, they'd be on their knees at his feet, begging him to kill them.

Foolish. Canaranth was convinced that Raygh was a narrow-minded, foolish beast. He had no idea what it had cost to collect the few Slayers housed below, or what it took to control them. If they were fed too little, they died. Too much, and they fought back, killing everything they could reach. The only reason it made any sense at all to keep them was because they healed so fast, regenerating gallons of blood that helped keep Canaranth's kind alive.

Killing them was stupid and wasteful, and at this rate, the few Slayers they had left would be dead by sunrise.

Perhaps it was time. Canaranth had spent every night since Ella's escape wondering how she was, wondering if their child had survived. He wasn't supposed to love her. He wasn't even supposed to be capable of love. But if what he felt for her wasn't love, it was as close to it as Canaranth was ever going to come.

He needed to be with her. He'd told her he'd come for her. And now his own cowardice held him back.

She wasn't going to want him. And even if she did, he had nothing to offer her. She was human. She needed a human life with a home and food and sunshine. All he had to offer her was a dark cave filled with blood and pain.

As much as he wanted to see her again, the only way he could was if she came back to him. And if she did, her life was at constant risk.

If Raygh would so carelessly drain a Slayer who offered unlimited blood, then what would stop him from doing the same to one fragile human woman?

And all of that was assuming that she still lived, which wasn't likely. Bearing a hybrid child was dangerous. Most of the women died. Even more of the offspring. Chances were Canaranth would be happier wondering about Ella's fate than actually knowing. At least that way, when he slept, he could dream that she was alive and well, playing with their child under a sun he could only imagine.

Chapter 26

Cain paced the floor of the Gerai house, wishing Ronan would hurry up.

"Will you sit down?" asked Rory. "You're making me nervous."

She had reason to be nervous. The demon was getting stronger. Even Cain could feel it swelling inside of her now, bulging against the confines of the cage Ronan had created.

The last thing he wanted to do was add to her anxiety, so he did as she asked and sat down next to her on the worn couch.

She didn't look at him as she spoke. "If this doesn't work, I want you to promise me that you'll do whatever you have to do to keep me from hurting anyone."

"I want to promise you, but I can't. I've already vowed to keep you safe. I can't now vow to do whatever it takes to stop you."

"Because you might have to kill me," she guessed.

"It won't come to that. Ronan will be here soon. And even if he doesn't make it in time, you're strong. I'm strong. We can fight the demon together."

"We couldn't last time."

"We didn't know the problem existed then. Now we do. We know what's coming, and we will face it."

She gave him a sad smile. "You have so much faith."

"No more than you deserve."

A car pulled up outside. Cain jumped to his feet and met Ronan at the door. He looked better than he had before, but still clearly not one hundred percent. Lines of strain bracketed his mouth, and his eyes were dull.

He barged into the small house without stopping for niceties. "Lie down," he ordered Rory.

"Uh. Sure. Not freaked out or anything over here. I'll just take a nice nap."

Ronan's jaw bunched as if he were biting back harsh words. "Just do it."

Cain didn't like the vibe coming off the Sanguinar. Not that he had much choice. Still, he went to stand next to the couch where Rory was lying down—close enough to stop Ronan if things got out of hand.

"I'll need blood," said Ronan.

Cain shook his head. "I don't—"

Ronan snarled, "Do not fight me on this. If you want the demon contained, I need blood."

"It's fine," said Rory. "Just do what you need to do."

Before Cain could argue further, Ronan went for her neck, leaning over her in a way that looked far too much like a lover's embrace.

Furious jealousy roared to the surface, making blood pound in Cain's ears. His hand was fisted on his sword, and it was all he could do to keep himself from drawing live steel.

Rory let out a soft sigh of contentment, which only fueled Cain's irrational burst of possessiveness. He knew Ronan was helping her. He knew that taking blood from her wrist would have taken much longer. And they were clearly running out of time. But none of that mattered as he watched another man hold Rory in his arms.

What if she decided to leave him for good? What if he had to witness her sharing her life with another man—one of his brothers?

He wasn't strong enough for that. Not even close.

Rory bucked on the couch, her body bowing up. She reached out blindly, her hands curling into fists.

Cain forgot all about his jealousy as a rush of panic hit him. He grabbed her hand, hoping to comfort her. Instead, the connection between them flared wide and a screaming bundle of fear lurched into him from Rory.

Acting on instinct, Cain opened himself up, reaching for her through the luceria. Silent screams vibrated between them. In her mind a battle was raging as Ronan struggled to contain the Synestryn who was working to control her through her blood.

It was hard to make sense of what was going on. There was so much pain radiating out from the point where Ronan's power glowed in a trembling, golden bubble. At the center of it was a coiled, black entity, covered in scales and flame. As the bubble shrank, the creature was forced to grow ever smaller. It thrashed at its cage, clawing and snarling.

And then Cain saw something else. Hovering just behind Ronan, another, larger creature perched in still silence. As Rory's beast shrank, Ronan's grew.

He wasn't beating back the demon, he was drawing it into himself.

Cain burned with the need to help, but there was nothing he could do. His sword was useless here. Physical strength meant nothing, and he would only distract Ronan if he tried to aid the man.

The bubble collapsed until it was the size of a marble. The demon within screamed in fury, letting out a high-pitched, tinny noise. Ronan kicked it away, into a steel box, sealing it shut.

He felt Rory relax. As he retreated from her mind, he saw her lying on the couch, panting and pale.

Ronan swayed. Cain grabbed his shoulders and helped him into a chair. When he looked up, his gaunt face was a stark mask of desperation. "You must find the demon soon. I can't hold out much longer. It's going to . . ." He trailed off, making horrible choking sounds.

"Ronan? Are you okay?"

"Restrain me," Ronan whispered, trembling.

Cain wasn't sure he'd heard right. "What?"

"Chain me. Now. I can't remain in control much longer."

The demon. It was going to come out and play.

Cain didn't dare waste a second. He drew his sword and slammed the butt of it against Ronan's temple. The Sanguinar slumped into unconsciousness, but there was no guarantee that would hold him for long.

Cain picked him up and carried him into the basement, where there was no risk of sunlight hitting his skin later. There was no way to know how long Ronan would need to be restrained.

"What are you doing?" asked Rory.

"What he asked me to do."

Her voice shook. "He's bad, isn't he?"

"Yeah. Help me look for something to tie him up."

A length of clothesline ran across the basement ceiling. Cain cut it down and bound Ronan's hands behind his back.

She handed him a roll of duct tape. "Is this going to be enough?"

Cain had felt how strong that demon was—how determined it was to take control. "I don't think so. Wish I had some chain."

"Hold on." She ran back upstairs and came back with her leather jacket. She used scissors to cut the leather away, leaving a three-foot length of chain. "Here."

It wasn't much, but it was better than what they had.

Cain bound the ends together with several coils of thick copper wire weaving through the links, and covered the whole thing with tape. By the time he was done, Ronan looked like a silver caterpillar.

"What are we going to do with him?" she asked.

"We'll have to leave him here. The only hope he has is if we kill that demon."

"We're going to have to find it first."

The way she said it made him turn around and look at her. "You have an idea."

"You're not going to like it."

"I don't have to like it if it works. Ronan's life is on the line." And after what he'd done for Rory, Cain owed him.

"I can feel it pulling on me. Even now, as weak as it is, there's still this little tug, drawing me toward it."

"You're right. I don't like it."

"That's not the part you're not going to like." She squared her shoulders like she was psyching herself up for battle. "The closer I get, the stronger it gets. I think that's why it was so close to breaking free."

"Because we're close."

She nodded. "Yeah. So, I can get us there, but I'm not sure who'll be behind the wheel once we arrive."

"Just point me in the right direction. I can go without you."

"No way. I've felt how strong it is. I know you're tough and all, but this thing controls an army. You can't fight it alone."

"You're right."

Cain used another several layers of tape to attach Ronan to a copper pipe, then he dialed Joseph. "I need help. Serious firepower. Who can you send?"

"No one."

"This is big, Joseph. Two lives are at stake."

"I'm sorry, but there's nothing I can do. Jackie, Andra and Nika are pregnant and on the bench. Lexi is in Africa. Viviana and Neal are in Pennsylvania, and Dakota and Liam are hip deep in demons down in Texas with the Defenders."

"What about Helen and Drake?"

"They left word they were going deep into a cave to

clean it out and collapse it from the inside. I can't reach them." Joseph sighed. "I'm sorry, Cain. You're on your own. We have our own crisis here."

"What crisis?"

"Connal stole a human woman and her child. We don't know why, but we know it's not good. Ella was hiding it, but her baby was half-Synestryn."

"Connal?" asked Cain, stunned.

"Yeah. He's our traitor. He's the one who let the demons through the walls to attack Lexi."

"Why? What possible reason could he have for doing any of that?"

"Does it matter?" asked Joseph. "I can't find any sense in it, but that doesn't change the fact that there's a little boy and his mother out there, and we're trapped in here, at least for a few more minutes."

"Trapped?"

"Connal forced two humans to help him. One destroyed the gate mechanism, and the other cut the fuel line to the chopper. We can scale the walls, but it will take a little while for the Gerai to get vehicles here. Andra wants to bust the gate open, but that would leave us open to attack."

"And if you send men out to find Connal, then they won't be there to defend Dabyr."

"Exactly. For all I know, that is their endgame—an undefended Dabyr. I won't risk putting any expectant mothers into battle. The area's crawling with those scorpion-looking things Ronan warned us about. No doubt they're out for blood. We have to keep batting them off the walls."

Cain glanced at Rory, who was watching him openly. "Do not let them get anyone's blood, Joseph. I've seen what they can do, and you don't want any part of it."

"Are they as bad as Ronan said?"

"Yes. He's completely disabled. That's where I'm headed now—to take out the demon who's controlling them. If anything happens to me, someone needs to come and cut Ronan loose." Assuming he survived.

"No. You're on the outside. I need you to go after Connal. Nicholas is sitting here, telling me you're close. Everyone else is busy, out of contact or too far away to help. I need you to hunt him down."

"We need to kill that demon, Joseph."

"The lives of a woman and child are at stake. I'm not asking you. Find Connal and stop him. That's an order."

Chapter 27

Something was wrong. Rory could feel it.

Cain's body had gone still. Not even his chest moved with his breath. He hadn't tried to put up another wall between them, and even though it was a raging invasion of privacy, Rory couldn't help herself. She tentatively poked at their connection, looking for what had upset him.

Fury hit her in a hard slap that made her bare her teeth. Fear wove around his fury, along with a heaping mass of guilt. Rory had no idea what it meant, but the emotions were so strong, she knew that something terrible had happened.

"Of course I want to help," he nearly screamed, "but Rory has to come first. You know that."

"No, Rory doesn't," said Rory.

Cain ignored her, making her want to punch him in the stomach. She hated being left out of the conversation, as if her opinion on whatever was going on didn't matter.

"I understand perfectly. And you need to understand that I'll do what I have to do. You and your orders can go fuck themselves." Cain hung up, his face mottled with anger.

She'd never seen him look like this before. He was beyond furious and well into homicidal rage.

"What happened?" she asked, unsure if she really wanted to know.

"One of the Sanguinar has kidnapped a human woman and her son."

"Well? What are you waiting on? Let's go find them."

"You can't go anywhere until I kill the demon—not with your degrading condition. And Ronan's."

"Are you kidding me?" she demanded. Touching his anger had sparked her own, making it burn bright. "Who the hell cares about my condition, degrading or otherwise, when there's a terrified woman and child who need us to save them? I'm sure Ronan will feel the same way. He nearly killed himself helping me. What do you think he'd do for an innocent child?"

"Others will be on the Sanguinar's trail soon. We need to get you somewhere safe."

"Safe? Really? Are you that stupid? Where the hell can you take me that I don't tote my brain along for the ride? Because as long as I'm wearing my head, and as long as there's a demon inside it, I'm pretty much fucked. I might as well be fucked while saving that poor woman and her kid."

"Once the demon is dead, then we can go after Connal."

"You really think that I'm going to worry about myself while there's a missing child at stake?"

"It's not safe for us to wait—not now that I've given the demon reason to fight even harder to free itself by implanting that knowledge in your head. Ronan can't help you again. He's too weak."

"Screw safe, Cain. I saw what your life was all about. You never once thought about your own safety when there were others in danger. Don't you dare try to feed me any bullshit now, because I know better." She sucked in a long breath, trying to find enough calm to sound reasonable. "Now, you and I are going after the asshole who abducted those people. We're going to find them and make sure that they're safe. And then we're going to find the demon in my brain and kill it. And then we're going to find the person who blocks my visions and take their magic ring or whatever so that I don't have to walk around blind half the time. Got it?"

She felt a heavy throb of frustrated anger pulse out of him, but when he spoke, there wasn't a single hint of it tinting his calm tone. "Is that what you really want?"

Rory didn't bother with words. Instead she gathered up her determination to do the right thing and shoved it at him. She let him see how he wasn't going to stop her, even if that meant she ditched him. Whatever it took, she would not let that woman and child end up trapped in a flooded basement filled with monsters the way she'd been.

Cain shuddered and gripped his phone until his knuckles popped. "This is the worst timing possible. You realize that, don't you?"

"Don't fucking care. It's the timing we've got."

"And if the demon emerges and takes control of your body again?"

"Knock me out. Kill me. Whatever you have to do. Until then, I'm going to fight."

She felt his grudging acceptance stomp through their link. "Get in the car. We don't have much time."

Cain said nothing as they drove back to the nearest highway. It was well past midnight, and there wasn't much traffic.

The car accelerated until they were pushing ninety. Regardless of what he said, Cain wanted to find that kid as much as she did.

His voice was hard, leaving no room for argument. "We keep the link open. That way I can monitor your thoughts. If the demon breaks free or starts whispering things to you, I'll know."

"Agreed. Though I would guess the first thing the demon would do would be to shut you out."

"Likely. Which is why if you try to block me, I will render you unconscious."

She still wasn't used to the idea of having Cain in her mind, touching her in such an intimate way, but so far, he'd been the one who'd been putting himself out there, exposing his entire life. He hadn't asked for much in return, and his request now was completely logical.

"You have my permission," she said. "Don't you dare let me hurt anyone who doesn't deserve it."

He nodded, his face grim. He handed her his phone. "Call Nicholas. Ask him where Connal is. He may be able to track his vehicle."

Rory didn't waste time asking questions. She didn't know these people, but she was willing to do anything that might help save that kid.

Nicholas answered fast. "Tell me you changed your mind, Cain."

"Hi, Nicholas. My name is Rory Rainey. I'm with Cain and he asked me to call you and have you tell us where Connal is."

"Thank God. Is Cain okay?"

"He's driving."

Suspicion was clear in his tone. "Let me speak to him."

Rory sighed in frustration, but held the phone to Cain's ear. "She's with me, Nicholas. . . . Yes, *with* me with me. Tell her what you know."

When Rory got back on the line, all of Nicholas's suspicion was gone, replaced with a kind of excited reverence she didn't understand. "Sorry about the confusion. I had to be sure who you were before I gave you information."

"Sure. Whatever. Now spill. This Connal asshat was the one who stole the woman and kid, right? Where is he?"

"Connal disabled the tracking device in his car, but Ella has a cell phone on her. We're tracking that. I'll send his coordinates to Cain's phone."

"Thanks."

"Tell Cain we have warriors on the way now, but they're at least twenty minutes behind you."

Rory relayed the message.

Cain nodded. "Ask him—"

She didn't need to hear the rest of his question. It had already slipped into her head fully formed. "Cain wants to know if you've got Gerai on the way to intercept him."

"No. It's too dangerous. We didn't want any more human victims. Connal has already killed one woman and damaged two men's minds with brutal force. Gerai don't stand a chance."

She didn't have to say a word: She felt Cain absorb the knowledge from her.

It was such a cool process she didn't spend time thinking about how creepy it was. Or would have been with anyone else. With Cain it wasn't so bad.

"Call us if anything changes," she said.

"Will do."

By the time she hung up, Nicholas had already sent a message with an attachment to Cain's phone. She opened it, and rather than listing coordinates as she expected, she saw a little dot moving across a map. She zoomed out and saw another dot where they were.

"He's heading south. If we turn east up ahead, we'll be on course to intercept him."

Cain gunned the engine. Apology laced his voice. "We're going to hit the edges of civilization soon."

"It's okay. I can take it."

"You're taking an awful lot right now."

"Good thing I'm tough then, huh?"

As they headed east toward the suburbs, visions began to flicker more frequently inside her eyes. The unpredictable motion of a dozen other people moving about made her queasy. She gripped the seat and focused on her breathing.

Cain's hand slipped under her hair, stroking the back

of her neck. Like a switch had been thrown, the visions disappeared, giving her some visual peace.

"Thanks."

"I wish I could do more. I wish that taking my luceria would have given you the ability to control the visions."

"Yeah, me, too. But having you touch me is a hell of a consolation prize."

"I won't always be around."

The thought made her heart squeeze with anxiety and something else she refused to acknowledge. "I know. But you're here now. That's good enough."

As each mile passed, she felt the demon swell with power. They were getting closer to it, making it hard for Rory to concentrate on anything else.

She checked the phone again and saw that Connal had just passed the road they were on. "Go right at the junction ahead. We're close."

Cain went where she told him, and once again they started leaving the populated areas for more isolated countryside.

The demon shook inside its cage. She could hear it now, growling in hunger and eagerness. It knew she was getting closer.

"How far away?" asked Cain.

She wasn't sure if he meant how far away was the demon or Connal, so she picked the one she could actually answer.

"Connal is a few miles in front of us, and he's flying." She watched the flashing red light as it seemed to slow. "Wait. I think he's stopping."

Rory zoomed in on the map until she could get a satellite image showing photographs of the area. It was an old picture that looked like it had been taken in the green heat of summer. All she could see was trees, and open expanses of uninhabited land.

"There's nothing there, but his dot isn't moving."

"Let me see."

She zoomed out so he could get an idea of the location and showed Cain the map. After a quick glance, he gave her a grim nod. "I know the area. It's riddled with caves."

"Great. Fun times."

"You know you don't have to—"

"Stop right there before you piss me off. I know I don't have to do anything. As if you could make me even if you tried. Quit reminding me of the obvious and let's go rescue a kid."

He let it drop, though she could feel a throb of his frustration sink into her. Alongside that, she also felt a slight tug, urging her to come closer. The demon.

Cain pulled off the road. A few yards away, a black van sat parked at the edge of a field, next to a jutting, rocky cliff. There were no houses in sight—no lights other than the stars overhead. They were too far out for streetlights. There weren't even any power lines, which reassured her that when Cain moved his hand from her neck, she wouldn't get blasted with a bunch of blinding TV images.

She wasn't ready for him to stop touching her yet, so as soon as he stopped, she put the car in park and killed the engine, leaving the keys in the ignition.

"Are you ready?" he asked.

"I can do this."

"We can wait for help."

"And let the demons do whatever it is they're going to do to that baby? Fuck that. Let's go get some."

He nodded and lifted his hand to open his door. The instant his skin left hers, she was hit with a thousand scenes of blood and rot. Filthy, oily beasts fought each other for scraps of rancid meat, giving her an up close and personal view of their jagged teeth and feral, glowing eyes.

Thank God she didn't see in smell-o-vision.

She had to make sense of the visions—to collect whatever information she could so that they didn't go in there blind. With only the two of them, they had to be careful.

Rory gripped the strand of power running through her and tugged hard. She focused in on her eyes, the way she'd done to make them see in the dark, hoping it would sort out her visions. Instead, they grew only more vivid and blinding. The harder she tried, the worse it became until she was nauseated and panting with effort.

Finally, she let go of Cain's power, feeling the ribbon snapping back into place.

Her normal fucked-up visions were back, but at least they weren't in IMAX 3D anymore. They faded down until she saw one sight that made sense. A lean, beautiful man had a woman's limp body over his shoulder. Under his other arm, he carried a toddler whose chubby limbs bounced as the Sanguinar hurried through a rocky passage.

Then, as she watched, another angle appeared, and another. Connal was being surrounded by creatures, and each one of them was closing in.

"We need to hurry," she squeaked out.

"I understand. Let's get you suited up."

Rory didn't waste time arguing. She felt his determination to see to her protection as an immovable force pounding through him. By the time she'd fumbled her way out of the car, he was there with a long leather coat. He slipped it on her arms, clearing away the rank visions as his skin brushed hers. A plastic shield went on over her head.

"I can't see," she admitted.

"Use my eyes."

"How?"

"The luceria. Our connection is wide open. Use it to see what I see. Or you can stay here. I'll go in and get them without you."

Her instant gut reaction to that was to scream at him in denial. Not only did she want to help, but she also didn't want to be standing around in the dark, blind and alone. But as rational thought seeped in, she realized the truth. She was going to slow him down. Maybe even get him killed. She hadn't considered what it would be like to be this close to a horde of demons. It was just as bad as being in the city, only with bloody chunks instead of crappy late night infomercials.

Rory wanted to fight. She *needed* to fight. The urge burned through her so bright it blinded her to any other possibility. Only now, she realized just how stupid her lack of forethought had been. If she couldn't see, how could she fight?

Cain grabbed her shoulders and gave her a little shake. "You're giving up on me now? You haven't even tried yet. Now pull yourself together and use the luceria."

He was right. She couldn't give up. Even now, that woman and her baby were being dragged deeper into the bowels of the earth.

Rory concentrated on the luceria, felt it hugging her neck. It warmed and vibrated in anticipation. She sensed his thoughts, felt his emotions. All she had to do now was filter all of that out and use his eyes. Certainly, seeing what he saw now shouldn't be any harder than seeing the memories of something he'd seen before.

With that strategy in mind, Rory closed her eyes. The demonic images flared in more gruesome detail, but she tried to ignore them—tried to ignore her own eyes altogether. Only Cain's eyes mattered.

Power wove around her, trickling out of the luceria to hug her close. She didn't even have to try to take it from him now. It simply came to her as if it belonged inside of her.

The strands of power thickened, turning into resonant ribbons of energy. Something clicked into place, and she saw her face. She grasped onto that image, concentrating on her pink hair, glowing bright under the moon. Suddenly, the sight slipped past her, out of reach.

"Almost," she heard Cain whisper.

More power glided into her, sinking into her skin and bone. She felt lighter, as if she could float away if she let go. Only Cain's hands on her leather-clad shoulders kept her fixed on the ground.

Like tuning a radio, she searched for the right frequency, discarding those visions flowing from the demons.

There. Right there. She saw her head again, and this time, when she clutched on to the image, it stuck with her.

Pride filled his tone. "That's it. Just like that."

Before she even had time to smile at her success, her control failed, and her vision dissolved into a flurry of teeth, blood and fur. The strand of power she'd been holding snapped back into Cain, leaving her feeling like a pile of suckful failure.

"It's okay," he said. His voice was gentle, but she could feel him fighting his disappointment. "We have time for you to figure it out."

"Just not now," she added. She grabbed his hand so that she could see his face clearly, and almost wished she hadn't.

His jaw was set with determination, and his shoulders were pulled back. Regret hovered in his eyes, and she knew she was going to hate the next words coming out of his lovely mouth. "I can't take you down there. Not when you're blind and compromised. I have to focus completely on getting that woman and her baby out."

Rory nodded as an avalanche of frustration pinned her in place. "I understand. I'll slow you down. Get in the way."

His voice rang with apology, "Rory, I'm so—"

"No. Don't be. It's okay. You go in there and save those people. I'll stay here."

"You're not fighting me."

"There's no time to argue. They need you. Go now. Before I change my mind."

"If things get dangerous, drive away or put up a shield to protect yourself. The sun will be up soon. Synestryn will be coming back to hide."

"I'll be fine. Just go."

Cain turned and left. A swarm of demon sights filled her eyes, making her sick.

Disappointment and rage shook her to her bones. She wasn't afraid. If the demons came, she knew she could protect herself. But that wasn't enough. Not even close. She wanted to be like Cain and help others, too. Her life had been all about her for too long. Isolation had managed to narrow her focus until she could hardly see past herself.

Cain had opened her eyes and shown her what she was missing. And now that she'd seen how it could be—how it was supposed to be—she knew she'd never again be happy settling for less.

She couldn't just stand around doing nothing, so she stumbled back to the car, got in, locked the doors and latched on to Cain's power. One way or another, she was going to make her brain see what she wanted it to see. And then she was going in after him.

Raygh felt his prey draw near. The urge to grab her mind and reel her in made him salivate, but he held fast, pretending he was still trapped and held in check. She'd stopped moving now, but the closer she got, the easier it became to feel her heartbeat. It would go still soon enough, but not until he'd given her the same pain and fear that had been visited upon his sons.

Once all of her screams were his, trapped for eternity within his memories, then he would drain her blood and carry her with him for all time. She would provide him with information and fuel his power, giving him the strength to find her friends—those who were also responsible for Raygh's grief.

In fact, one of them was with her now. He sensed the

man's power radiating through her, and sent his demons out to gather the man's blood.

It had been a long time since Raygh had tasted the power of a male Theronai's blood. But that was about to change. Her mate possessed great knowledge. If anyone knew how to reach the Gate and the Athanasian blood that lay on the other side, it would be this man. And everything he knew, Raygh would soon know as well.

Chapter 28

Canaranth smelled Ella before he saw her. The sweet, light fragrance of her skin was unmistakable. His heart jumped with excitement and joy, and he broke out in a dead run, sprinting toward her.

Before he'd gone ten feet, his mind caught up with his emotions. If she was here, she was in terrible danger. Raygh destroyed all he touched. He didn't care about how foolish it was to kill three Slayers when cultivating their blood was far smarter. He'd already killed one of the human children they needed. Nothing mattered to him beyond his rage, hunger and his whims. Zillah had been ruthless, but at least he had some sense of preserving their future.

Raygh was on a rampage of anger and grief, and Canaranth knew he wouldn't stop until everyone who'd witnessed the death of his sons had been destroyed.

He had to get Ella out to safety—back into the hands of the Sentinels.

As Canaranth rounded a curve in the tunnel leading to the surface, he saw her body draped over the shoulder of a Sanguinar they'd had dealings with in the past—Connal. In his other arm was a small child—one who smelled familiar.

His son. The boy hanging limp in Connal's arm was Canaranth's son. He'd survived.

Shock and joy swelled under his ribs, stealing his breath.

That his son had lived was a miracle. Being able to see the boy with his own eyes was more than Canaranth deserved or expected. And Ella was here as well, her heart beating out reassurance that she was alive.

He took a step forward, reaching for his family before he realized he couldn't let anyone know he was the boy's father. Or how much he loved Ella. Down here, they would be tools used against him. If anyone suspected their connection to him, they would suffer for it.

So instead of revealing how much he ached to take them in his arms, he put on a mask of indifference and addressed the Sanguinar. "Why are you here?"

Connal stopped in his tracks. His pale eyes flared with light as he gathered his power. "I seek asylum. I bring tribute to Zillah."

"Zillah is . . . no more. You need to take your tribute and leave now."

Canaranth silently willed Ella to wake so he could see her face again, even as he begged her to stay asleep. Seeing him would be hard on her. And she might say something to give them away.

"Who is leader here?"

"I am," lied Canaranth. "Now go before I gut you and feed you to my demons."

Connal's eyes narrowed. "You lie. Your heart is racing. Now, why would you lie to me?"

"Give me your tribute. I will take it to Raygh and request an audience for you."

"No. I'll take it to him myself. Take me to him."

Connal's eyes flared brighter, and Canaranth felt the sting of compulsion scamper over his mind. He tried to fight it, but he hadn't fed in days, knowing that they needed to conserve what blood they had left. He was weak, and because of that, he turned and began walking.

There was nothing Canaranth could do now. Not until Connal let go of his mind. But once he did, Canaranth would go and feed. And then he would come back for his family. He would take them by force if he had to, killing whoever got in his way, even if he had to drain every last Slayer they had to make it happen.

Apparently, he was more like Raygh than he'd thought.

This labyrinth of underground tunnels was much more extensive than Cain had suspected. Claw marks were evident on the walls where the rock had been scraped away to widen the passages. It had been done methodically, intentionally, as if they needed the space to move something big.

He made a mental note of it, but that was all the attention he could spare. This place was crawling with lesser demons, when it should have been mostly empty. The sun would be up soon, but until then, there shouldn't have been nearly as many demons present as there were.

The sheer number of creatures kept him on his toes as he cut them down. The smell of their blood and his sweat was going to alert others of his presence, but there wasn't much he could do about that. His priority had to be Ella and her baby.

Besides, the sooner he got this job done, the sooner he could get back to Rory. He didn't like leaving her out there alone, unguarded. If not for her constant tug on his power, he would have been distracted with worry. But as long as she was drawing energy from him, she was alive. He took what solace he could from that.

A pair of sgath slinked out from a narrow crevice, their green eyes glowing with hunger. They were small, young, but they were also fast and ferocious. They worked in tandem, circling him so that he was continually flanked.

He bided his time, waiting for one of them to attack. With each second that ticked by, he felt the urge to hurry, but if he got himself killed, he'd be of no help to the humans.

Finally, the one on his left coiled to pounce. As it flew up toward Cain's throat, he stepped aside and cut through its brother's snout. One of its eyes winked out as the other sgath hit the cave wall. Cain used its moment of stunned confusion to lop off its head, then made quick work of the injured beast.

From down the corridor, he heard the telltale scratching of claws on stone. Hundreds of them. The scent of the sgath's black blood pooling beneath them was like ringing a demon dinner bell.

The time for patience was over.

The instant Raygh smelled the child draped over the Sanguinar's arm, he knew what it meant. The boy looked completely human upon first glance, but his scent gave him away.

Not only was the child half-Synestryn, he was Canaranth's offspring.

Raygh stretched out his hands. "Give the child to me."

The sudden tension that overcame Canaranth was more proof that Raygh's first guess was correct. Still, his servant took the child from the Sanguinar and slowly carried him closer.

The slight hesitation to let go of the boy thrilled Raygh, showing him one more of the many weaknesses Zillah's previous lieutenant possessed.

With a thought, Raygh woke the child, freeing him of the Sanguinar's thrall. There were no tears or cries of fear. The child regarded him with calm, steady interest.

"He is ours," announced Raygh.

"Of course," said the Sanguinar. "Tribute in exchange for asylum. And food."

"Come closer."

The Sanguinar handed the sleeping woman to Canaranth, who cradled her as if she were a rare and precious thing.

Yet another weakness waiting to be used against him. It truly was disgusting to watch.

The Sanguinar knelt at Raygh's feet, as was proper.

"I will accept your tribute. And your blood."

"No," said the Sanguinar. "My blood is my own. I will not allow you to control me."

"I already do," said Raygh. "You came here bearing gifts, seeking asylum. That means you have nowhere else to go. You are in my home, in my presence. You are already stripped of all control. The rest is mere formality."

"Let me take the child from you, my lord, so you may more comfortably feed," said Canaranth.

Raygh tossed the boy at him, watching in amusement as he chose between which precious thing he let hit the ground. In the end, Canaranth eased the woman down just in time to throw his body under the boy's, allowing himself to take the brunt of the impact.

Interesting. And useful. If Canaranth was willing to suffer for the woman and child, then perhaps he wasn't a lost cause after all. Raygh could use the humans to turn Canaranth into a true leader, rather than the weakling he currently was. Their kind needed more strong rulers.

"I will not give you my blood," said the Sanguinar.

"I don't expect you to give it. But I will take it." And before the other man was able to move out of the way, Raygh grabbed him by the head and shoved his will into the Sanguinar's mind.

Connal was his name. He was desperate. Lost. Weak.

Raygh held him still while he fed, sucking both blood and information from him.

Zillah had tricked Connal into drinking his blood by masking it inside a pregnant human. And now that he'd had a taste, he wanted more. Human blood, Sentinel blood—none of it sated him—only the blood of an altered human breeding vessel had filled the void.

Raygh pulled his mouth away, heedless of the blood that poured from Connal's neck. "You think I'm going to give you the blood of my breeders?"

"Zillah did."

Connal tried to break free, but he was weak compared to Raygh, who held him still without effort. "Zillah was a fool."

The Sanguinar's voice became a desperate whine. "I was useful. I helped him."

"Yes, but now your people know of your treachery. You are useless to me."

Connal healed his wounds shut, but the process was slow, proving just how little strength was left in him. "I can help. I can find more women for you—women like Beth."

"Whom you killed." Raygh had seen that in Connal's memories.

"I needed her blood."

Raygh studied him for a moment. Perhaps he could be of use, but if he would betray his own kind, he would betray Raygh as well. Better to not risk what was bound to fail. Besides, with the rest of the Sanguinar's blood, Raygh would be strong enough to break through the last of the female Theronai's defenses. Then she would come to him without a fight.

"And I need your blood." He gripped Connal's hair and bent his head back. The Sanguinar hardly even struggled as he died.

Chapter 29

Cain wasn't going to make it. Rory could feel his calm assessment of the situation as he tore through possible options for survival. She saw the wall of little demons sweeping toward him, like a fury, scaly flash flood. There was no way he was going to be able to take them all on before they killed him.

It took only one bite to take him down. One little poisonous scratch.

And then she realized what had just happened. All of the other visions had faded from her sight. She saw only through Cain's eyes now. Her focus on him and his safety had been absolute, allowing her to control her sight.

Not that it did her much good. That's all she could see, as if she were right there with him. How the hell was she going to make it into the cave and to his side when she couldn't see to get out of the car?

Something tickled in the back of her mind, drawing her attention. Her fear for Cain grew until she was shaking with it. The only thing that mattered was getting into the cave. She had to go. Now. Before it was too late.

Rory pushed out of the car, landing on the cold ground. She scrambled to her feet, using the car as a frame of reference. The only sight she saw was of Cain's powerful arms cutting through dozens of demons, their black blood making the earth beneath his feet slick.

The hood of the car was still warm. She tried to remember which direction the cave entrance was from here, but she'd never been good with directions, and had no clue which angle to take.

Still, the need to move drove her forward. She tripped on dips in the ground, but stayed on her feet, walking in shuffling steps in what she hoped was the right direction.

She must have veered off course, because she was pulled back to her left, as if an invisible rope had given her a hard tug.

This way. She heard the thought whisper across her mind, its rasping voice cold and alien.

A surge of fear rose up in Cain and he shouted a wordless warning in her head.

Ignore him, said the voice. *He needs you. Hurry.*

Of course Cain didn't want her to come and help. He was always worried about her safety. But this time, he was the one in trouble. Not her. He needed her, and she was not going to let him down.

Good pet. Hurry!

Pet? That didn't seem right, but she didn't waste time worrying about it. The river of demons flooding around Cain's feet was not slowing. He needed her to shield him.

Rory hurried as fast as she could. She fell twice, but was back on her feet in seconds, pushing forward. When her hands hit the cold rock near the entrance of the cave, a sense of elation cascaded over her, making her shiver.

More demons had surrounded Cain, but he had worked his way back into a crevice, protecting himself from attack on all sides. Each powerful swing was a killing blow, sending the heads and paws of multiple demons flying.

Stay away! he warned. *It's a trap.*

A trap for him, based on the look of things.

He needs you, whispered the cold voice.

Rory agreed. She found the curve in the rock, smelled the dank, fetid stench of decay and knew she'd located the opening. With one hand on the wall to guide her, she picked up speed and raced blindly toward Cain.

The demon had broken free inside of Rory's mind, and she didn't even realize it.

Cain forced his body to keep moving, his sword to keep swinging while he shouted continual warnings for Rory to stay away.

Nothing he'd said had gotten through. She was convinced that he needed her. The demon had tricked her into believing the lie.

He kept fighting. Sweat dripped into his eyes, burning. Most of the demons at his feet were small and easy to kill, but toward the back of the swarming mass he saw larger beasts shoving their way forward.

As soon as they reached him and he had to turn his attention to them, the smaller Synestryn would break through his defenses. There was no way his sword could be in so many places at one time.

He didn't want to die. Not now, not when he'd just found Rory. He'd come to care for her, deeply. He loved her feisty spirit and her refusal to back down from what she believed was right. He loved her willingness to risk herself for others. He even loved her ridiculous pink hair and how it felt as it brushed his skin.

They'd hardly had any time together. The luceria made him feel like he'd known her for years, and yet it only highlighted how little time they'd really had.

But his regrets for what he'd never have were selfish compared to what that baby would never have. If Cain lost this battle, little Ethan would be lost as well. He couldn't let that happen.

His resolve fueled his limbs, forcing them to move faster. He didn't spare any attention on what was behind the demons right in front of him. He focused only on cutting them down, watching as the Synestryn behind them pulled the corpses back to feed on them.

Rory drew closer. He felt her pull energy from him so fast, it nearly burned. He couldn't tell what she was doing with it—whether she would use it to help him or kill him. With the demon free in her mind, there was no way to know whose side she was on.

Cain lifted his sword for another countless attack, but by the time his swing landed, the targets in front of him were gone. They'd been ripped away, screaming in fury as something shoved them back against the cave wall.

Dozens of demons squirmed behind a faintly glowing blue wall. Some of them burst under the pressure, causing others to go into a feeding frenzy for the blood.

Rory stood nearby, staring blindly into space. She wasn't even facing the right way to see what she was doing.

Her breathing was hard, and her skin was too pale. Her body shook under the strain of crushing the demons.

More power flowed out of him, feeding her magic. She let out a hoarse cry of effort, and the demons behind the glowing wall were crushed into oily black slurry. The few that had escaped, rushed over to feed from the blood leaking out along the ground.

Cain didn't wait to see what she'd do next. While the demon in her head was still alive, she was a threat. Perhaps she wouldn't kill him and cut off the source of her power, but that didn't mean she wouldn't use his power to kill others. There were innocents down here, and it was Cain's duty to make sure Rory didn't hurt them.

So, as he promised, he reached into her mind with the intent to render her unconscious. Only nothing happened. She stayed on her feet.

That same blue light that had crushed the demons against the wall formed around him in a cylinder, pinning his arms to his sides. He felt his feet leave the ground, and as she walked deeper into the caves, Cain bobbed beside her like a balloon on a string.

A slow, wicked smile curved her pretty mouth, and when she spoke, the voice that came out was not hers. It was a low, hissing threat. "She's mine now. And so are you."

Chain the human to my bed. Lock the child in a kennel in my room to ensure her cooperation.

Those had been Raygh's orders to Canaranth, given in such an arrogant, assuming tone it was obvious he didn't even question whether or not Canaranth would obey.

Is that what he'd become? A lackey who did what he was told without thought or opinion?

Yes, Raygh could kill him with little more than a twitch of his finger. And yes, he was one of the Synestryn lords who ruled with ruthless control. But that didn't mean Canaranth was a coward.

He loved Ella as much as a monster like him was capable of loving anyone. And his child . . . he'd never thought to feel such profound hope as he had when he'd held his son in his arms.

He'd helped Ella escape once. And while he'd broken his promise to come find her, he'd done it for her own good. She was supposed to be safe behind the Sentinels' hidden walls.

If it weren't for Connal, she still would be.

Canaranth was partially responsible for the events that had led up to Ella being back inside the caves. If he'd defied Zillah, refusing to feed Connal, none of this would have happened.

But it had, and now it was Canaranth's job to protect his family.

He carried Ella into a small stone chamber. Their son sat atop his mother, staring at Canaranth with huge, dark eyes. As he watched, plumes of inky black swirled within his irises, barely visible against the rich brown color.

"I'm your father," he told the boy. "I'm going to get you out of here. You and your mother will be safe."

He wasn't sure how he was going to make that happen—Raygh would be furious that he'd been disobeyed. Still, it was worth whatever punishment he suffered to see his family back in the hands of the Sentinels.

There were two of them here, now. He could smell them nearby. All he had to do was make sure they got out of here alive to take Ella and the boy away.

It struck him that he didn't even know his son's name. What kind of father didn't know such a fundamental fact about his own flesh and blood?

With a twist of regret for things he knew he could never have, Canaranth shoved the compulsion of sleep away from Ella's mind, waking her.

She blinked several times. "Hello? Who's there?"

Her human eyes were no longer used to the dark the way they had been. And even then, she'd always needed some light to see. The lighter he carried had reminded him of her, and he once again put it to good use.

The flame flared to life, shining over her face. The golden glow wrapped around her, as if it wanted to be a part of her. So pretty, so clean and soft.

He'd missed everything about her, and only now had he realized how inadequate his memory had been compared to the real thing.

"Canaranth?" she asked in disbelief.

"Yes. You're safe now, but you must leave here. It's not safe for you or our son."

The child had remained utterly silent—no fussy cries or babbling squawks.

Ella pulled the boy to her chest in a hug. "You knew he was yours?"

"Instantly. His scent."

She swallowed and nodded. "I won't leave without you. Come away with us."

"I can't. You know I can't. They would hunt me down."

"We'll run. We'll hide."

"There is nowhere you and I can live in safety. How you managed to keep our son alive for so long is a wonder. He's so big."

"Ethan. I named him Ethan. He's strong, like you. All he needs is us to love him. And the sun."

The sun. If he hadn't already been aware of the giant rift between them, that made it clear. "Sunlight keeps him alive?"

"Yes. Like the other boy. I heard rumors. I hid his Synestryn side. No one knows."

Canaranth stroked Ethan's silky cheek. "Your mother loves you. I love you. Don't ever forget that."

"Don't talk like you'll never see him again," said Ella. "We're going to be together now."

She would fight him if he told the truth. There was no time for that now. Later, she would be angry over his lie, but it was for the best.

He forced himself to give her a reassuring smile. "If that's what you really want."

"I do."

"Okay, then you need to listen carefully. We don't have much time. I need you to stay here, hidden, until I come for you."

"No, don't leave. The monsters—"

"Will leave you alone. I'll see to it. Just stay here and stay quiet. I won't be long."

She nodded.

Canaranth had little power, thanks to the human blood running through his veins. But he was powerful enough to protect his family.

He used his teeth to cut open his wrist, and laid a line of blood across the entrance to the chamber. Within the blood, he wove a warning to his kind to stay away.

The scent of possession filled the space, marking this area as his.

His measures wouldn't keep Raygh or any of the other Synestryn lords out, but none of the lesser beasts would bother Ella and their son.

All he had to do now was find the Theronai he smelled and make sure they stayed alive long enough to save his family.

Chapter 30

Rory realized what she was doing too late. She'd been tricked. The demon in her head—Raygh was what he called himself—had been lurking there, waiting silently for an opportunity to strike, and had used her fear for Cain against her. Like a dog following a trail of bacon, she'd gone where Raygh had led, not even realizing that she was no longer in control.

And now she was trapped inside her own body, unable to do anything more than scream in silent frustration and anger.

Visions of hundreds of demons filled her eyes. She saw herself in front of a horrible, monstrous beast.

Raygh.

Its face was sunken, its body hairless, tinted the same color as new bruises. Its flat, open nostrils leaked snot onto its lips and chin, which it licked away with a scaly, black tongue.

She knelt before him, still and pliant, fighting for control. Cain floated at her side, wrapped tightly inside the cage Raygh had crafted using her body. She tried to cut off the flow of power to release him, but it was like the connection between her mind and body was severed.

"You're wasting your energy," Raygh hissed at her.

Mucus flew from where it leaked over his lips, making her stomach give a queasy heave.

She reached for the luceria, hoping to find some way to touch Cain's mind. Surely he had a plan. All those thousands of battles he'd shown her were filled with winning strategies. She hadn't had time to sort through them all and make sense of them, but Cain had been around forever. He had to have a plan.

"Such a dilemma," said the snot monster. "I really want to kill your beau, but if I do, then all that pretty power of yours will be lost. Just think of what I can do with a trained, bonded pair of Theronai at my command."

She was definitely thinking about it. At least she was new to all of this, and relatively harmless, unlike some of the other women from Cain's memories.

Another man walked into the room. Dozens of eyes slid in his direction, giving Rory a clear view. He was tall, pale, and compared to Raygh, beautiful. He could easily have passed as a human—at least from a distance. His voice was soft and mesmerizing, almost gentle. "I think we should cage them. Separately, of course. That will give you time to decide what to do with them." He moved closer, and small demons parted to allow him to pass. "I will take them now if it pleases you."

"It does not. I want his blood first. Then there will be no question of their obedience. He will do as I will, just as she does."

"Of course. You'll need to lower the barrier holding him." He had a dagger in his hand, which he held at Cain's throat with an air of menace. "If you fight, I will kill you."

Rory felt the flow of power going through her ease as the glowing cylinder of light dissipated down to Cain's elbows. He struggled, but the tight shield held firm.

She was unable to do anything except witness the event through too many eyes to count. The different angles gave her a disturbingly 3D view, forcing her to witness Cain's fury from all angles.

"If you hurt her, I will kill you," growled Cain.

Raygh laughed, sending streamers of mucus flying onto his lap. "I'm going to hurt her. You can be sure of that. In a minute, you're going to help me hurt her."

"Never going to happen. I'm bound by my vow."

"I'm not. You two are simply meat puppets for my amusement. It's my will that matters. Not yours."

A ripple of comfort that felt like Cain brushed her mind, gone so soon, she wasn't sure she'd felt it at all.

"How sweet," said Raygh. Then to the man with the dagger, "Bring him to me."

Cain's body bobbed along the floor as the pale man pulled him by one ear toward Raygh. All she had to do was regain a second of control and Cain would cut those fuckers down before they could blink. His sword was in his hand, pressed tight against his leg. If she could just find the strength to shove the demon back into its box, they'd make it out of this alive.

Rory remembered what Ronan had done when he'd barricaded the demon inside that cage. She could picture the metal box in her mind, open and waiting for her to shove him inside. She was strong. She could do this.

Instinctively, she reached for Cain's power to aid her efforts, but she couldn't touch it. Something huge and evil loomed in her way. As she struggled, the visions flared to sickening brightness, shoving their way into her eyes like electrified knitting needles. Within some of those visions, she saw Raygh flinch. Whether he was also reacting to her visions or if she was gaining some ground, she had no idea. Either worked for her.

She refocused her efforts, trying to picture the demonic presence as bound and shrinking.

Sweat trickled down her back. Her muscles trembled with strain. The Godzilla of headaches rampaged through her brain like it was Tokyo. A stifled cry of pain erupted from her lips, but she'd made the sound herself with no demon-fueled compulsions.

"She's beating you," said Cain, his deep, gravelly voice warming her like sunshine. "She's going to smash your mind flat until it's nothing more than chunky pulp."

His cheerleading efforts helped her ignore the pain and fight harder.

Something inside one of her visions caught her attention. Raygh was glaring at her, teeth bared as it growled in frustration. He wasn't paying attention to the man with the dagger—the one who had lifted it to just the right angle to plunge it into Raygh's neck.

The demon saw what she saw. She felt his awareness spark. He turned just in time to block the attack from his servant. The pale man's wrist snapped audibly as it was bent down. The tip of the dagger dug into his forearm. Raygh's anger was so powerful, she felt it blow back against her like hot, rotten breath.

But he was distracted now. Busy.

Rory shoved every scrap of willpower and strength she had at the demon's presence in her mind, trapping it within a glowing bubble the way Ronan had done. The cage only lasted for a split second, but it was enough to break his hold on her.

She let go of the power holding Cain against his will. He hit the floor, landing on his feet. His sword came up in a powerful arc, slicing the demon's chest open from stomach to chin. On the downswing, Raygh threw the man who'd tried to stab him in the way. Cain's sword went right through him before he could slow or stop.

Rory felt his horror at what he'd done, his fury at the creature that had caused him to harm someone who'd tried to help.

Raygh tossed the pale man at Cain, knocking him off balance. He regained his footing and charged. An enraged bellow echoed off the cave walls.

She felt the demon gather his power, bursting free of

the glowing bubble to take over her body once again. She fought back, screaming as pain sliced through her skull. The visions flowing into her from the monsters surrounding them grew brighter, more vivid. One part of her saw a mass of creatures swarming toward the man with the dagger. He was bleeding badly, struggling to swat them away.

Rory wanted to help, but she couldn't move. Raygh had regained control of her limbs, locking her in place. She tried to fight him off, but she was so tired. Weak. Her heart was skipping beats, jerking around in her chest as if trying to break free.

That's when she realized what was happening. Raygh was bleeding out, dying. And Rory was going to die right along with him.

"No!" screamed Cain. His desperation reverberated in her ears and inside her thoughts. He knew what was happening. She felt the dark knowledge seep into him, making him hesitate.

If Cain killed the demon, he would kill her as well.

Chapter 31

Ronan crouched in a small corner of his mind, waiting to strike at the demon that controlled his body. It had ravaged him, fighting the chains and tape that bound him until blood flowed freely from his broken skin.

Ronan couldn't even muster the control he needed to heal himself. The demon didn't care if he lived or died, it only cared about freeing his body to use as it willed.

As Ronan waited, feeling his body weaken drop after drop, he felt a sudden change. A flickering break in the demon's control.

Without hesitation, Ronan sprang from where he waited, forcing his consciousness to swell and surge so there would be no room left for the demon.

It realized what had happened and fought back, snarling for control. Ronan wasn't going to get another chance. He was too weak to do this again, and now the demon knew he was lying in wait. If Ronan was to be free, now was his chance.

His cells burned as he ripped power from them. His muscles trembled as they shrank. The tape binding him loosened as he turned his tissue into fuel, growing skinny and frail.

For a fleeting second, he felt Rory's presence, recognizing her fighting spirit instantly. He'd had her blood. The demon inhabited both of them. They shared a space, linked together in a way Ronan had no time to understand. He simply accepted her presence as fact.

The demon was powerful, but its strength was fading. Something had happened. It was dying.

And it was going to take both Ronan and Rory with it.

No. He refused to allow that. His people needed Rory to survive and provide them with sustenance. One fewer Sanguinar left to feed was no tragedy. One fewer female Theronai left to feed his kind—left to bear children whose blood was strong—was.

As starvation ravaged his body, he knew what he had to do. He wouldn't let his kind suffer as he did now, fighting back hopelessness, pain and despair. She and her future children were the key to Sanguinar survival. She had to live, no matter what.

Strengthened by his decision, Ronan did the only thing he could think to do. He found the lingering, weakened presence of the demon in her mind and pulled it from her. It fought his hold, but was no match for a Sanguinar with nothing to lose.

We'll die together, he whispered to the creature. *And I will torture you for eternity.*

Cain felt it the moment Ronan had freed Rory from the demon's hold. He didn't understand how Ronan had done it, but there was no time to figure it out now. Later, he would ask Ronan. And thank him. Whatever blood he needed, Cain would give him. He deserved no less.

Assuming he survived.

If Ronan was tied to the demon in the same way Rory had been, then chances were killing it would kill him as well.

Sadly, there was no choice. Rory's life was at stake as long as the demon lived, and Cain's vow forced his hand. He could, however, kill the beast slowly, giving Ronan time to slip away.

Cain sliced a shallow cut across the demon's arm. The sound of scratching, chittering creatures grew louder as the scent of blood sent them into a frenzy.

A flicker of panic bursting out of Rory was the only warning Cain had of the impending attack. She sent him an image of hundreds of those small, scorpion-tailed demons skittering toward his back.

His mind spun through the options and came to rest on the only conclusion possible. The little demons weren't poisonous. The Synestryn lord in front of him was the real danger.

Raygh lifted his hand, and the cave walls began to shudder. Rocks tumbled from the ceiling, stinging Cain's arms and back.

If he didn't kill the demon, it would bring the cave down on top of them. There was no more time to delay and give the Sanguinar time to escape.

I'm sorry, Ronan.

The mass of scorpion-tailed demons swarmed over Cain's back. Their barbs dug into his skin, shoving their way right through his leather. He ignored them and adjusted his swing for the additional weight riding his body.

Raygh cowered back in his stone throne, slipping on his blood as he saw Cain's intent. There was nowhere for the demon to run. At least that's what Cain had thought.

The demon lifted from his seat, rising steadily out of reach. Cain jumped onto the throne, but the added weight of the small demons threw him off balance. He slipped in the blood and began to fall, the stone floor of the cave and hungry mass of demons waiting for him.

Something stopped his fall. Rory. He felt her presence caress him as she batted away the demons with a sharp gust of wind. She buoyed him up, lifting him until he was within striking distance.

He had no leverage inside her invisible grip, but she was so firmly fixed in his mind, she acknowledged the problem in an instant, giving him a solid surface on which to stand. He didn't know how far out his temporary floor expanded, but he trusted her to give him what he needed.

A bolt of fire shot from Raygh's fingers, searing along Cain's ribs. He held his cry of pain behind clenched teeth and swung for the demon's neck. It couldn't move out of the way. It was trapped against a rock jutting from the ceiling. Instead, it dropped out of sight.

Cain dove after it, knowing he couldn't let it get away. As he fell, he caught sight of the floor below. Hundreds of Synestryn lined the floor, waiting to pounce as he hit the ground. Rory stood near the man who'd dared attack Raygh, holding the creatures back with a brilliant circle of fire.

As she split her attention to slow his fall, the flames sputtered and a few demons leaked through.

Let me go, he told her. *Protect yourself.*

Little busy. Mind your own damn business.

Raygh hit the floor running. Cain was right on its tail, but not close enough. The demon reached a passageway—the one leading out—and put its scaly blue hands on the walls. The cave shook and more rock spilled down.

A wall of demons blocked Cain from his target. The scent of his blood had them nipping at his heels. They hadn't hit him from behind only because Rory was there, shielding his back.

He cut through them, shoving his way forward. A couple managed to get through his defenses, but there was nothing he could do to stop them. Poison entered his blood, slowing him down. It hadn't sapped his strength yet, but it would. Soon.

Before that could happen, he threw everything he had into reaching the Synestryn lord. The rumble of the walls, crash of falling rock, and screams of crushed demons was deafening. Raygh slumped in the opening, but the twisted sneer of determination on its monstrous face made it clear that it was going to pull the cave down on them, even if it had to die to make it happen.

Cain shouldered a larger demon out of the way, taking a deep bite in the bargain. His right arm cracked and went instantly numb. He grabbed up his sword in his left hand and used every bit of his strength to lunge forward.

The tip of his sword went right through Raygh's throat. A hard pivot to the side and its spinal cord was severed. It fell to its knees. Cain finished the job, lopping off Raygh's head completely.

The Synestryn lord was dead. Cain had stopped him from collapsing the cave. But it didn't matter. There were too many demons left to fight. He was poisoned, fading fast. His right arm was broken. He couldn't possibly fight them all. And neither could Rory.

They were all going to die down here and share Raygh's tomb.

Chapter 32

So this was how it ended.

Rory wasn't one to give up, but she knew overwhelming odds when she saw them—especially when she saw them from so many angles. Cain's assessment reverberated in her mind, agreeing with her own. He couldn't see a way out, either.

He was in bad shape. He could barely fight. She was struggling to keep the demons off of him and keep them away from her. She didn't know how much longer she could hold up the flow of magic. As it was, she was shaking and having trouble breathing. And that weakness he'd warned her about? It was here, crushing her under a mountain of sudden exhaustion.

Maybe if he touched her—if the two halves of the luceria connected—she could find the strength to carry them out. It was worth a shot.

Cain was nearer the exit, and the flames surrounding her and the dying man were flickering out.

"Hold on," she told him. "I'm going to get you outside."

"No. Can't go. The sun. I always wanted to see the sun."

Right. She'd almost forgot he was one of the Synestryn, unable to stand sunlight.

"What can I do?" she asked, her desperation obvious even to her own ears.

"My son. His mother. I put them here." He touched her head, giving her an image of where Ella and Ethan were stashed. "Save them."

"I'll try," she said, and as she spoke, the vision of her face—the one coming from him—winked out.

He was dead.

The weight of the promise she'd made to him bowed her shoulders. She didn't know how she was going to manage to save them, much less herself, but she wasn't going to give up yet. Not when there was still time to fight for survival.

Rory lifted herself up out of the ring of fire, letting it die down. She stood on a disk of solidified air, hoping she didn't fall off into the black sea of teeth and claws. As she moved, she saw herself from hundreds of eyes. A single ray of sunlight bounced off her pink hair.

Hope filled her up. If there was sunlight, there was a way out. All she had to do was find it. And yet not one of the demons dared look in that direction. She couldn't use their eyes. She had to find a way to take control of her own.

A pulse of power spilled into her, an offering from Cain. She clasped on to it, struggling to use it to do her will. But no matter how hard she tried, she could not force even one of the demons to look toward the sunlight so she could see where to punch through.

Cain was safe inside a dome of protection, but the poison was acting fast, stealing his strength. Hers was fading with his, their connection vibrating under the strain. He couldn't open his eyes. She couldn't use him to see, either.

Rory turned her head in the right direction, but the flood of visions was too dense, blinding her. She focused Cain's power into a wedge, hoping to shove all the other sights aside.

A flash of light filled her eyes. Her real eyes. The beam

was shining directly on her face, giving her a tiny glimpse of the rising sun. Brilliant golds and oranges flowed through the tiny crack. Freedom was so close, she could feel its heat, but the opening was way too small for her and Cain to fit through.

I always wanted to see the sun.

That man or demon or whatever he was had given his life in an effort to save them. She wished now that he'd lived long enough for her to show him this beautiful sight.

He was gone, cursed to eternal darkness, but she could show all of those demons what she saw. Maybe she could scare them away.

A flare of hope lit inside of Cain. He was still with her, feeding her the power she needed to stay aloft.

Show them. Show me. *Show me the sun.*

Rory gathered Cain's strength into herself, and concentrated on making one single demon see what she saw. At first she wasn't sure if it was going to work, but then her target below began to scream a high, painful cry. It ran in stark terror, slamming so hard into the wall that it went still.

That was it. She'd done it. Now all she had to do was do that again about two hundred times.

She wasn't sure she could do it, but she was sure she was going to try. The thrill of the challenge strengthened her. Cain felt it, too, offering her silent encouragement and complete trust. He truly thought she could do this. His faith in her did not waver in the slightest.

She'd witnessed it before when he'd leapt after the falling demon, trusting her to catch him. She hadn't had time to marvel over it then, but she couldn't help but do so now. He didn't see her as weak or helpless. He didn't see her as someone who needed to be saved. He saw her as an equal. A partner. To him, she was not broken, but whole and solid and beautiful. She *was* going to save them.

Something in her clicked, some fundamental understanding that she'd been overlooking dawned, and everything fell into an orderly array. Her eyes started to work properly. She was no longer ruled by the visions of those around her. She ruled them.

She began sorting through the things she saw, taking in knowledge from everything she witnessed through every creature present. Cain's breathing was shallow. His heart was slowing. Ella was trapped in a room nearby, and dark, twisted demons began to tentatively cross a wet line drawn across the doorway. She wrapped herself around her baby, protecting him with her body as the monsters closed in.

Rory had no more time to learn how to do what she needed to do. She sucked in huge gulps of Cain's power, hearing him groan as she forced him to give her what she needed. The air in front of her shimmered as she reshaped it, forcing it to focus the beam of sunlight into a tiny band. It hit her eyes, searingly bright and perfect for her needs.

Rory stared into the light until tears wet her cheeks. She forced the creatures below to see what she saw. She gave them no way to hide. No way to escape. Even when they shut their eyes, her vision was still there, forcing its way into their brains—the way her visions had always done to her.

The smell of smoke choked her. The agonized screams of dying demons filled the air. Her eyes burned as the blinding light drove into them. She welcomed the pain, refusing to blink until the last shrill, hissing scream faded into silence.

She floated down until her feet hit something solid. Globs of blotchy color faded from her sight, leaving her standing in blackness. She couldn't see Cain or Ella. She couldn't see anything. She was blind, and Cain was dying.

She felt Cain's presence, felt the luceria tying them together, and followed that connection. She pushed her way through piles of dead demons, using her boots to shove them aside. Cain's clothes were wet with blood. She could feel the burn of poison in his skin, but had no idea how to fix it.

Her hands shook with fatigue, and it was all she could do to stay upright. Weariness weighed her down, and she could no longer tell if what she was feeling was coming from him or her.

With an excruciating effort of will, she pulled on his power, channeling it over his skin to close his wounds. She had no idea if it worked. He was still slick with blood.

A second later, she fell, too weak to sit up. His hard body cushioned her fall, and beneath the stench of demons, smoke and blood, she smelled his skin. So warm, so familiar. Like home.

Rory had lost everyone she'd ever loved. Her mother, Nana. She'd lost her quiet little life and her home. She would not lose Cain, too. Not as long as there was even a single spark of power left in either of them.

She grabbed his big hand and held it to her throat so that his ring latched on to her necklace. There was only a faint trickle of power, but she took hold of it and pulled, demanding that it go on a seek-and-destroy mission inside his body. As the magic spilled out of her, she deflated, sagging over his body. She couldn't move anymore. She could barely pull in her next breath, but she kept funneling power into him, ordering it to clean away the poison.

Cain jerked under her hand, letting out a pained gasp. A terrible choking sound rose between them, and a second later, she heard him vomit. Then he went still.

Only the steady beat of his pulse kept her from spiraling into complete panic.

Nothing mattered except keeping him alive. She no longer cared about anything beyond feeling his next breath fill his chest. She didn't care if she lived. She didn't care if she spent the rest of her life plagued by debilitating visions. She didn't even want to find the person who made them go away anymore. That would only separate her from Cain, which would make her life a far bleaker place than temporary blindness ever could.

She needed him to pull through. She needed him in her life, at her side, safe and happy. She swore that if she lived, she'd give up her search for freedom from her visions and learn to accept them. Whatever price she had to pay in exchange for Cain's life would be a bargain. Whatever the universe demanded of her, she would gladly give up. Even her life.

Please don't let him die.

Rory saw nothing but blackness, but heard a faint quivering sound. Motion. Footsteps.

Someone was coming. She didn't know if it was friend or foe, but it didn't matter. She'd done all she could. There was no fight left in her. Whatever came would come, and if she died, at least she'd die holding the man she loved.

Chapter 33

Justice had no idea where she was going. All she knew was that she was late, thanks to an accident on I-35.

Impatience burned in her gut, making her hands fidget on the steering wheel. Her Porsche didn't like these pockmarked, backcountry roads, but that was too bad. If it didn't behave, she'd ditch it and find another ride. Maybe a nice pickup truck that wouldn't complain so damn much.

A freight train's light caught her attention, coming from the west. Sunrise shone off of its metal cars, which stretched out in the distance. If she didn't beat the train, it would slow her down even more, and she didn't have that kind of time.

She gunned the engine, enjoying the smooth shift in gears and the powerful hum sliding through her. Up ahead, the striped, wooden barricades were falling slowly, the lights and bells chiming to warn her of the impending danger.

A rush of excitement trilled through her, stretching her mouth with a grin. She was going to make it. Probably. Maybe.

The Porsche went airborne as it hit the slight ramp in the road leading to the tracks. She sailed through the railroad crossing, the hood of her car clipping the wooden barricade.

She landed hard enough to rattle her teeth. The back end of the Porsche swayed with the wind the train created.

Justice watched the train pass in her rearview mirror, wondering what it would have been like if she'd been just half a second slower. She'd woken up years ago, naked, alone and confused, with no memory of who she was. As she crouched beneath a looming billboard advertising a seedy law firm, the giant, glowing letters asking the question "Seeking justice?" mocked her. She'd been seeking a lot more than that since that night, and now, years later, she was still no closer to finding answers. She didn't even know her own name.

If that freight train had hit her, would she have disappeared just as suddenly as she'd appeared, going back to wherever it was she'd come from?

Apparently, she wasn't going to find out this time. Maybe tomorrow.

She slowed at the next intersection and took a left. She didn't know why, but after more than a decade of bouncing around the country like a pinball, she'd stopped questioning why she went anywhere. She followed her gut, and ignored the world spinning past her. Nothing these people did could touch her. She, however, touched them often. Sometimes hard.

As she neared her target, she couldn't help but feel like this time was different. Special. She could feel it radiating in her bones, filling her lungs with anticipation.

Whatever waited for her this time was going to be one for the diary. She only wished she knew how it would end. Would she need a kind word this time, or her gun?

Only one way to find out.

Justice slewed over the gravel roads, ignoring the Porsche's complaints about chipped paint and dust. As she took the last turn, she saw a little house sitting back, snuggled inside a dense ring of trees.

She parked the Porsche next to a black van and got out, the sense of urgency growing with every passing second.

When she knocked on the door, no one answered. Ditto with the doorbell. The place was locked, but she wasn't going to let that stop her.

She circled around back and peered in through the sliders. No one.

With the butt of her gun, she smashed the window and let herself in. The place was dark, quiet. The scent of something spicy and sweet filled the air, like someone had been baking recently.

A quick search of the living areas and bedrooms told her no one was here. Only she was here for some reason—and that reason was becoming increasingly desperate.

Justice started opening doors, searching closets, looking behind shower curtains and under beds. Finally, she opened a door leading down into a basement. That sweet scent was stronger here, pulling her in.

With her gun in hand, she descended the wooden steps. When she was about halfway down, she saw a man bound from shoulders to ankles. He was slumped forward. Blood pooled under him. A trickle had worked its way over the concrete floor to a drain.

Panic hit her in the chest, and she stood there, gawking in shock for a moment. It had been a long time since she'd felt anything this powerful—good or bad. Maybe she never had felt anything like this. Emotions seemed to slide around her, mostly, never touching her in any meaningful way.

Until now.

She was afraid. Scared completely and utterly shitless.

Justice hurried down the steps to the bleeding man. Her fingers pressed against his throat, feeling for a pulse, but the chill of his skin told her she was too late.

He let out a quiet moan, and again, she was shocked. He was still alive. She wasn't too late.

The question was, why was she here? What was she supposed to do?

She pulled out her knife and cut through the tape. Stopping his bleeding seemed to be the first order of business.

Her blade hit metal. He'd been chained, too. Whoever he was, someone had really wanted to make sure he stayed put.

Maybe he was a bad guy. Maybe she was here to finish the job and kill him.

Something about that didn't ring true. If he was supposed to die, then all she would have had to do was stay away. Whatever powers compelled her wouldn't have had to waste the effort to send her here.

By the time she'd cut the bloody man free, his breath was wheezing in and out of his scrawny chest. His clothes were too big, and he was so thin he felt brittle as she moved him, trying to locate the bleeding.

As far as she could tell, he had no cuts. Which changed things.

"Whose blood is this?" she demanded.

His head fell back against her arm, and she was struck by the way she cradled him, as if he were something precious. But that wasn't true. No one was precious to her.

His pale blue eyes opened. Pain churned there, along with endless hunger and desperation. His lips moved and a faint whisper puffed out. "Blood. Need."

The sound of his voice made hidden memories churn in her head. She reached for them, trying to grab even one, but they all fell away, abandoning her.

Frustration made her arms tighten around his body. She lowered her head closer, hoping to hear another word—something, anything to give her back what was taken. "What do you need?"

He licked his dry lips. Swallowed. His gaze focused on her throat. "Blood. Please."

That power that drove her—God, fate, karma—whatever it was, spoke to her now, silently urging her to give him what he needed.

With a shaking hand, she pulled her curly black hair away from her neck and lifted him higher. His lips brushed her skin in what she thought a kiss would feel like. A tingling sense of familiarity spilled down her spine. She knew what he was going to do, but she wasn't afraid.

Then again, she hadn't been afraid of a speeding freight train, either.

A sharp pain broke her skin, and his mouth began to move against her, suckling. Pleasure unlike anything she could have imagined stroked over her, lighting up parts of herself she'd assumed were dead or missing. Other people felt joy and sadness. Other people laughed and cried. For Justice, that had all been fake—an act designed to fit in. And now those things were hers, streaking through her like lightning.

The man in her arms grew heavy. She was no longer holding him up. His body swelled and shifted, gripping her like his life depended on it. Maybe it did.

She grew weaker. The chill from the concrete floor sank into her, stealing her warmth. Her heart sped, and a sense of fear rose up.

He was killing her. And even more startling: she didn't want to die.

Justice tried to pull away, but he was too strong. The knife lay on the floor nearby, discarded and forgotten. But her gun was tucked in her waistband.

She fumbled to reach it. Her hands didn't quite work right. She wasn't holding it right and couldn't figure out which way to move it so she could fire. So instead, she lifted the heavy metal and slammed it down into the man's head.

He went limp. Blood flowed down her neck. She covered the wound and scrambled away, leaving him sprawled on the floor. By the time she stood, he was already moving.

She didn't wait to see what he'd do next. She just ran. Up the stairs, out the front door and into her Porsche. While she was struggling to find the right key, she saw him inside the house, holding back, just out of the light.

Whatever he was, she was out of here. That nagging sense that drove her to do the things she did was gone now. Apparently, saving his life was why she'd come, and now that her job was done, she was getting the hell away.

Ronan cursed the sun as he watched the woman flee. Power sang in his veins, and for the first time in memory, he was no longer hungry. She had done that for him, and now she was gone. But no matter how much power he possessed, he couldn't go after her. Not in the sunlight. He was trapped here until nightfall, by which time, she'd be long gone.

He memorized her license plate number. Perhaps someone at Dabyr could help him track her down while he slept.

If not, then he'd seek her out at nightfall. He had her blood now. There was nowhere she could hide from him. He would find her, and when he did, he would make sure she never ran from him again.

Chapter 34

Rory woke to utter blackness. She reached for Cain, but all she felt was soft bedding. The scent of laundry soap filled her nose, so welcome after the stench of burned demons.

A huge, gaping hole loomed right in her middle, but she was too groggy and confused to figure out what was wrong.

She reached out, searching for a lamp. A warm, bony hand found hers and held it in a loving grip.

"The lights are already on, honey."

Rory went still in shock. She knew that voice—remembered it from her childhood. "Mom?"

"Yes." That single word was filled with regret and lost chances.

"I'm dead, aren't I?"

"You're very much alive. Everything is going to be okay."

"Rory," said a deep, cultured voice. "It's Logan. You're safe at Dabyr. Your mother is right. You're going to be fine."

Mom was alive. That was so bizarre, Rory couldn't wrap her head around it. She struggled to make sense, but all she could find was happy relief.

She clasped her mother's hand, refusing to let go for

fear she'd disappear. "I thought you were dead. Nana said you were gone."

"I promised her I'd stay away if she took care of you. She didn't want my drug problem affecting you. Neither did I. I know I was a horrible mom, but I'm clean now."

Confusion swamped Rory, making her head spin. "I don't understand."

Logan said, "We found your mother with the other humans Krag held hostage. We brought her here, drove the toxins from her body and gave her refuge. We had no idea who she was until we brought you here and she saw you."

"I dreamed I saw you before but was too high to care. I'm so sorry, Rory. For everything."

She followed Mom's arm until she could pull her in for a hug.

Rory didn't care about the past. She'd made her own share of mistakes—hurt too many people. Maybe she was a fool to forgive her mom for the crappy things she'd done, but she didn't care. Life was too short not to forgive. So she did. She let all the shit fall away, leaving only a bright, clean slate stretching out in front of them.

As Mom's scent wrapped around her, the pieces of the puzzle began to click together. Mom had been on the streets for years. She'd probably been at Sister Olive's shelter. And she'd been there when Rory had been tossed down in that flooded basement.

Mom was the one who blocked Rory's visions. She always had. That's why they'd gotten so much worse after she'd left, and why they'd disappeared from time to time when Rory had been near her without knowing it.

Happiness settled through her and she let herself feel hope for the future. Instinctively, she reached out for Cain's mind so she could share her joy with him, only to find him missing—utterly and completely gone. Panic stole over her, sucking her breath from her lungs.

Rory pulled away from her mom and looked toward where Logan's voice had originated. "Where's Cain?"

"Sleeping," said Logan. "You drove the poison from him, but he was in bad shape."

"Is he going to live?" *Please let him live.*

"Yes. He'll wake soon and I'm sure he'll want to see you."

Relief brought tears to her eyes, making them burn. "What happened? How did we get out of there?"

"The warriors Joseph sent after Ella and Ethan found you."

"Are they okay?"

"Ethan is fine. His mother didn't make it. She died protecting him."

Rory couldn't process that right now. She was already dealing with too much. "I want to talk to Cain, but I don't want him to see me like this—blind and helpless. How long will it take you to fix my eyes?"

Sadness hung in Logan's voice. "I'm sorry, Rory. I've already tried to correct your blindness. There's nothing more I can do."

Chapter 35

Cain woke up at Dabyr. Joseph was at his bedside, looking like he needed about a year's worth of sleep.

He couldn't feel Rory. He reached for her, but there was . . . nothing.

Panic had him jackknifing out of bed. "Where's Rory?"

"Take it easy. She's alive. She's here. Safe."

"I want to see her." He threw back the covers, finding himself naked.

Joseph tossed him a wad of clothing. "She's refusing to see anyone. Most specifically you."

"What? Why?"

Joseph's gaze hit Cain's neck with an obvious message.

Cain reached up, felt his luceria back in place. His lifemark was nearly bare again.

"Logan kept you asleep while your leaves fell. We didn't see any point in making you suffer through that."

"How long?" demanded Cain. "How long since my luceria fell?"

"Just over a day."

A whole day for Rory to think about changing her mind. And yet she chose to avoid him. "I don't understand. What did I do wrong? The last thing I remember she was burning the eyes out of all the demons at once. Did something happen after that?"

"Her mother is here."

"Alive?"

"Yes. She was one of the victims we rescued last spring. Drug addict in Krag's thrall. The Sanguinar cleaned her up and she's been living here ever since."

"She was the one Rory was looking for," guessed Cain. "The one who blocked her visions."

Joseph nodded. "Your luceria fell shortly after she woke and realized what was going on. She asked me to return it to you."

Cain pulled on his jeans and buckled his sword in place. "Where is she?"

"She doesn't want to see you."

"I don't give a fuck. Where is she?"

Joseph sighed. "The suite across the hall. I wanted her close in case she changed her mind."

Cain's legs were a bit wobbly, but he ignored the weakness and stalked across the hall. Joseph was right at his back, yammering, as if he could actually stop Cain from seeing the woman he loved.

He paused with his hand on the door to her suite as the knowledge sank in, driving away all darkness and doubt. His soul was filled with the blinding light of complete and perfect truth. He loved her—in a forever kind of way—and he was not going to let her go so easily.

"There's something you need to know," said Joseph.

Cain didn't care what the man had to say. There was nothing that would change Cain's mind. The door swung open and Rory stood suddenly, her head turning toward him. She was looking right at him, but there was no hint of recognition. No anger, no excitement or relief. Just empty blankness.

"Rory is blind," whispered Joseph.

The shock of that news hit him hard, but it vanished

in a moment, doing nothing to shake his decision. He still loved her. He still wanted her. "It changes nothing."

"Cain?" said Rory. She took a step toward him and ran into the coffee table. She caught herself before he'd made it to her side. Shame burned in her cheeks. "Go away."

"Not going to happen. You and I are going to talk."

"There's nothing to talk about. I made my decision."

"So did I." Cain turned to Joseph. "Leave."

"I don't think that's a good idea. If Rory doesn't want you here—"

Cain cut him off. "Then she can kick me out. After we've talked."

Joseph nodded. To Rory, he said, "I'll be right outside if you need me."

"She won't," said Cain.

Joseph shut the door on his way out.

Cain didn't wait to dive in. The longer she was away from him, the worse he felt. And it was more than just his lifemark that was suffering. He missed having her in his thoughts, feeling her so deeply a part of him that he could hardly tell the difference between them.

"I need you," he admitted, not giving a fuck about his pride.

"No, you need someone to fight by your side. That's all you've ever wanted." Her voice went quiet. "That and a child."

"Are you saying you don't want the same thing? You loved having my power at your fingertips. I felt every second of your exhilaration when you were kicking ass. You can't now lie and pretend you didn't love it."

"Of course I did. But in case you didn't hear Joseph, I'm blind. The Sanguinar can't fix it."

"So?"

"So, that makes it pretty hard to fight, don't you think?"

"Not for you. Sure, it's a challenge, but since when have you ever backed away from a challenge?"

"The stakes are too high. I'll get someone killed. Maybe even you."

"Maybe. Maybe not. What I do know is that without you I don't have much time left."

"So this is about saving yourself. I see."

"No, you don't. But if I have to use pity to get you back at my side, then I will. Whatever it takes, Rory. I love you too much to let you walk away."

She went still. "Love? I'm way too fucked up for you to love."

He was silent as he went to her. He cupped her face, making her jerk with surprise. Then she settled into his touch, her eyes, fluttering closed in pleasure.

"Is that what you think?" he asked.

"It's what I know. I'm helpless now, Cain. I can't be what you want me to be—except for the baby mama part, which I'm totally not ready for."

"I'll wait. As long as you need. And if you're never ready, I'll still love you. How can I not when you're so strong and fearless?"

She settled her hands on his chest, flinching away for a second as she realized he was bare. Tingling ribbons of excitement wove between them. The branches of his lifemark swayed under her touch.

"I'm not fearless now, Cain. I'm scared as hell. I don't know what I'm going to do."

"Take a chance on me. Let me love you."

"You don't really mean that. It's just the magical bullshit talking."

"Is that what you tell yourself? That what you feel for me isn't real?"

"It can't be. Nothing this good is real."

"Don't you want to find out if you're wrong? Take my luceria again, Rory. Once you do, you'll see how real my love for you is. I won't be able to hide the truth. You'll see it bright and clear, just the way I feel it."

"What if you're wrong? What if whatever this thing between us is goes away? Do you really want to be stuck with a woman who can't fight?"

He knew his Rory. She was a fighter at heart. She'd find a way to help them battle the demons regardless of whether or not she could see. One day, she'd realize that, too, but until then, it was his duty—his privilege—to keep trying to show her the truth.

"If you're really that worried, then word your vow carefully. You can give me whatever time you choose. I'll use that time to prove to you that my love is real and not dependent on something you can or can't do."

"I love you, too," she whispered.

Her words filled him up, making him feel invincible. He was the luckiest man who'd ever drawn breath, and he intended to spend every day making sure she knew how he felt.

He took her hands and guided them to his neck. "Then take my luceria, Rory. Give me your vow. You won't be sorry."

Her hands shook as she touched the band. It fell away easily, slipping down his chest into her grip. He took it from her and fastened it around her lovely throat.

Rory swallowed. Her voice trembled. "I promise to stay with you for as long as you really love me."

Every cell in his body rose up, crying out in victory. She was his now. Forever. Because that's how long his love for her would last.

Cain hurriedly finished the ceremony, cutting himself, giving her his vow, watching as the luceria shrank close to fit her skin. It immediately deepened to a dark, rich purple that made her skin glow in contrast. The Amethyst Lady. Forever his.

Her eyes widened with surprise and a smile lifted her mouth. "I can see me."

"What?"

Her smile grew bigger. "I can see through your eyes. And others'. Your power . . . the visions no longer blind me. They let me see."

Cain felt her joy shimmer into him, filling him up and making him whole. It was magnified by his own, so powerful he wasn't sure he could contain it all.

She hugged him tight and he folded himself around her, knowing that he'd never get enough of her, no matter how many more centuries he lived.

"What do we do now?" she asked.

"Whatever makes you happy."

"First, I'm going to take you into the bedroom and use you shamelessly."

"I like where this plan is going."

A fierce growl entered her voice. "And then, when it gets dark, we're going to go out and kick some demon ass."

Cain laughed. He simply couldn't hold in so much happiness. "Whatever you want, Rory. Whatever you want."

Chapter 36

Sibyl resisted the urge to call Cain. She didn't want to interrupt his happiness. After all of his years of faithful service to her, he deserved no less.

She picked up her porcelain doll and laid it on the top of her packed suitcase. The blond ringlets were tangled now, the blue dress marred with smudges of dirt. A few months ago, Sibyl had looked just like the doll, but no longer. She was a woman now, still growing used to her woman's body and all of its strange quirks.

"You're going back, aren't you?" asked the doll.

"Yes. I only left for Cain's sake. If I hadn't pushed him away, he never would have left my side. He found the woman. I can go home now."

The doll's black eyes blinked, and within that glassy stare, Sibyl saw her sister Maura's presence.

"You're going to try to find me, aren't you?" Maura's voice wavered between fear and hope.

"You can't be alone. It's not safe. Come home."

The doll's mouth did not move, but Maura's voice spilled out all the same. "I have no home."

"Mother and Father forgave you. As did I. Others will as well."

"Forgiveness is for those who no longer intend to do harm."

Sibyl's blood chilled at her sister's veiled threat. "Your powers have returned."

"As have yours. Unlike you, I can't help but use them. Eventually."

"It doesn't have to be that way. You can find a man whose power you can use to control yourself."

"And what Theronai would have me? Who values his honor so little that he would unite with his enemy? And who can I touch without killing him?"

Sibyl had no answers.

"Don't bother searching for me," said Maura. "It's a waste of your time."

"You could save a dying man. There is value in that. Redemption."

"Not for me. I'm . . . broken."

"Mother and Father are dead. Cain has found his mate. I'm alone now. I need you."

"You've never needed me. You have everything."

"Not my sister."

"We were never meant to be sisters."

"We were never meant to be separated. You're part of me, as I am part of you. Please. Come home."

There was a long, bleak silence. Finally, Maura said, "Don't try to contact me again."

The doll's eyes lost the sparkle of life, leaving Sibyl alone in her room.

Maura had been different this time. Insistent. Intent. Sibyl feared that wherever Maura was, whatever she was doing, she suffered. And because of that, Sibyl refused to leave her alone.

Despite the things Maura had done, she was not beyond redemption. And Sibyl was going to make sure she found it.

Turn the page for a special look
at the first book in the Edge series,

LIVING ON THE EDGE

by Shannon K. Butcher.
On sale now from Signet Eclipse.

Lucas Ramsey's target stood out from the swirling masses of perfumed, sequined gold diggers on the ballroom floor. There was something different about her—a watchful, focused quality that none of the other women at this fancy shindig possessed. Then again, there were three other women flirting with the flabby, older man she was hanging on. Maybe she was worried she'd lose her sugar daddy.

Too bad Lucas wasn't a rich man, 'cause he'd love to sign up for that job, even if for only one night.

The weapon in his shoulder holster felt odd through the thin cotton of his tuxedo shirt, and the shiny leather shoes didn't have the same gripping traction of his combat boots. He was as far out of place here as a man could get, but Sloane Gideon was here, so he was, too.

She was his last chance to repay a man he owed everything to. And the job was simple. All he had to do was keep her from catching her flight on a private jet in ninety-eight minutes.

No sweat. Even a washed-up soldier like him could handle that. In fact, Lucas could think of more than one way to make her miss that flight. The Old Man had said to use any means necessary to keep her in Texas, and as the list of the more interesting possibilities formed in

Lucas's head, his body temperature kicked up a couple of degrees.

There were hundreds of people here, all as well dressed as the room itself. Silk draped the walls, and fine linen cloths covered the tables. No polyester there.

A tidy crew of unobtrusive waiters wove among the guests, offering an endless supply of champagne in crystal flutes. Live music swelled from the raised platform where a small orchestra played. Elegant harmonies wove their way through the room, and on the far left, couples danced to a waltz Lucas recognized but could not name.

He was more of a beer and rock-and-roll kind of guy, but that didn't mean he couldn't appreciate the finer things in life.

Like Sloane Gideon. She was definitely fine.

Sloane was lovely in an untouchable sort of way. Perfect hair, perfect makeup, perfect dress flowing over perfect curves. She was walking perfection, and he'd bet his last dollar that she knew it. Decked out in diamonds and a dress that probably cost more than his car, she was way out of his league. Of course, if a man managed to strip her of all that flash and sparkle, the playing field would be a lot more even. And a lot more interesting.

All he had to do was pry her off the arm of Moneybags.

Lucas made his way across the ballroom, through the glittering upper-crust socialites. He ignored the women who glanced his way, and the men who sized him up, staring at him as if trying to calculate his net worth. Not much, he knew, but he'd played enough roles in his life that this one wasn't much of a stretch. At least here no one was shooting at him, which made this a walk in the park by comparison.

He mimicked the rigid posture of the other men here, donned an air of casual indifference to the ridiculous amounts of wealth being displayed, and moved toward his target.

His knee throbbed as he forced it to accept his weight

without limping. He wasn't sure how he was going to hit the dance floor with Sloane without giving away his weakness, but he'd think of something. Maybe a nice, long slow dance would come their way.

Even with a busted knee, Lucas could still come up with at least a dozen ways he could make her forget about her flight. Hell, if he wasn't too rusty, he might even be able to make her forget what day of the week it was. That would be a nice change of pace from his recent, unwelcomed, lengthy celibacy.

Any means necessary held a cargo ship load of possibilities.

Lucas had a hotel room upstairs all ready and waiting, stocked with enough wine to knock a man his size unconscious. Come morning when his debt to the Old Man was repaid, he'd leave Sloane satisfied and sleeping while he walked away from his old life with a clean slate and a clean conscience.

His new life held little appeal, but that, thankfully, was a problem for another day.

A movement in his peripheral vision stopped him dead in his tracks. He wasn't yet sure what he'd seen, but his instincts were: trouble. The urge to duck and cover screamed inside him, making his pulse skyrocket.

He turned his head, just enough to see the threat.

On a raised platform behind the orchestra was a thick arrangement of huge potted trees and plants. Sticking out of those plants was the last six inches of a rifle's barrel.

And it was aimed right at Sloane.

The man crossing the ballroom toward Sloane had been born to wear a tux.

She let her gaze slide up and down his body, appreciating the way the fabric hugged his broad shoulders and accentuated his trim waist. The fit was so good it almost hid the bulge of the weapon beneath his jacket. Almost.

She tightened her grip on the arm of her client, signaling to him there was trouble.

"Time to go," she whispered into his ear, smiling as though she'd just said something seductive.

Edward Henning looked at the three cosmetically engineered gold diggers fawning over him and giggling, then back at her like she was crazy. "I don't think so."

Sloane squeezed his arm harder. "Move. Now."

She'd scoped out the place earlier, and her best bet was the eastern stairwell exit. She gave her client a not so gentle tug, but the man refused to budge. Hanging on whatever bimbette number three was saying, he stayed glued to the spot.

Mr. Tuxedo and his concealed weapon were still fifty feet away, but he was making progress through the crowds easily. Men parted from his path, pulling their wives and dates out of his way. Not that she could blame them. Any woman in that man's path was a target—whether for sex or violence, Sloane wasn't sure, but it was definitely one of the two. Maybe both.

The bimbo trio giggled at something her client said, and she felt his chest puff up. At sixty-three, Edward Henning was turning to flab, spending too much time at a boardroom table and not enough in a gym. Then again, if he'd been in better shape, maybe he wouldn't have needed to hire her to watch his back. Out-of-shape flab with deep pockets was her job security. And Sloane loved her job—loved the danger and adrenaline rush. If it hadn't been for her friend Gina, she never would have even considered taking vacation time.

But Gina needed her. Now. Another half hour of guard duty and Sloane was officially off the clock. Her private flight left in ninety minutes, and it couldn't happen soon enough. It had taken all day and she'd called in a lot of favors, but she'd managed to make arrangements for a whole lot of firepower to be waiting for her in Colombia. No matter how deep a mess Gina had gotten herself into this time, one way or another, Sloane was going to get her out of that godforsaken country in one piece.

Mr. Tuxedo stopped for a split second, then fixed his gaze on her and picked up speed with more than a hint of desperation hurrying his pace.

Now it was *really* time to go.

Sloane plastered a vapid smile on her face and stomped over whatever bimbette number two was saying. "It's time to go, Edward. I have twin twentysomethings back in our room waiting for us, and the girls won't wait naked all night."

Edward's eyes rounded with shock, and her absurd distraction worked well enough that when she tugged on his arm this time, he went.

"What is going on?" he asked under his breath as they hurried toward the exit.

"A man with a gun is headed right this way. I thought now would be a really good time to leave."

Edward cast an apologetic look over his shoulder at the girls. "Why didn't you say so?"

"I did," said Sloane, refusing to allow her frustration to enter her tone.

"No, you said it was time to go. You didn't say anything about a gun."

"You hired *me* to protect you, rather than one of the big, beefy men I work with. That tells me that you really didn't want a lot of people knowing you needed a bodyguard. I was trying to be discreet."

"By telling everyone I'm going to have sex with twin girls?"

Sloane shrugged, urging Edward to hurry the hell up. The exit was only twenty feet away. "Would you have preferred guys?"

He sputtered in outrage, but at least she'd gotten his blood moving enough that he had picked up speed.

Just not enough.

Hot, strong fingers closed around her bare arm, jerking her to the side. Her grip on Edward failed, and she stumbled toward Mr. Tuxedo.

"Run," she shouted at Edward.

"Get down," barked Mr. Tuxedo.

He tried to push her to the floor, but Sloane had other plans. She had a perfect track record at the Edge, and she wasn't about to ruin that now by leaving her principal unprotected.

She spun her arm, breaking Mr. Tuxedo's grip. She needed to reach Edward and get him out of harm's way. Running in heels was an art all its own—one she'd spent hours working on—but the laws of physics hadn't changed because of that training, and she found herself slipping on the glossy ballroom floor.

Edward hadn't moved. He stood staring at her in shock, his mouth hanging open, his flabby body trembling with indecision.

"Go!" yelled Sloane. She'd catch up with him on the stairwell once she'd disarmed Mr. Tuxedo.

Behind Edward, only inches from his head, a glass wall sconce exploded into shrapnel. A large gaping hole opened up in the drywall where a bullet had shredded it.

"Gun!" shouted Mr. Tuxedo, an instant before he tackled her to the floor, covering her with his bulk.

Screams filled the ballroom. Confused panic skittered through her system.

Mr. Tuxedo's heavy body crushed the air from her lungs, and black spots formed in her vision. Through them, she saw Edward turn tail and run, pushing open the heavy stairwell door.

Now all she had to do was get out from under Mr. Tuxedo and join Edward. Not that she was going anywhere until she got a little oxygen.

Another shot went off, fracturing a section of the exit door, and people started stampeding.

"We're going to get trampled." Mr. Tuxedo's mouth

was right next to her ear, allowing her to hear him over the panicked screams of the partygoers.

His weight disappeared, and in the next instant, she felt weightless as he lifted her to her feet and pulled her toward the exit. She jerked away, dodging him in the crowd. The doorway was already clogged with people, pushing and shoving as if that would help them escape faster.

For one split second, she thought about going back to find the shooter and take out the threat to her principal. She knew better; she knew her job was to keep Edward safe, not hunt down scum, but the urge was still there, and she had to fight it every step of the way. There were at least two gunmen here so far. Who knew how many more there might be flooding out the doors toward her unprotected client?

Someone stepped on her foot, hard, but she didn't dare look down to figure out who it was. Beside her, an old woman gasped and slipped beneath the shoving bodies.

Sloane reached for her but was too late, and the frail woman went down beneath a herd of lethal spiked heels.

Sloane tried to turn around to face the mob, hoping to stop them before they killed the woman. She was swept along in their wake, forced to move with them or fall herself. The crush of shoving limbs was unrelenting, and it took her too long to face the oncoming crowd. She pulled in a breath to scream for them to stop when she saw Mr. Tuxedo behind her with the frail woman in his arms.

He gave her a grim, determined nod. "Go," he told Sloane. "I've got her."

Seeing him protect the old lady gave Sloane pause. He was supposed to be the bad guy. Wasn't he?

Okay, so clearly he wasn't the shooter—that shot had come from across the room. But if he wasn't here to hurt Edward, why had he been heading their way with a gun under his jacket?

There wasn't a whole lot of time to contemplate that question before Sloane squeezed through the door, and down the steps, and found Edward waiting for her on the ground floor.

She didn't even slow, but grabbed his arm and headed for the rear exit of the hotel, where the armored limo was supposed to be ready and waiting to pick them up.

Mr. Tuxedo still had an elderly woman in his arms to deal with, and Sloane hoped that by the time he did, she and Edward would be long gone. She really would have liked to know what his part in all of this had been, but her job was to get her principal out safely, and that was exactly what she was going to do.

Lucas had lost her. One minute she was right in front of him, and the next, she was gone.

He set the little old lady on a bench and checked to make sure she was going to stay upright. Her white hair had come free of its sparkling combs and was now a mess. The sleeve of her silk gown was torn, but she looked healthy enough.

"Are you okay?" he asked.

She gave him a shaky nod.

"Are you hurt?"

"Just banged around a bit. I'll be fine. Thank you." She sounded breathless, but Lucas figured she had a right to be. That whole mess had probably scared the hell out of her.

She reached up to pull at her mangled sleeve, and her hands were shaking so badly, they looked like they might fly off her wrists. A dark bruise was forming on her forearm, beneath pale, papery skin.

Shit. He couldn't leave her like this. What if she'd hit her head?

"Sit tight. I'm going to find you some help."

Lucas flagged down one of the confused bellboys and

hauled his pimply ass over to the woman. "You stay with her," he ordered the kid, jabbing a finger into his skinny chest. "Do not let her out of your sight until a paramedic has checked her out. Understand?"

"Yes, sir," said the kid.

Police and other emergency vehicles were swarming into the parking lot. Lucas flagged down the first paramedic he saw and dragged him bodily to the old woman. The wide-eyed EMT went to work, glancing nervously over his shoulder every few seconds. At least he seemed capable enough to handle the situation.

It was going to have to be good enough. Lucas still had to find Sloane and keep her off that flight to Colombia. His best chance now was to intercept her at the small airport where her plane would depart.

In eighty-eight minutes.

As he headed for his car, he dialed the Old Man.

"Is she with you?" he answered on the first ring.

"No, sir. There was a situation here. Shots fired. She got away."

"Shots? Is she okay?"

"Yes, sir."

"I swear to God, Ramsey, if so much as one hair on her head is harmed, I'll hold you personally responsible."

Lucas slid behind the wheel of his car. "Yes, sir."

"Find her. Stop her. Do not let her step foot on that jet. I don't care what it takes."

He eased out of the parking lot as more emergency vehicles came into view down the street. "I'm on it, sir."

"I chose you for this because you're not a man who knows how to fail. Was I wrong?"

"No, sir. This was just a minor setback."

"Any idea why there were shots fired at some charity ball?"

"None. But I can tell you that the shooter was aiming right for her."

"Dear God," breathed the Old Man, sounding like

he'd just aged twenty years in a heartbeat. "Are you sure he wasn't aiming at her principal?"

Lucas merged onto the highway, heading away from Dallas toward the airstrip. "Principal, sir?"

"She's a bodyguard, of all things." He spoke like the mere thought chapped his ass raw. "Are you sure the shooter wasn't aiming for her client?"

A bodyguard? Seriously? Well, that would certainly explain how she knew how to break his hold without so much as batting an eye.

Lucas wondered why this little bit of info hadn't been passed on to him earlier. Must've been need-to-know.

"No, sir. I guess he could have been the target. She was hanging all over him, so it's hard to be sure exactly where the gunman was aiming. I assumed that since she was my target, she was also the shooter's."

"Anything's possible with that woman, but I hope you're wrong."

"Is there anything else about her I should know, sir?"

"Now that you've lost her, you mean?"

Lucas gritted his teeth and gunned the engine, maneuvering around the late-night traffic. "Yes, sir."

"Like what?"

"Like why it's so important that I stop her from getting on that flight. What's so important about some chick bodyguard?"

"That chick bodyguard happens to be my daughter."

Daughter? No way. The Old Man couldn't have a child. He wasn't human. He was frigid logic. He lived and breathed strategy and tactics. He was walking death with any weapon created by man, and had at his disposal some of the most lethal men on the planet. All of whom feared and respected him. He couldn't have a kid. That was just . . . spooky.

"Uh. Sorry, sir. I didn't realize you had a daughter."

"Not many people do. See that you keep it that way."

"Yes, sir."

The Old Man hung up, leaving Lucas reeling. The stakes had just been raised, big-time. If he failed to stop Sloane and she ended up heading toward one of the most dangerous countries on the planet, he wouldn't have to worry about a new line of work. The Old Man would kill him.

Also available from

NATIONAL BESTSELLING AUTHOR

Shannon K. Butcher

They are the Sentinels: three races descended from ancient guardians of mankind, each possessing unique abilities in their battle to protect humanity against their eternal foes.

The Novels of the Sentinel Wars

Burning Alive
Finding the Lost
Running Scared
Living Nightmare
Blood Hunt
Dying Wish

"Enter the world of Shannon K. Butcher and prepare to be spellbound."

—*New York Times* bestselling author Sherrilyn Kenyon

Available wherever books are sold or at penguin.com

facebook.com/ProjectParanormalBooks

S0337

Also available from
NATIONAL BESTSELLING AUTHOR

Shannon K. Butcher

DYING WISH

A Novel of the Sentinel Wars

Jackie Patton has been rescued by the Theronai from her captivity and torture at the hands of the Synestryn, only to learn that she's a potential match for the Theronai warriors who need a woman to literally save their lives.

Forced to choose, she unexpectedly selects Iain, a cold-hearted warrior who doesn't want to be saved. Iain is convinced that it's too late—that his soul is already as dead as his former betrothed, killed by the Synestryn. Still, he is the only man Jackie feels a measure of peace around and the only one she wants. But is Iain indeed beyond saving?

"Enter the world of Shannon K. Butcher and prepare to be spellbound."
—Sherrilyn Kenyon

Available wherever books are sold or at penguin.com

S0151

Also available from
NATIONAL BESTSELLING AUTHOR

Shannon K. Butcher

EDGE OF SANITY

An Edge Novel

Working for private security firm The Edge, Clay Marshall has seen it all. But the recent blackouts he's been having are new. So is waking up with blood on his hands and clothes, with no memory of what happened. He knows he needs help. Dr. Leigh Vaughn has treated other Edge employees before, but from the moment she sees him, Clay strikes her as a special breed of man. She knows he's dangerous, and distrustful of doctors, but is drawn to him even as his own steely exterior gives way to his growing desire for her. But neither can foresee the secret danger that will soon threaten them both...

"Butcher is...phenomenal."
—Affaire de Coeur

Available wherever books are sold or at
penguin.com

facebook.com/LoveAlwaysBooks

S0442

Also available from

NATIONAL BESTSELLING AUTHOR

Shannon K. Butcher

RAZOR'S EDGE

An Edge Novel

Roxanne "Razor" Haught is an expert in stealth security for corporate espionage cases. But now she's a target. Tanner O'Connell has no intentions of leaving Razor's side. Despite her objections to having a "babysitter," his orders as the newest member of the Edge are to watch her back. With a brainwashed assassin after his partner, Tanner cannot afford to let his desire for Razor interfere with his duty. His special ops skills may be all that stand between saving Razor—or losing her forever.

Available wherever books are sold or at penguin.com

facebook.com/LoveAlwaysBooks

S0422